D0117688

SPECIAL THANKS TO...

Kaare Andrews
James Asmus
Evan Bailey
Jeff Boison
Jacob Chabot
Albert Ching
Charlie Chu
Tze Chun
Thomas Crowell
Pete The Dog
Gerry Duggan
Maura Dwyer
Nathan Fairbairn
Tom Fowler
Nathan Fox
Atom Freeman

David Gallaher
Drew Gill
Hunter Gorinson
Sanford Greene
Nicoll Hunt
Josh Johns
Daniel Warren
Johnson
Duncan Jones
Robert LeHeup
Nick Lowe
Andrew Maclean
Benjamin Marra
Shanna Matuszak
Robb Mommaerts
Jerome Opeña

Pornsak Pichetshote
Jeff Powell
Brendan Ratliff
Rick Remender
Paolo Rivera
Andrew Robinson
Robbi Rodriguez
Kat Salazar
Jeff Stang
Eric Stephenson
Andy Suriano
Jhonen Vasquez
Sheldon Vella
Doan Whito
Skottie Young
Victoria Zoellner

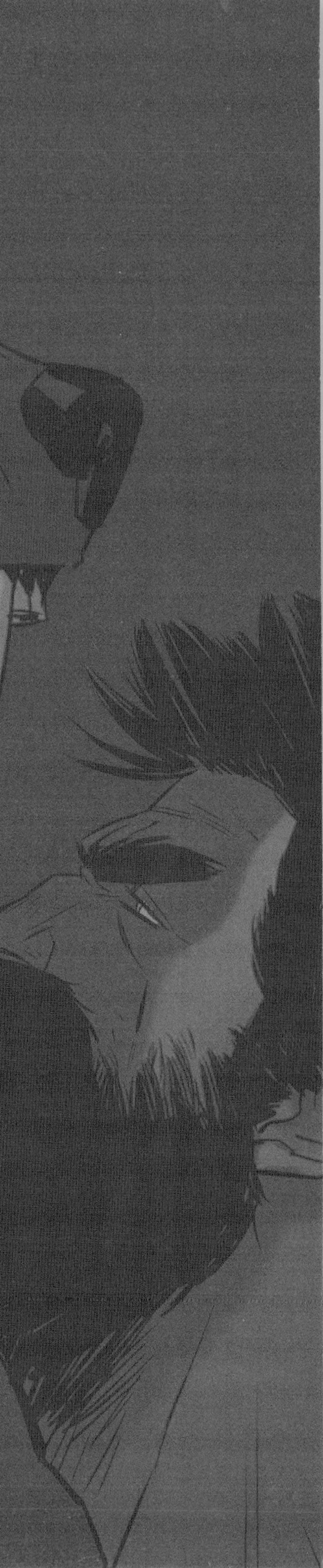

I have a beard & I do not like to wear pants. But I know full well I do not have the cojones to punch a bear, let alone take on a pack of bloodthirsty Ursidaes alone. As much as I may admire Shirtless Bear-Fighter, he is made of far furrier stuff than I. I'm ok with that. We all need someone to look up to.

As agent Burke explains, "…sometimes, God makes a mistake… and makes a man… too much of a man."

I am not a religious collector of comics, either. In fact, it's been many years since one has grabbed my attention the way *SBF* has, but from the first issue out, it crackled with an energy, humor & daftness that spoke to my soul. Nil Vendrell's art is so sharp it looks like he chiseled it into the paper. Mike Spicer's vibrant, contrasting palette only adds to the electricity running through the pages, and Dave Lanphear? I haven't misread a beat yet!

In the best possible way, it reminded me of reading issue 1 of Eastman & Laird's *Teenage Mutant Ninja Turtles* many decades ago. That & its less well-known sibling, *Adolescent Radioactive Black Belt Hamsters* (in 3D, don't ya know!). Jody and Sebastian let loose their manic imaginings but play them straight and true like an early Stalone film. Every twist is a torturous ordeal for our protagonist. Every battle, a picked scab. History weighs on him like a wet bearskin…

Like *Axe Cop* before it, it's beyond silly! But it has such conviction, that every tear into the absurd feels utterly justified. You just want to know, "how far are we going?!"

And isn't that what we all want from a comic, anyway? To have it take you away from all of… whatever it is you're doing? Let me ride along with Shirtless as he saves cities, one pummeled bear at a time. Let me see the world through his furious, ever-squinting blue eyes. Maybe I can't be Shirtless, but issue by issue, I sure as hell can cheer him on!

So stop reading this introductory crap and read the damn book! But be warned…

Jody, Sebastian & Nil have created an archetype, so dense with testosterone & anachronism, pixelation of the comic form is the only way it can be safely consumed.

It's probably best you squint while you read it too.

Keep punching, Shirtless.

Duncan Jones
2017

*Duncan Jones is a Bafta award-winning film director and screenwriter best known for directing feature films **Moon**, **Source Code**, **Warcraft**, and **Mute**.*

IMAGE COMICS, INC.

Robert Kirkman: Chief Operating Officer / Erik Larsen: Chief Financial Officer / Todd McFarlane: President / Marc Silvestri: Chief Executive Officer
Jim Valentino: Vice President / Eric Stephenson: Publisher / Corey Murphy: Director of Sales / Jeff Boison: Director of Publishing Planning & Book Trade Sales
Chris Ross: Director of Digital Sales / Jeff Stang: Director of Specialty Sales / Kat Salazar: Director of PR & Marketing / Branwyn Bigglestone: Controller
Kali Dugan: Senior Accounting Manager / Sue Korpela: Accounting & HR Manager / Drew Gill: Art Director / Heather Doornink: Production Director
Leigh Thomas: Print Manager / Tricia Ramos: Traffic Manager / Briah Skelly: Publicist / Aly Hoffman: Events & Conventions Coordinator
Sasha Head: Sales & Marketing Production Designer / David Brothers: Branding Manager / Melissa Gifford: Content Manager
Drew Fitzgerald: Publicity Assistant / Vincent Kukua: Production Artist / Erika Schnatz: Production Artist / Ryan Brewer: Production Artist
Shanna Matuszak: Production Artist / Carey Hall: Production Artist / Esther Kim: Direct Market Sales Representative / Emilio Bautista: Digital Sales Representative
Leanna Caunter: Accounting Analyst / Chloe Ramos-Peterson: Library Market Sales Representative / Maria Eizik: Administrative Assistant

imagecomics.com

sbf! logo design by	series production by	collection design by
JARED FLETCHER	SHANNA MATUSZAK & DAVE LANPHEAR	JEFF POWELL

SHIRTLESS BEAR-FIGHTER, VOLUME 1. First Printing. December 2017. Published by Image Comics, Inc. Office of publication: 2701 NW Vaughn Street, Suite 780, Portland, OR 97210. Copyright © 2017 Fuzzy Wipes, LLC. All rights reserved. Originally published in single magazine form as SHIRTLESS BEAR-FIGHTER #1-5. SHIRTLESS BEAR-FIGHTER™ (including all prominent characters featured herein), its logo and all character likenesses are trademarks of Fuzzy Wipes, LLC, unless otherwise noted. Image Comics® and its logos are registered trademarks of Image Comics, Inc. No part of this publication may be reproduced or transmitted, in any form or by any means (except for short excerpts for review purposes) without the express written permission of Fuzzy Wipes, LLC or Image Comics, Inc. All names, characters, events and locales in this publication are entirely fictional. Any resemblance to actual persons (living or dead), events or places, without satiric intent, is coincidental. PRINTED IN THE U.S.A. For information regarding the CPSIA on this printed material call: 203-595-3636 and provide reference #RICH-769880. For international rights inquiries, contact: Law Offices of Harris M. Miller II, P.C. (rights.inquiries@gmail.com). All other inquiries contact Jody LeHeup at fuzzywipes@gmail.com.

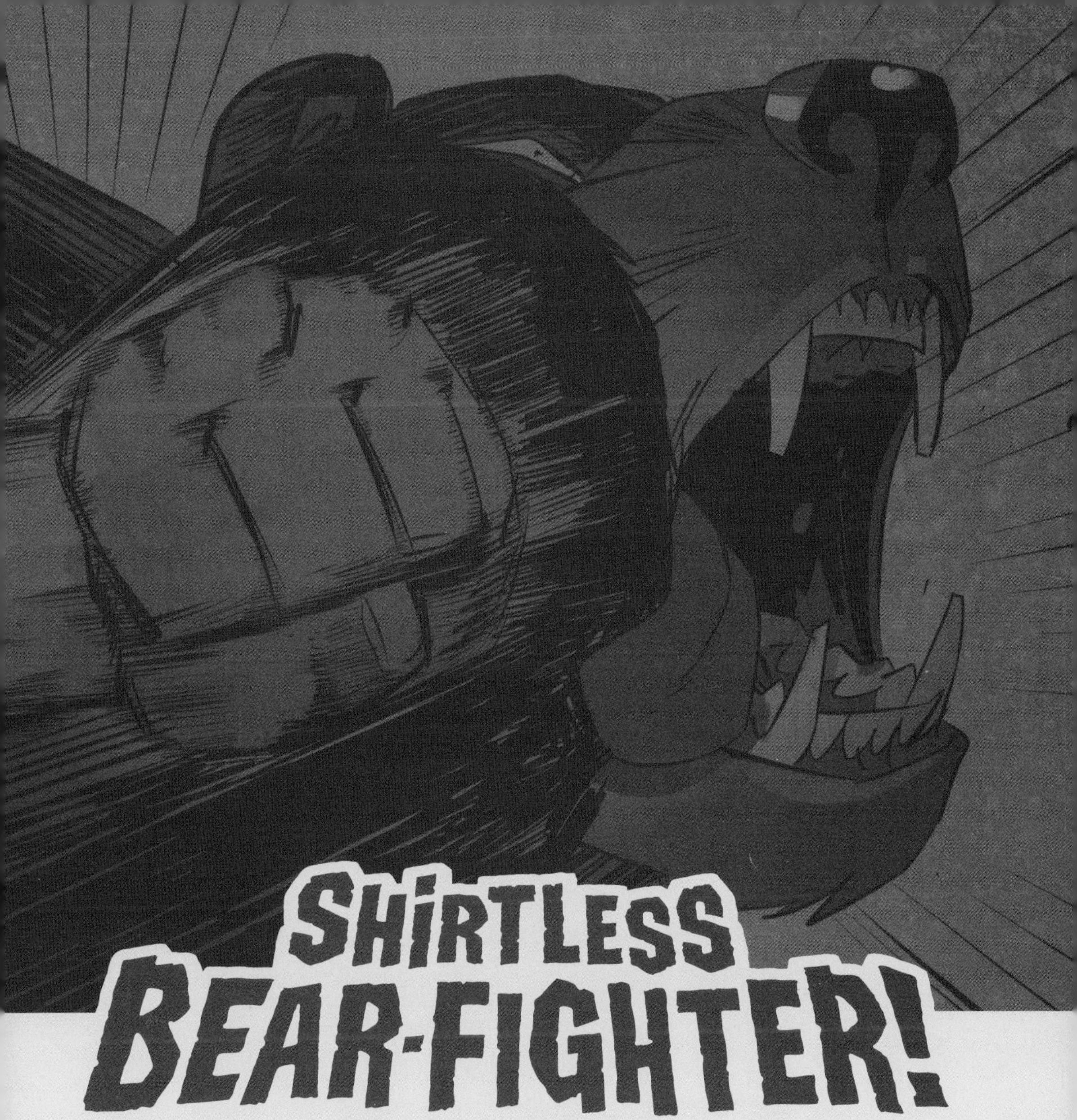

SHIRTLESS BEAR-FIGHTER!

written by

JODY LEHEUP AND SEBASTIAN GIRNER

art

NIL VENDRELL

color

MIKE SPICER

letters

DAVE LANPHEAR

covers by

ANDREW ROBINSON

created by

JODY LEHEUP, SEBASTIAN GIRNER AND NIL VENDRELL

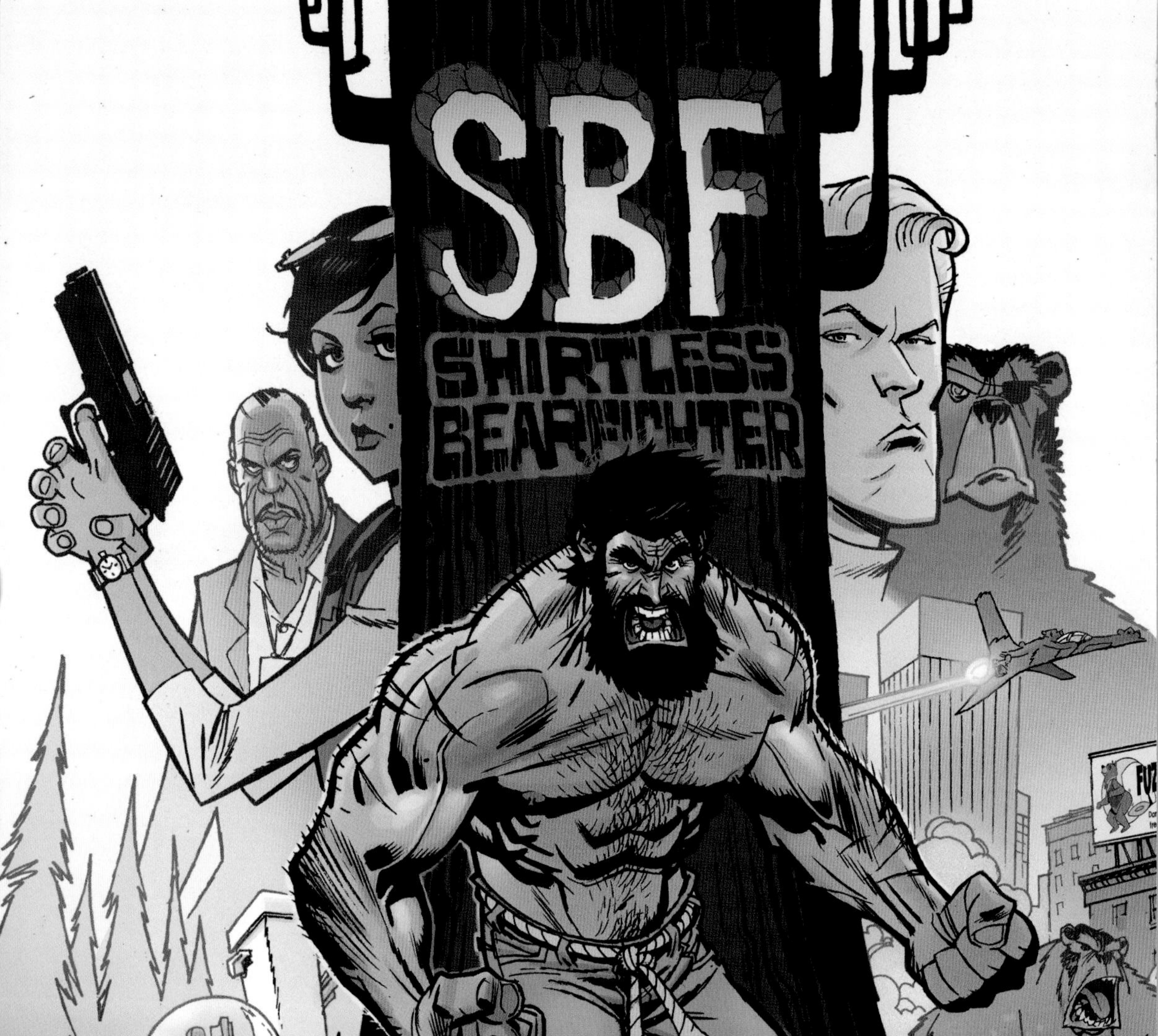
SBF
SHIRTLESS

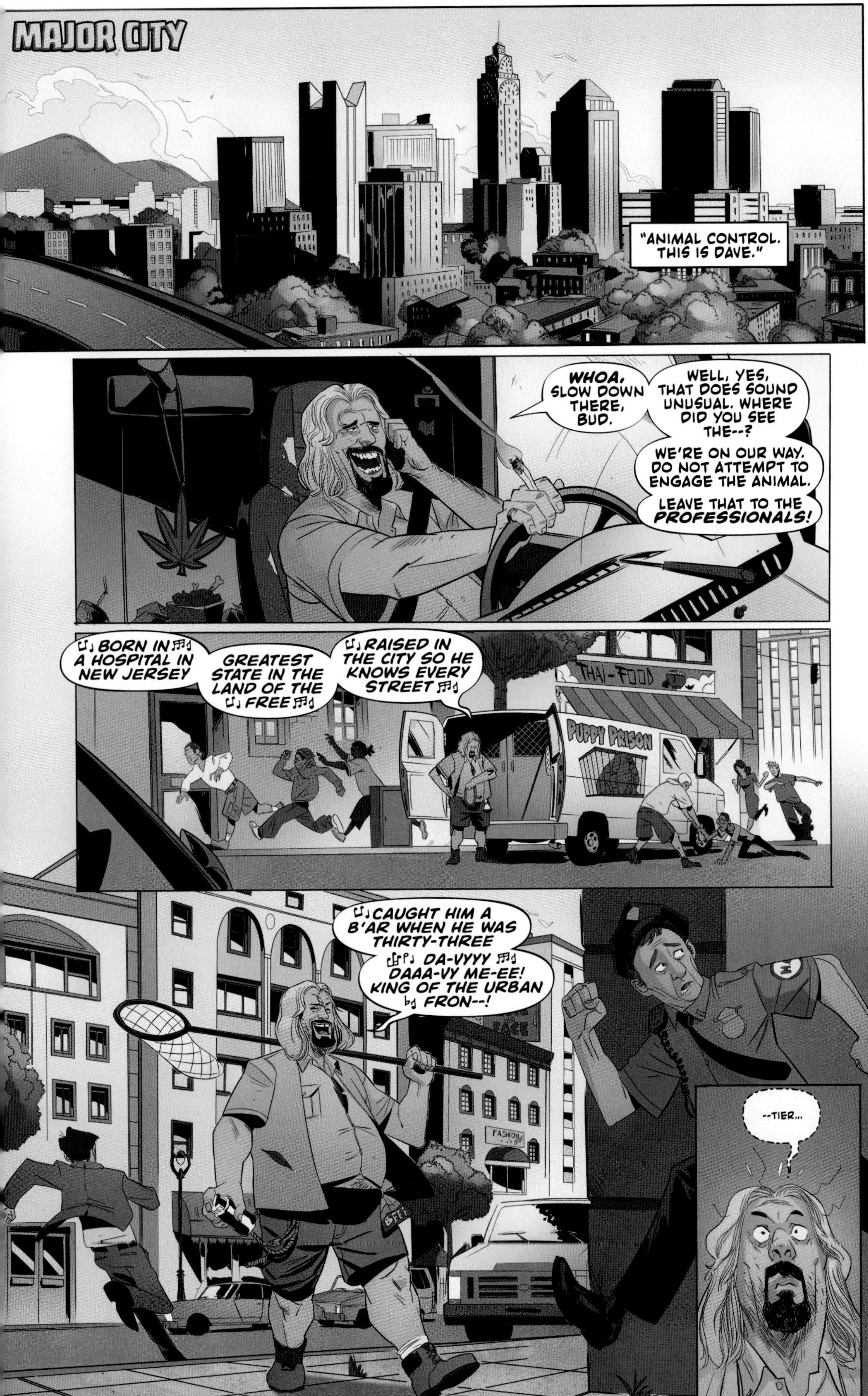
MAJOR CITY
"ANIMAL CONTROL. THIS IS DAVE."
WHOA, SLOW DOWN THERE, BUD.
WELL, YES, THAT DOES SOUND UNUSUAL. WHERE DID YOU SEE THE--?
WE'RE ON OUR WAY. DO NOT ATTEMPT TO ENGAGE THE ANIMAL.
LEAVE THAT TO THE PROFESSIONALS!
BORN IN A HOSPITAL IN NEW JERSEY
GREATEST STATE IN THE LAND OF THE FREE
RAISED IN THE CITY SO HE KNOWS EVERY STREET
THAI-FOOD
PUPPY PRISON
CAUGHT HIM A B'AR WHEN HE WAS THIRTY-THREE
DA-VYYY DAAA-VY ME-EE! KING OF THE URBAN FRON--!
FASHION
--TIER...

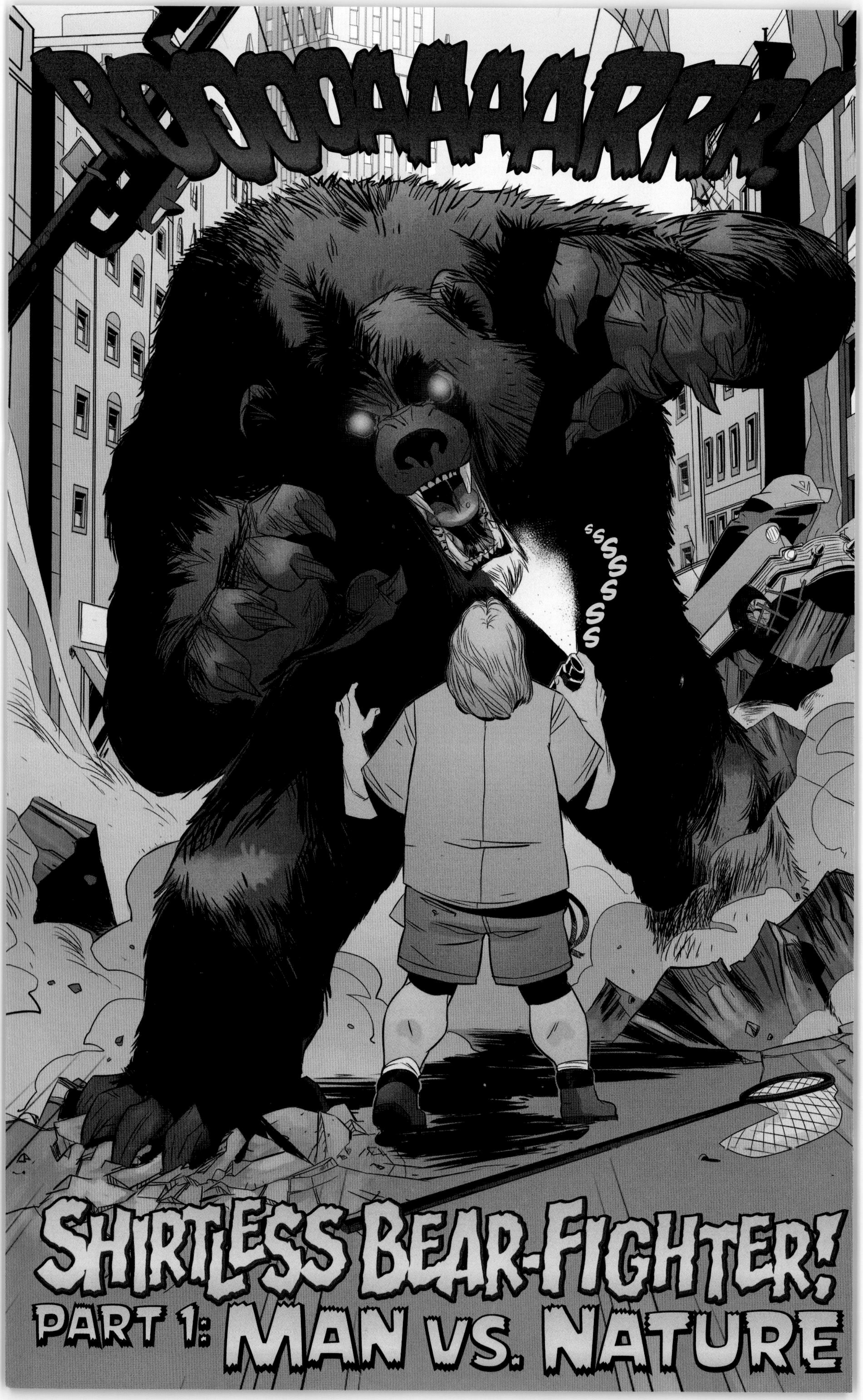
ROOOOAAAARRR!
SSSSSS
SHIRTLESS BEAR-FIGHTER!
PART 1: MAN VS. NATURE

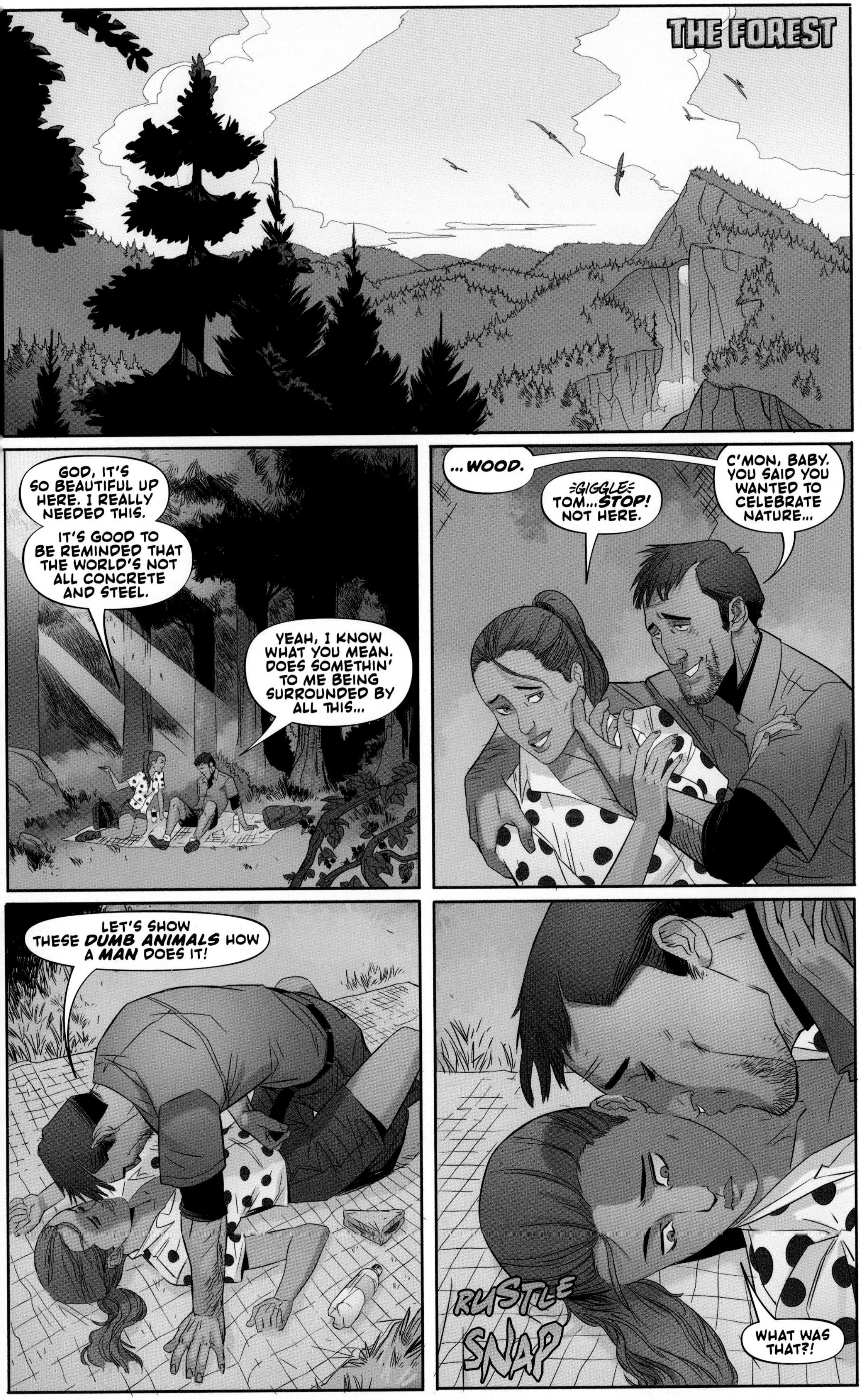
THE FOREST
GOD, IT'S SO BEAUTIFUL UP HERE. I REALLY NEEDED THIS.
IT'S GOOD TO BE REMINDED THAT THE WORLD'S NOT ALL CONCRETE AND STEEL.
YEAH, I KNOW WHAT YOU MEAN. DOES SOMETHIN' TO ME BEING SURROUNDED BY ALL THIS...
...WOOD.
GIGGLE TOM...STOP! NOT HERE.
C'MON, BABY. YOU SAID YOU WANTED TO CELEBRATE NATURE...
LET'S SHOW THESE DUMB ANIMALS HOW A MAN DOES IT!
RUSTLE
SNAP
WHAT WAS THAT?!

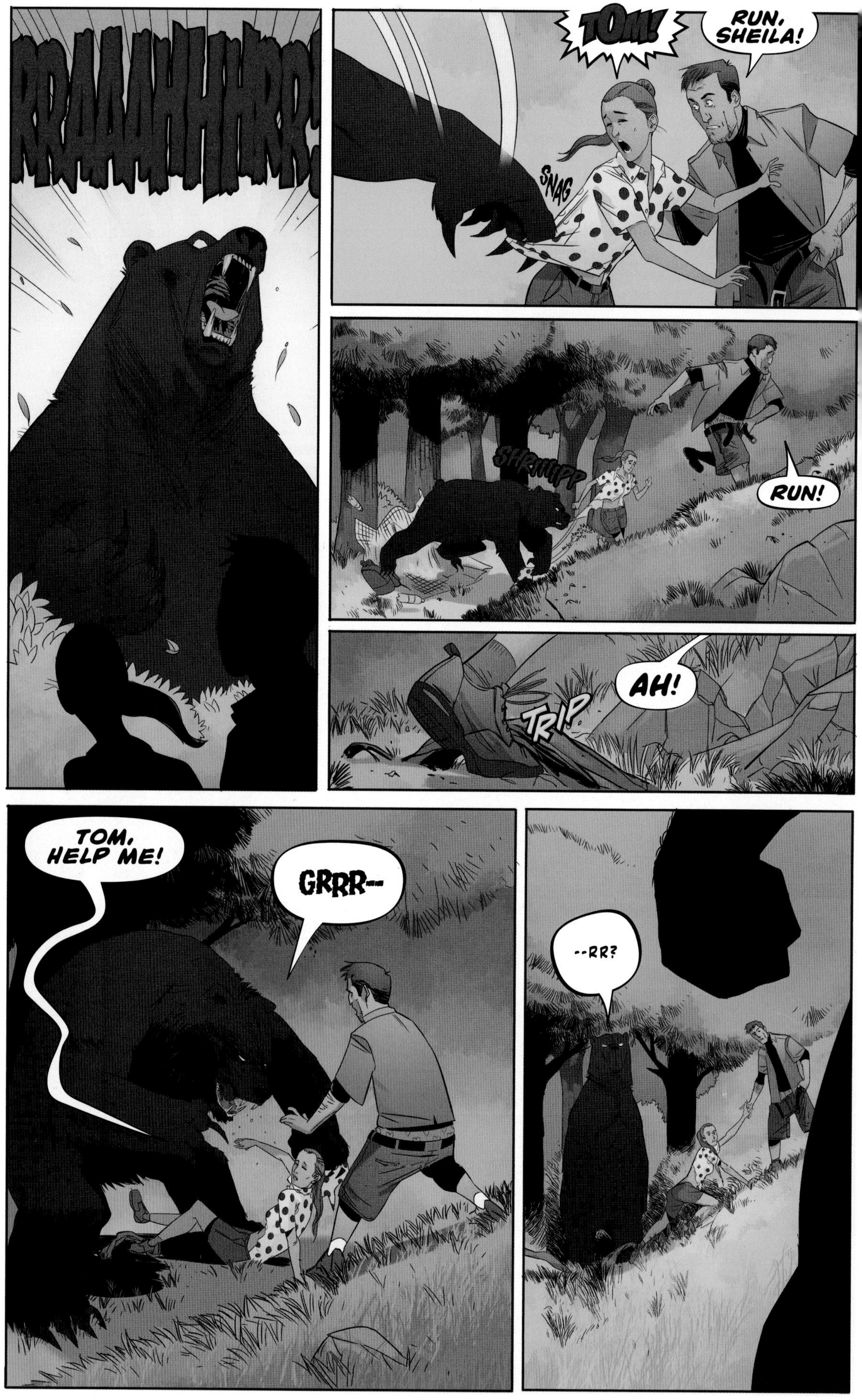
RRAAAHHHRR!
TOM!
RUN, SHEILA!
SNAG
SHRIIIPP
RUN!
TRIP
AH!
TOM, HELP ME!
GRRR--
--RR?

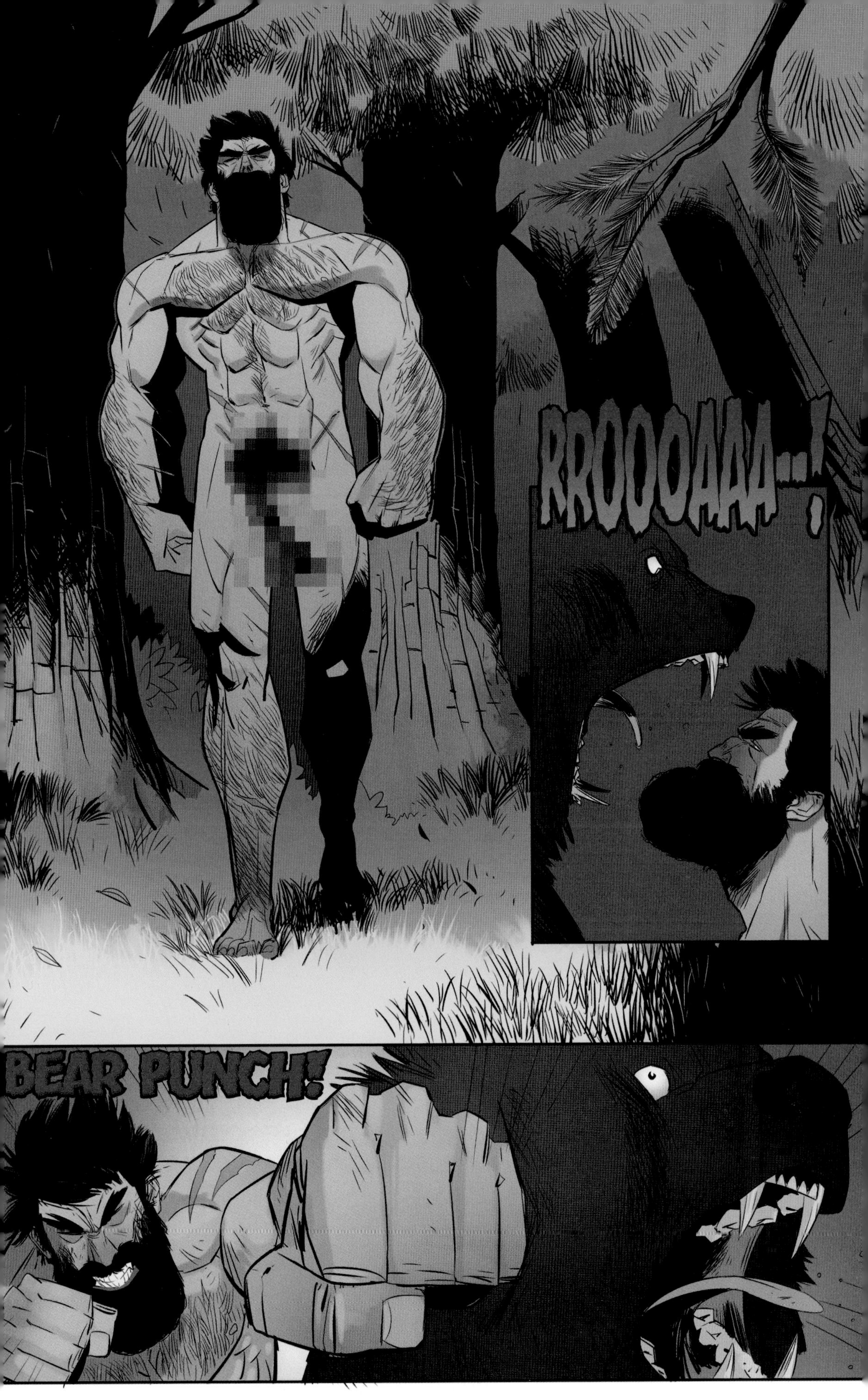
RROOOAAA..!
BEAR PUNCH!

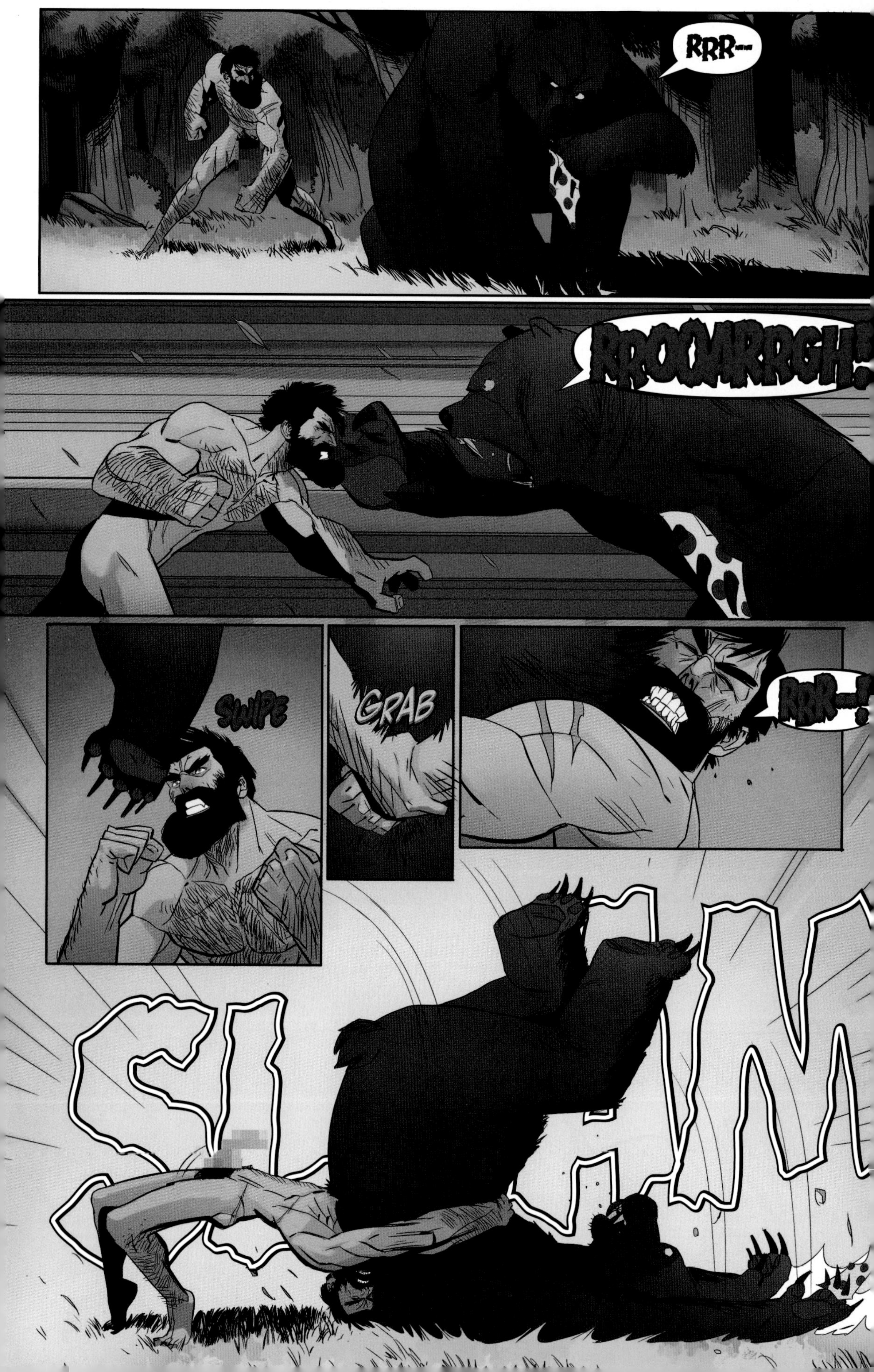
RRR--
RRROOARRRGH!
SWIPE
GRAB
RRR--!
SLAM

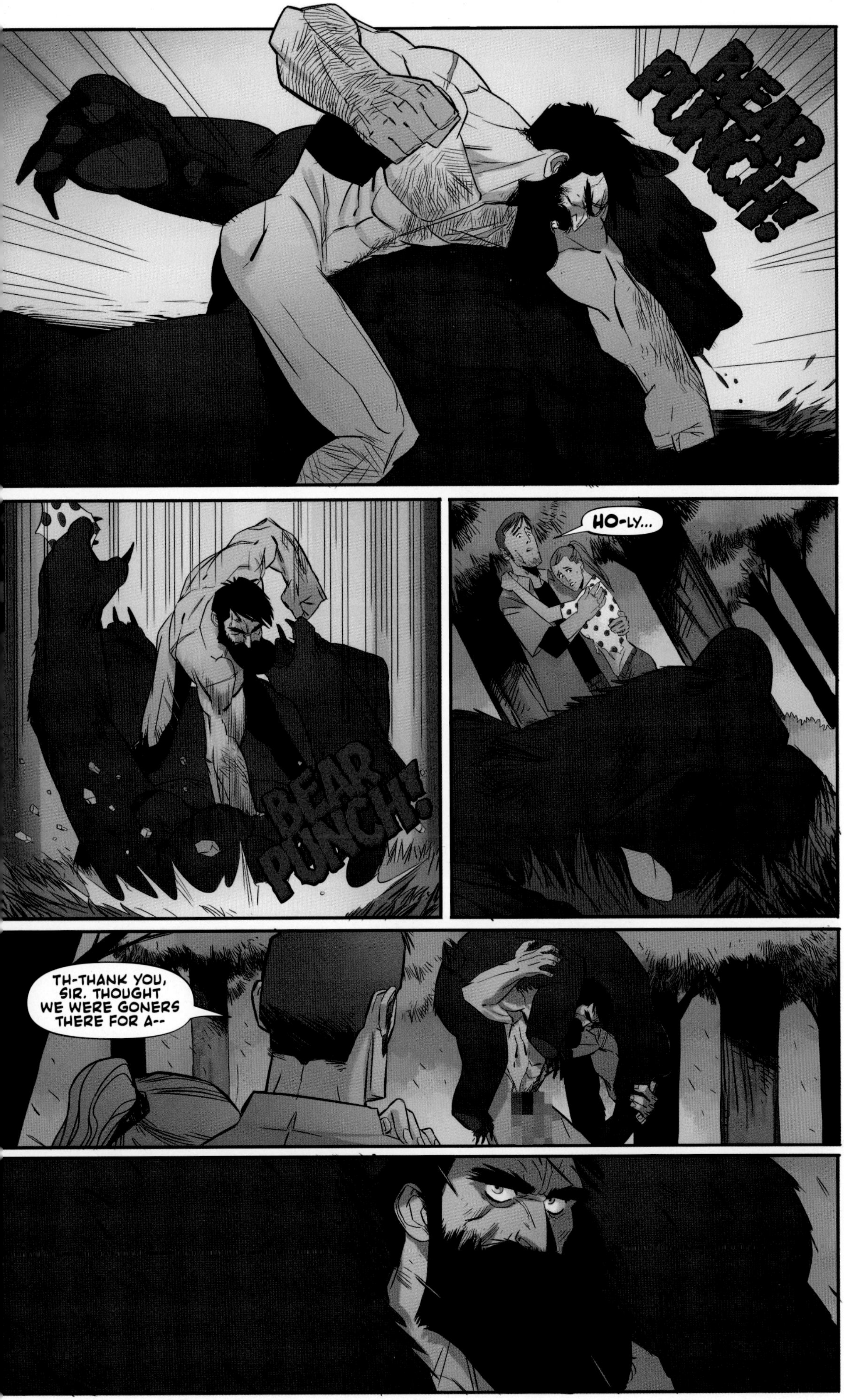
BEAR PUNCH!
BEAR PUNCH!
HO-LY...
TH-THANK YOU, SIR. THOUGHT WE WERE GONERS THERE FOR A--

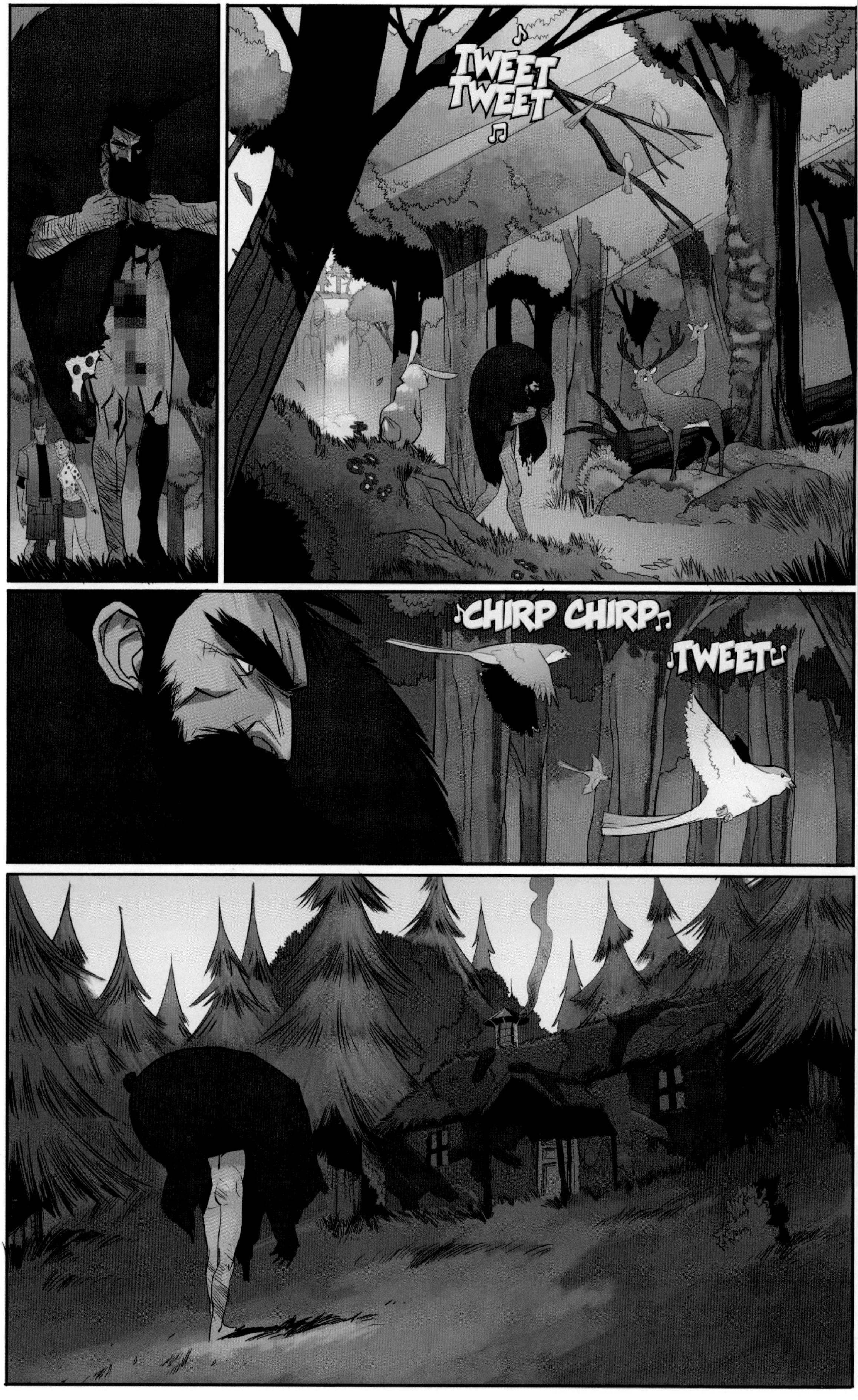
TWEET TWEET
CHIRP CHIRP
TWEET

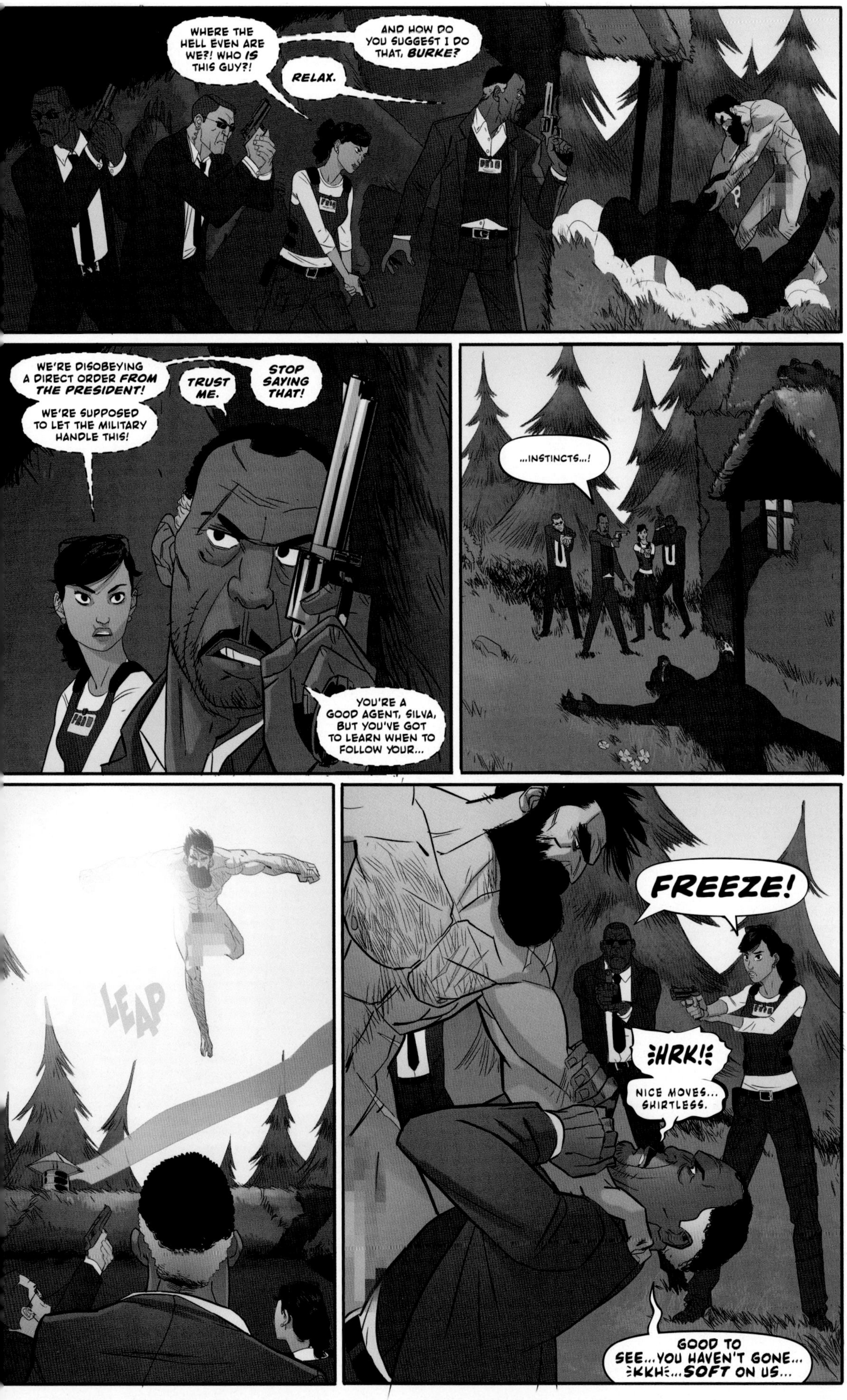
WHERE THE HELL EVEN ARE WE?! WHO *IS* THIS GUY?!
AND HOW DO YOU SUGGEST I DO THAT, *BURKE?*
RELAX.
WE'RE DISOBEYING A DIRECT ORDER *FROM THE PRESIDENT!*
TRUST ME.
STOP SAYING THAT!
WE'RE SUPPOSED TO LET THE MILITARY HANDLE THIS!
YOU'RE A GOOD AGENT, SILVA, BUT YOU'VE GOT TO LEARN WHEN TO FOLLOW YOUR...
...INSTINCTS...!
LEAP
FREEZE!
HRK!
NICE MOVES... SHIRTLESS.
GOOD TO SEE... YOU HAVEN'T GONE... KKH... *SOFT* ON US...

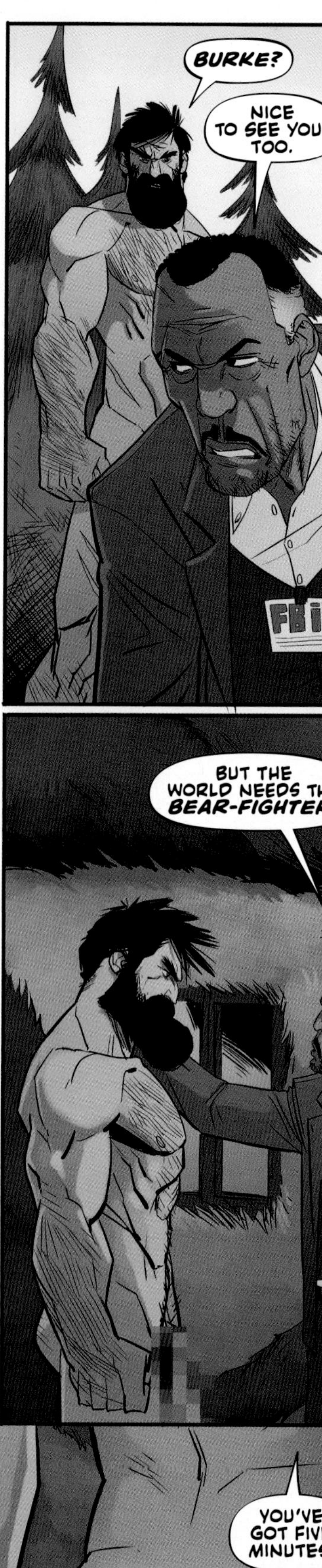
BURKE?
NICE TO SEE YOU TOO.
FBI
BUT THE WORLD NEEDS TH
BEAR-FIGHTER
YOU'VE GOT FIVE MINUTES

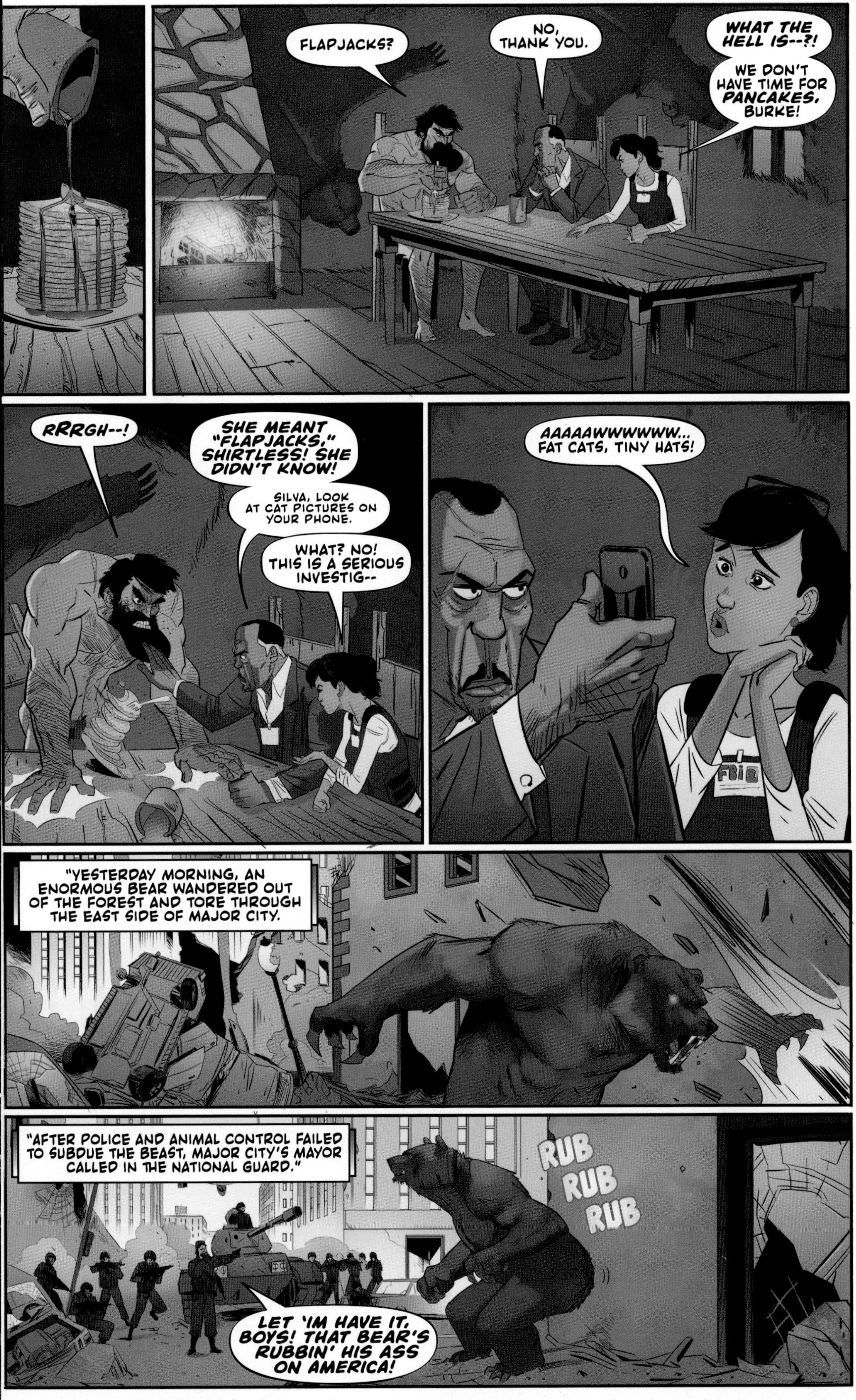

FLAPJACKS?
NO, THANK YOU.
WHAT THE HELL IS--?!
WE DON'T HAVE TIME FOR PANCAKES, BURKE!
RRRGH--!
SHE MEANT "FLAPJACKS," SHIRTLESS! SHE DIDN'T KNOW!
SILVA, LOOK AT CAT PICTURES ON YOUR PHONE.
WHAT? NO! THIS IS A SERIOUS INVESTIG--
AAAAAWWWWWW... FAT CATS, TINY HATS!
FBI
"YESTERDAY MORNING, AN ENORMOUS BEAR WANDERED OUT OF THE FOREST AND TORE THROUGH THE EAST SIDE OF MAJOR CITY.
"AFTER POLICE AND ANIMAL CONTROL FAILED TO SUBDUE THE BEAST, MAJOR CITY'S MAYOR CALLED IN THE NATIONAL GUARD."
RUB RUB RUB
LET 'IM HAVE IT, BOYS! THAT BEAR'S RUBBIN' HIS ASS ON AMERICA!

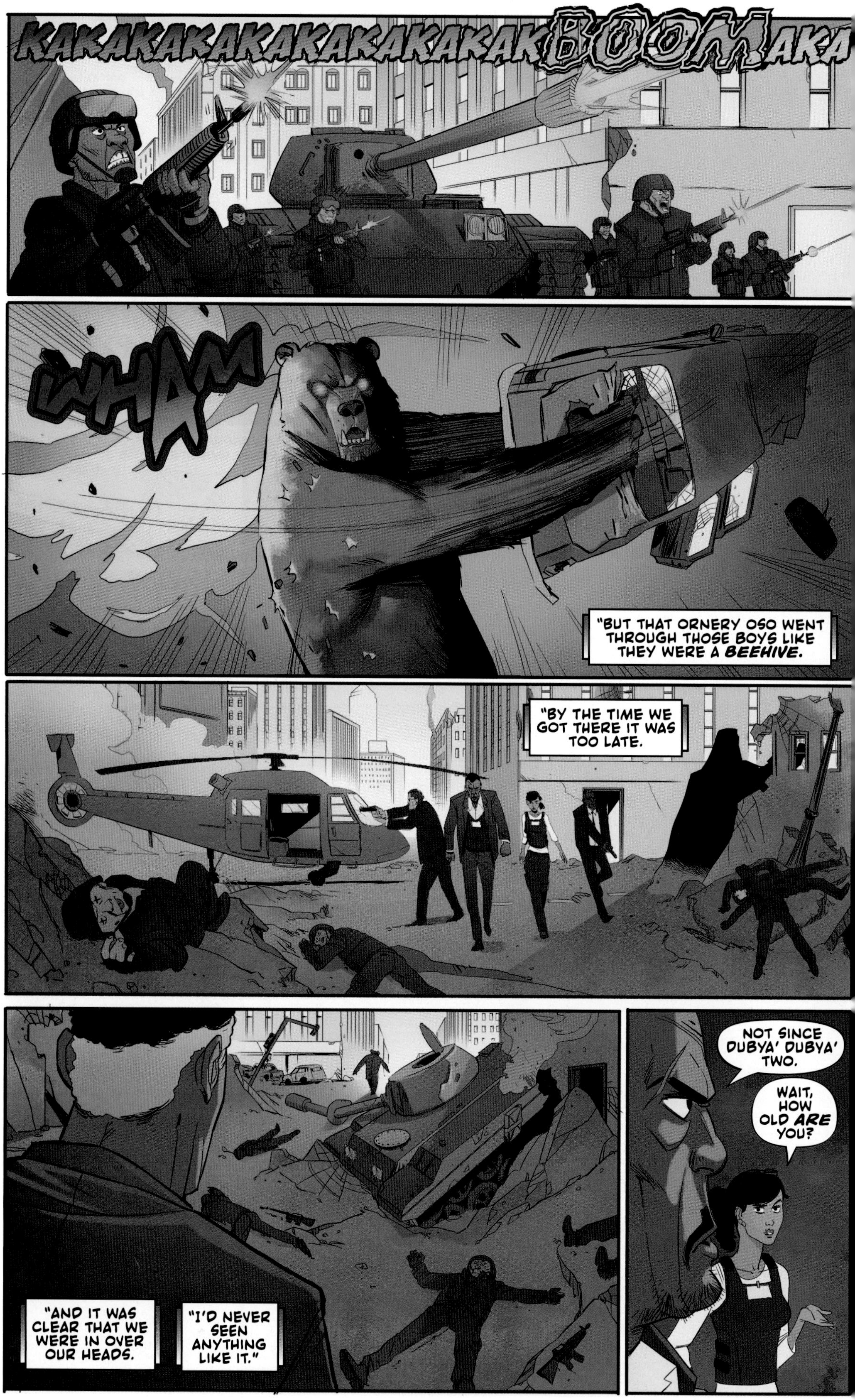
KAKAKAKAKAKAKAKAKAKAKAKBOOMAKA
WHAM
"BUT THAT ORNERY OSO WENT THROUGH THOSE BOYS LIKE THEY WERE A *BEEHIVE*.
"BY THE TIME WE GOT THERE IT WAS TOO LATE.
"AND IT WAS CLEAR THAT WE WERE IN OVER OUR HEADS.
"I'D NEVER SEEN ANYTHING LIKE IT."
NOT SINCE DUBYA' DUBYA' TWO.
WAIT, HOW OLD *ARE* YOU?

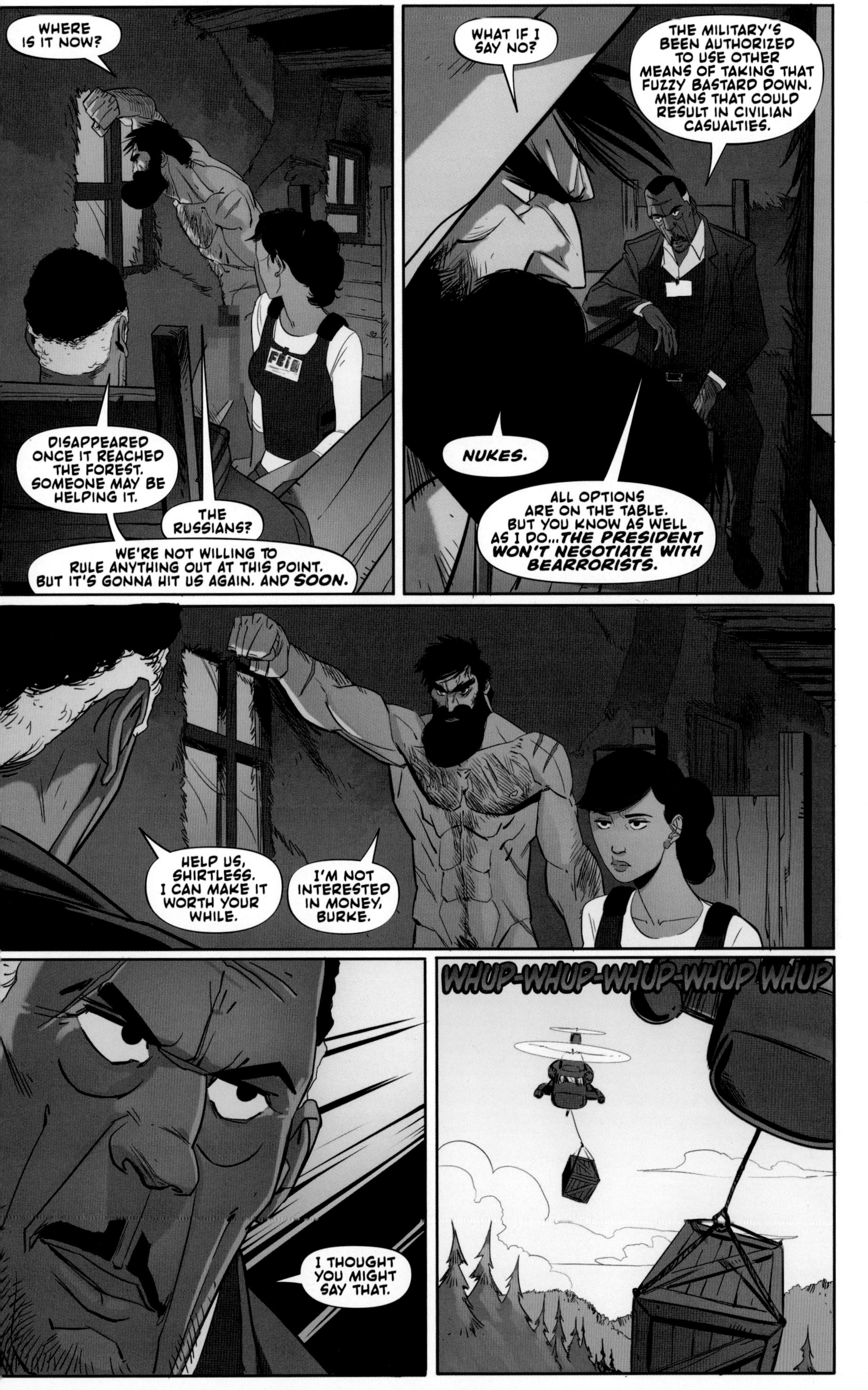
WHERE IS IT NOW?
DISAPPEARED ONCE IT REACHED THE FOREST. SOMEONE MAY BE HELPING IT.
THE RUSSIANS?
WE'RE NOT WILLING TO RULE ANYTHING OUT AT THIS POINT. BUT IT'S GONNA HIT US AGAIN. AND SOON.
WHAT IF I SAY NO?
THE MILITARY'S BEEN AUTHORIZED TO USE OTHER MEANS OF TAKING THAT FUZZY BASTARD DOWN. MEANS THAT COULD RESULT IN CIVILIAN CASUALTIES.
NUKES.
ALL OPTIONS ARE ON THE TABLE. BUT YOU KNOW AS WELL AS I DO...THE PRESIDENT WON'T NEGOTIATE WITH BEARRORISTS.
HELP US, SHIRTLESS. I CAN MAKE IT WORTH YOUR WHILE.
I'M NOT INTERESTED IN MONEY, BURKE.
I THOUGHT YOU MIGHT SAY THAT.
WHUP-WHUP-WHUP-WHUP WHUP

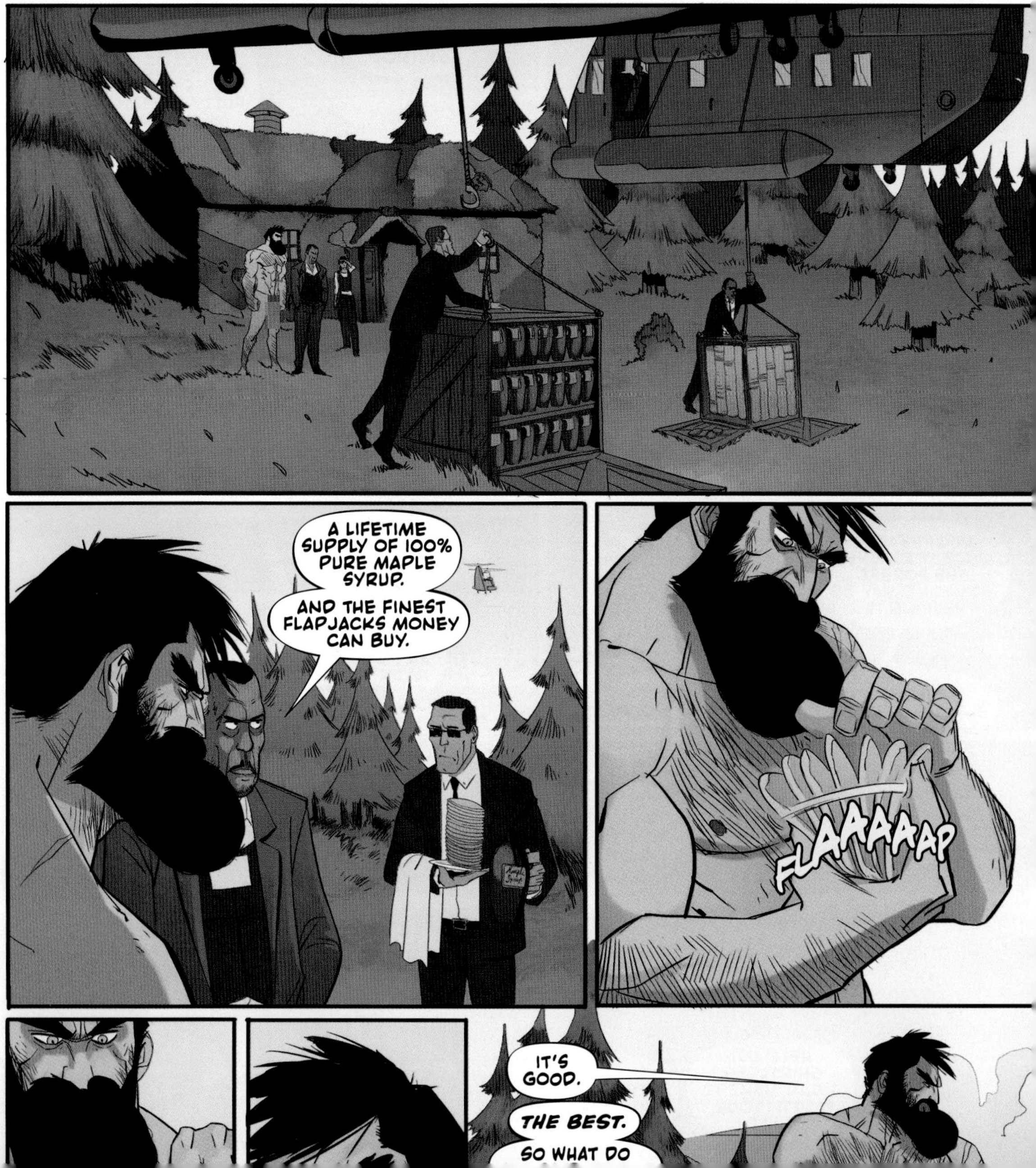
A LIFETIME SUPPLY OF 100% PURE MAPLE SYRUP.
AND THE FINEST FLAPJACKS MONEY CAN BUY.
FLAAAAAP
IT'S GOOD.
THE BEST.
SO WHAT DO

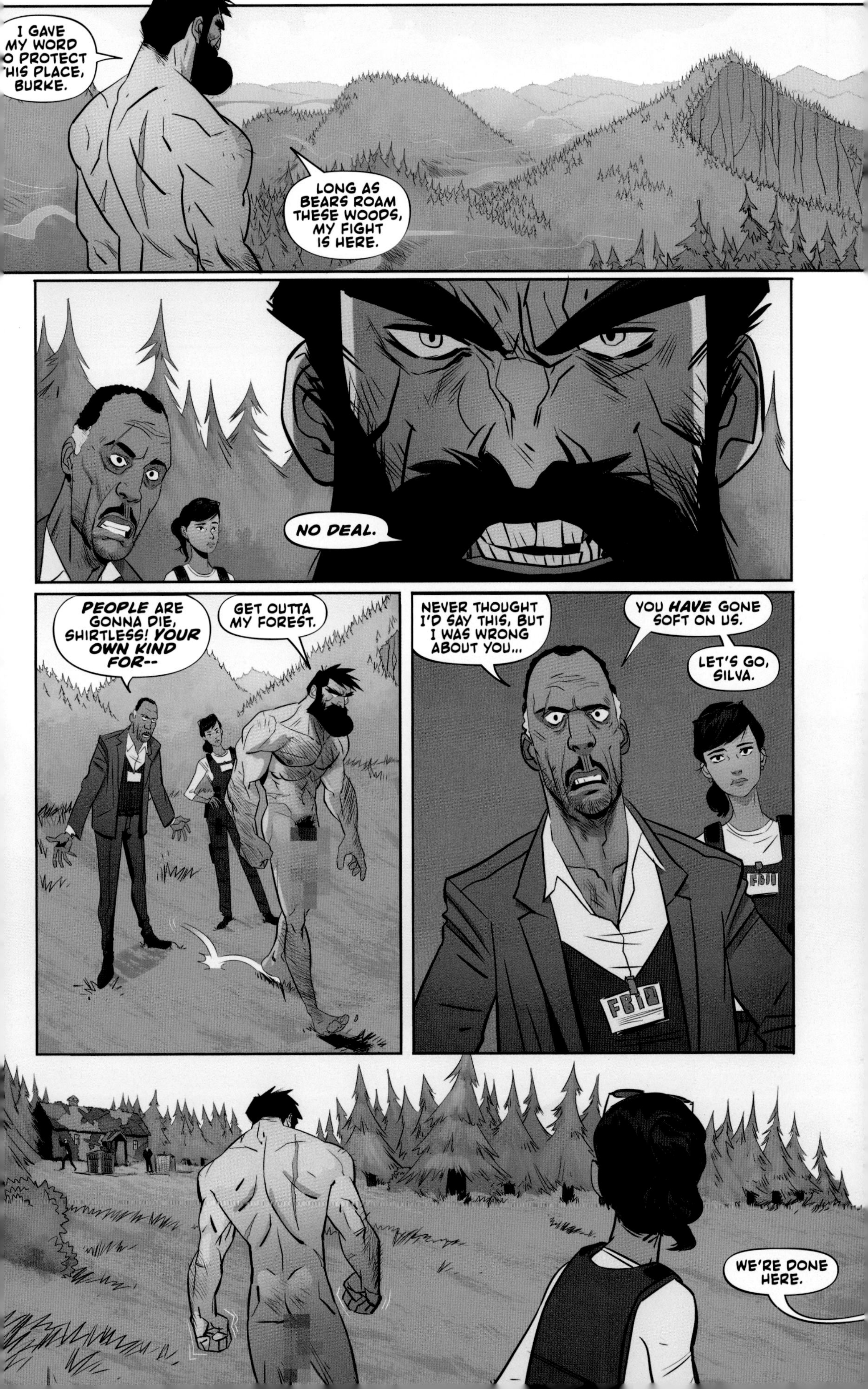

I GAVE MY WORD TO PROTECT THIS PLACE, BURKE.
LONG AS BEARS ROAM THESE WOODS, MY FIGHT IS HERE.
NO DEAL.
PEOPLE ARE GONNA DIE, SHIRTLESS! YOUR OWN KIND FOR--
GET OUTTA MY FOREST.
NEVER THOUGHT I'D SAY THIS, BUT I WAS WRONG ABOUT YOU...
YOU HAVE GONE SOFT ON US.
LET'S GO, SILVA.
WE'RE DONE HERE.

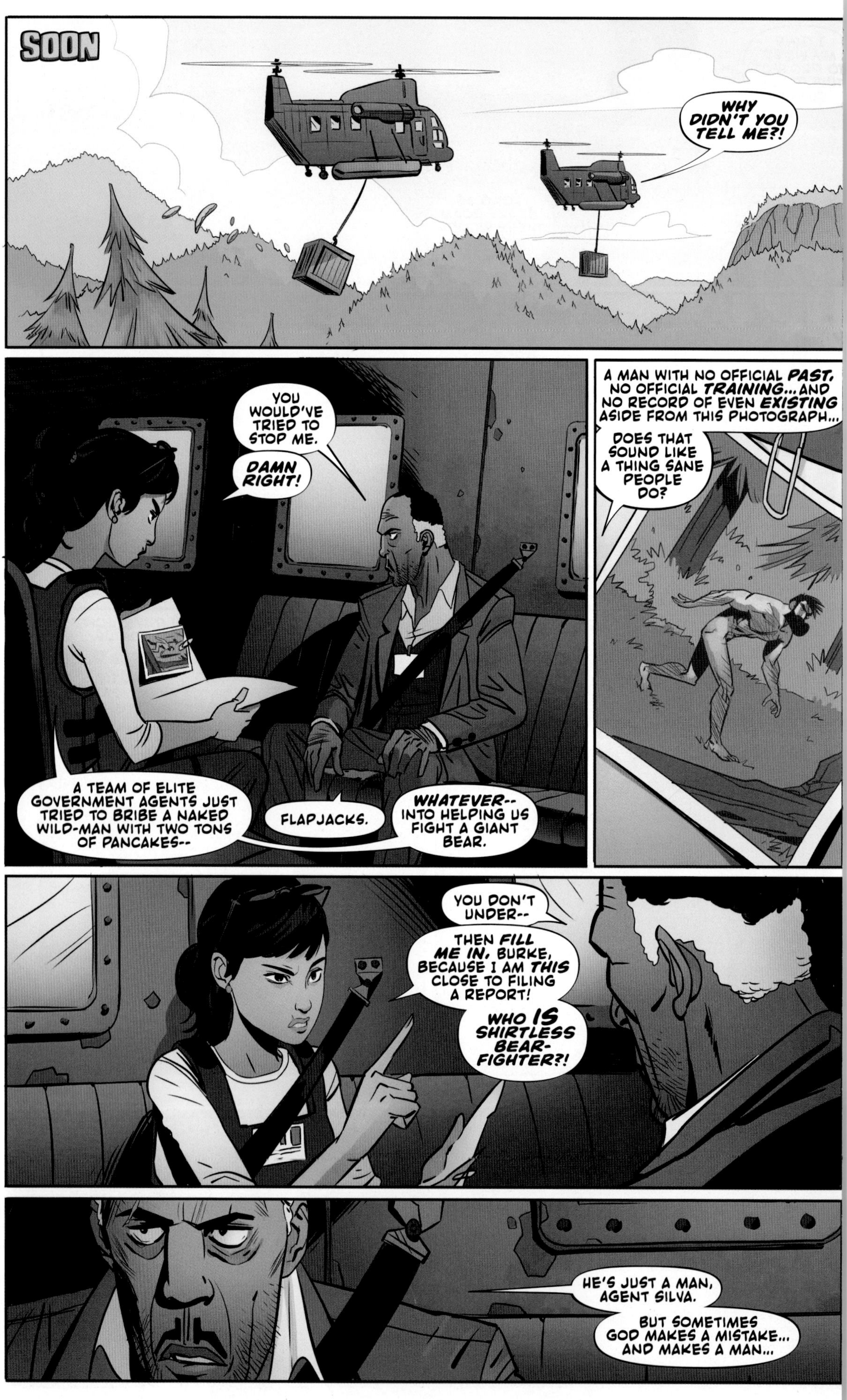
SOON
WHY DIDN'T YOU TELL ME?!
YOU WOULD'VE TRIED TO STOP ME.
DAMN RIGHT!
A MAN WITH NO OFFICIAL PAST, NO OFFICIAL TRAINING... AND NO RECORD OF EVEN EXISTING ASIDE FROM THIS PHOTOGRAPH...
DOES THAT SOUND LIKE A THING SANE PEOPLE DO?
A TEAM OF ELITE GOVERNMENT AGENTS JUST TRIED TO BRIBE A NAKED WILD-MAN WITH TWO TONS OF PANCAKES--
FLAPJACKS.
WHATEVER-- INTO HELPING US FIGHT A GIANT BEAR.
YOU DON'T UNDER--
THEN FILL ME IN, BURKE, BECAUSE I AM THIS CLOSE TO FILING A REPORT!
WHO IS SHIRTLESS BEAR-FIGHTER?!
HE'S JUST A MAN, AGENT SILVA.
BUT SOMETIMES GOD MAKES A MISTAKE... AND MAKES A MAN...

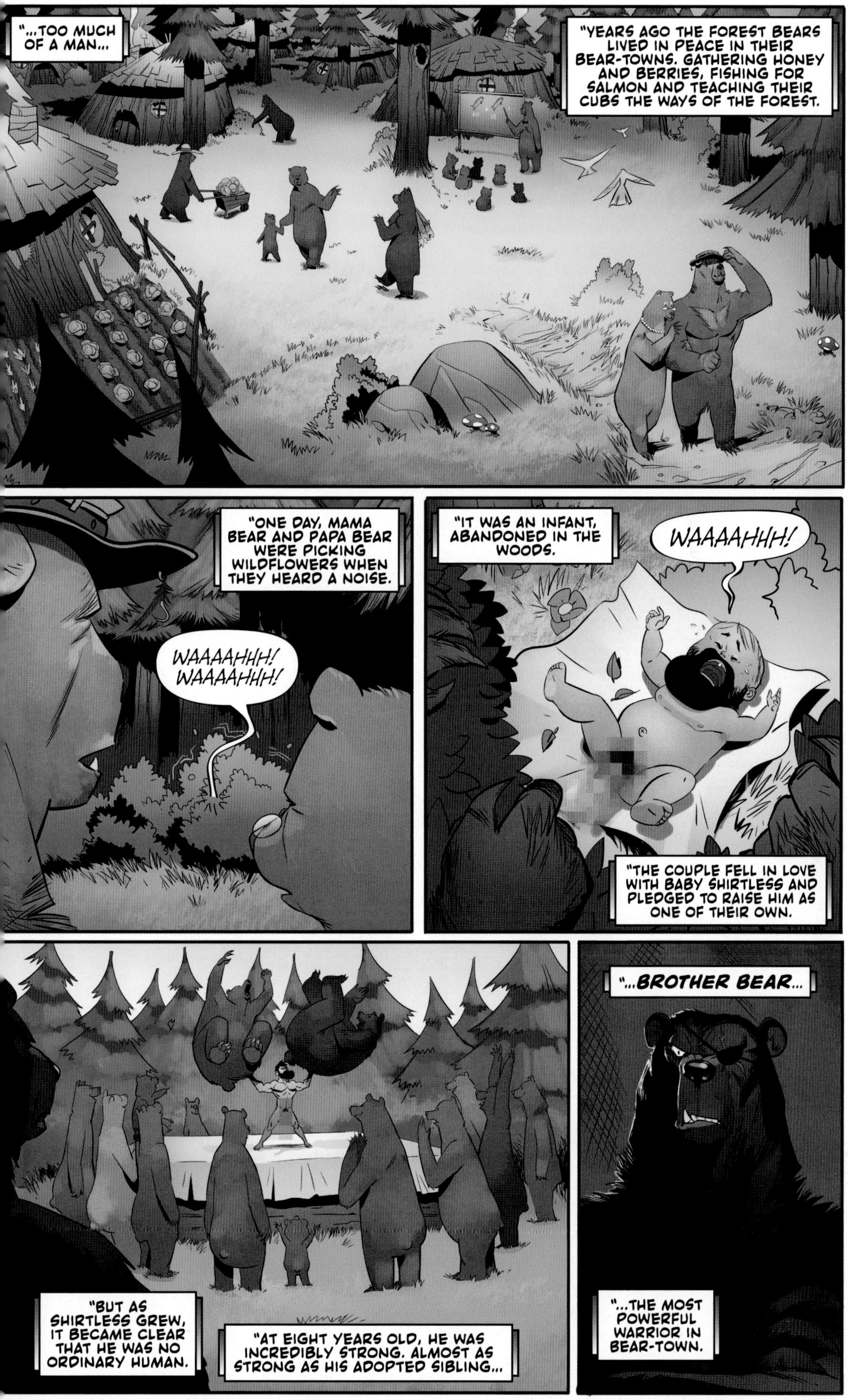
"...TOO MUCH OF A MAN...
"YEARS AGO THE FOREST BEARS LIVED IN PEACE IN THEIR BEAR-TOWNS. GATHERING HONEY AND BERRIES, FISHING FOR SALMON AND TEACHING THEIR CUBS THE WAYS OF THE FOREST.
"ONE DAY, MAMA BEAR AND PAPA BEAR WERE PICKING WILDFLOWERS WHEN THEY HEARD A NOISE.
WAAAAHHH! WAAAAHHH!
"IT WAS AN INFANT, ABANDONED IN THE WOODS.
WAAAAHHH!
"THE COUPLE FELL IN LOVE WITH BABY SHIRTLESS AND PLEDGED TO RAISE HIM AS ONE OF THEIR OWN.
"BUT AS SHIRTLESS GREW, IT BECAME CLEAR THAT HE WAS NO ORDINARY HUMAN.
"AT EIGHT YEARS OLD, HE WAS INCREDIBLY STRONG. ALMOST AS STRONG AS HIS ADOPTED SIBLING...
"...BROTHER BEAR...
"...THE MOST POWERFUL WARRIOR IN BEAR-TOWN.

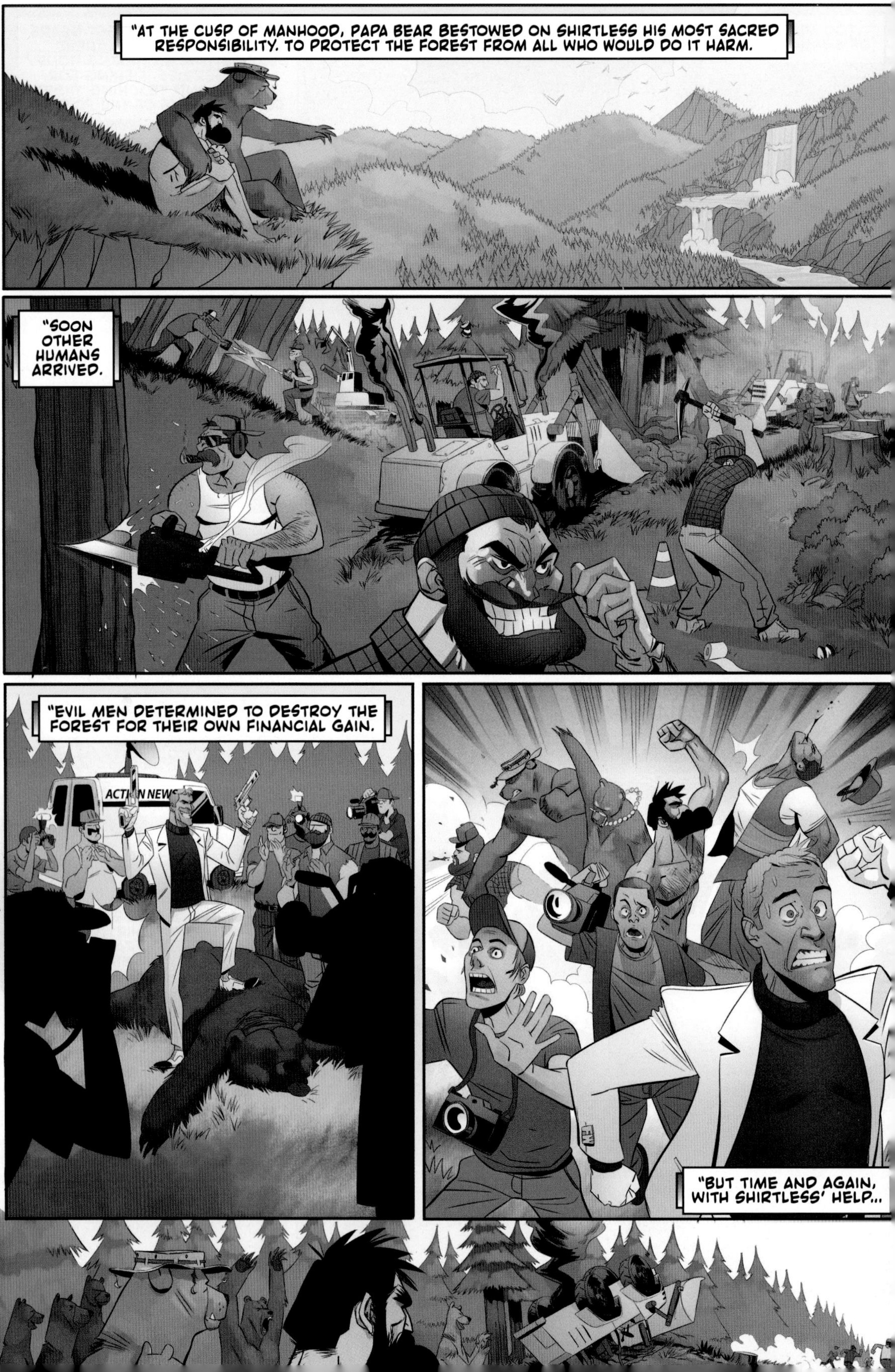
"AT THE CUSP OF MANHOOD, PAPA BEAR BESTOWED ON SHIRTLESS HIS MOST SACRED RESPONSIBILITY. TO PROTECT THE FOREST FROM ALL WHO WOULD DO IT HARM.
"SOON OTHER HUMANS ARRIVED.
"EVIL MEN DETERMINED TO DESTROY THE FOREST FOR THEIR OWN FINANCIAL GAIN.
ACTION NEWS
"BUT TIME AND AGAIN, WITH SHIRTLESS' HELP...

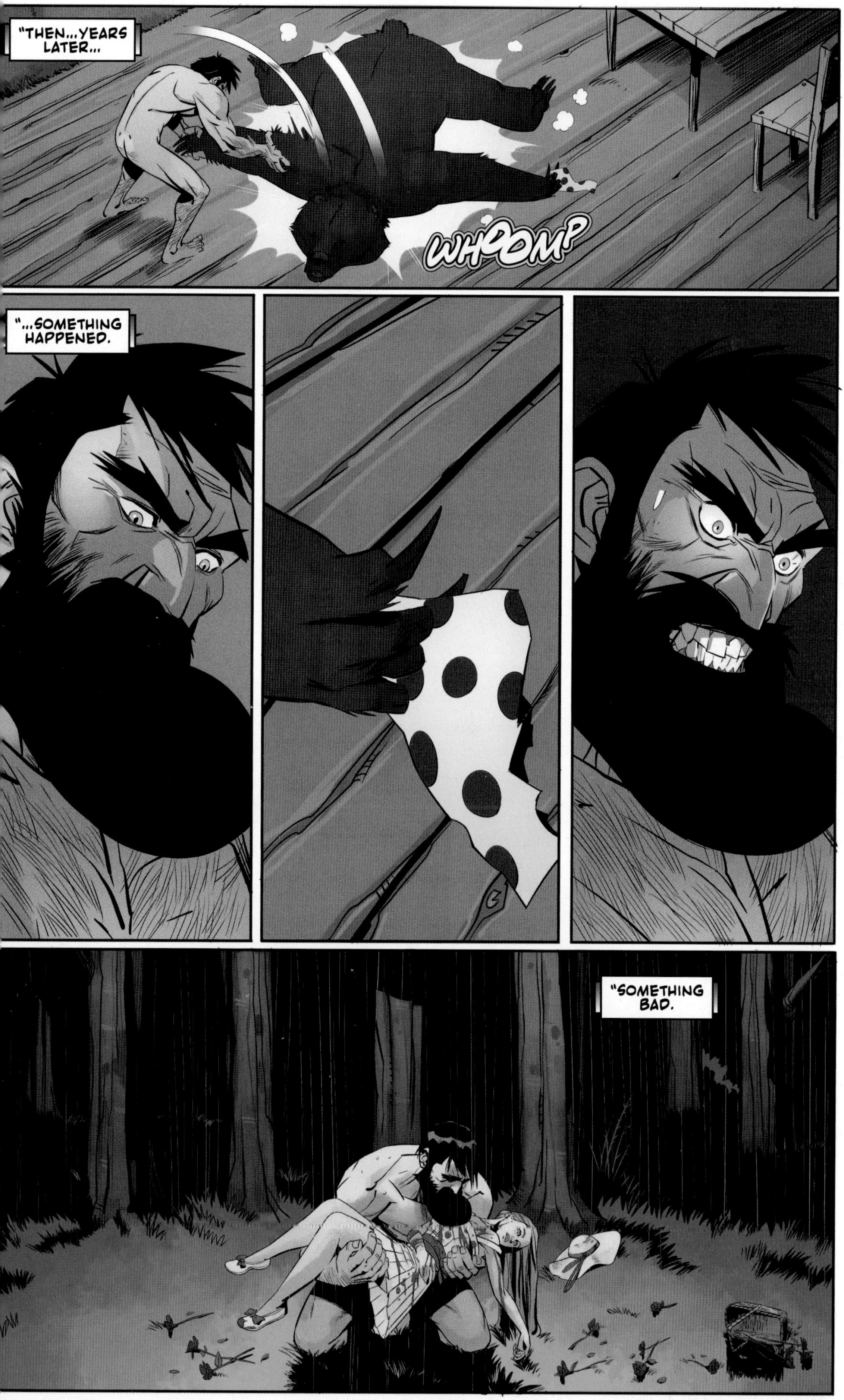
"THEN...YEARS LATER...
WHOOMP
"...SOMETHING HAPPENED.
"SOMETHING BAD.

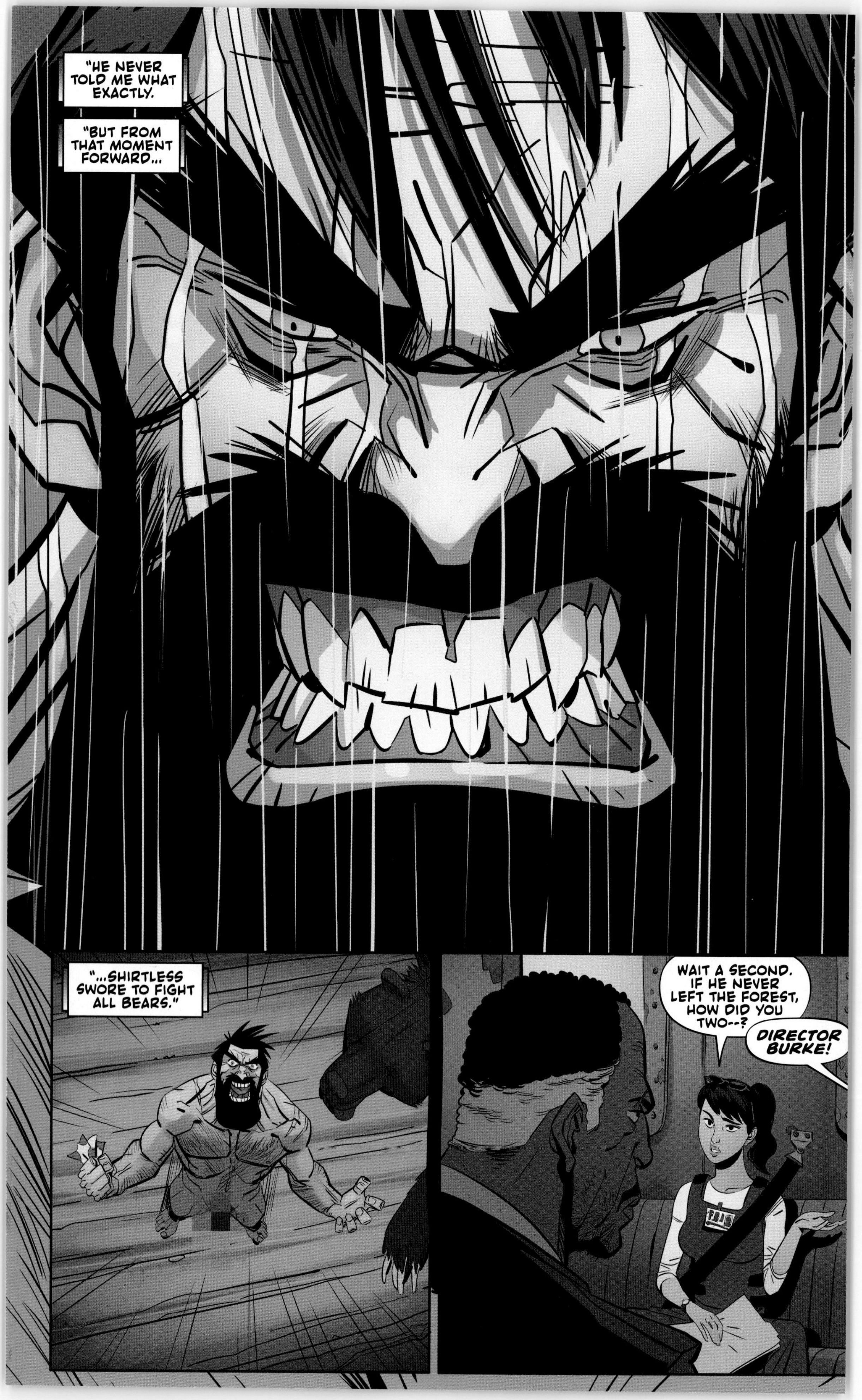
"HE NEVER TOLD ME WHAT EXACTLY.
"BUT FROM THAT MOMENT FORWARD...
"...SHIRTLESS SWORE TO FIGHT ALL BEARS."
WAIT A SECOND. IF HE NEVER LEFT THE FOREST, HOW DID YOU TWO--?
DIRECTOR BURKE!

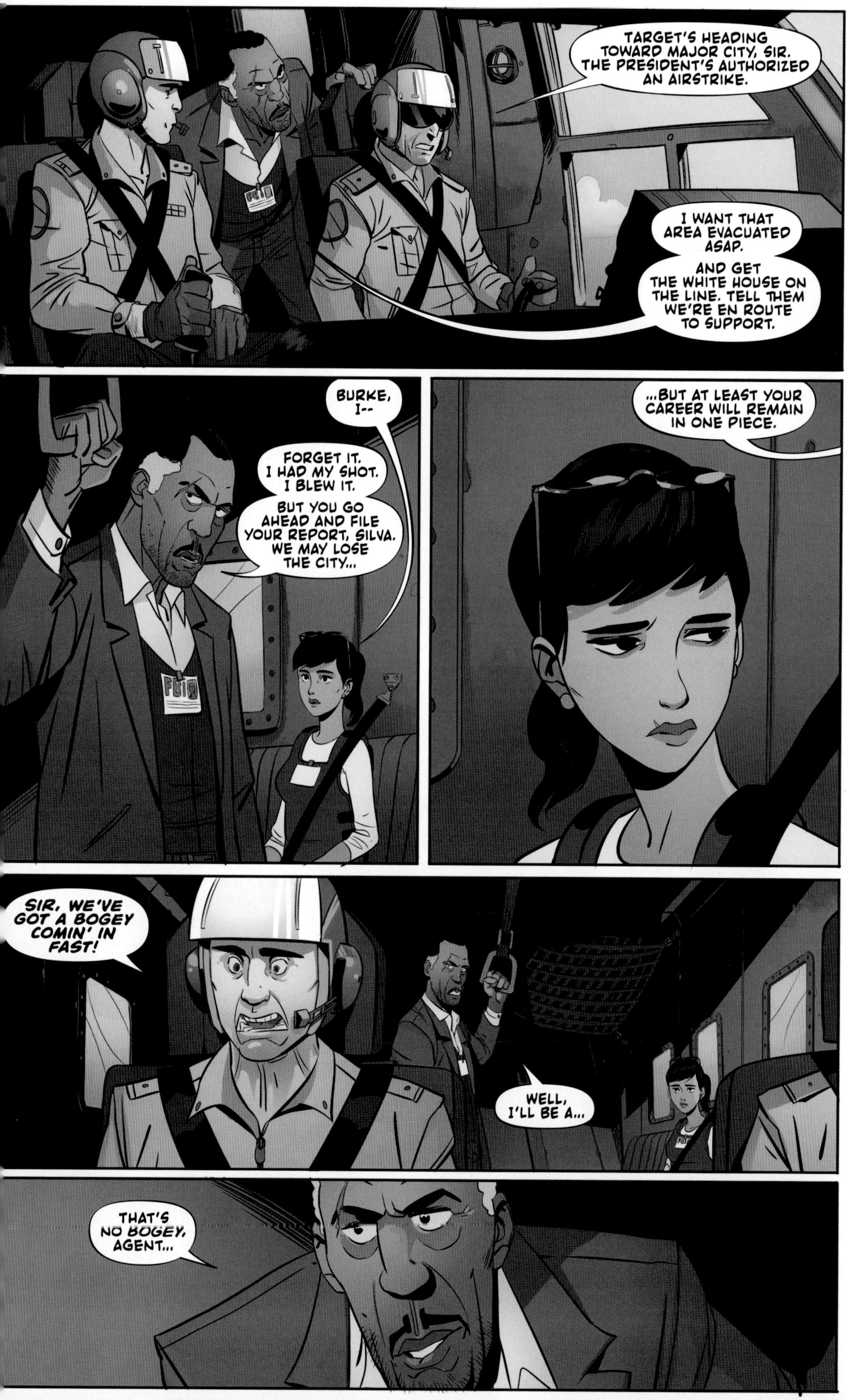
TARGET'S HEADING TOWARD MAJOR CITY, SIR. THE PRESIDENT'S AUTHORIZED AN AIRSTRIKE.
I WANT THAT AREA EVACUATED ASAP.
AND GET THE WHITE HOUSE ON THE LINE. TELL THEM WE'RE EN ROUTE TO SUPPORT.
BURKE, I--
FORGET IT. I HAD MY SHOT. I BLEW IT.
BUT YOU GO AHEAD AND FILE YOUR REPORT, SILVA. WE MAY LOSE THE CITY...
...BUT AT LEAST YOUR CAREER WILL REMAIN IN ONE PIECE.
SIR, WE'VE GOT A BOGEY COMIN' IN FAST!
WELL, I'LL BE A...
THAT'S NO BOGEY, AGENT...

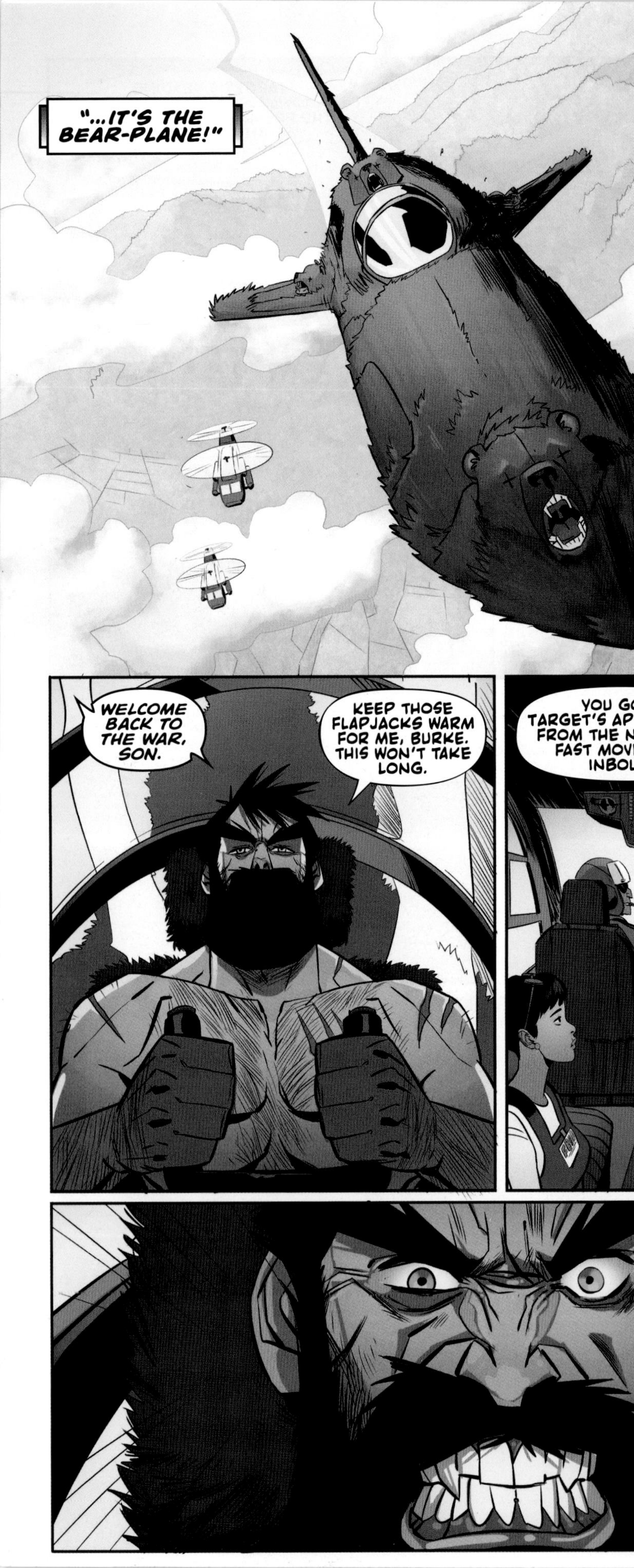
"...IT'S THE BEAR-PLANE!"
WELCOME BACK TO THE WAR, SON.
KEEP THOSE FLAPJACKS WARM FOR ME, BURKE. THIS WON'T TAKE LONG.
YOU GO
TARGET'S AP
FROM THE N
FAST MOVI
INBOL

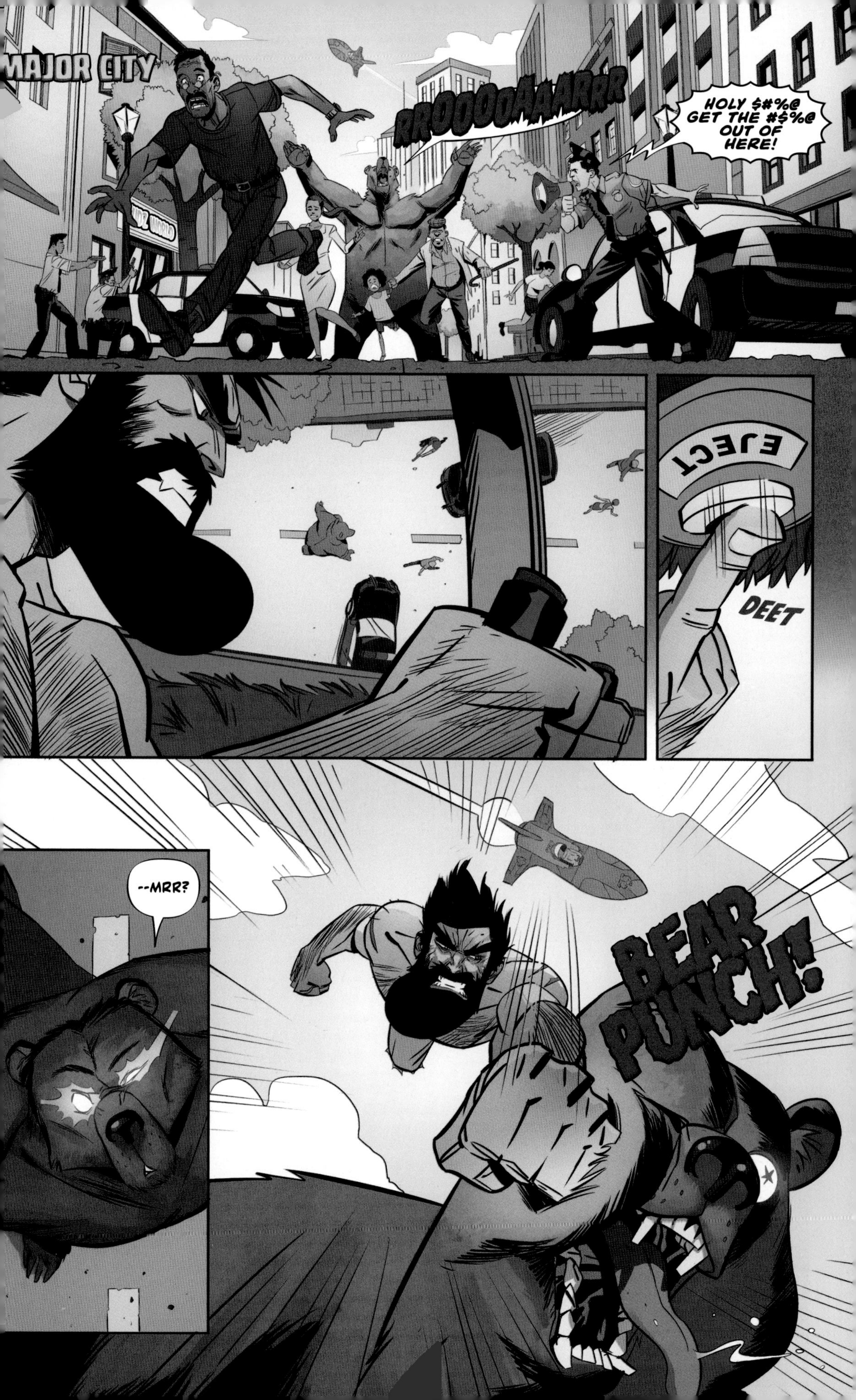
MAJOR CITY
RROOOOAAAARRR
HOLY $#%@ GET THE #$%@ OUT OF HERE!
EJECT
DEET
--MRR?
BEAR PUNCH!

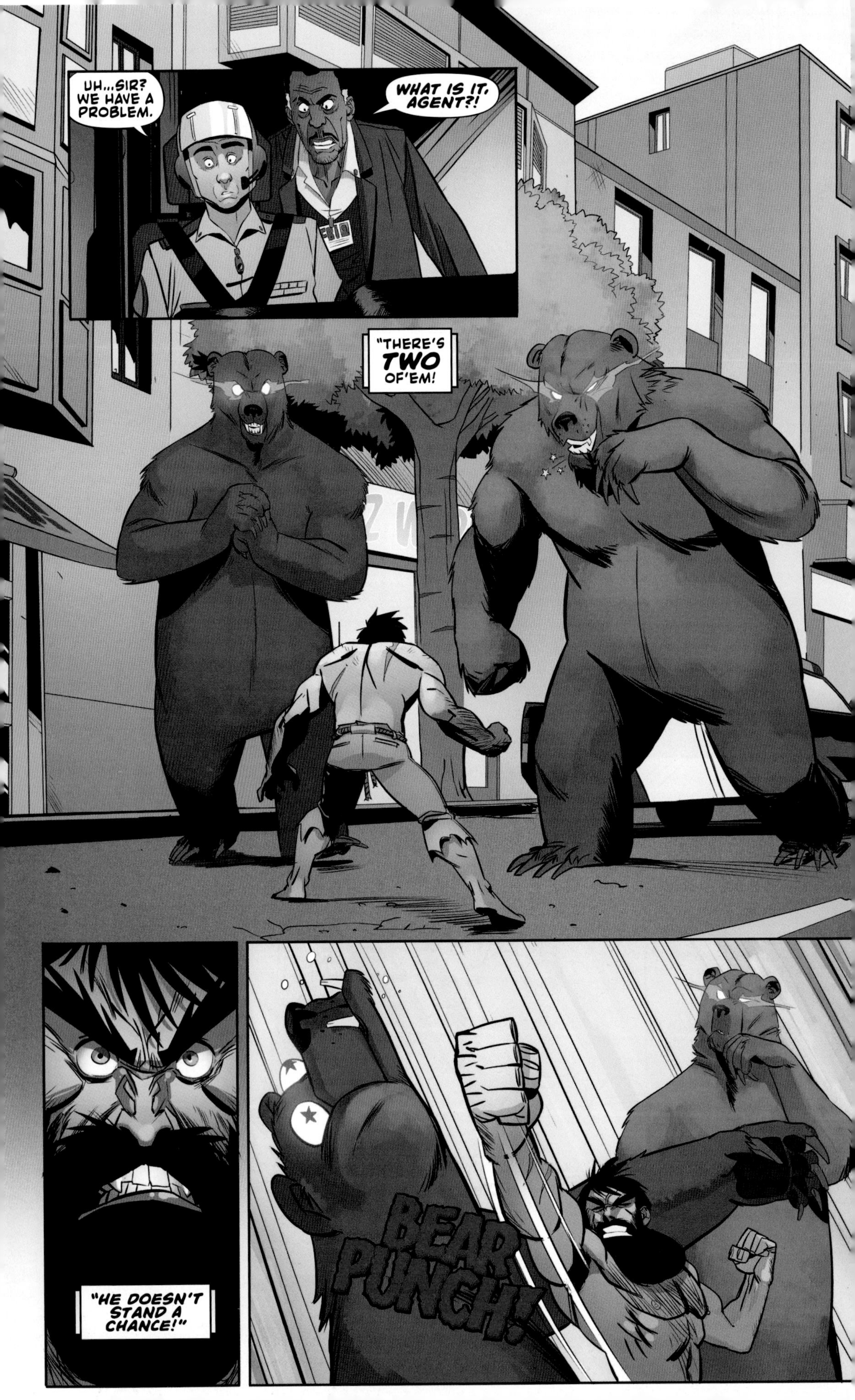
UH...SIR? WE HAVE A PROBLEM.
WHAT IS IT, AGENT?!
"THERE'S TWO OF'EM!
"HE DOESN'T STAND A CHANCE!"
BEAR PUNCH!

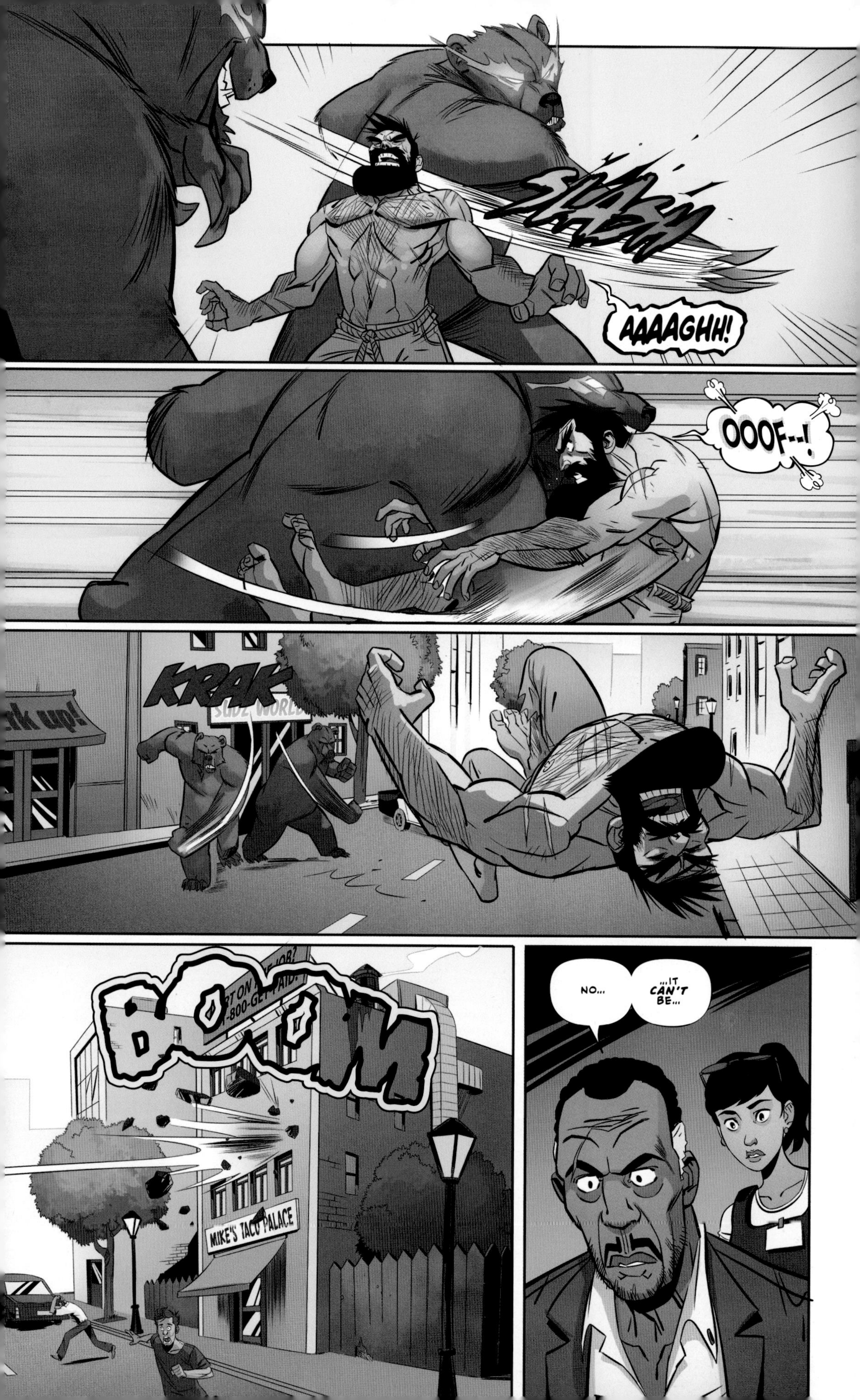
AAAAGHH!
OOOF--!
KRAK
BOOM
MIKE'S TACO PALACE
NO...
...IT CAN'T BE...

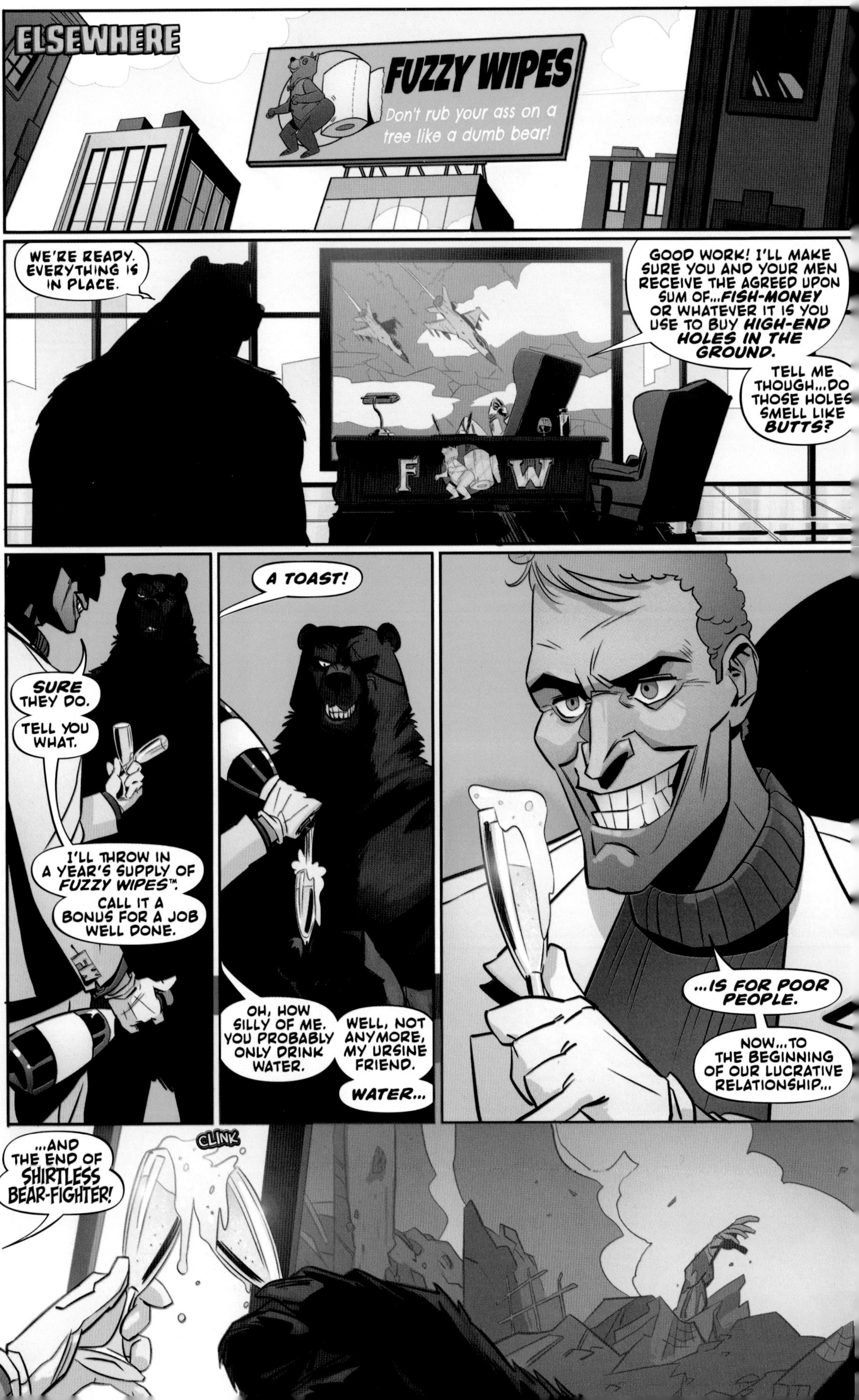
ELSEWHERE
FUZZY WIPES
Don't rub your ass on a tree like a dumb bear!
WE'RE READY. EVERYTHING IS IN PLACE.
GOOD WORK! I'LL MAKE SURE YOU AND YOUR MEN RECEIVE THE AGREED UPON SUM OF...FISH-MONEY OR WHATEVER IT IS YOU USE TO BUY HIGH-END HOLES IN THE GROUND.
TELL ME THOUGH...DO THOSE HOLES SMELL LIKE BUTTS?
F W
SURE THEY DO.
TELL YOU WHAT.
I'LL THROW IN A YEAR'S SUPPLY OF FUZZY WIPES™.
CALL IT A BONUS FOR A JOB WELL DONE.
A TOAST!
OH, HOW SILLY OF ME. YOU PROBABLY ONLY DRINK WATER.
WELL, NOT ANYMORE, MY URSINE FRIEND.
WATER...
...IS FOR POOR PEOPLE.
NOW...TO THE BEGINNING OF OUR LUCRATIVE RELATIONSHIP...
...AND THE END OF SHIRTLESS BEAR-FIGHTER!
CLINK

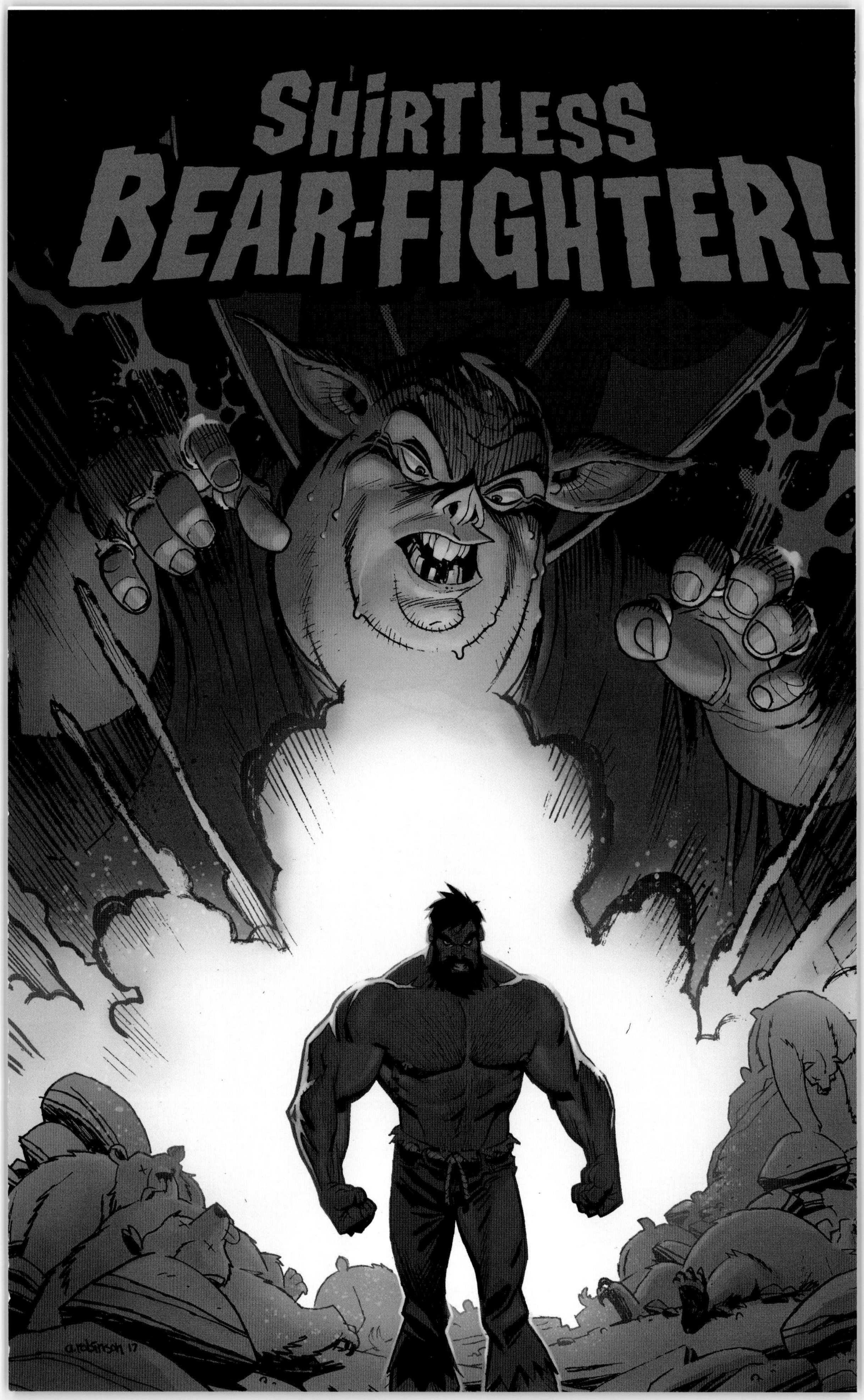
SHIRTLESS
BEAR-FIGHTER!

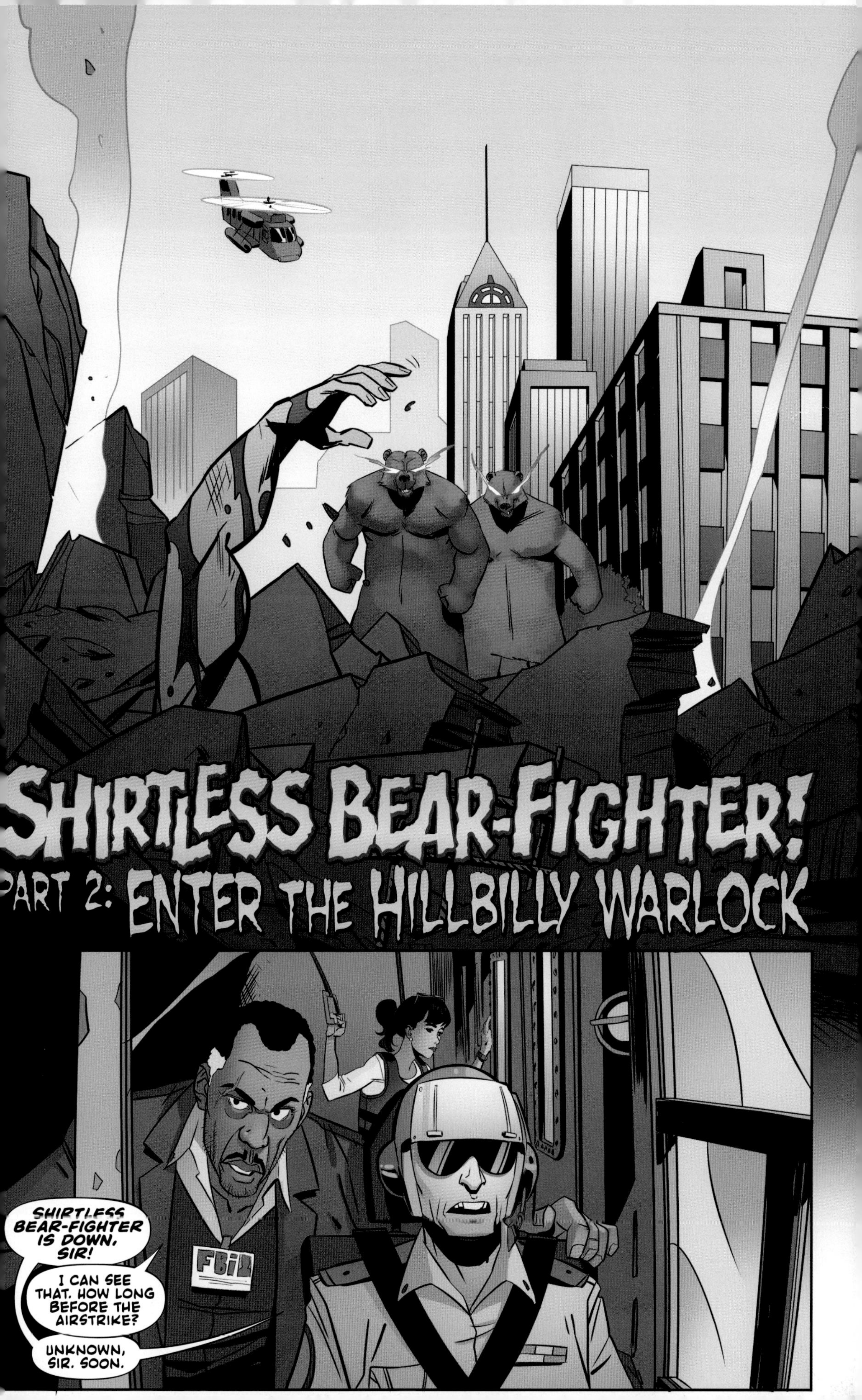
SHIRTLESS BEAR-FIGHTER!
PART 2: ENTER THE HILLBILLY WARLOCK
SHIRTLESS BEAR-FIGHTER IS DOWN, SIR!
I CAN SEE THAT. HOW LONG BEFORE THE AIRSTRIKE?
UNKNOWN, SIR. SOON.
FBI

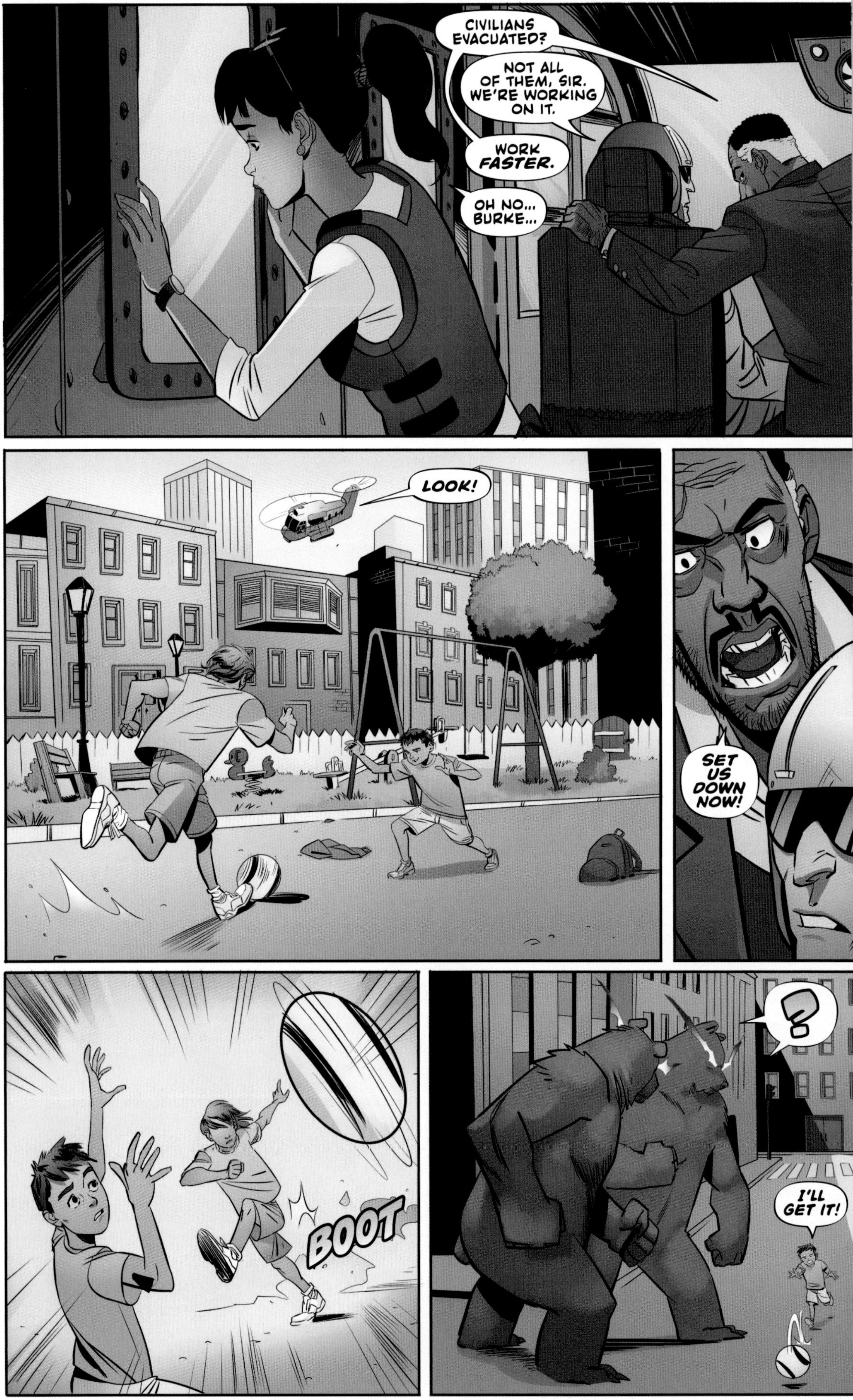
CIVILIANS EVACUATED?
NOT ALL OF THEM, SIR. WE'RE WORKING ON IT.
WORK FASTER.
OH NO... BURKE...
LOOK!
SET US DOWN NOW!
BOOT
?
I'LL GET IT!

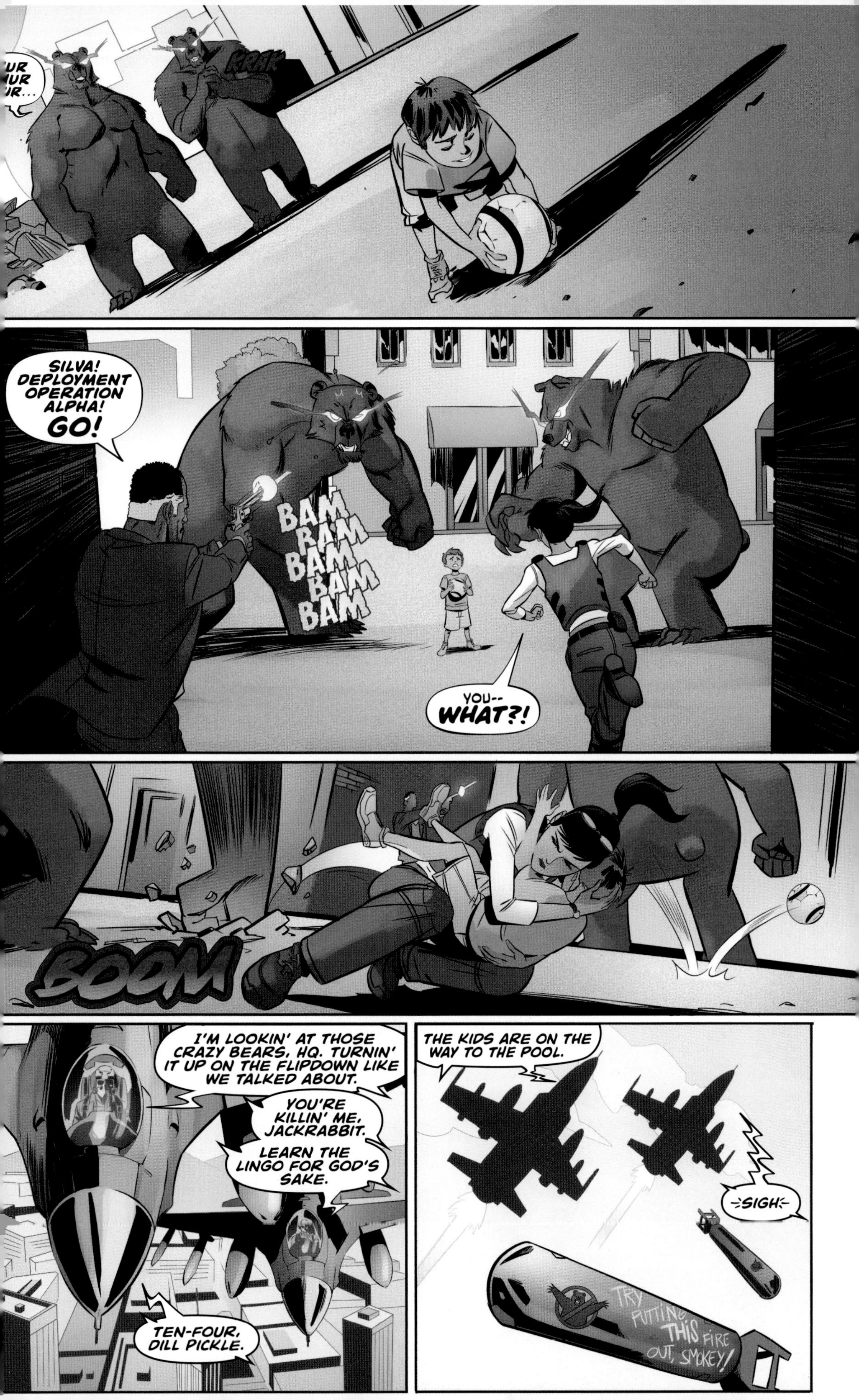
KRAK
SILVA! DEPLOYMENT OPERATION ALPHA! GO!
BAM BAM BAM BAM BAM BAM
YOU-- WHAT?!
BOOM
I'M LOOKIN' AT THOSE CRAZY BEARS, HQ. TURNIN' IT UP ON THE FLIPDOWN LIKE WE TALKED ABOUT.
YOU'RE KILLIN' ME, JACKRABBIT.
LEARN THE LINGO FOR GOD'S SAKE.
TEN-FOUR, DILL PICKLE.
THE KIDS ARE ON THE WAY TO THE POOL.
SIGH
TRY PUTTING THIS FIRE OUT, SMOKEY!

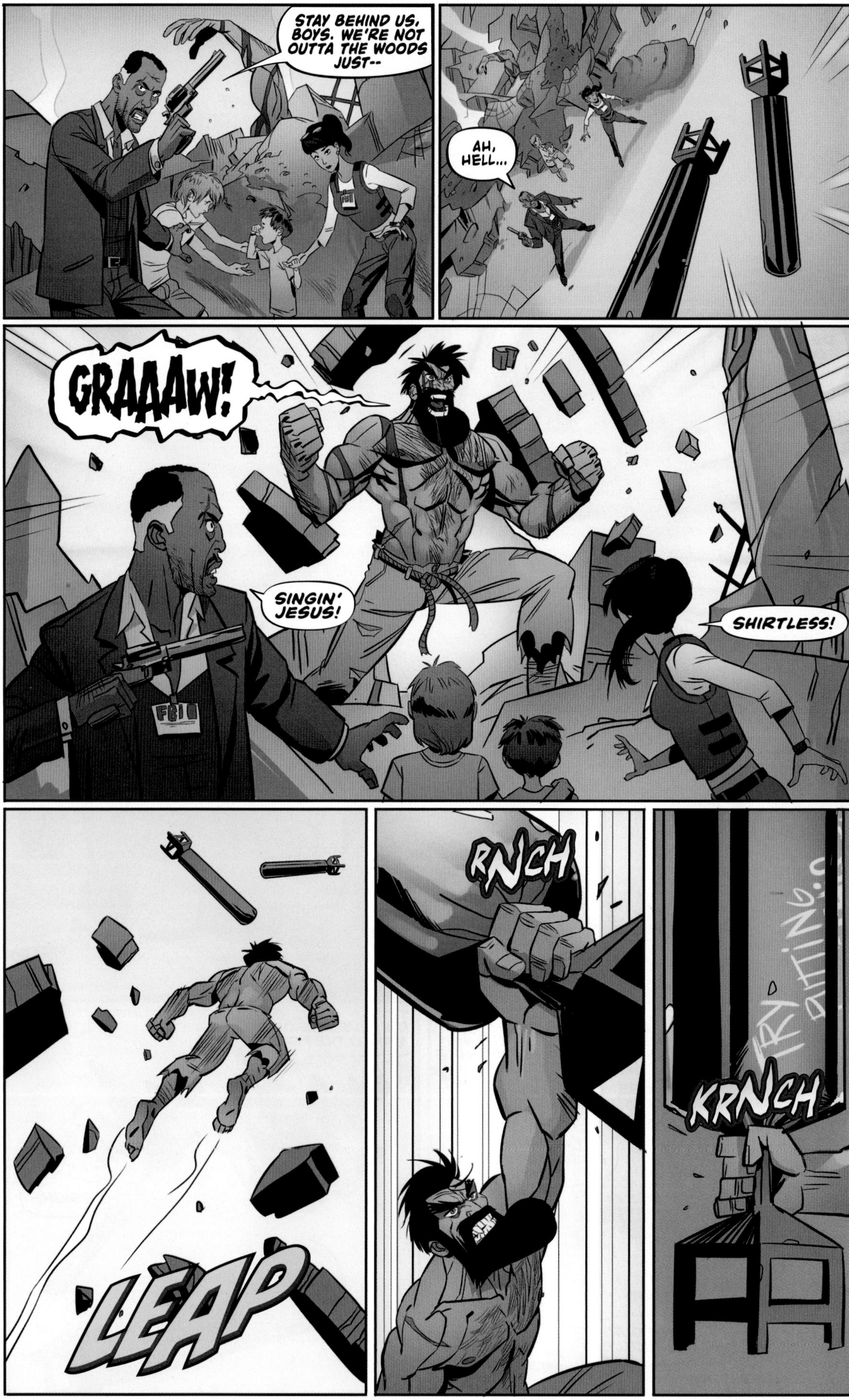
STAY BEHIND US, BOYS. WE'RE NOT OUTTA THE WOODS JUST--
AH, HELL...
GRAAAW!
SINGIN' JESUS!
SHIRTLESS!
LEAP
RNCH
KRNCH

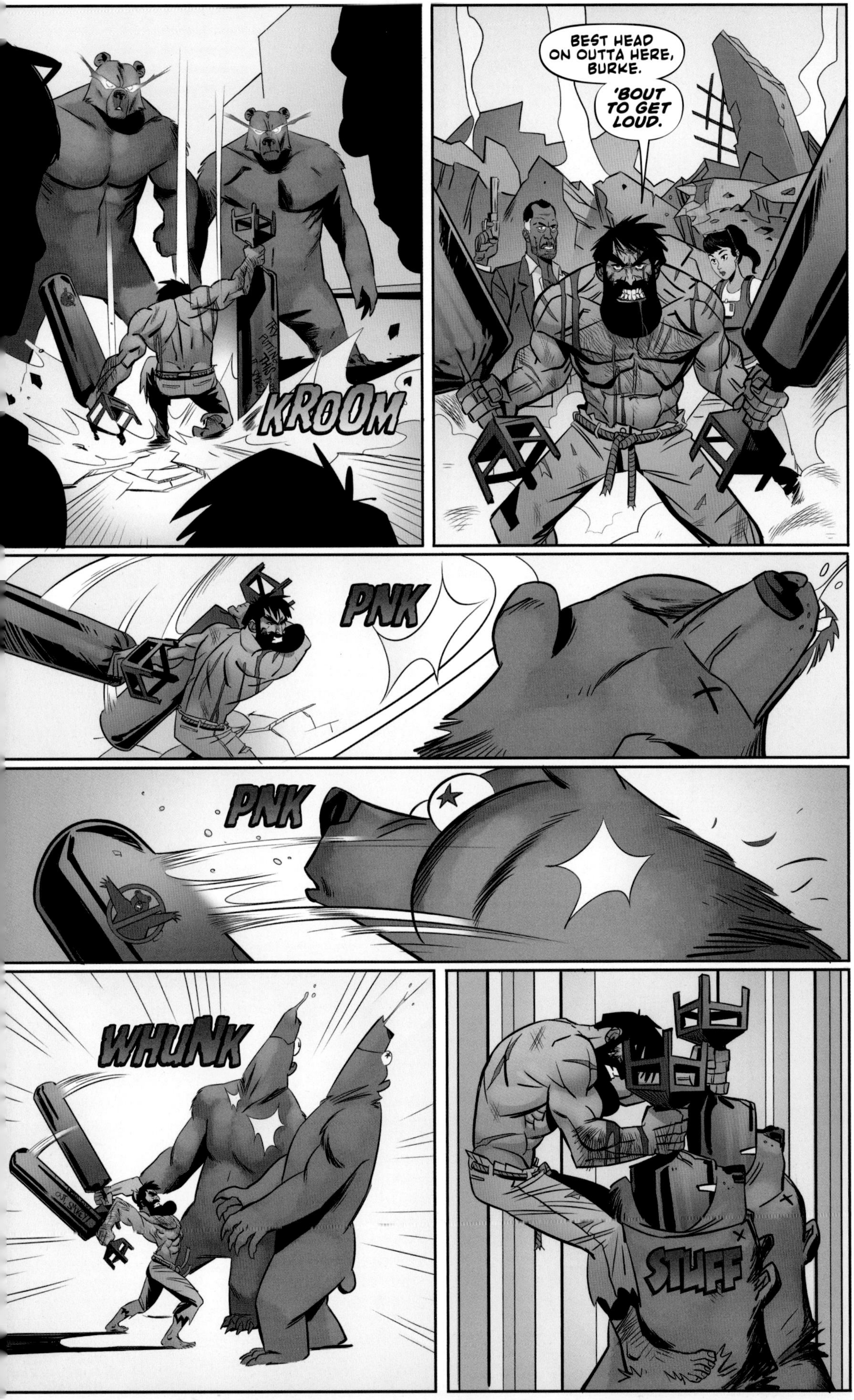
TRY PUTTING THIS
KROOM
BEST HEAD ON OUTTA HERE, BURKE.
'BOUT TO GET LOUD.
PNK
PNK
WHUNK
STUFF

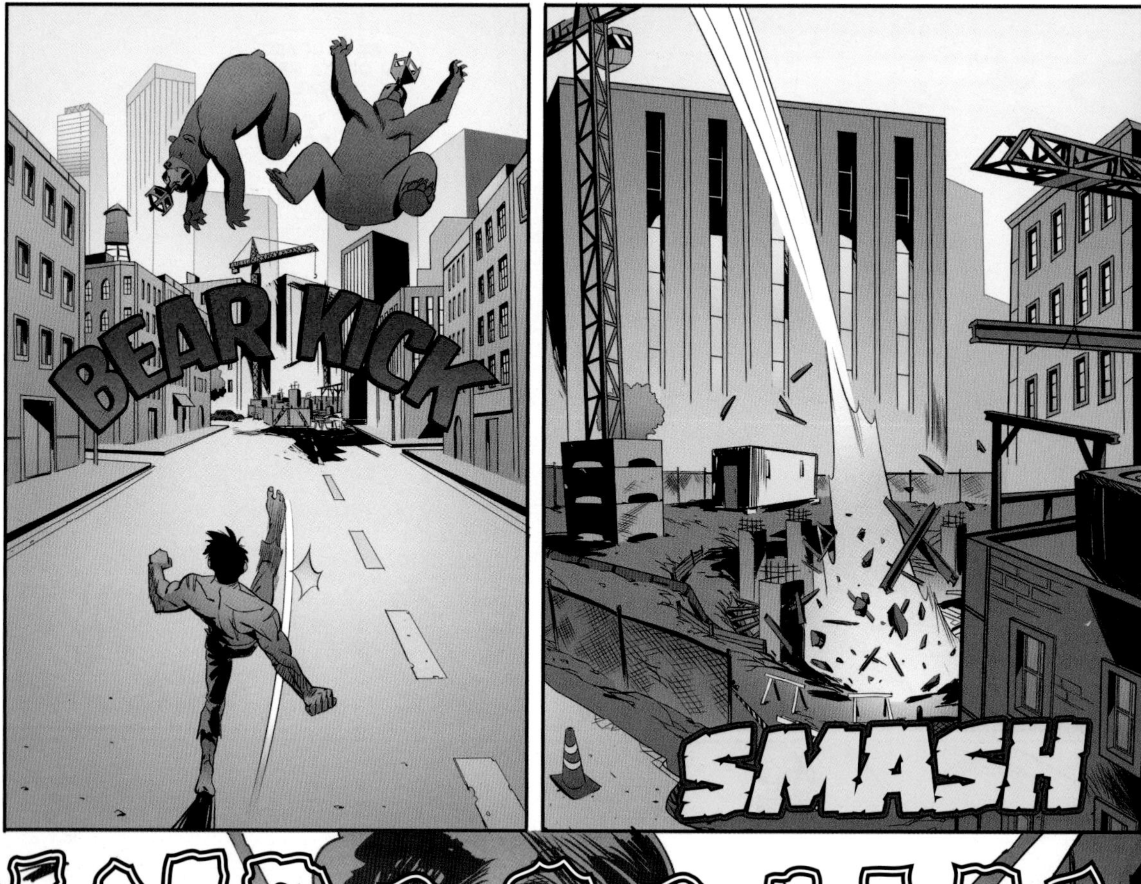
BEAR KICK
SMASH

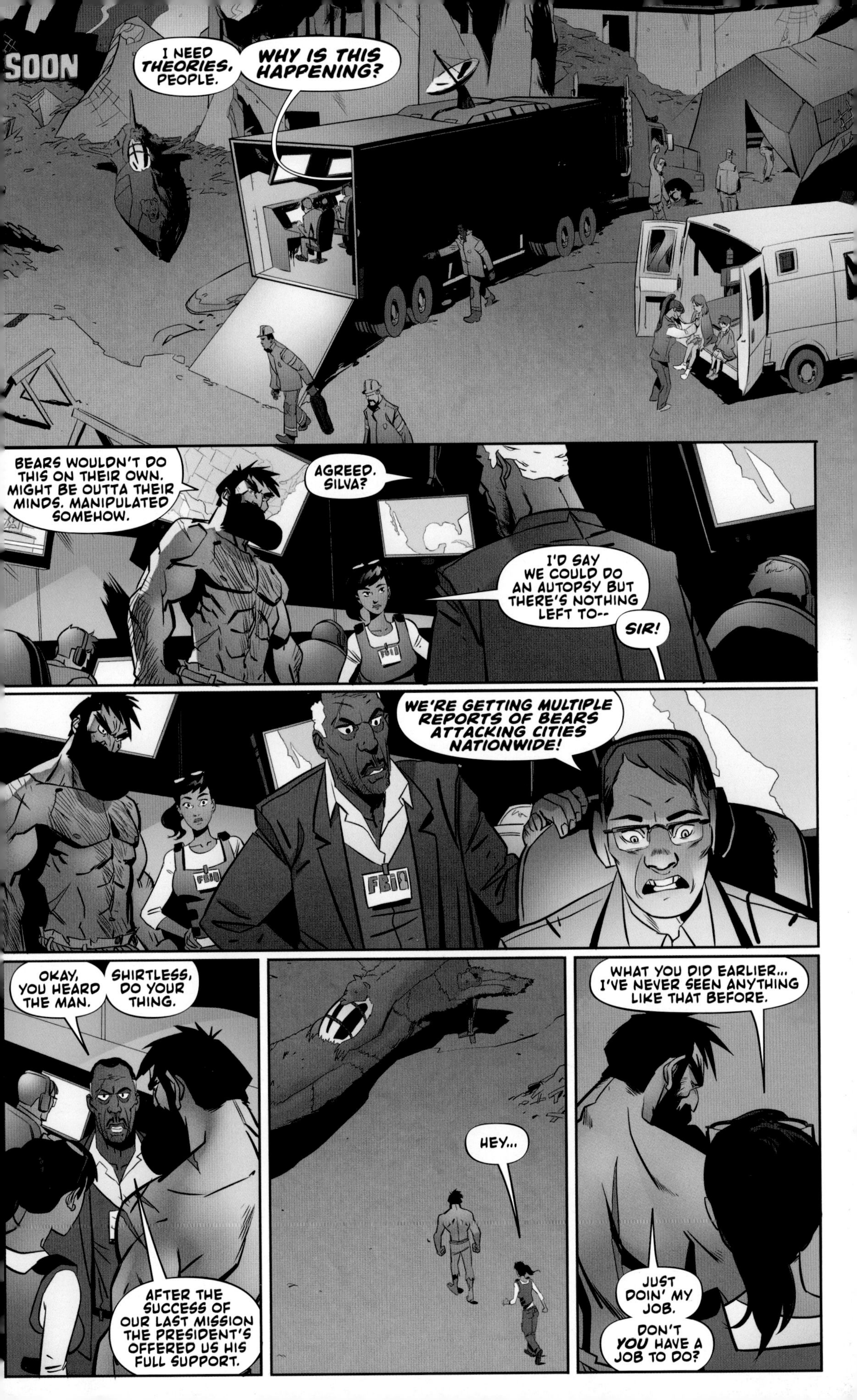
SOON
I NEED THEORIES, PEOPLE.
WHY IS THIS HAPPENING?
BEARS WOULDN'T DO THIS ON THEIR OWN. MIGHT BE OUTTA THEIR MINDS. MANIPULATED SOMEHOW.
AGREED. SILVA?
I'D SAY WE COULD DO AN AUTOPSY BUT THERE'S NOTHING LEFT TO--
SIR!
WE'RE GETTING MULTIPLE REPORTS OF BEARS ATTACKING CITIES NATIONWIDE!
OKAY, YOU HEARD THE MAN.
SHIRTLESS, DO YOUR THING.
AFTER THE SUCCESS OF OUR LAST MISSION THE PRESIDENT'S OFFERED US HIS FULL SUPPORT.
HEY...
WHAT YOU DID EARLIER... I'VE NEVER SEEN ANYTHING LIKE THAT BEFORE.
JUST DOIN' MY JOB.
DON'T YOU HAVE A JOB TO DO?

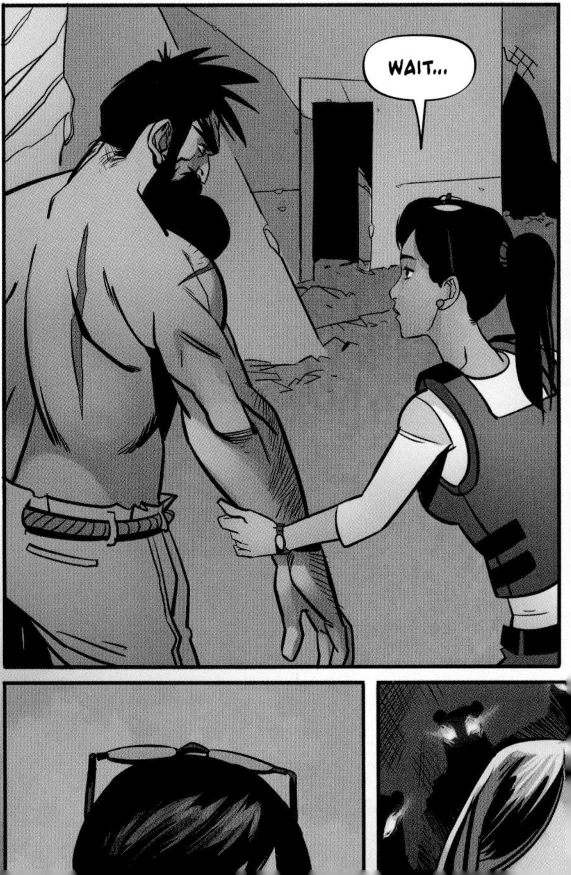
WAIT...

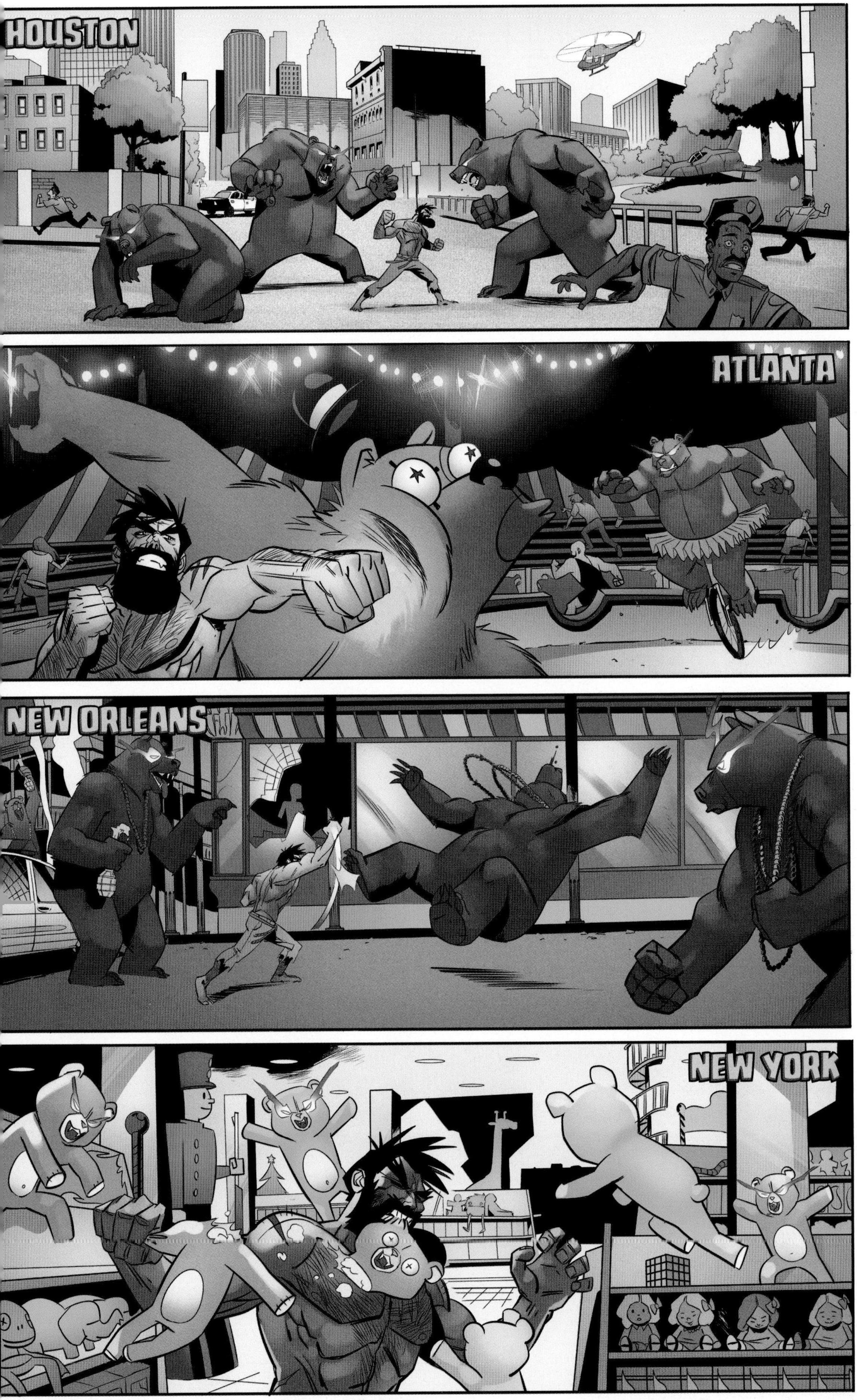
HOUSTON
ATLANTA
NEW ORLEANS
NEW YORK

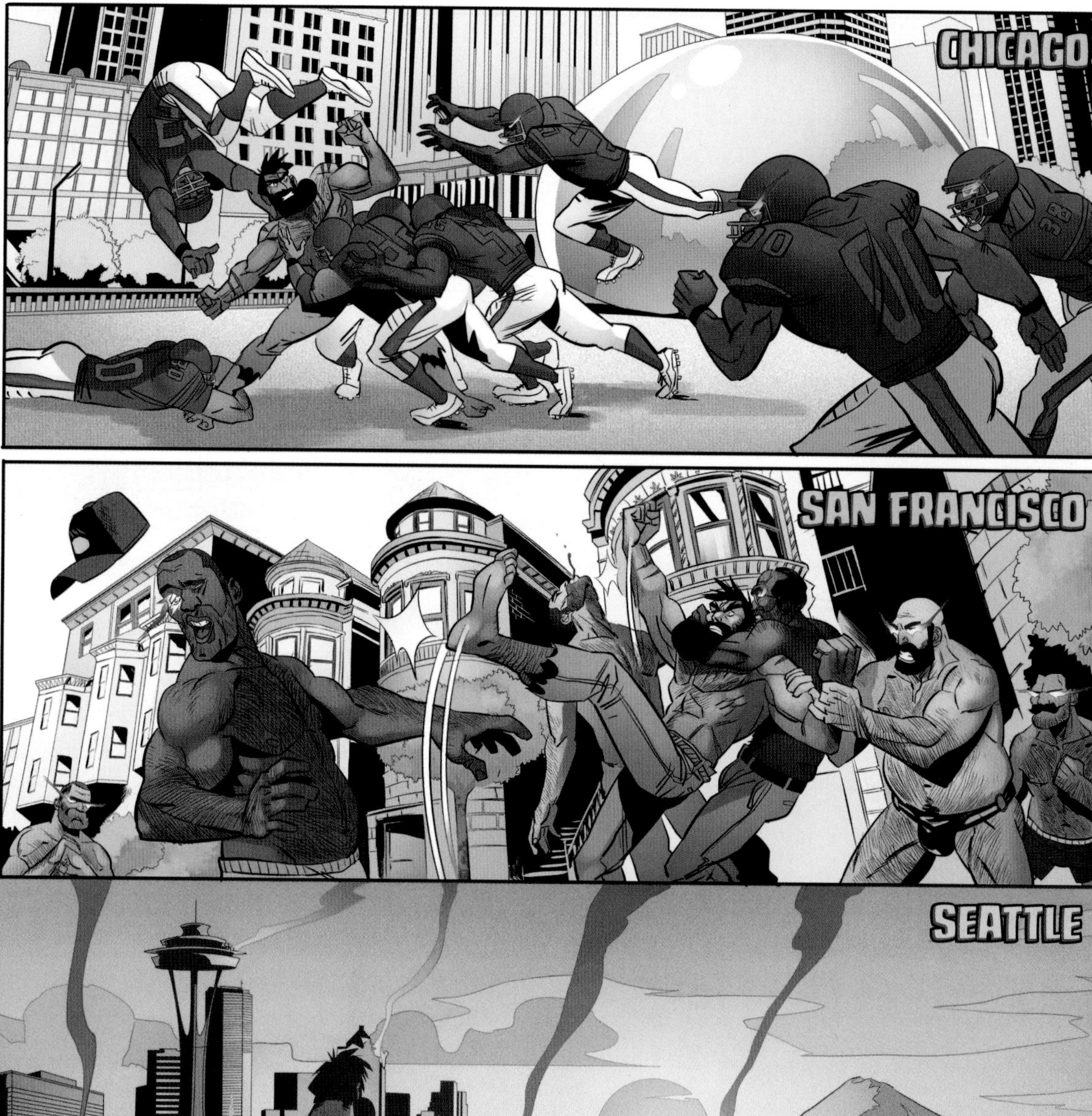
CHICAGO
SAN FRANCISCO
SEATTLE

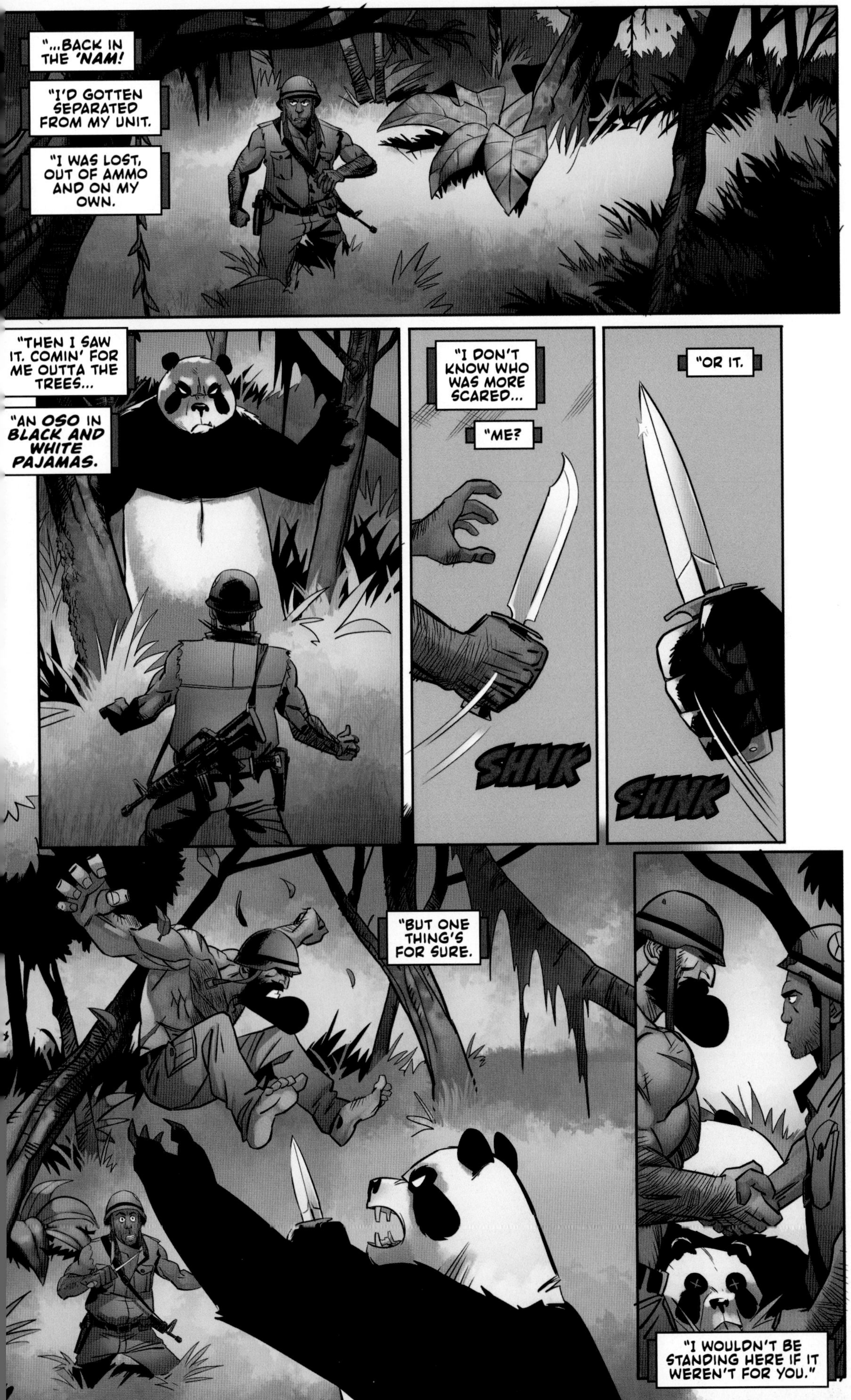
"...BACK IN THE 'NAM!
"I'D GOTTEN SEPARATED FROM MY UNIT.
"I WAS LOST, OUT OF AMMO AND ON MY OWN.
"THEN I SAW IT. COMIN' FOR ME OUTTA THE TREES...
"AN OSO IN BLACK AND WHITE PAJAMAS.
"I DON'T KNOW WHO WAS MORE SCARED...
"ME?
SHNK
"OR IT.
SHNK
"BUT ONE THING'S FOR SURE.
"I WOULDN'T BE STANDING HERE IF IT WEREN'T FOR YOU."

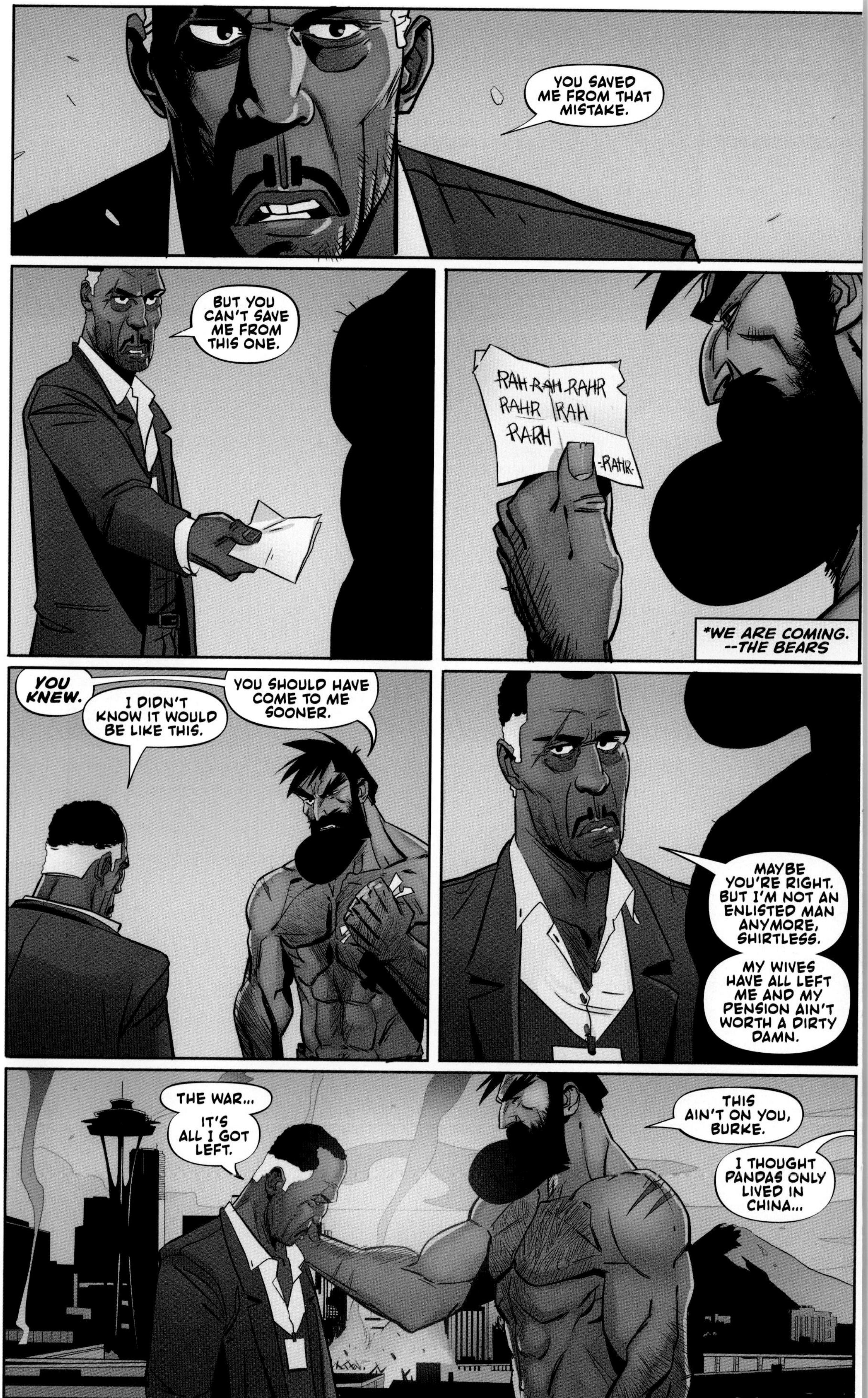
YOU SAVED ME FROM THAT MISTAKE.
BUT YOU CAN'T SAVE ME FROM THIS ONE.
RAH RAH RAHR
RAHR RAH
RARH
-RAHR-
*WE ARE COMING. --THE BEARS
YOU KNEW.
I DIDN'T KNOW IT WOULD BE LIKE THIS.
YOU SHOULD HAVE COME TO ME SOONER.
MAYBE YOU'RE RIGHT. BUT I'M NOT AN ENLISTED MAN ANYMORE, SHIRTLESS.
MY WIVES HAVE ALL LEFT ME AND MY PENSION AIN'T WORTH A DIRTY DAMN.
THE WAR...
IT'S ALL I GOT LEFT.
THIS AIN'T ON YOU, BURKE.
I THOUGHT PANDAS ONLY LIVED IN CHINA...

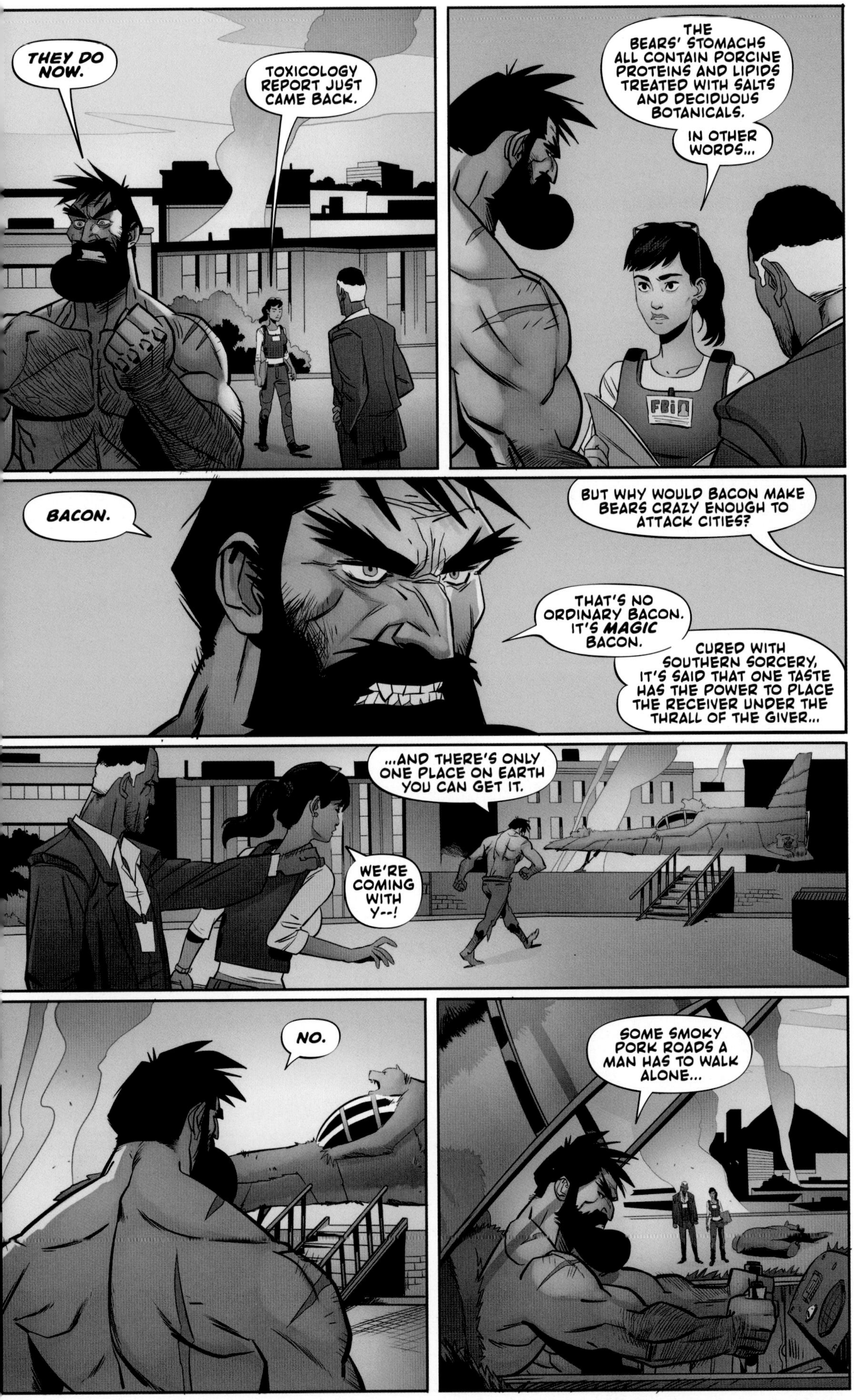
THEY DO NOW.
TOXICOLOGY REPORT JUST CAME BACK.
THE BEARS' STOMACHS ALL CONTAIN PORCINE PROTEINS AND LIPIDS TREATED WITH SALTS AND DECIDUOUS BOTANICALS.
IN OTHER WORDS...
FBI
BACON.
BUT WHY WOULD BACON MAKE BEARS CRAZY ENOUGH TO ATTACK CITIES?
THAT'S NO ORDINARY BACON. IT'S MAGIC BACON.
CURED WITH SOUTHERN SORCERY, IT'S SAID THAT ONE TASTE HAS THE POWER TO PLACE THE RECEIVER UNDER THE THRALL OF THE GIVER...
...AND THERE'S ONLY ONE PLACE ON EARTH YOU CAN GET IT.
WE'RE COMING WITH Y--!
NO.
SOME SMOKY PORK ROADS A MAN HAS TO WALK ALONE...

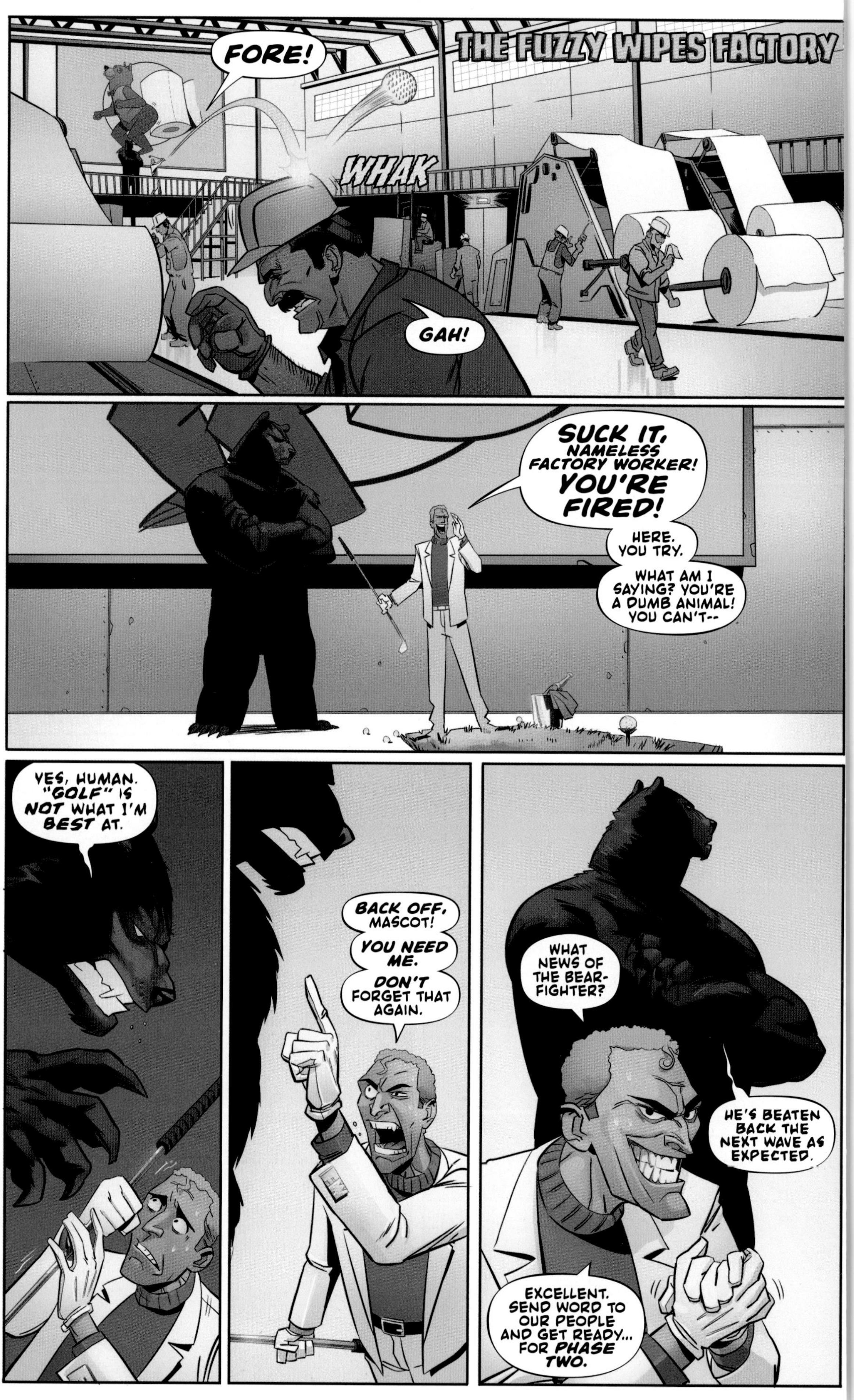
THE FUZZY WIPES FACTORY
FORE!
WHAK
GAH!
SUCK IT, NAMELESS FACTORY WORKER! YOU'RE FIRED!
HERE. YOU TRY.
WHAT AM I SAYING? YOU'RE A DUMB ANIMAL! YOU CAN'T--
YES, HUMAN. "GOLF" IS NOT WHAT I'M BEST AT.
BACK OFF, MASCOT!
YOU NEED ME.
DON'T FORGET THAT AGAIN.
WHAT NEWS OF THE BEAR-FIGHTER?
HE'S BEATEN BACK THE NEXT WAVE AS EXPECTED.
EXCELLENT. SEND WORD TO OUR PEOPLE AND GET READY... FOR PHASE TWO.

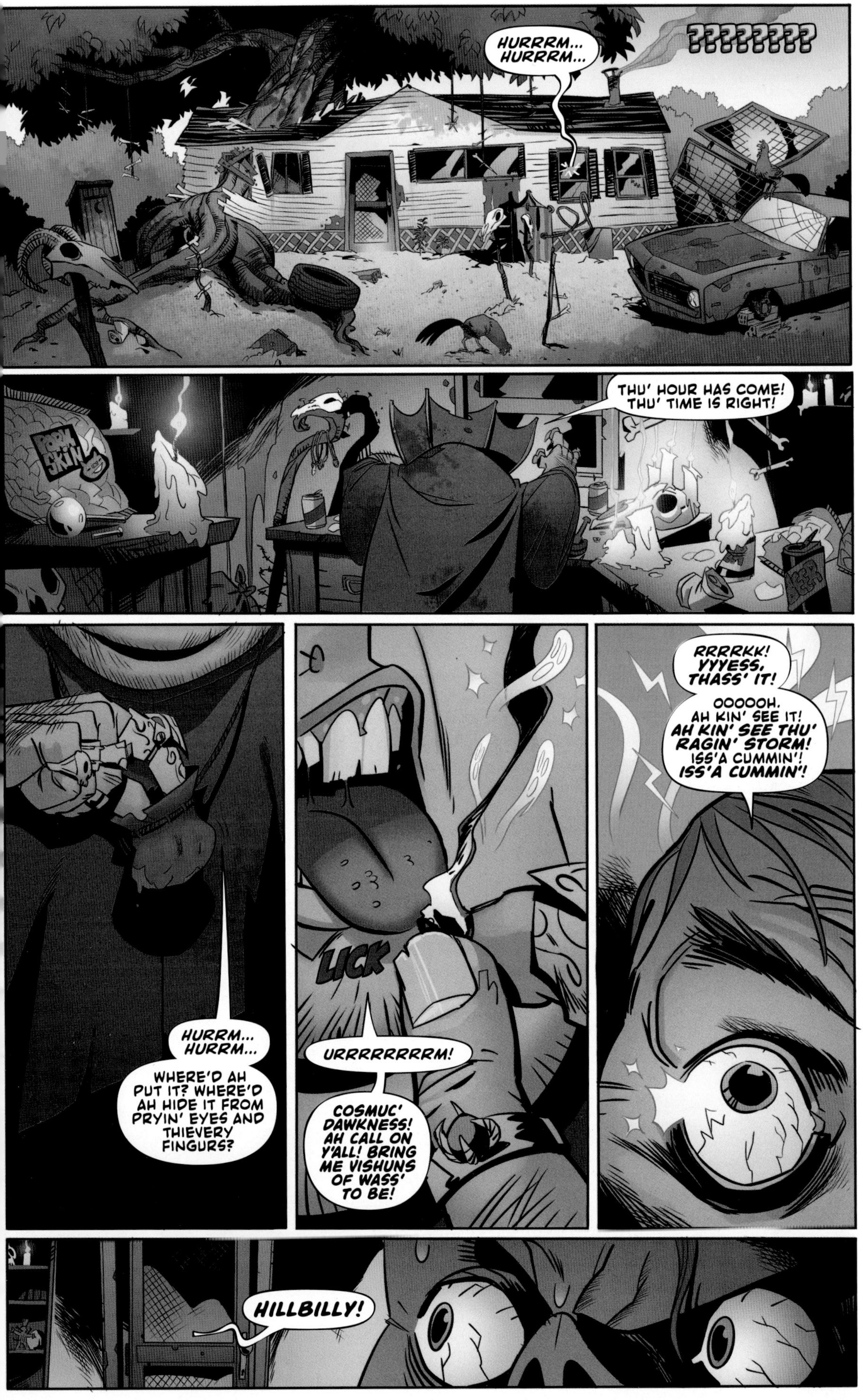
????????
HURRRM... HURRRM...
THU' HOUR HAS COME! THU' TIME IS RIGHT!
PORK SKIN
HURRM... HURRM...
WHERE'D AH PUT IT? WHERE'D AH HIDE IT FROM PRYIN' EYES AND THIEVERY FINGURS?
LICK
URRRRRRRRM!
COSMUC' DAWKNESS! AH CALL ON Y'ALL! BRING ME VISHUNS OF WASS' TO BE!
RRRRKK! YYYESS, THASS' IT!
OOOOOH. AH KIN' SEE IT! AH KIN' SEE THU' RAGIN' STORM! ISS'A CUMMIN'! ISS'A CUMMIN'!
HILLBILLY!

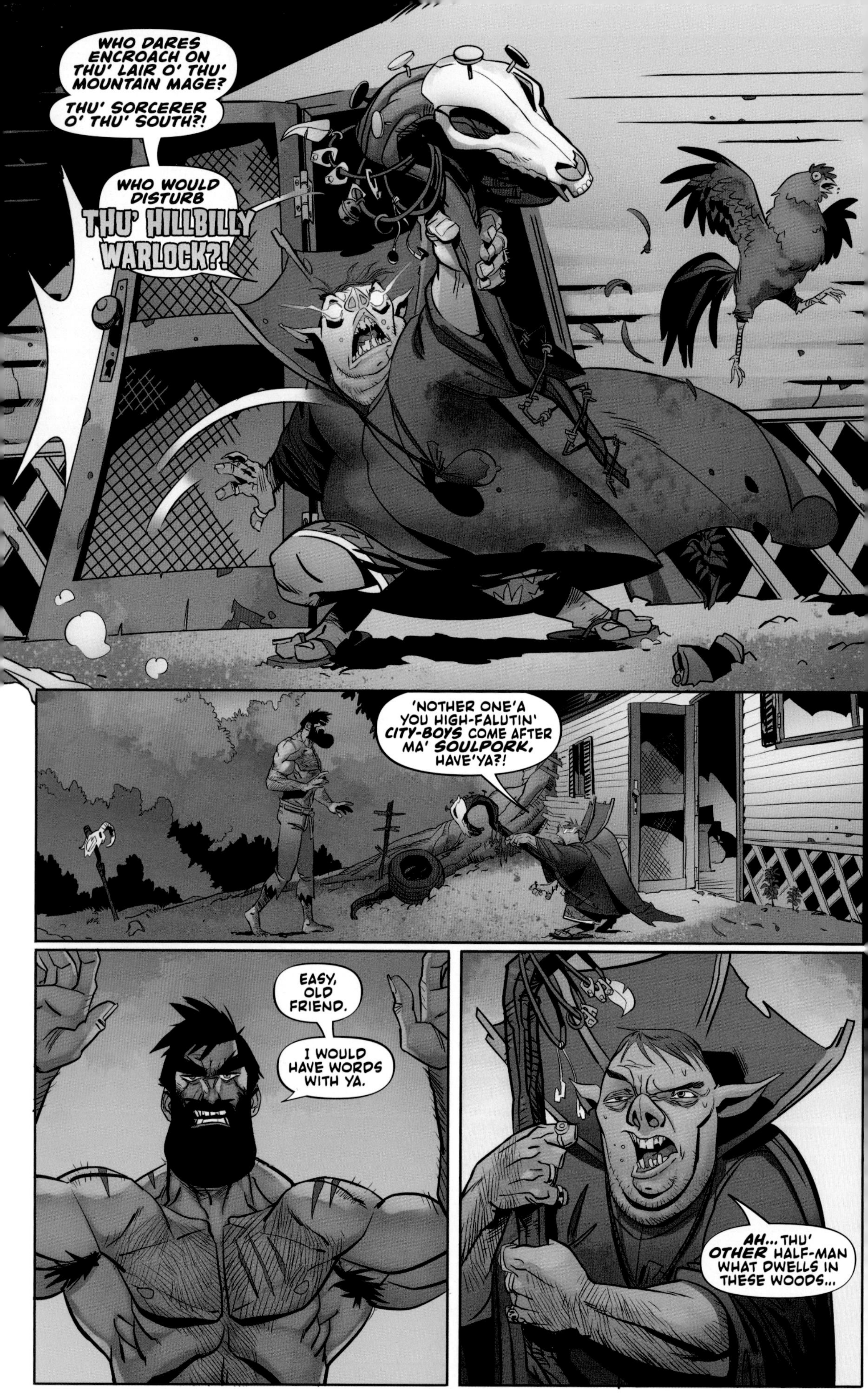
WHO DARES ENCROACH ON THU' LAIR O' THU' MOUNTAIN MAGE?
THU' SORCERER O' THU' SOUTH?!
WHO WOULD DISTURB THU' HILLBILLY WARLOCK?!
'NOTHER ONE'A YOU HIGH-FALUTIN' CITY-BOYS COME AFTER MA' SOULPORK, HAVE'YA?!
EASY, OLD FRIEND.
I WOULD HAVE WORDS WITH YA.
AH... THU' OTHER HALF-MAN WHAT DWELLS IN THESE WOODS...

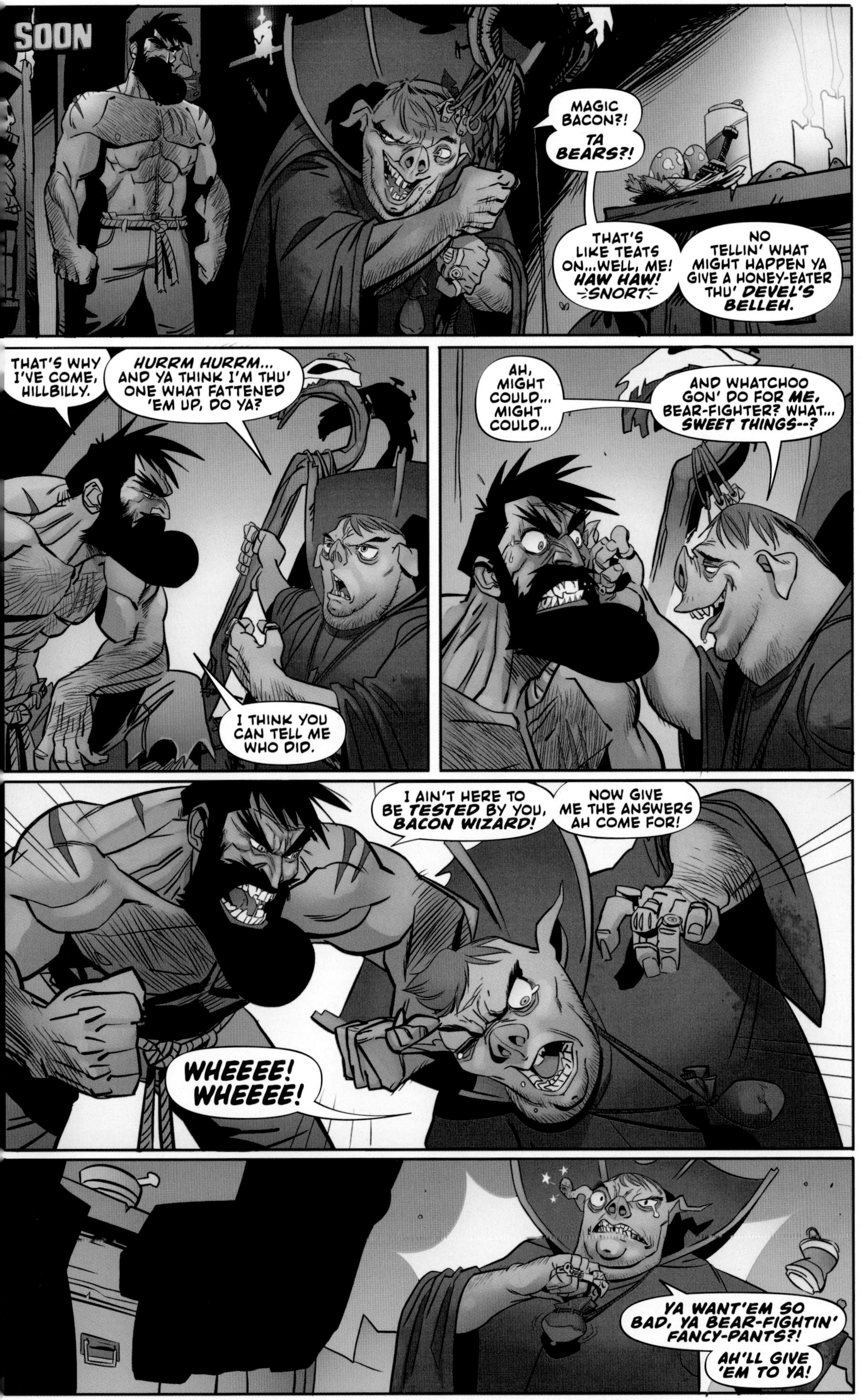
SOON
MAGIC BACON?! TA BEARS?!
THAT'S LIKE TEATS ON...WELL, ME! HAW HAW! SNORT
NO TELLIN' WHAT MIGHT HAPPEN YA GIVE A HONEY-EATER THU' DEVEL'S BELLEH.
THAT'S WHY I'VE COME, HILLBILLY.
HURRM HURRM... AND YA THINK I'M THU' ONE WHAT FATTENED 'EM UP, DO YA?
I THINK YOU CAN TELL ME WHO DID.
AH, MIGHT COULD... MIGHT COULD...
AND WHATCHOO GON' DO FOR ME, BEAR-FIGHTER? WHAT... SWEET THINGS--?
I AIN'T HERE TO BE TESTED BY YOU, BACON WIZARD!
NOW GIVE ME THE ANSWERS AH COME FOR!
WHEEEE! WHEEEE!
YA WANT'EM SO BAD, YA BEAR-FIGHTIN' FANCY-PANTS?!
AH'LL GIVE 'EM TO YA!

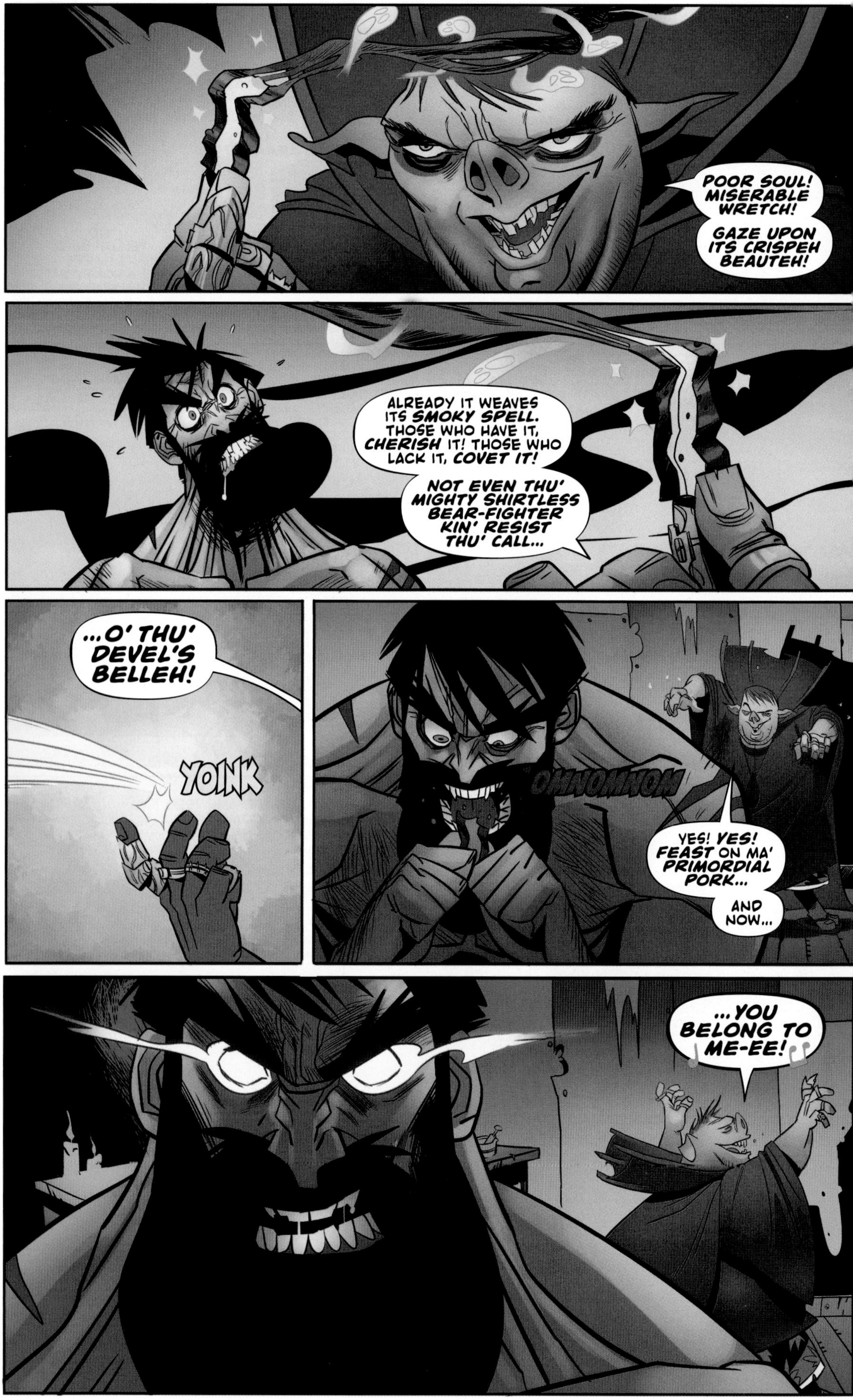
POOR SOUL! MISERABLE WRETCH!
GAZE UPON ITS CRISPEH BEAUTEH!
ALREADY IT WEAVES ITS SMOKY SPELL. THOSE WHO HAVE IT, CHERISH IT! THOSE WHO LACK IT, COVET IT!
NOT EVEN THU' MIGHTY SHIRTLESS BEAR-FIGHTER KIN' RESIST THU' CALL...
...O' THU' DEVEL'S BELLEH!
YOINK
OMNOMNOM
YES! YES! FEAST ON MA' PRIMORDIAL PORK...
AND NOW...
...YOU BELONG TO ME-EE!

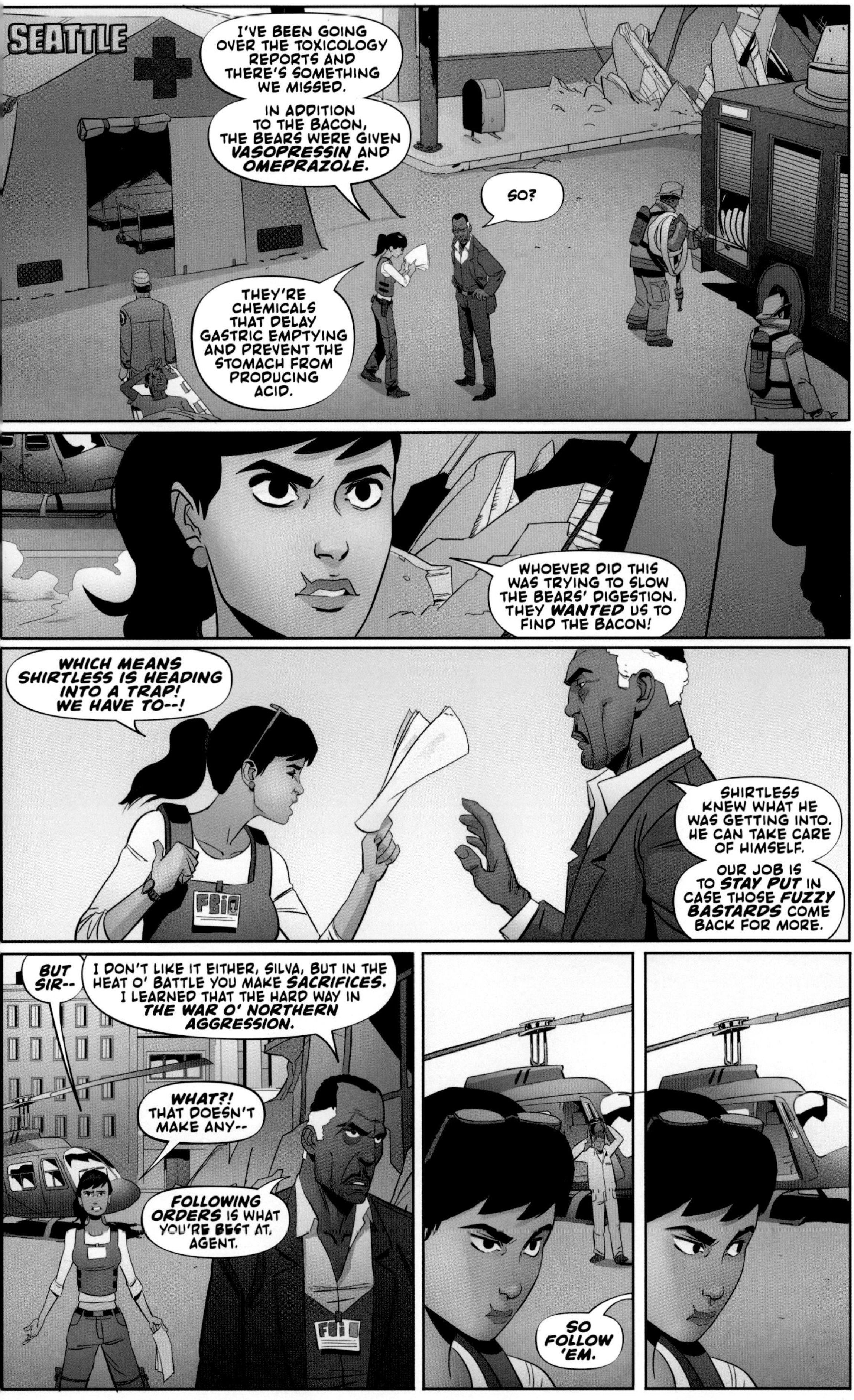
SEATTLE
I'VE BEEN GOING OVER THE TOXICOLOGY REPORTS AND THERE'S SOMETHING WE MISSED.
IN ADDITION TO THE BACON, THE BEARS WERE GIVEN VASOPRESSIN AND OMEPRAZOLE.
SO?
THEY'RE CHEMICALS THAT DELAY GASTRIC EMPTYING AND PREVENT THE STOMACH FROM PRODUCING ACID.
WHOEVER DID THIS WAS TRYING TO SLOW THE BEARS' DIGESTION. THEY WANTED US TO FIND THE BACON!
WHICH MEANS SHIRTLESS IS HEADING INTO A TRAP! WE HAVE TO--!
SHIRTLESS KNEW WHAT HE WAS GETTING INTO. HE CAN TAKE CARE OF HIMSELF.
OUR JOB IS TO STAY PUT IN CASE THOSE FUZZY BASTARDS COME BACK FOR MORE.
BUT SIR--
I DON'T LIKE IT EITHER, SILVA, BUT IN THE HEAT O' BATTLE YOU MAKE SACRIFICES. I LEARNED THAT THE HARD WAY IN THE WAR O' NORTHERN AGGRESSION.
WHAT?! THAT DOESN'T MAKE ANY--
FOLLOWING ORDERS IS WHAT YOU'RE BEST AT, AGENT.
SO FOLLOW 'EM.

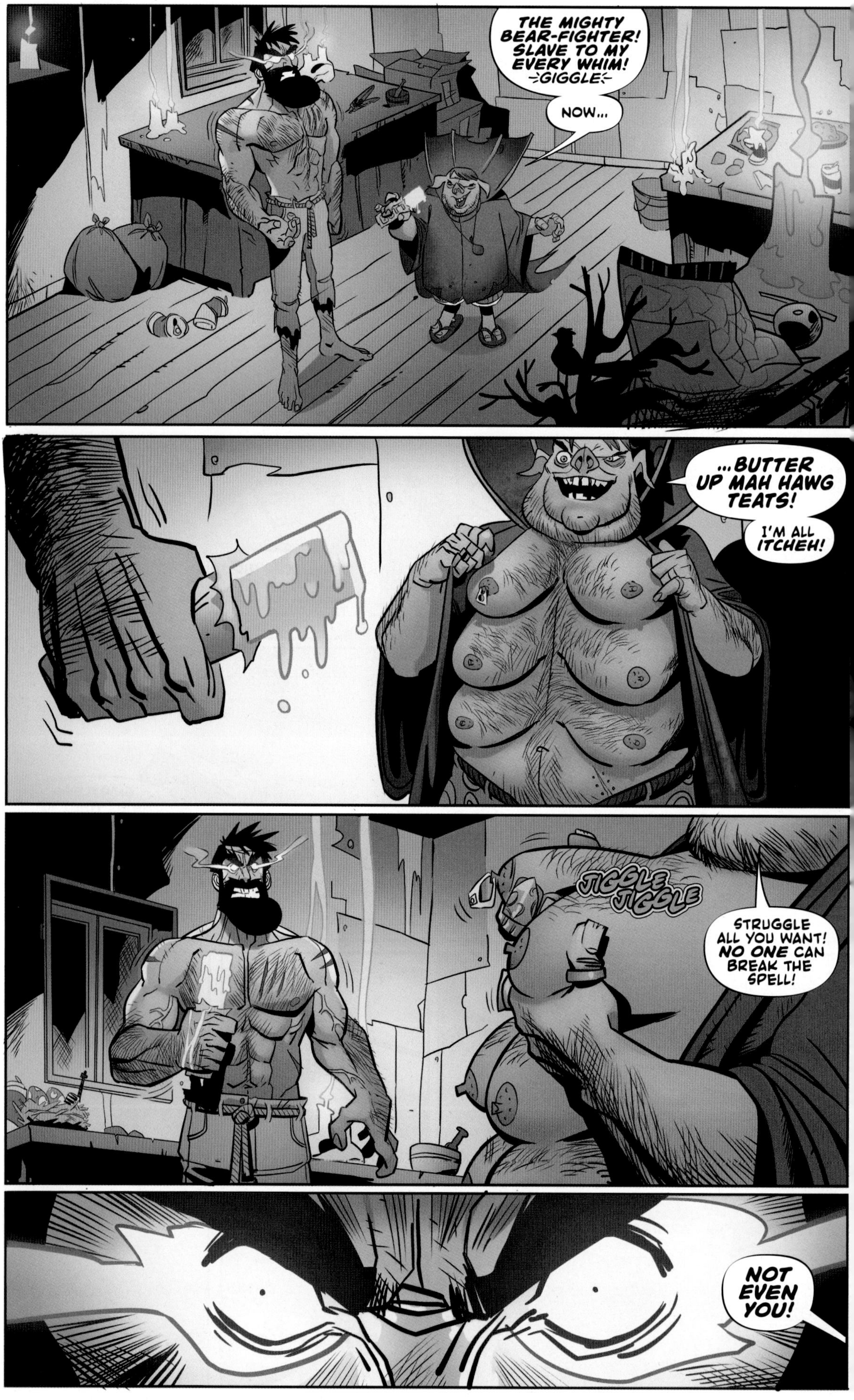
THE MIGHTY BEAR-FIGHTER! SLAVE TO MY EVERY WHIM! -GIGGLE-
NOW...
...BUTTER UP MAH HAWG TEATS!
I'M ALL ITCHEH!
JIGGLE JIGGLE
STRUGGLE ALL YOU WANT! NO ONE CAN BREAK THE SPELL!
NOT EVEN YOU!

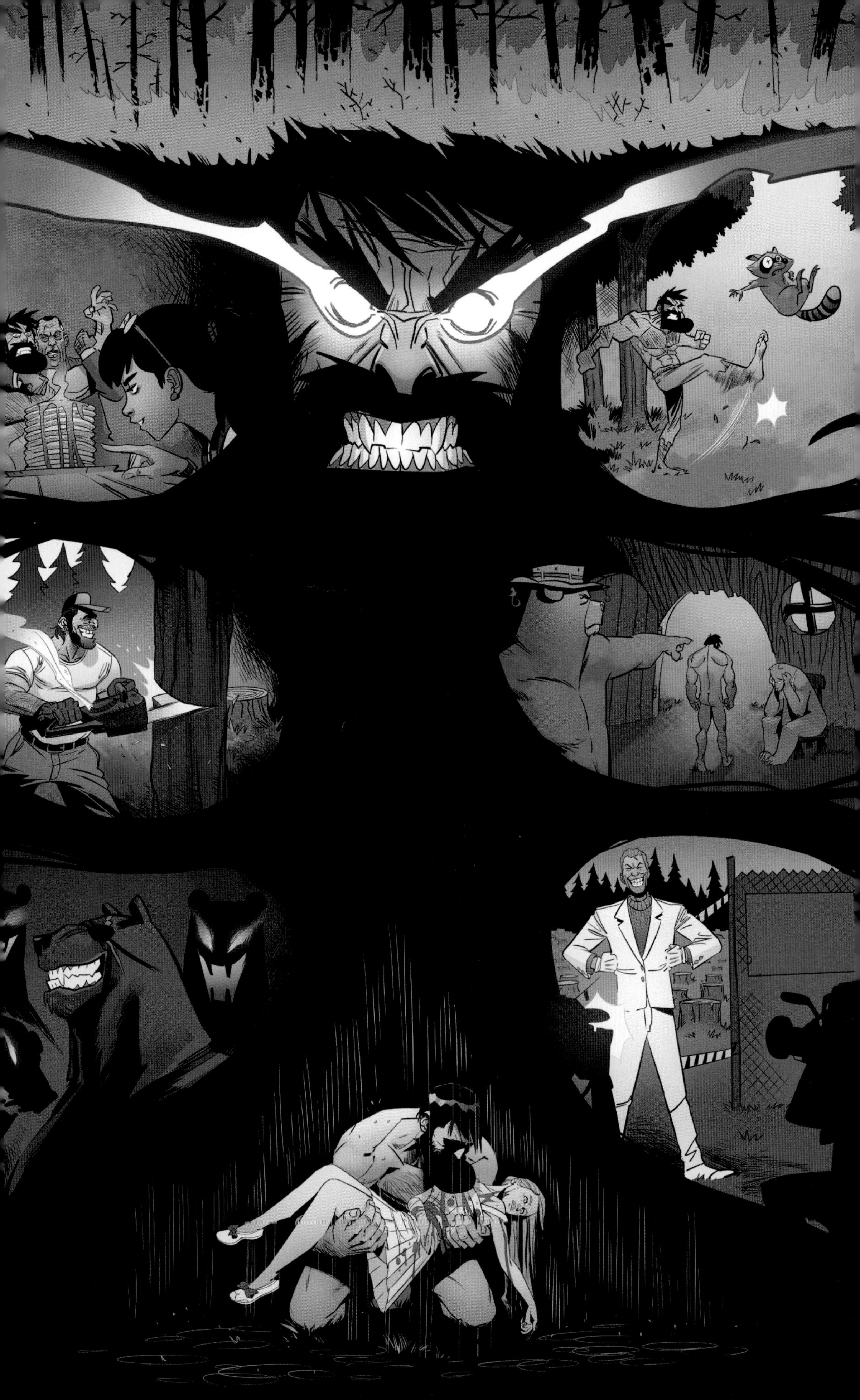

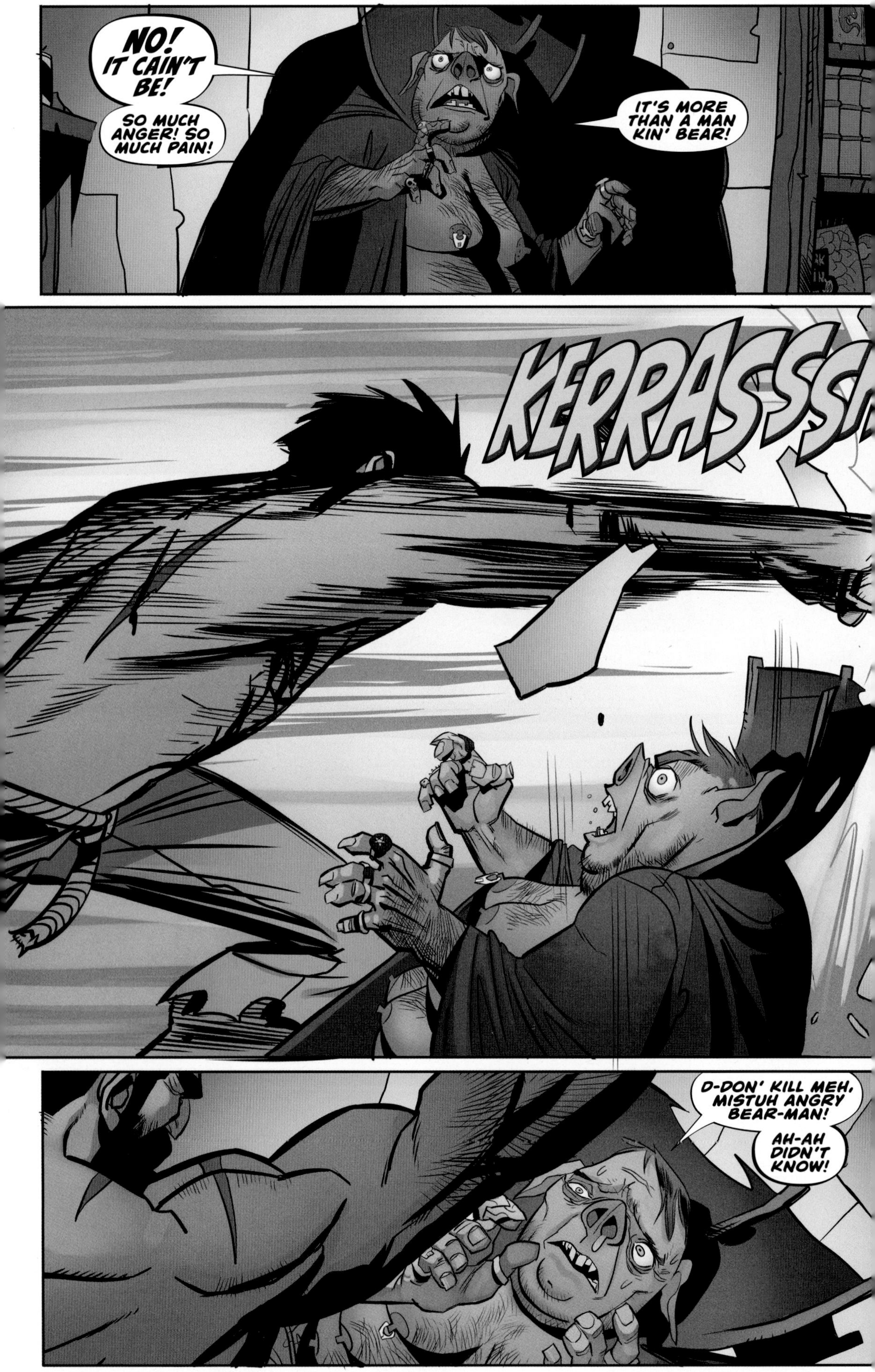
NO! IT CAIN'T BE!
SO MUCH ANGER! SO MUCH PAIN!
IT'S MORE THAN A MAN KIN' BEAR!
KERRASSSH
D-DON' KILL MEH, MISTUH ANGRY BEAR-MAN!
AH-AH DIDN'T KNOW!

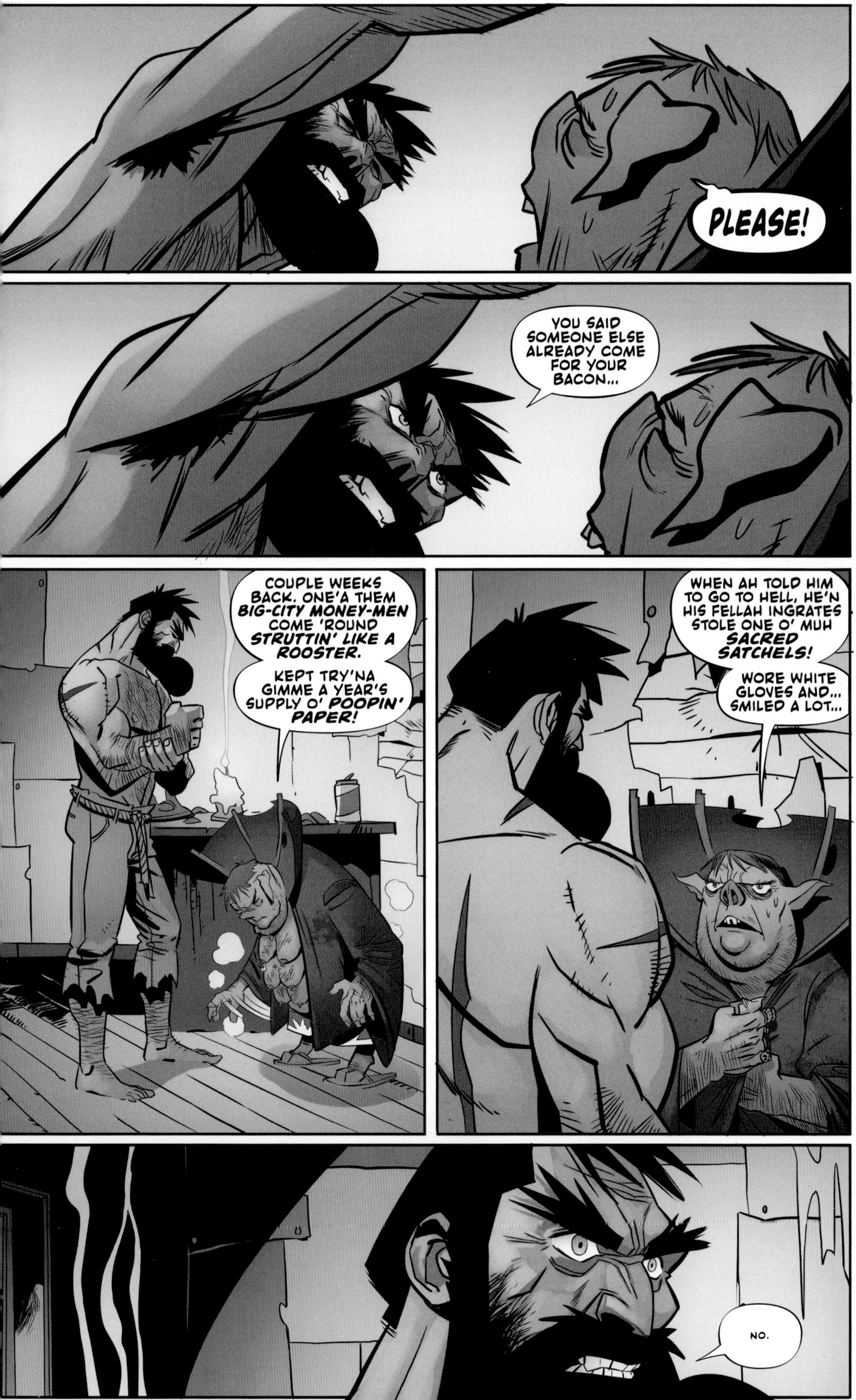
PLEASE!
YOU SAID SOMEONE ELSE ALREADY COME FOR YOUR BACON...
COUPLE WEEKS BACK. ONE'A THEM BIG-CITY MONEY-MEN COME 'ROUND STRUTTIN' LIKE A ROOSTER.
KEPT TRY'NA GIMME A YEAR'S SUPPLY O' POOPIN' PAPER!
WHEN AH TOLD HIM TO GO TO HELL, HE'N HIS FELLAH INGRATES STOLE ONE O' MUH SACRED SATCHELS!
WORE WHITE GLOVES AND... SMILED A LOT...
NO.

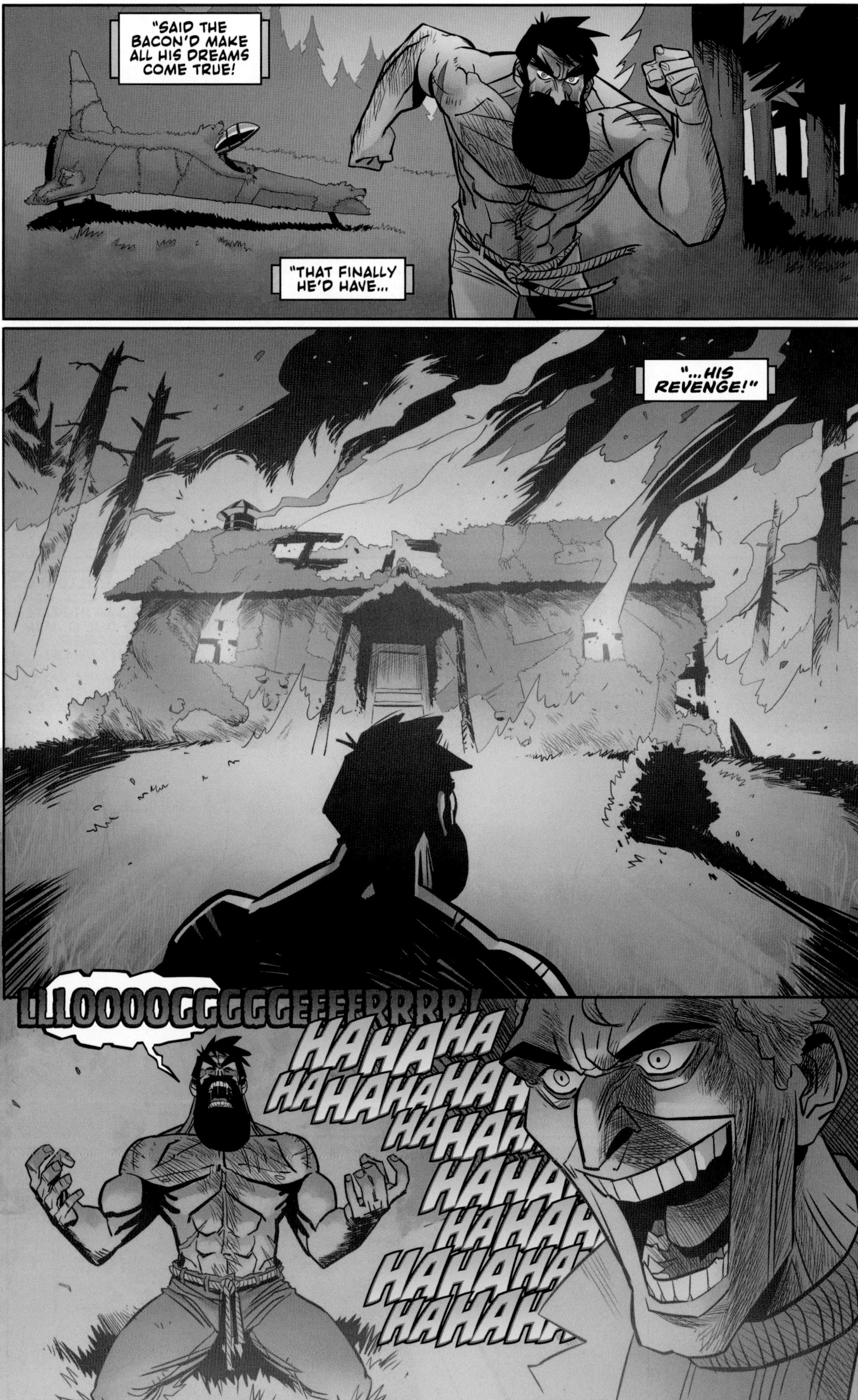
"SAID THE BACON'D MAKE ALL HIS DREAMS COME TRUE!
"THAT FINALLY HE'D HAVE...
"...HIS REVENGE!"
LLLOOOOOGGGGGEEEERRRRP!
HAHAHA HAHAHAHAH HAHAH HAHAH HAHAH HAHAHA HAHAH

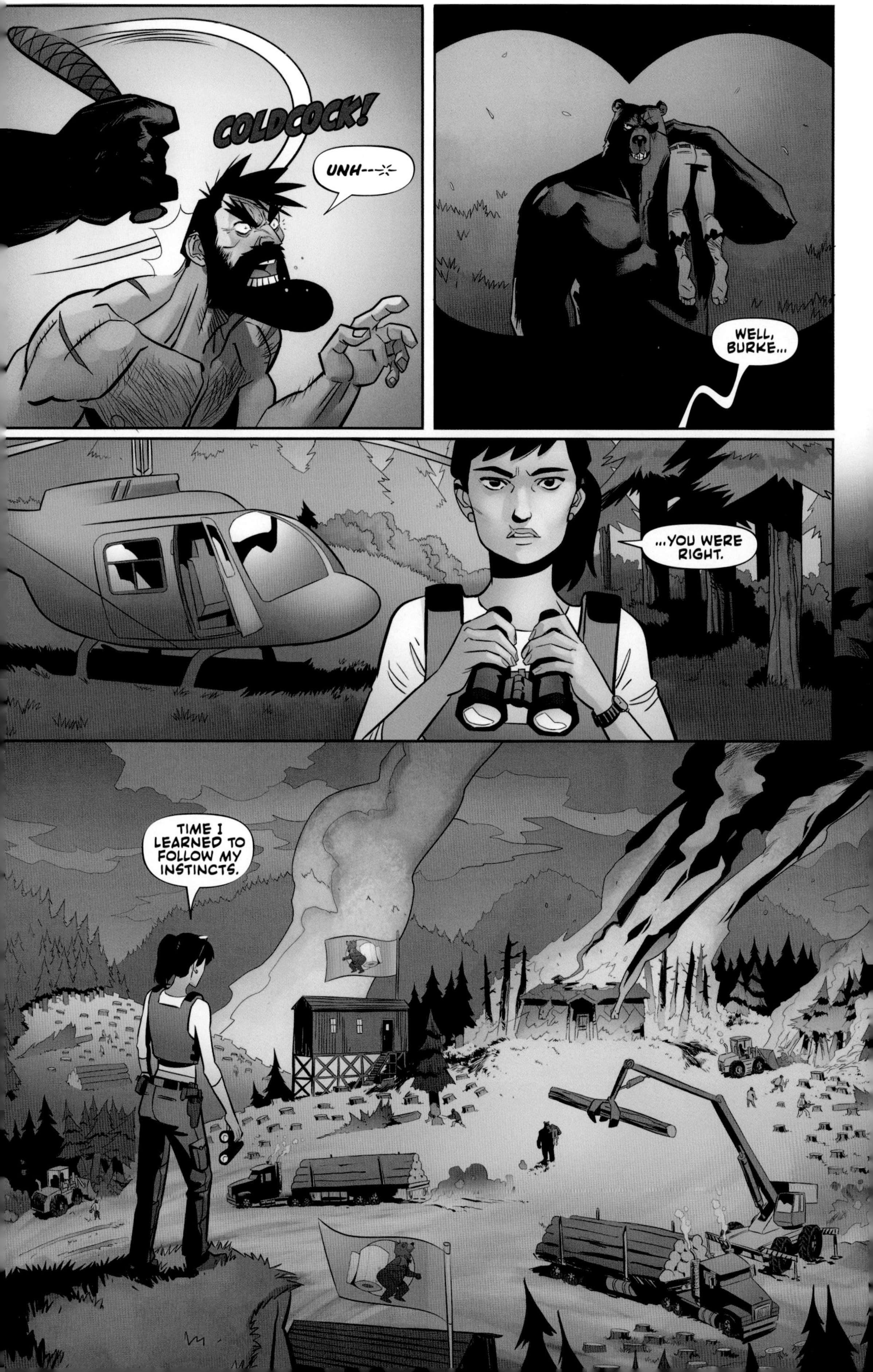
COLDCOCK!
UNH---
WELL, BURKE...
...YOU WERE RIGHT.
TIME I LEARNED TO FOLLOW MY INSTINCTS.

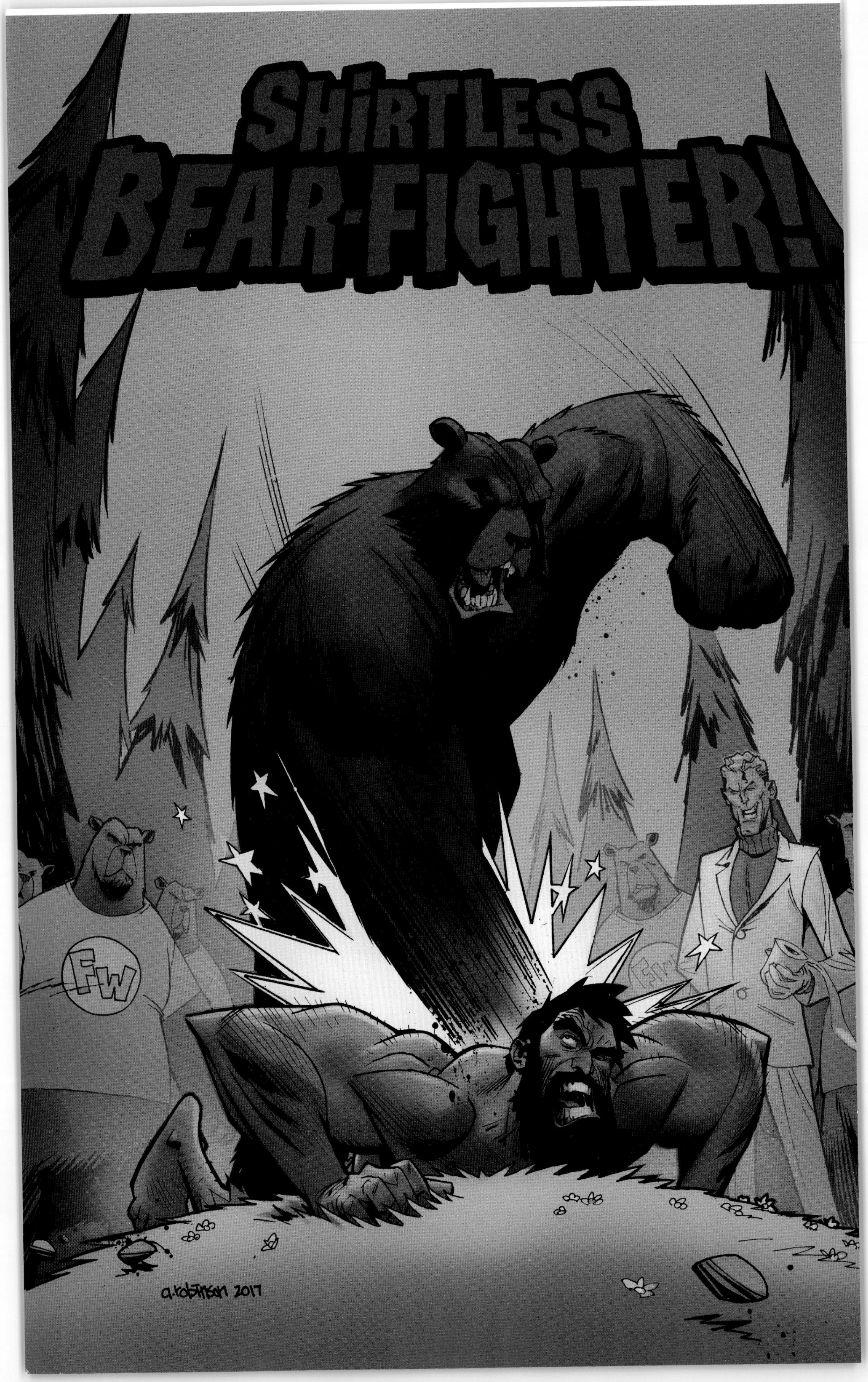
SHIRTLESS
BEAR-FIGHTER!
a.robinson 2017

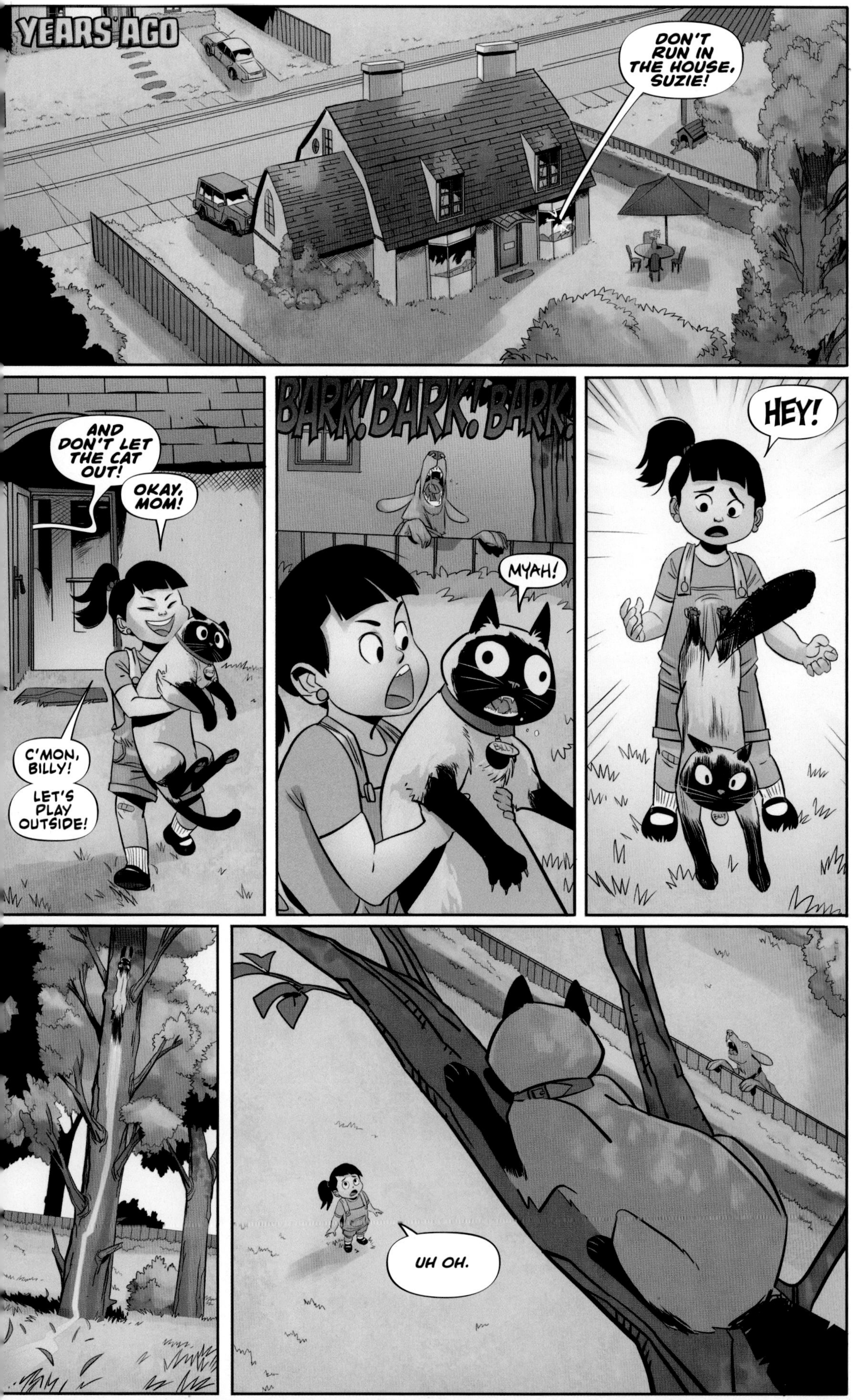
YEARS AGO
DON'T RUN IN THE HOUSE, SUZIE!
AND DON'T LET THE CAT OUT!
OKAY, MOM!
C'MON, BILLY!
LET'S PLAY OUTSIDE!
BARK! BARK! BARK!
MYAH!
BILLY
HEY!
UH OH.

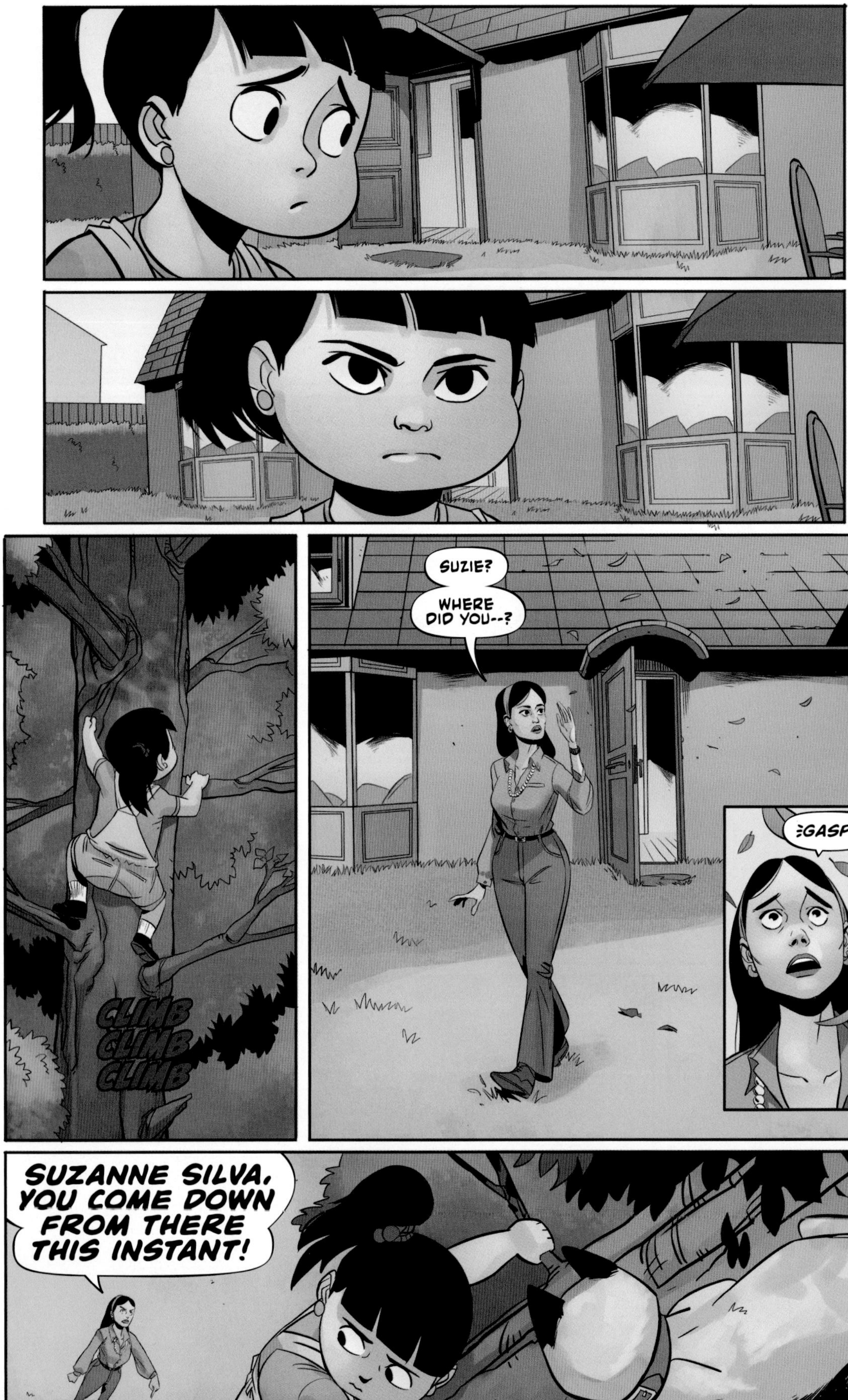
CLIMB
CLIMB
CLIMB
SUZIE?
WHERE DID YOU--?
GASP!
SUZANNE SILVA, YOU COME DOWN FROM THERE THIS INSTANT!

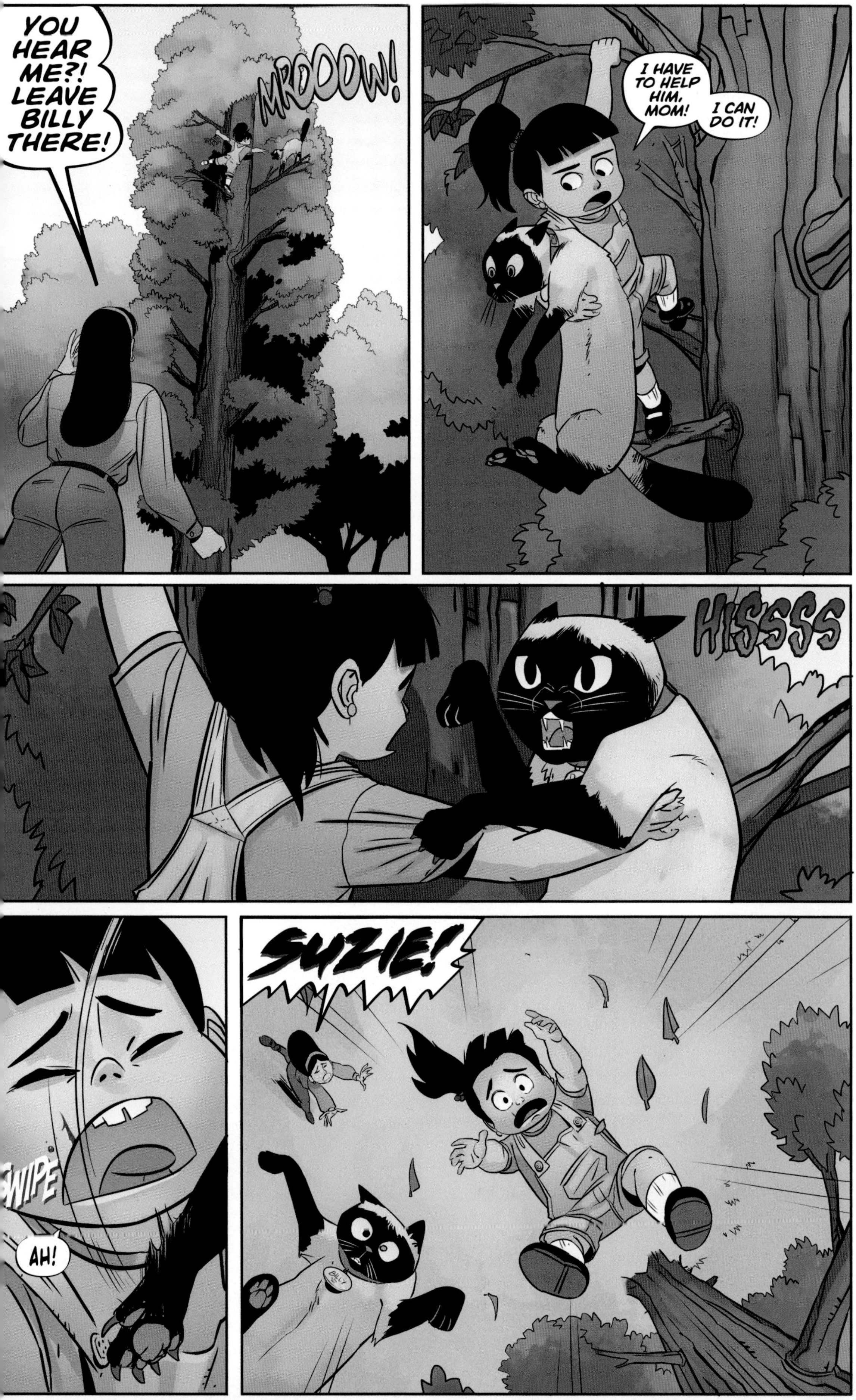
YOU HEAR ME?! LEAVE BILLY THERE!
MROOOW!
I HAVE TO HELP HIM, MOM!
I CAN DO IT!
HISSSS
SWIPE
AH!
SUZIE!

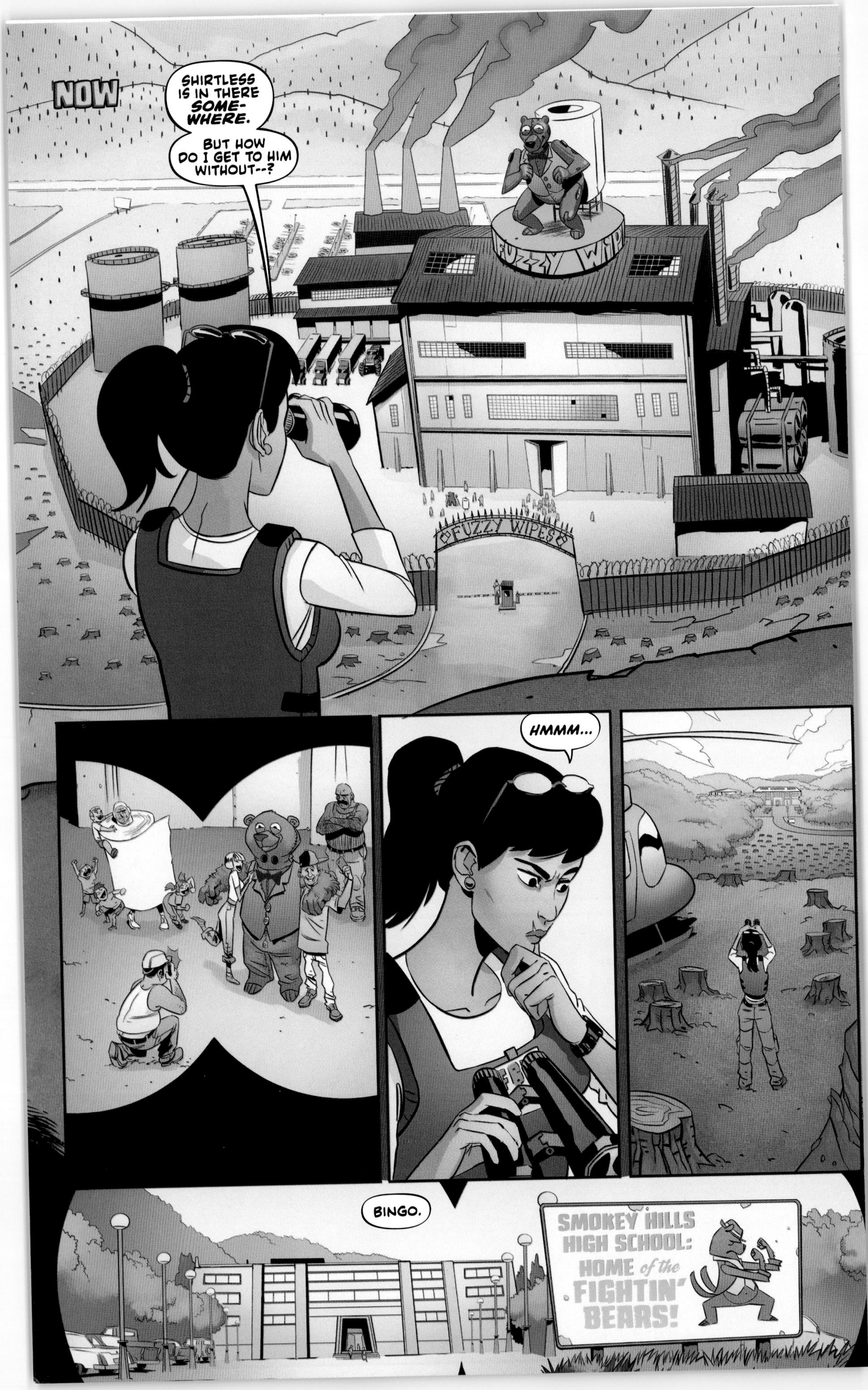
NOW
SHIRTLESS IS IN THERE SOME-WHERE.
BUT HOW DO I GET TO HIM WITHOUT--?
FUZZY WIPES
HMMM...
BINGO.
SMOKEY HILLS HIGH SCHOOL: HOME of the FIGHTIN' BEARS!

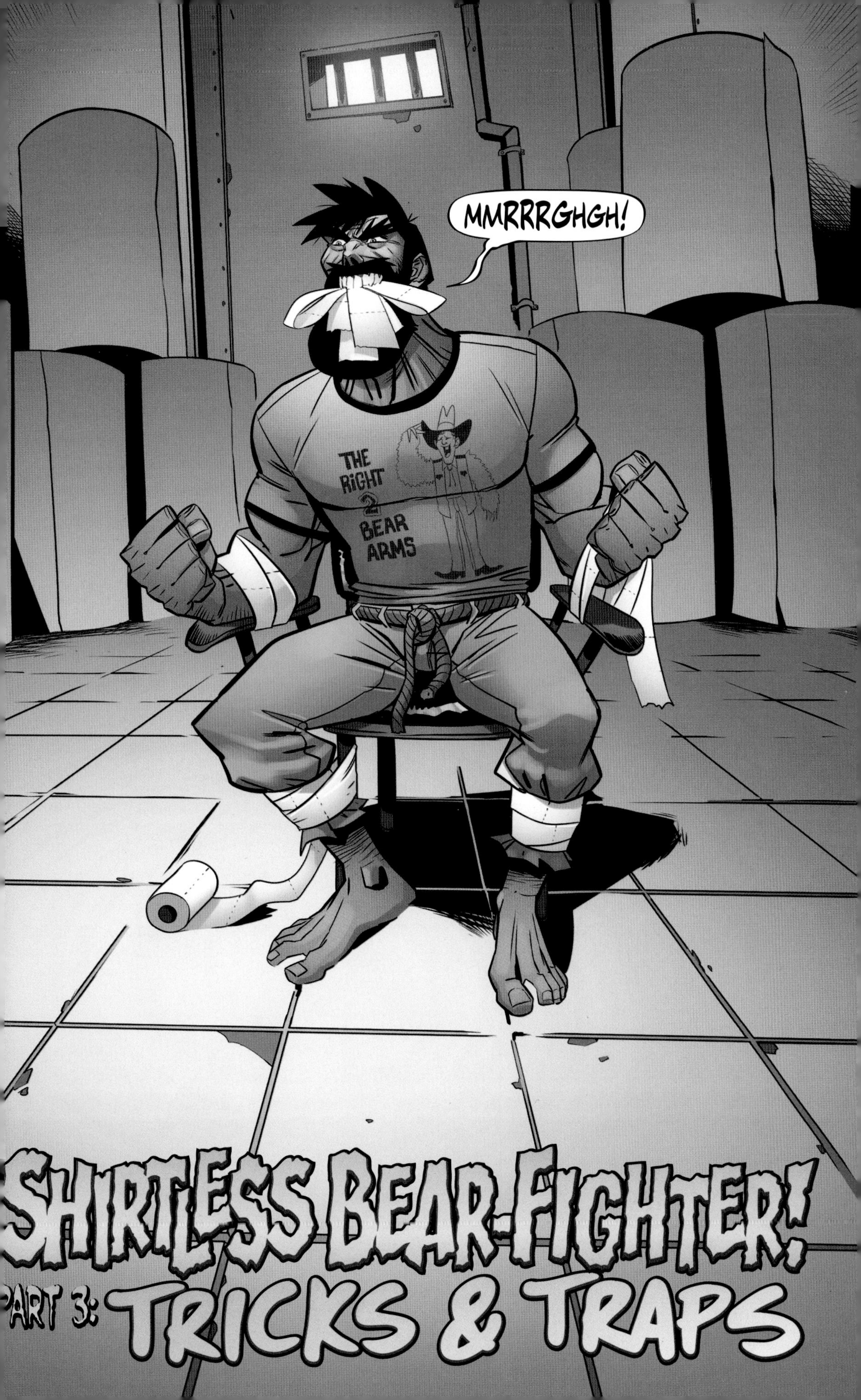
MMRRRGHGH!
THE RiGHT 2 BEAR ARMS
SHIRTLESS BEAR-FIGHTER!
PART 3: TRICKS & TRAPS

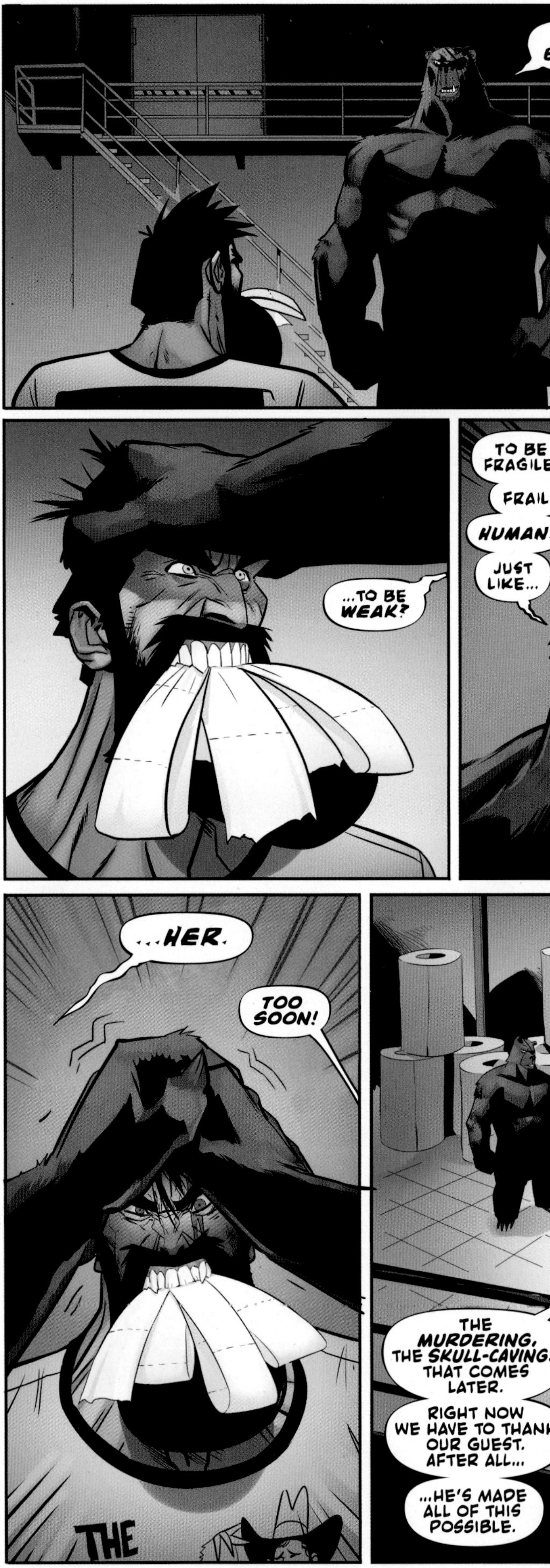

...TO BE WEAK?
TO BE FRAGILE
FRAIL
HUMAN.
JUST LIKE...
...HER.
TOO SOON!
THE MURDERING, THE SKULL-CAVING, THAT COMES LATER.
RIGHT NOW WE HAVE TO THANK OUR GUEST. AFTER ALL...
...HE'S MADE ALL OF THIS POSSIBLE.
THE

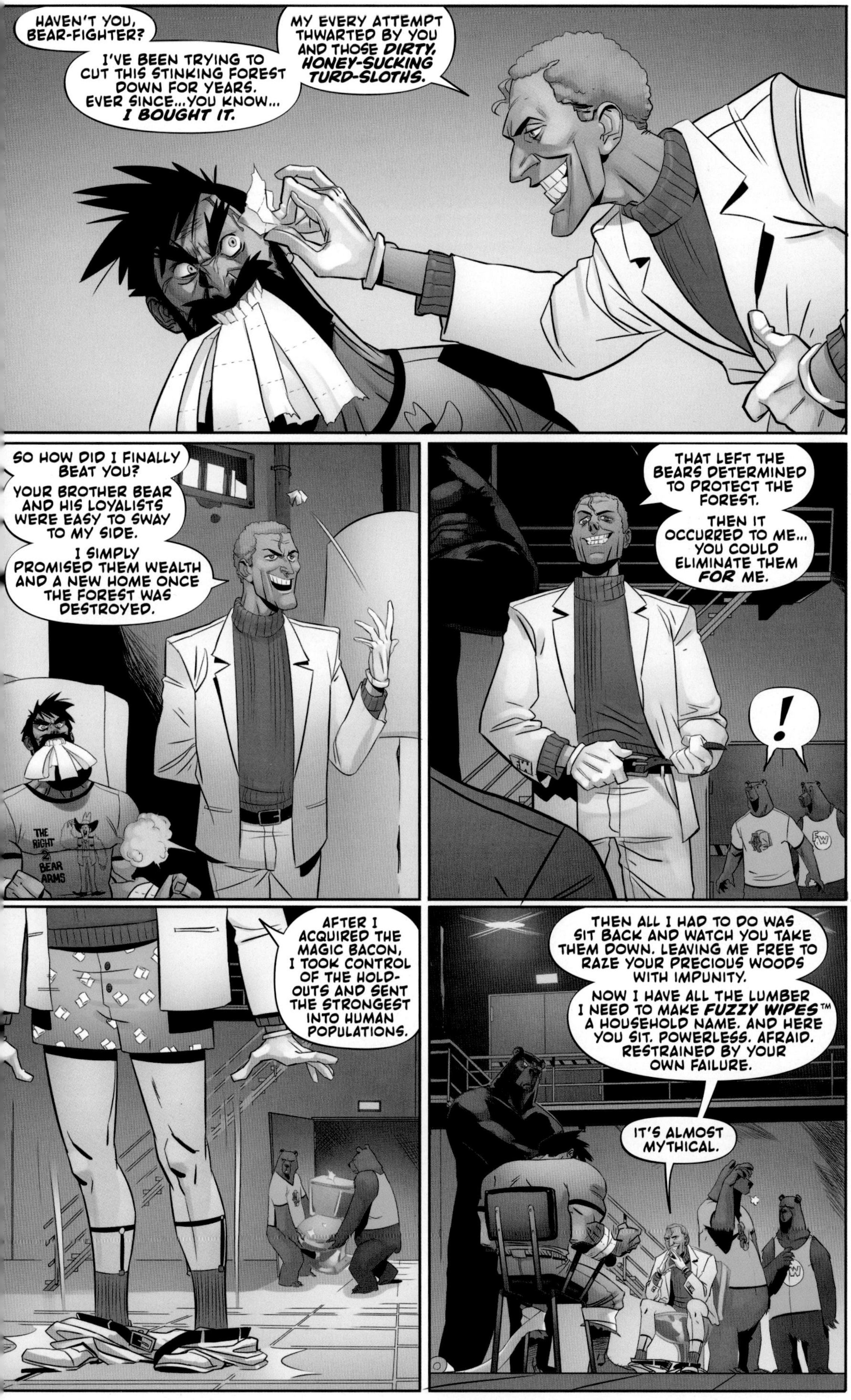
HAVEN'T YOU, BEAR-FIGHTER?
I'VE BEEN TRYING TO CUT THIS STINKING FOREST DOWN FOR YEARS. EVER SINCE...YOU KNOW... *I BOUGHT IT.*
MY EVERY ATTEMPT THWARTED BY YOU AND THOSE *DIRTY, HONEY-SUCKING TURD-SLOTHS.*
SO HOW DID I FINALLY BEAT YOU?
YOUR BROTHER BEAR AND HIS LOYALISTS WERE EASY TO SWAY TO MY SIDE.
I SIMPLY PROMISED THEM WEALTH AND A NEW HOME ONCE THE FOREST WAS DESTROYED.
THE RIGHT 2 BEAR ARMS
THAT LEFT THE BEARS DETERMINED TO PROTECT THE FOREST.
THEN IT OCCURRED TO ME... YOU COULD ELIMINATE THEM *FOR* ME.
!
AFTER I ACQUIRED THE MAGIC BACON, I TOOK CONTROL OF THE HOLD-OUTS AND SENT THE STRONGEST INTO HUMAN POPULATIONS.
THEN ALL I HAD TO DO WAS SIT BACK AND WATCH YOU TAKE THEM DOWN. LEAVING ME FREE TO RAZE YOUR PRECIOUS WOODS WITH IMPUNITY.
NOW I HAVE ALL THE LUMBER I NEED TO MAKE *FUZZY WIPES*™ A HOUSEHOLD NAME. AND HERE YOU SIT. POWERLESS. AFRAID. RESTRAINED BY YOUR OWN FAILURE.
IT'S ALMOST MYTHICAL.

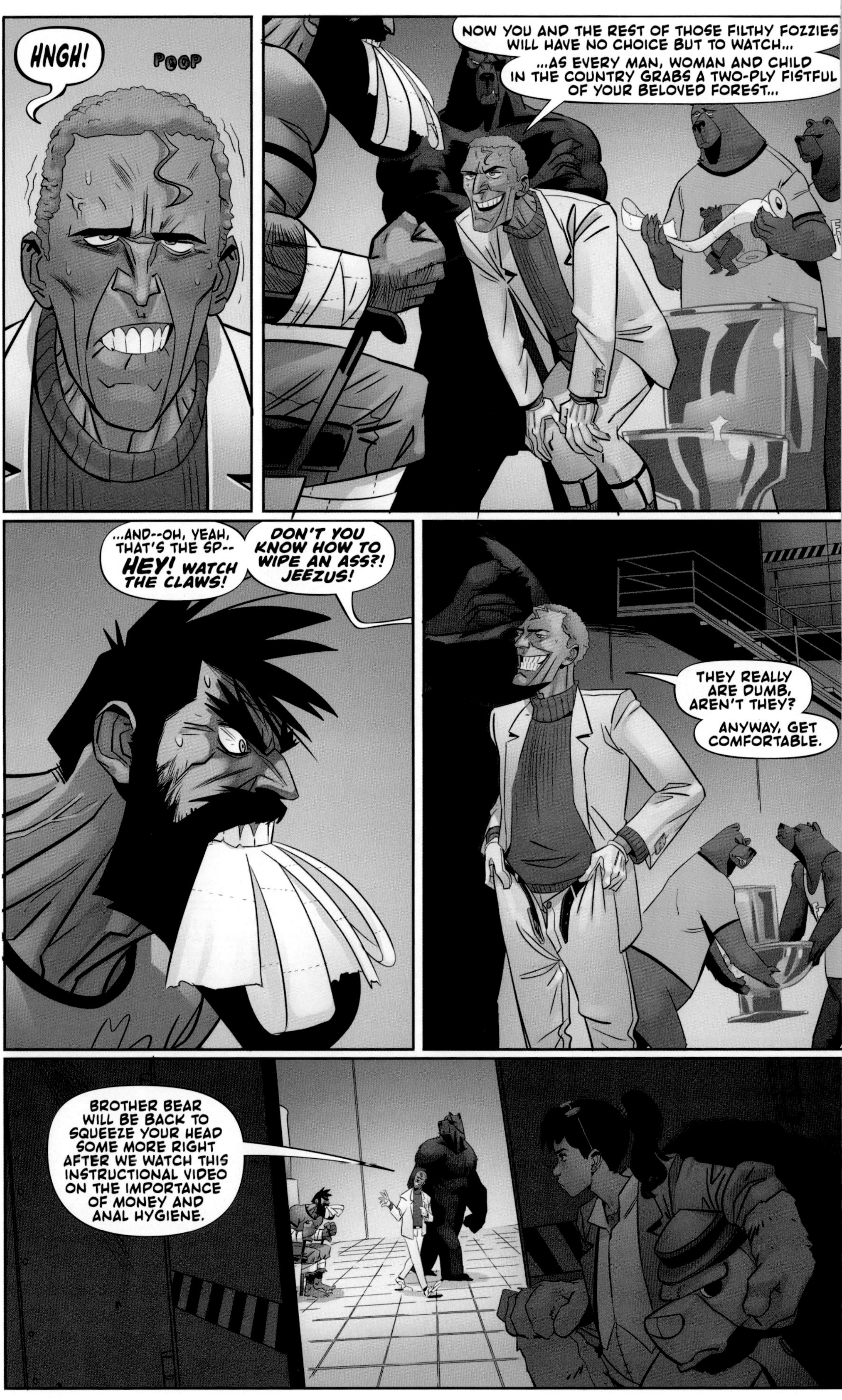
HNGH!
POOP
NOW YOU AND THE REST OF THOSE FILTHY FOZZIES WILL HAVE NO CHOICE BUT TO WATCH...
...AS EVERY MAN, WOMAN AND CHILD IN THE COUNTRY GRABS A TWO-PLY FISTFUL OF YOUR BELOVED FOREST...
...AND--OH, YEAH, THAT'S THE SP-- HEY! WATCH THE CLAWS!
DON'T YOU KNOW HOW TO WIPE AN ASS?! JEEZUS!
THEY REALLY ARE DUMB, AREN'T THEY?
ANYWAY, GET COMFORTABLE.
BROTHER BEAR WILL BE BACK TO SQUEEZE YOUR HEAD SOME MORE RIGHT AFTER WE WATCH THIS INSTRUCTIONAL VIDEO ON THE IMPORTANCE OF MONEY AND ANAL HYGIENE.

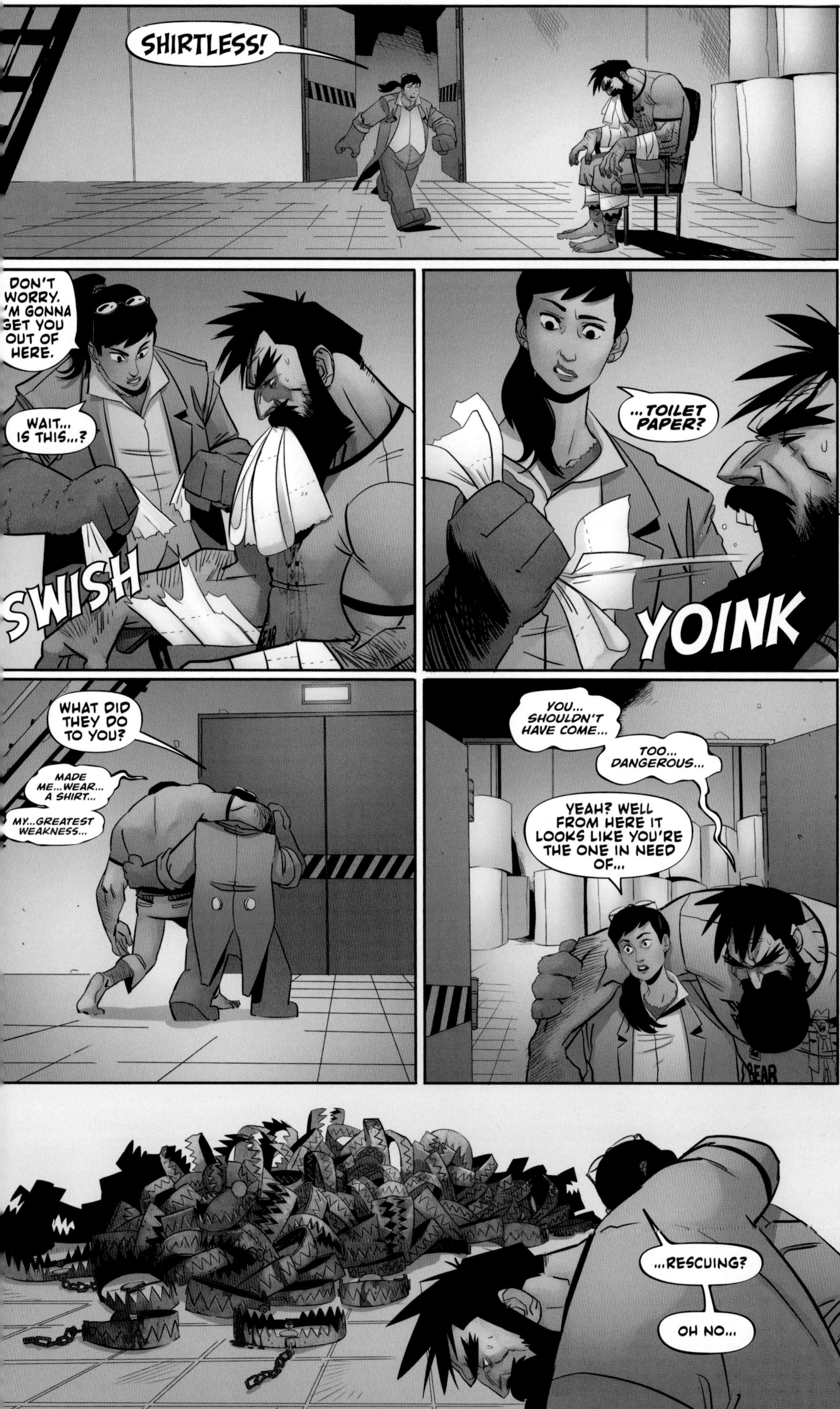
SHIRTLESS!
DON'T WORRY. I'M GONNA GET YOU OUT OF HERE.
WAIT... IS THIS...?
SWISH
...TOILET PAPER?
YOINK
WHAT DID THEY DO TO YOU?
MADE ME...WEAR... A SHIRT...
MY...GREATEST WEAKNESS...
YOU... SHOULDN'T HAVE COME...
TOO... DANGEROUS...
YEAH? WELL FROM HERE IT LOOKS LIKE YOU'RE THE ONE IN NEED OF...
...RESCUING?
OH NO...

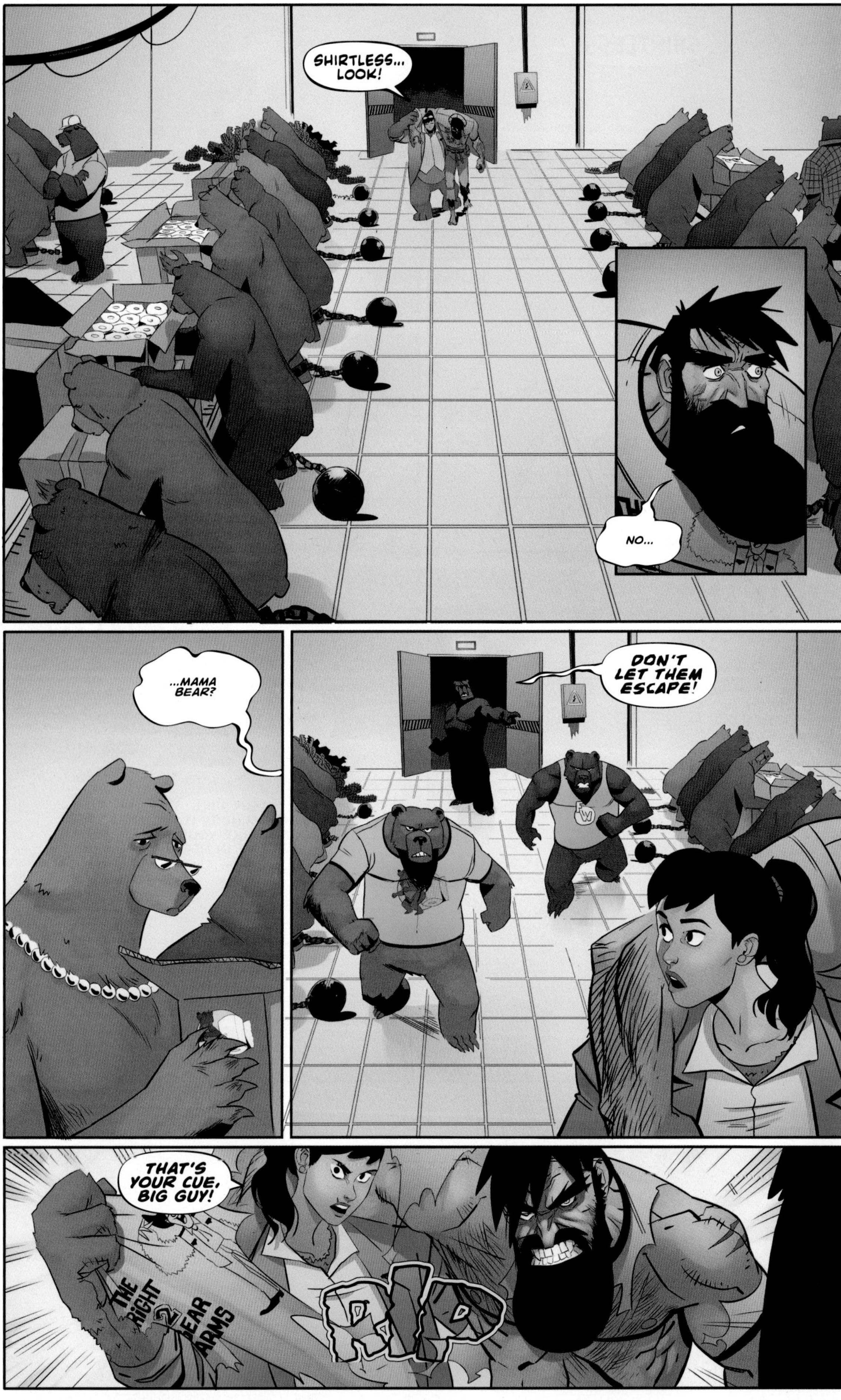
SHIRTLESS... LOOK!
NO...
...MAMA BEAR?
DON'T LET THEM ESCAPE!
THAT'S YOUR CUE, BIG GUY!
THE RIGHT 2 BEAR ARMS
RIP

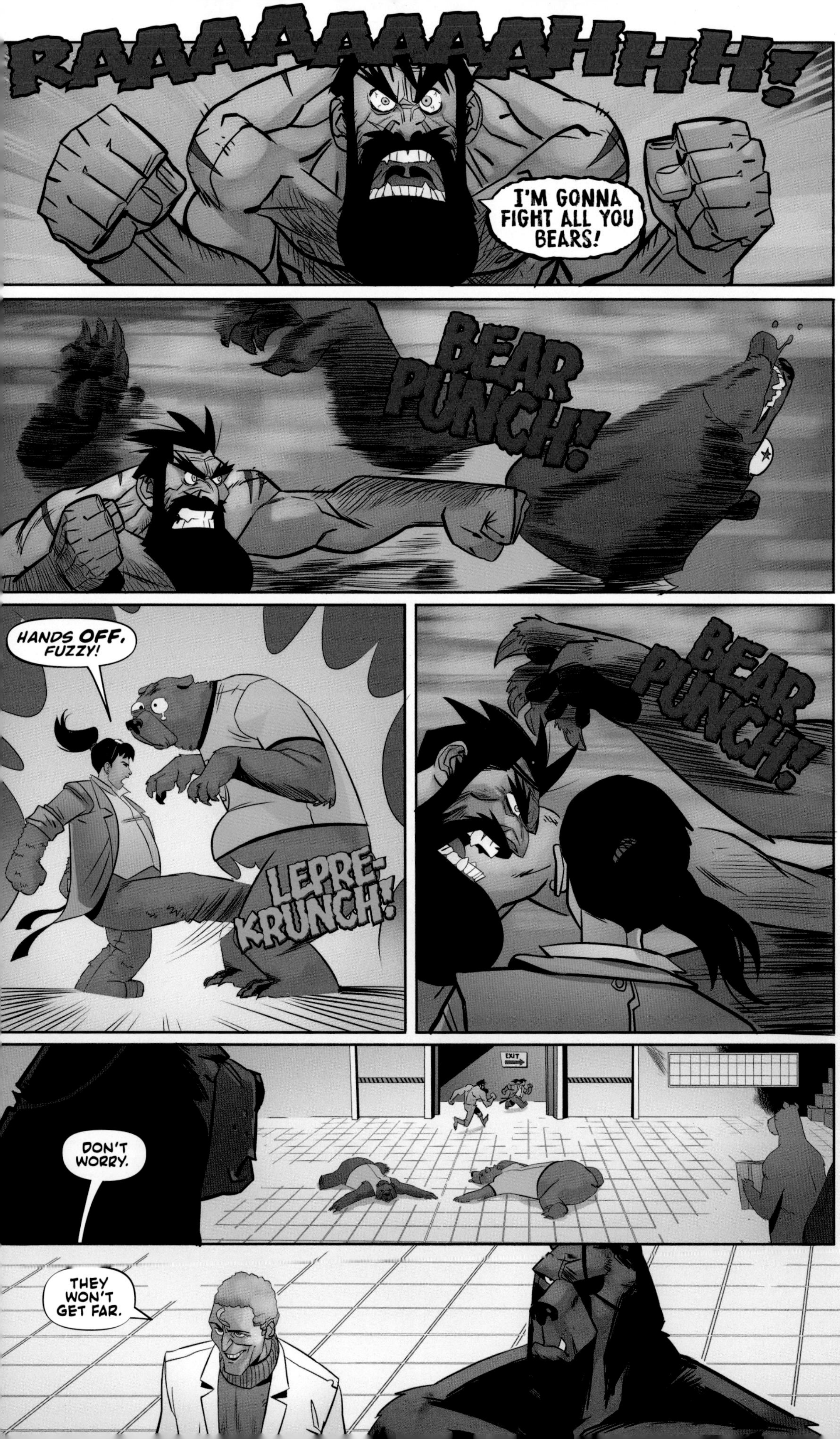
RAAAAAAAAAHHHH!
I'M GONNA FIGHT ALL YOU BEARS!
BEAR PUNCH!
HANDS OFF, FUZZY!
LEPRE-KRUNCH!
BEAR PUNCH!
EXIT
DON'T WORRY.
THEY WON'T GET FAR.

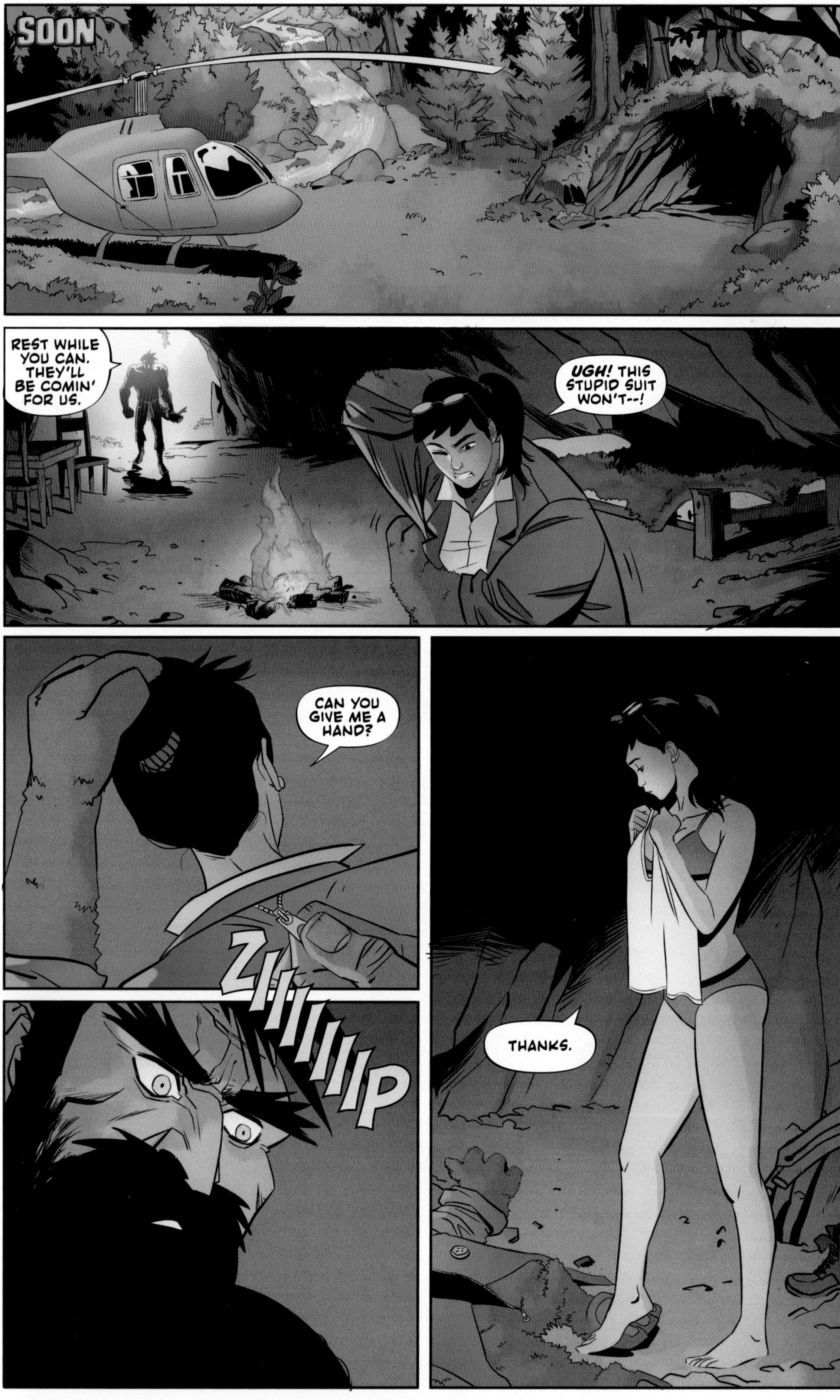
SOON
REST WHILE YOU CAN. THEY'LL BE COMIN' FOR US.
UGH! THIS STUPID SUIT WON'T--!
CAN YOU GIVE ME A HAND?
ZIIIIIIIP
THANKS.

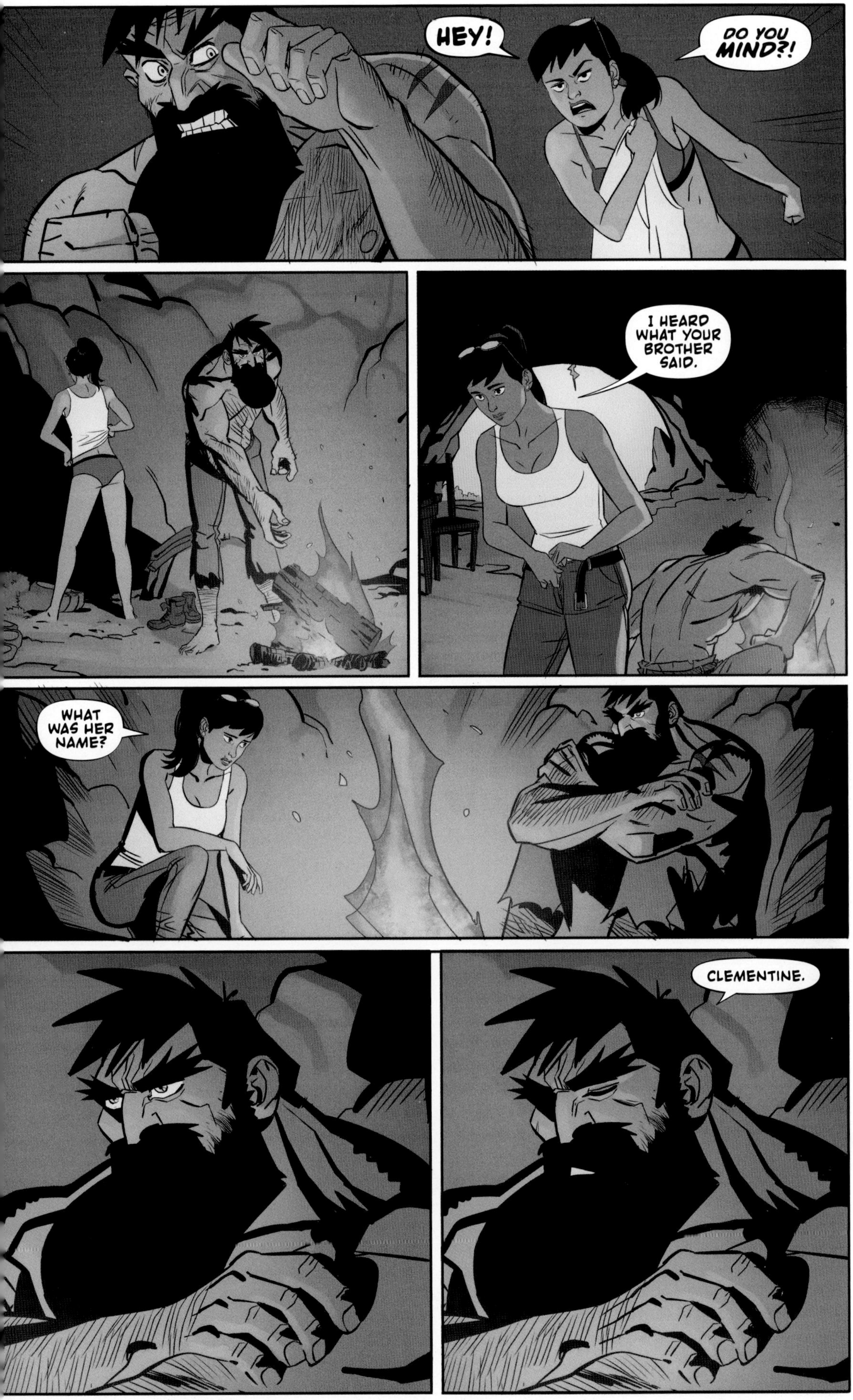
HEY!
DO YOU MIND?!
I HEARD WHAT YOUR BROTHER SAID.
WHAT WAS HER NAME?
CLEMENTINE.

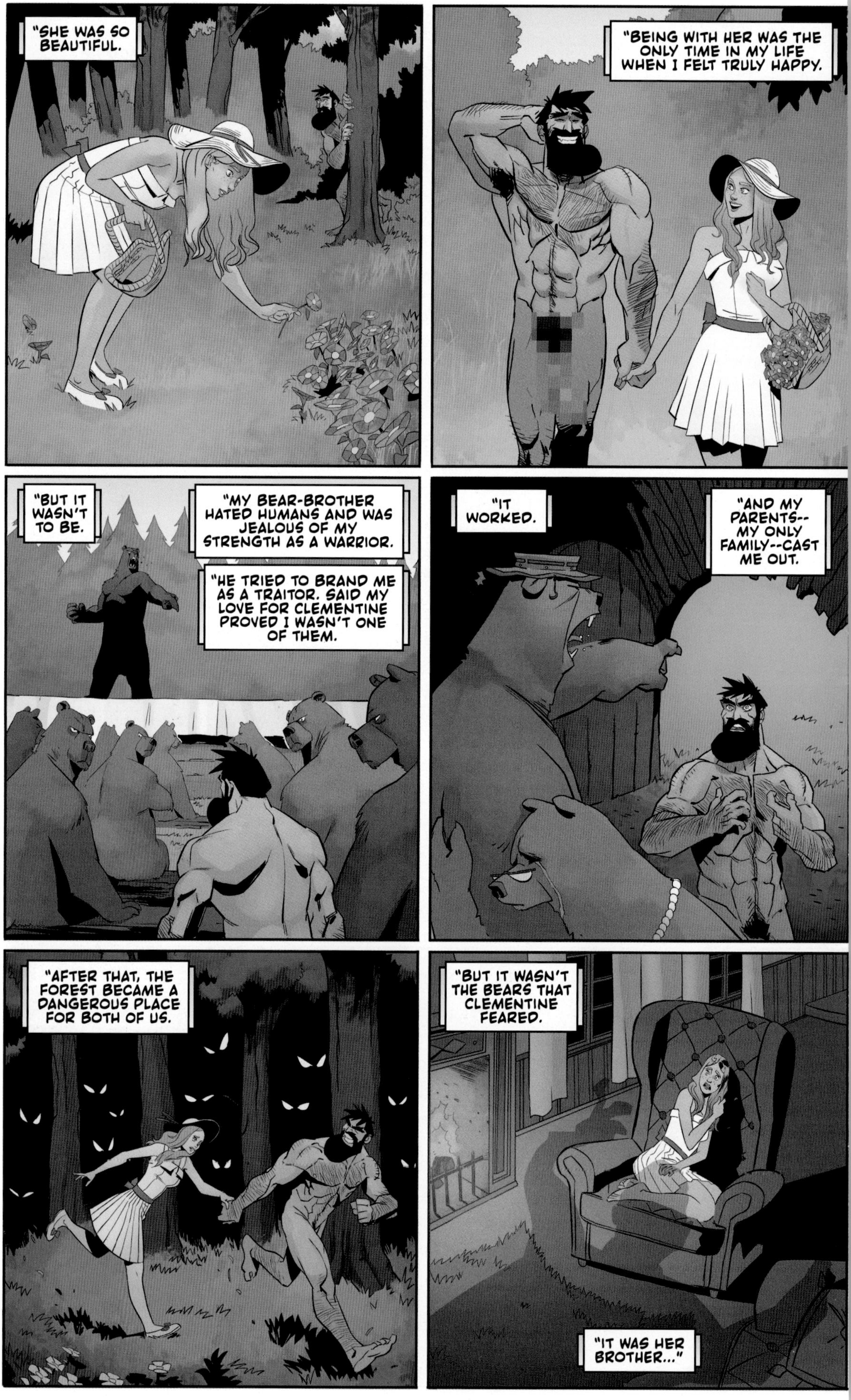
"SHE WAS SO BEAUTIFUL.
"BEING WITH HER WAS THE ONLY TIME IN MY LIFE WHEN I FELT TRULY HAPPY.
"BUT IT WASN'T TO BE.
"MY BEAR-BROTHER HATED HUMANS AND WAS JEALOUS OF MY STRENGTH AS A WARRIOR.
"HE TRIED TO BRAND ME AS A TRAITOR. SAID MY LOVE FOR CLEMENTINE PROVED I WASN'T ONE OF THEM.
"IT WORKED.
"AND MY PARENTS-- MY ONLY FAMILY--CAST ME OUT.
"AFTER THAT, THE FOREST BECAME A DANGEROUS PLACE FOR BOTH OF US.
"BUT IT WASN'T THE BEARS THAT CLEMENTINE FEARED.
"IT WAS HER BROTHER..."

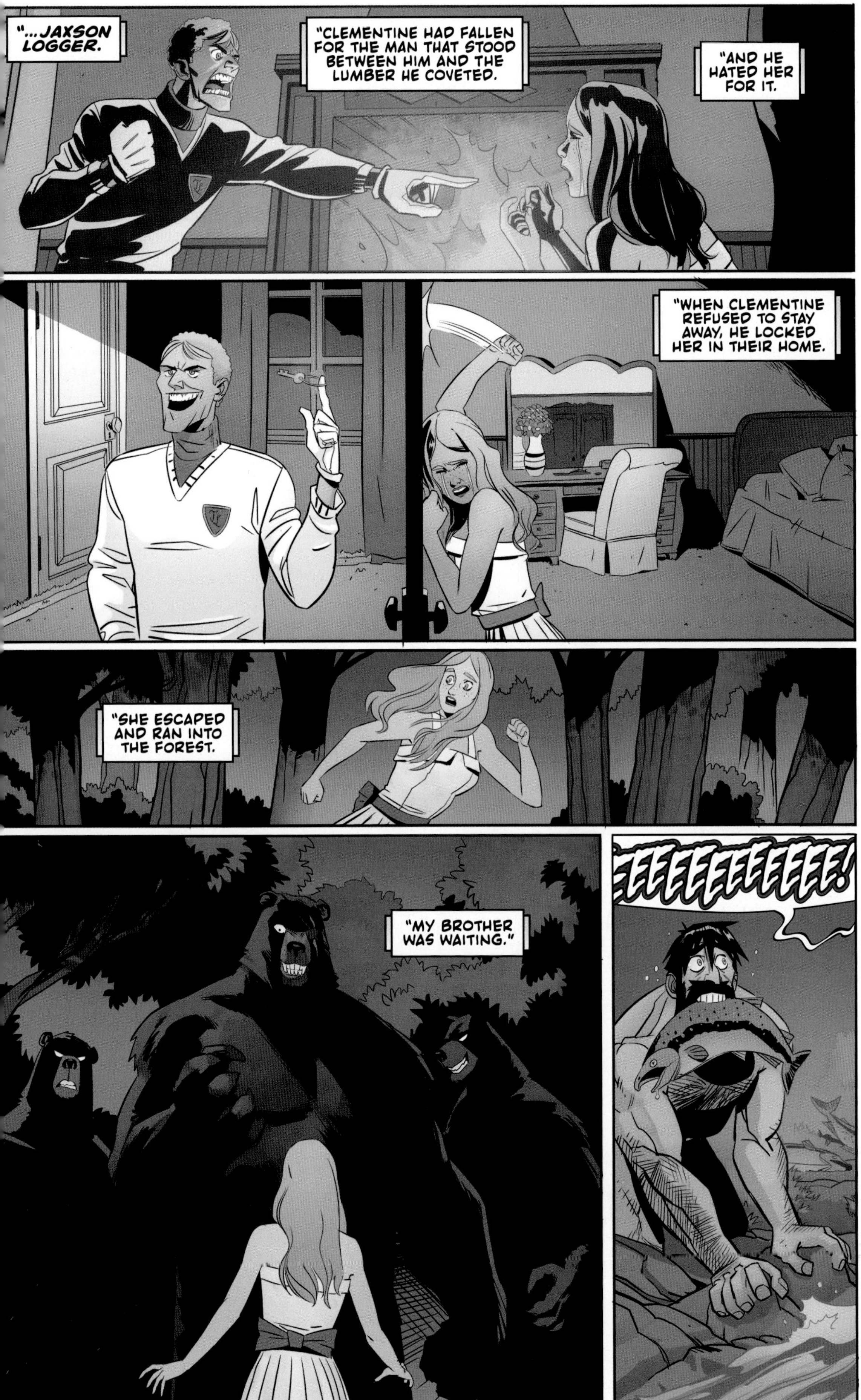
"...JAXSON LOGGER.
"CLEMENTINE HAD FALLEN FOR THE MAN THAT STOOD BETWEEN HIM AND THE LUMBER HE COVETED.
"AND HE HATED HER FOR IT.
"WHEN CLEMENTINE REFUSED TO STAY AWAY, HE LOCKED HER IN THEIR HOME.
"SHE ESCAPED AND RAN INTO THE FOREST.
"MY BROTHER WAS WAITING."
EEEEEEEEEEEEE!

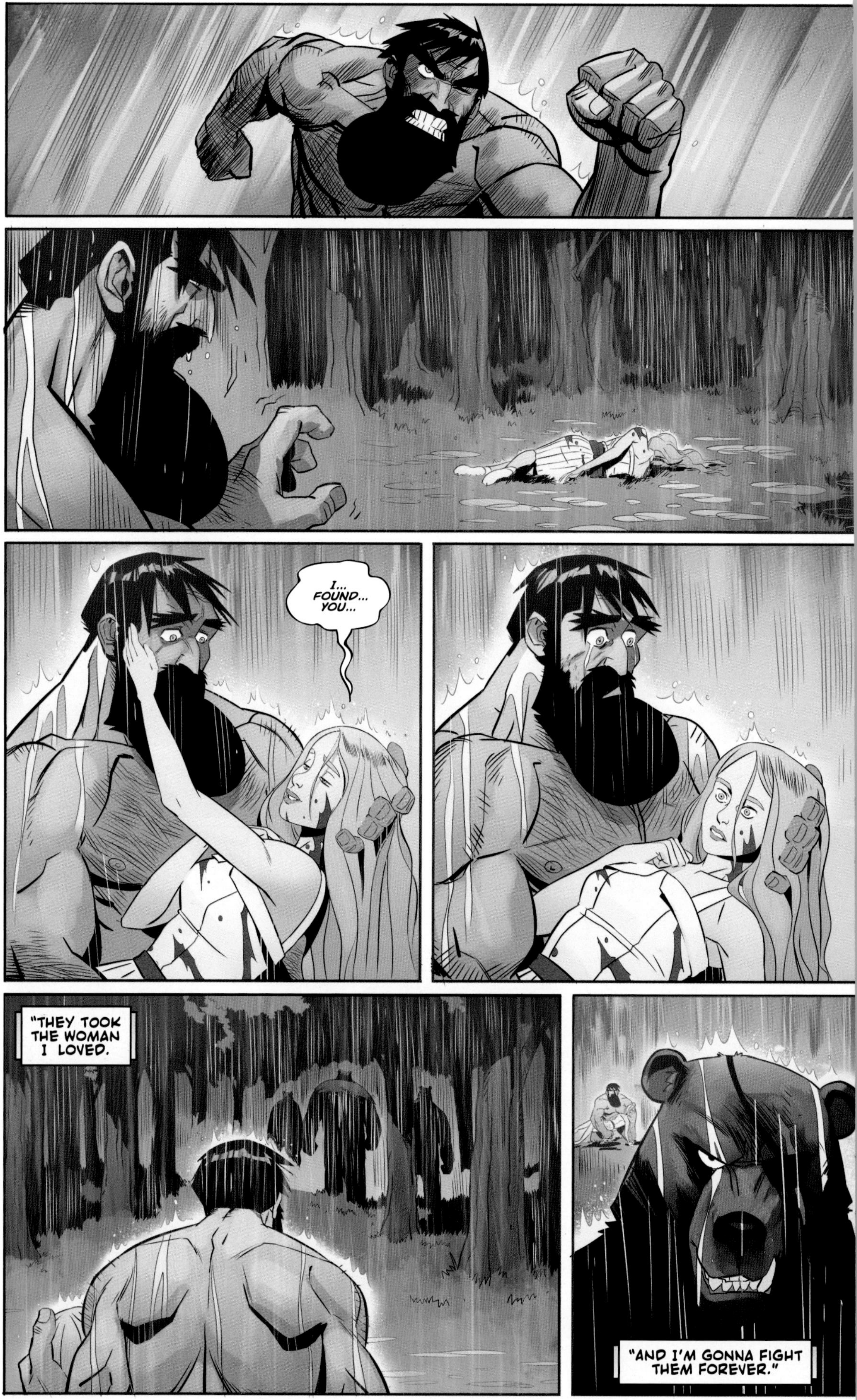
I... FOUND... YOU...
"THEY TOOK THE WOMAN I LOVED.
"AND I'M GONNA FIGHT THEM FOREVER."

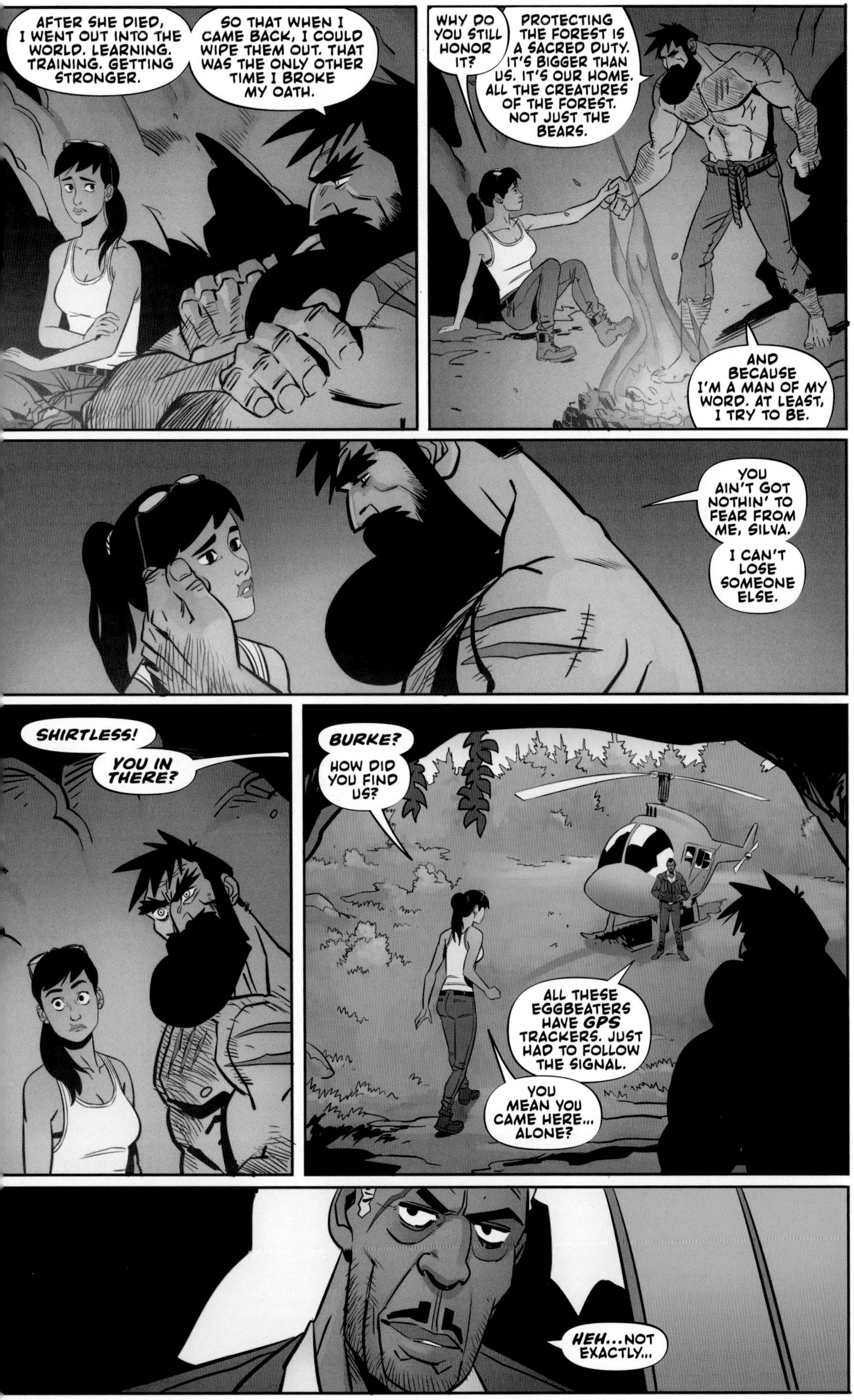
AFTER SHE DIED, I WENT OUT INTO THE WORLD. LEARNING. TRAINING. GETTING STRONGER.
SO THAT WHEN I CAME BACK, I COULD WIPE THEM OUT. THAT WAS THE ONLY OTHER TIME I BROKE MY OATH.
WHY DO YOU STILL HONOR IT?
PROTECTING THE FOREST IS A SACRED DUTY. IT'S BIGGER THAN US. IT'S OUR HOME. ALL THE CREATURES OF THE FOREST. NOT JUST THE BEARS.
AND BECAUSE I'M A MAN OF MY WORD. AT LEAST, I TRY TO BE.
YOU AIN'T GOT NOTHIN' TO FEAR FROM ME, SILVA.
I CAN'T LOSE SOMEONE ELSE.
SHIRTLESS!
YOU IN THERE?
BURKE?
HOW DID YOU FIND US?
ALL THESE EGGBEATERS HAVE GPS TRACKERS. JUST HAD TO FOLLOW THE SIGNAL.
YOU MEAN YOU CAME HERE... ALONE?
HEH...NOT EXACTLY...

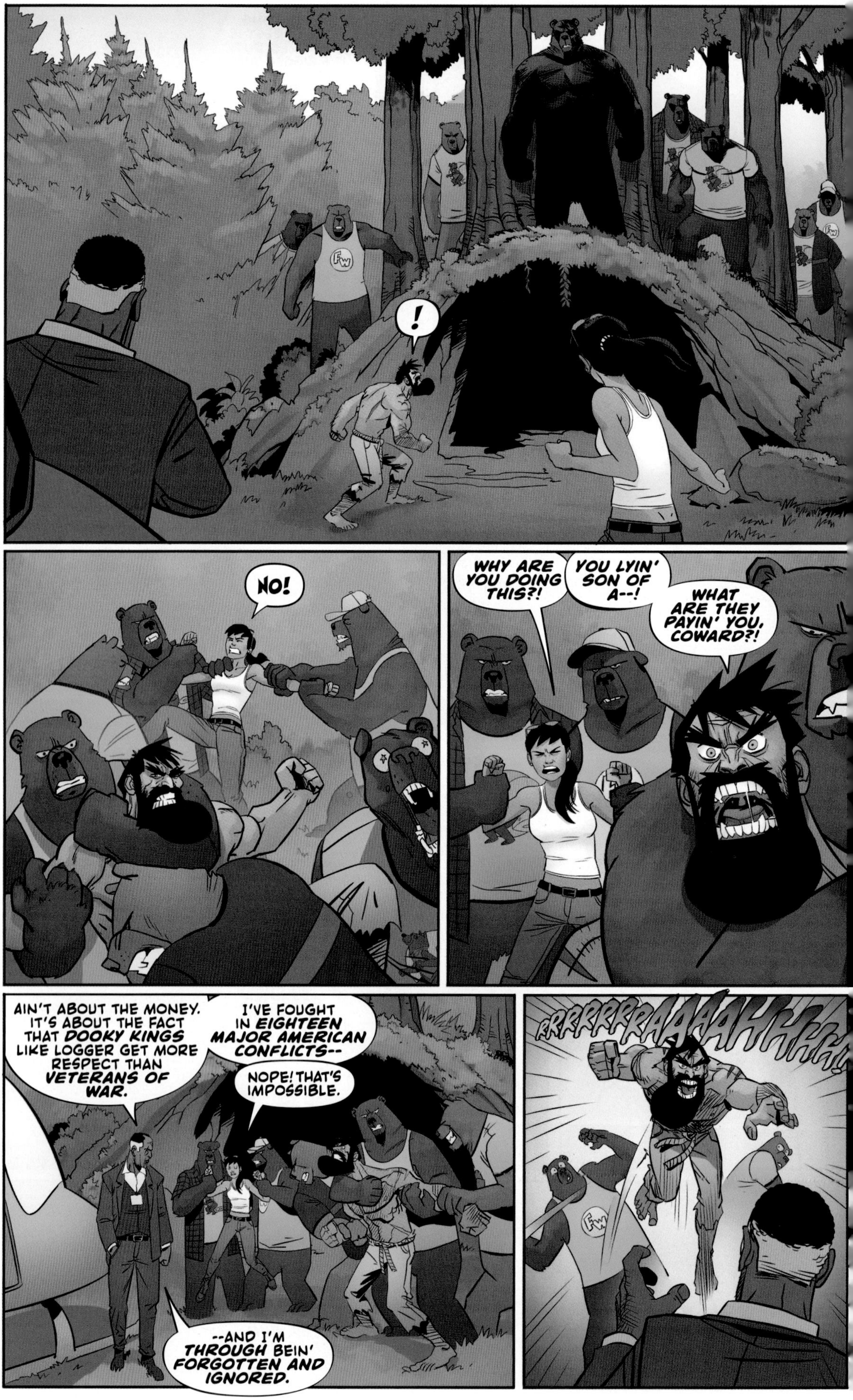
!
NO!
WHY ARE YOU DOING THIS?!
YOU LYIN' SON OF A--!
WHAT ARE THEY PAYIN' YOU, COWARD?!
AIN'T ABOUT THE MONEY. IT'S ABOUT THE FACT THAT DOOKY KINGS LIKE LOGGER GET MORE RESPECT THAN VETERANS OF WAR.
I'VE FOUGHT IN EIGHTEEN MAJOR AMERICAN CONFLICTS--
NOPE! THAT'S IMPOSSIBLE.
--AND I'M THROUGH BEIN' FORGOTTEN AND IGNORED.
RRRRRRRAAAAAHHHH

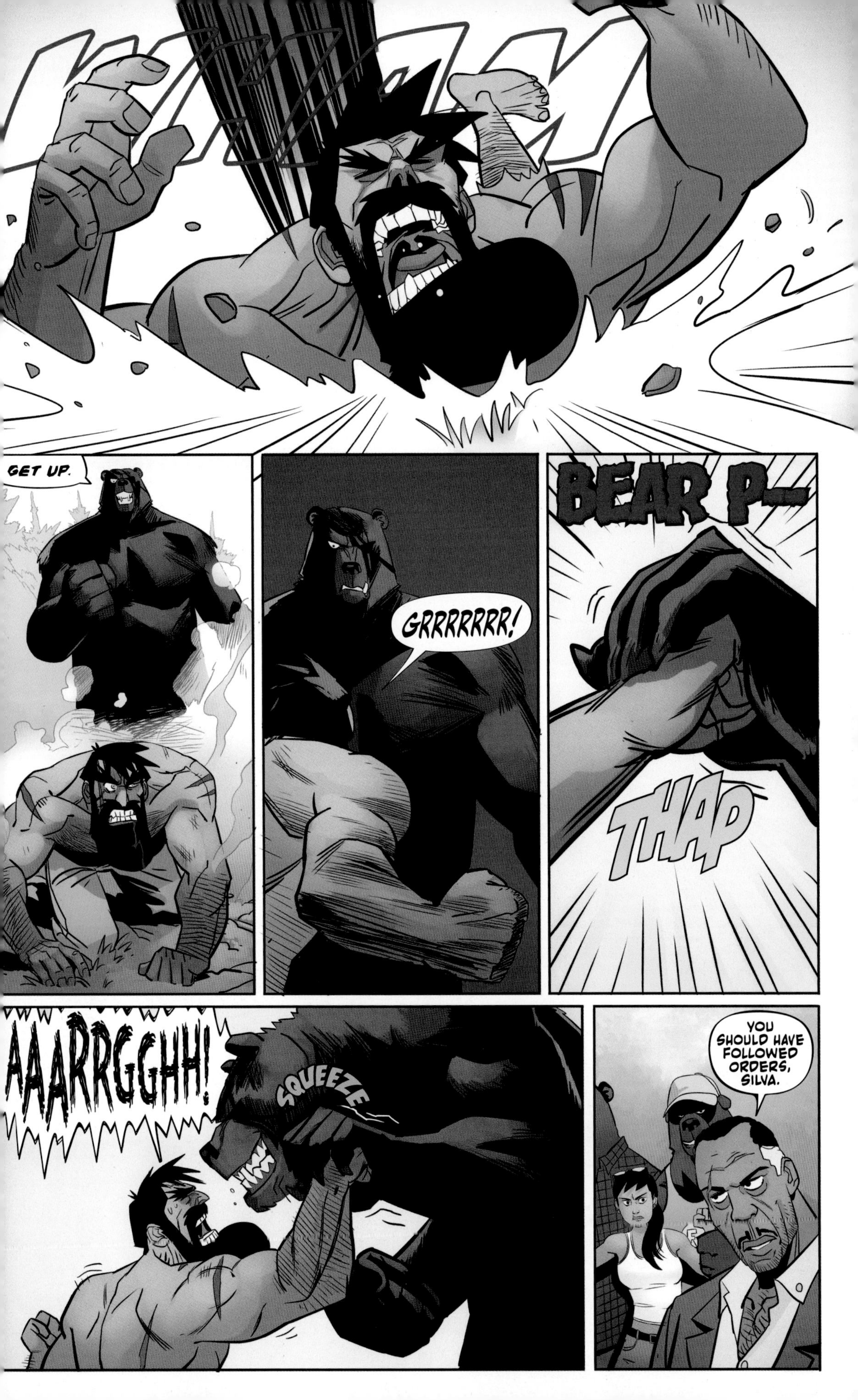
GET UP.
GRRRRRRR!
BEAR P--
THAP
AAARRGGHH!
SQUEEZE
YOU SHOULD HAVE FOLLOWED ORDERS, SILVA.

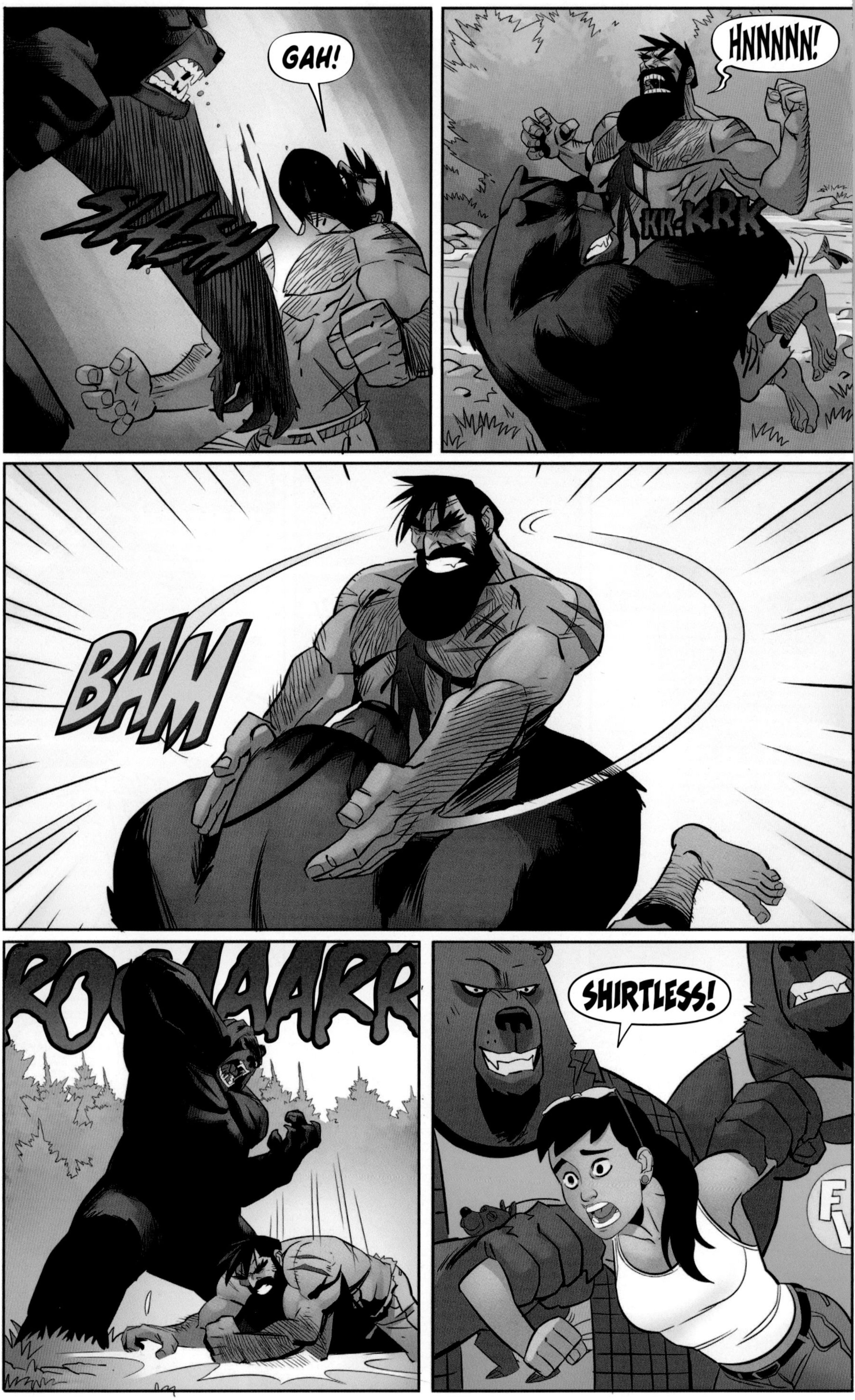
GAH!
HNNNNN!
KK-KRK
BAM
SHIRTLESS!

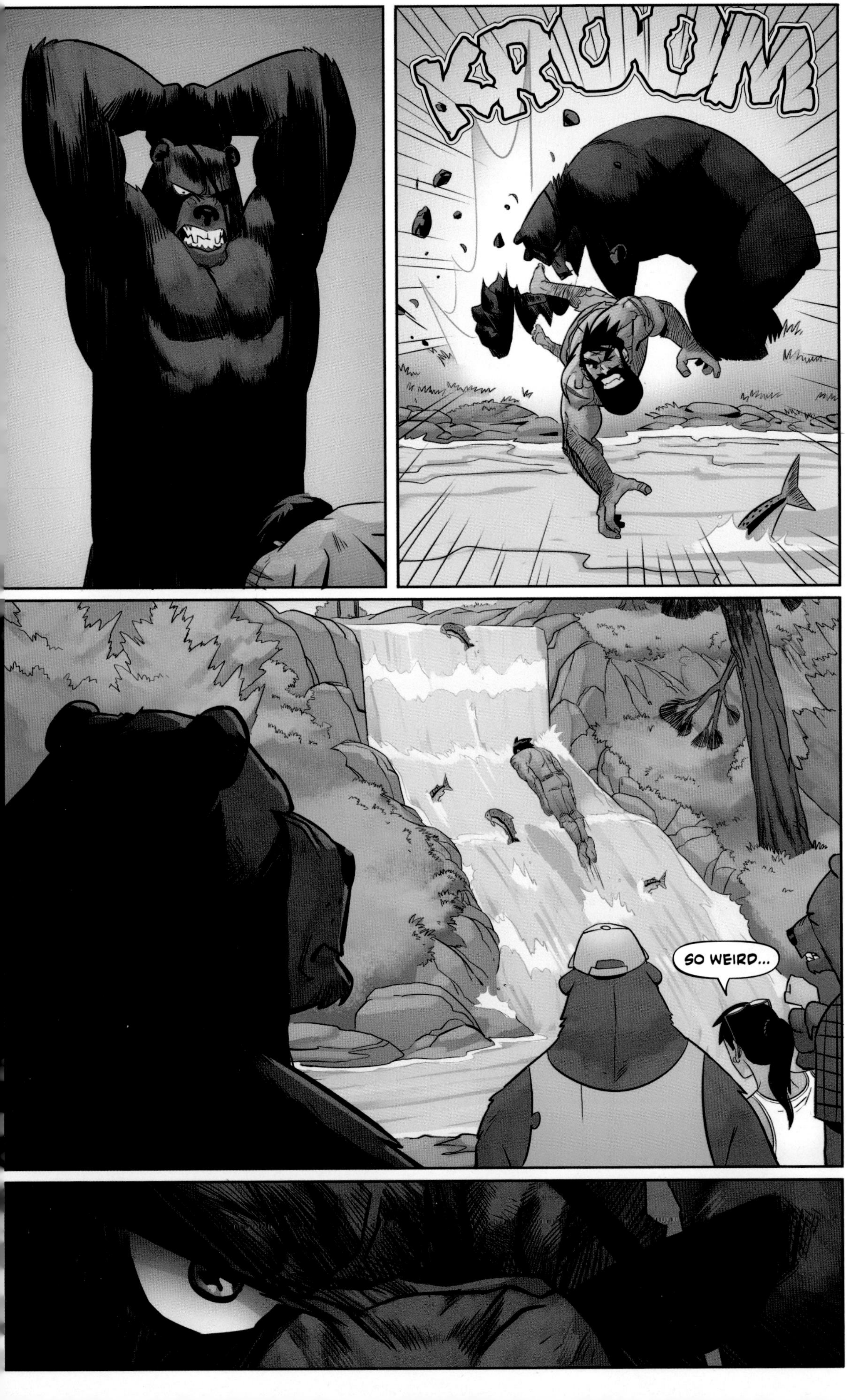
KRAKOOM
SO WEIRD...

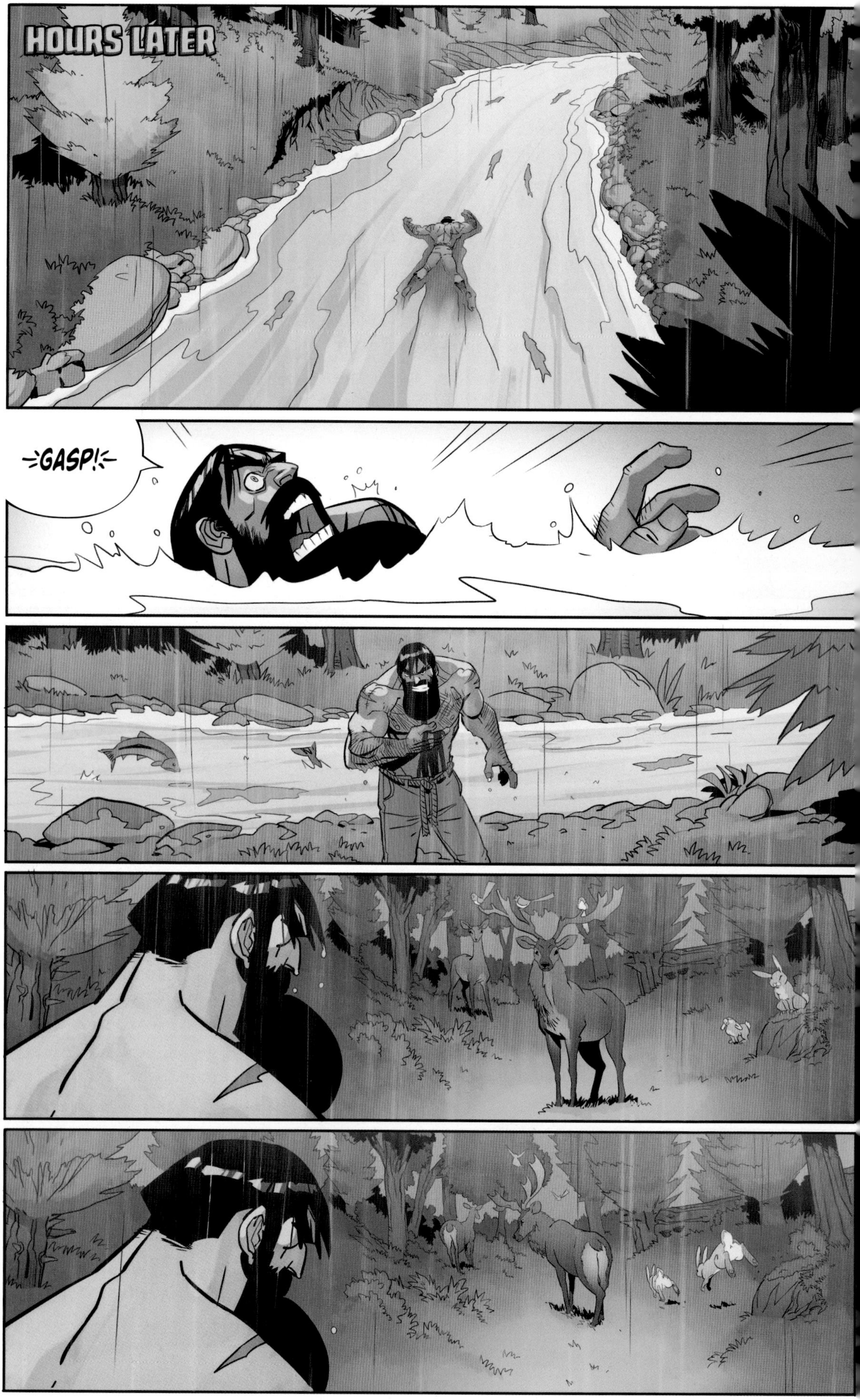
HOURS LATER
GASP!

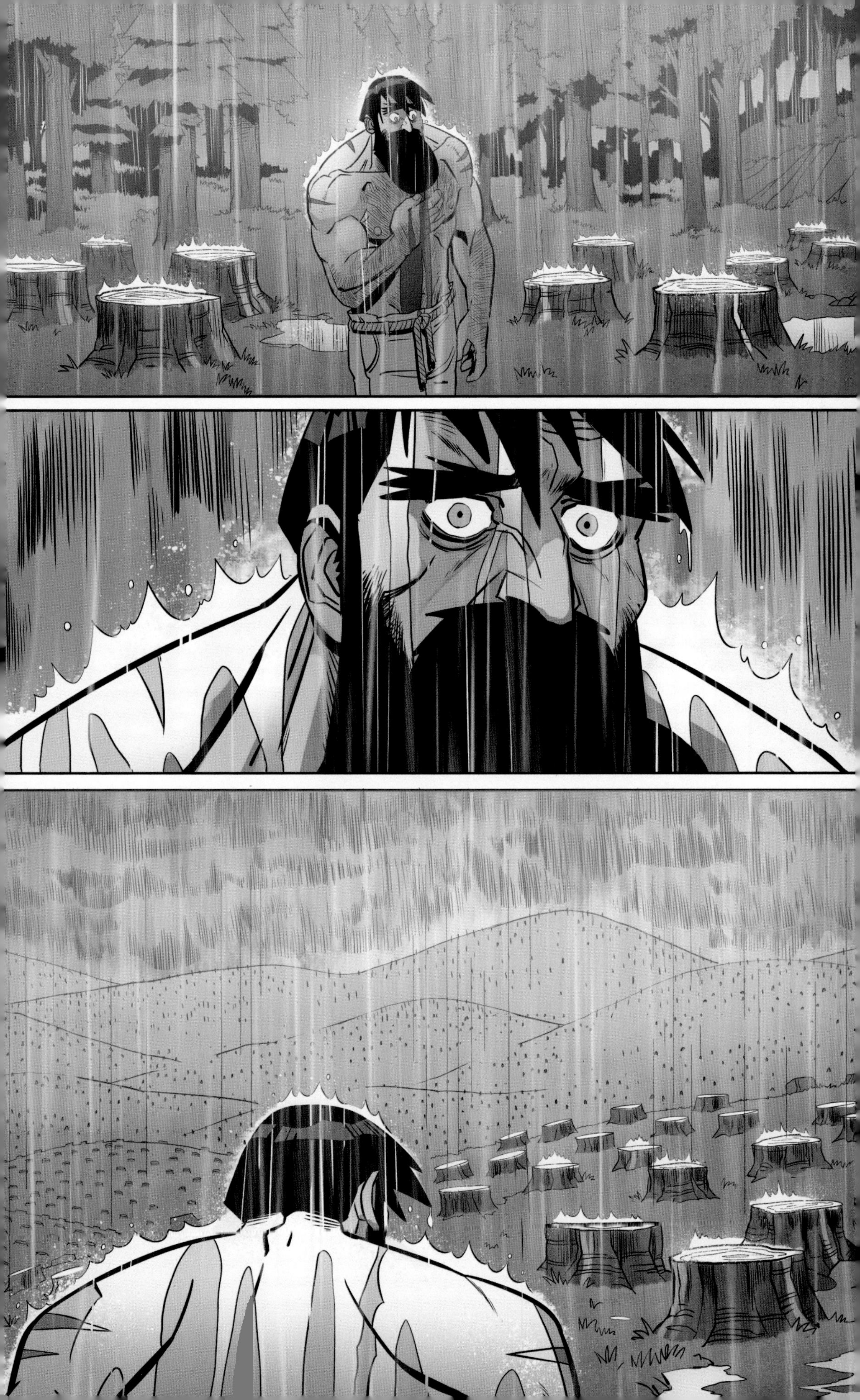

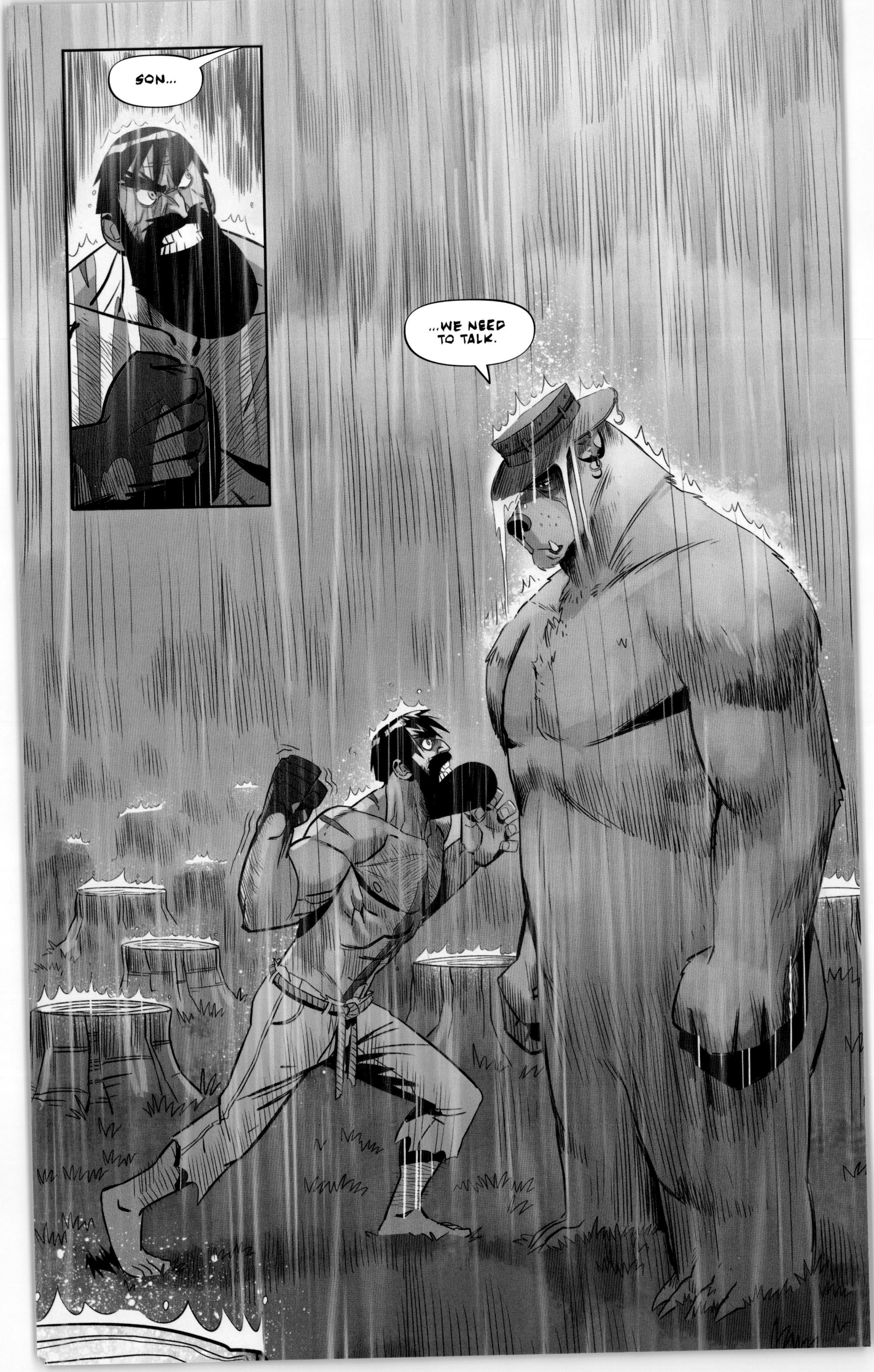
SON...
...WE NEED TO TALK.

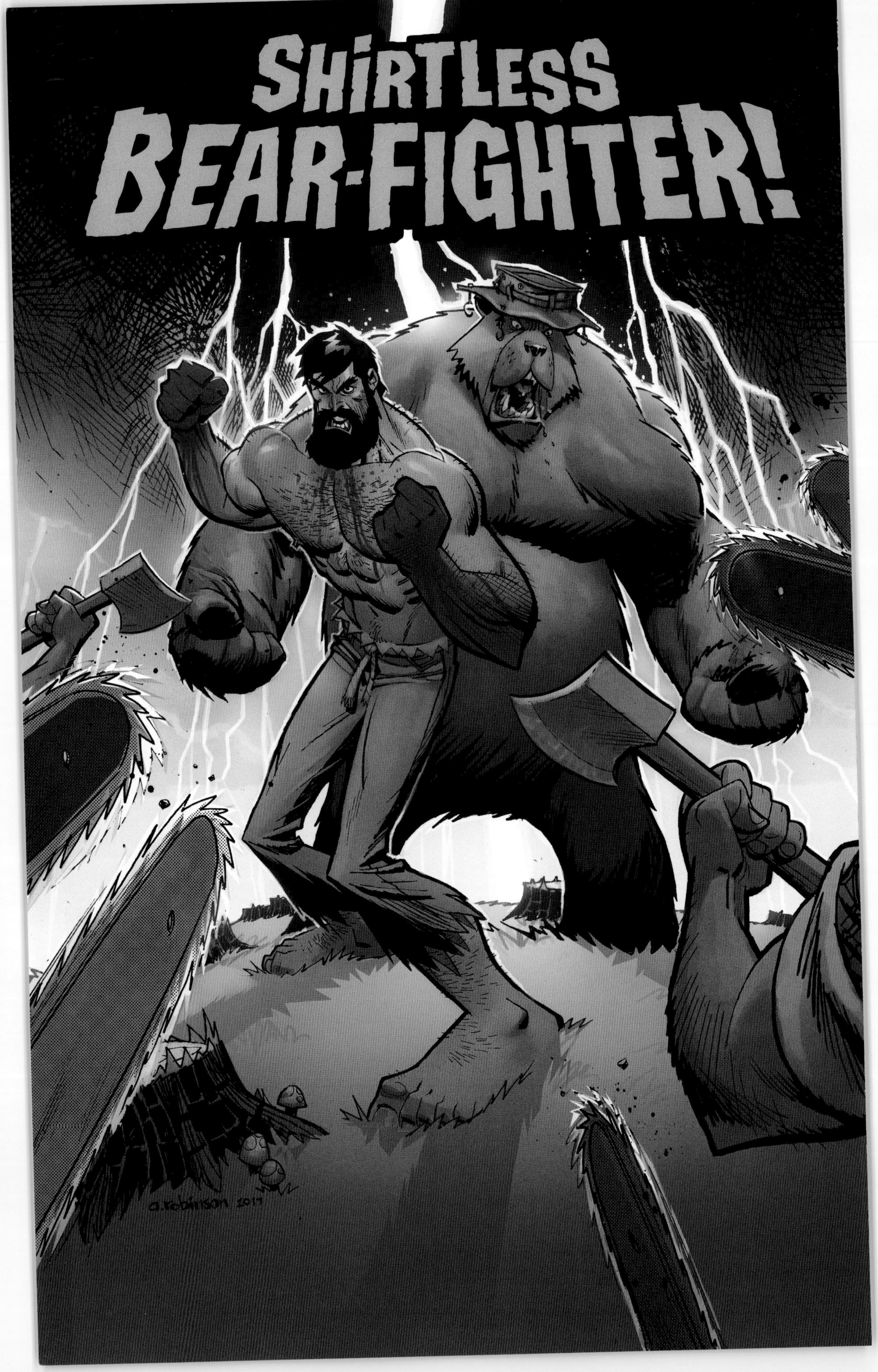
SHIRTLESS
BEAR-FIGHTER!
a.robinson 2017

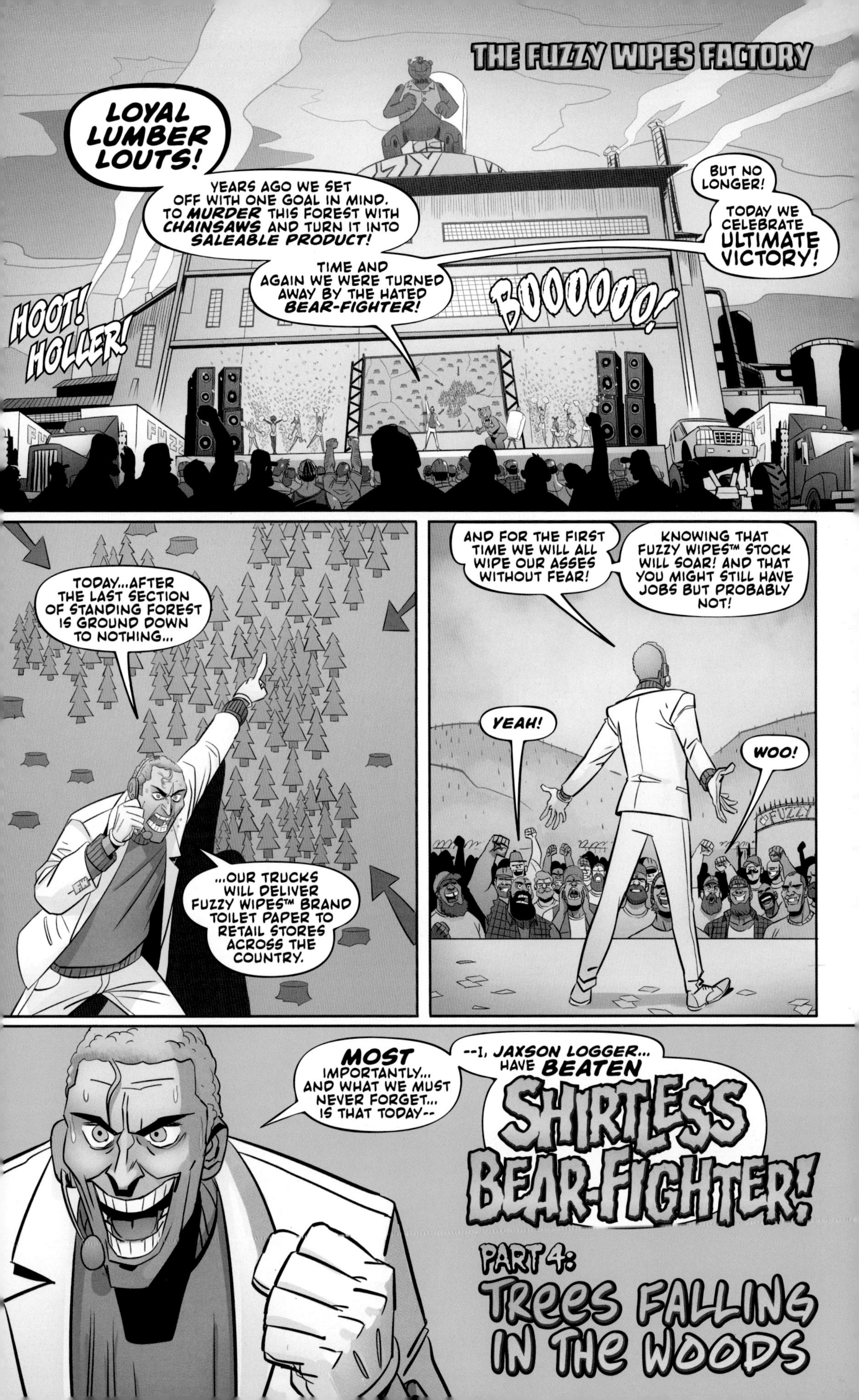
THE FUZZY WIPES FACTORY
LOYAL LUMBER LOUTS!
YEARS AGO WE SET OFF WITH ONE GOAL IN MIND. TO MURDER THIS FOREST WITH CHAINSAWS AND TURN IT INTO SALEABLE PRODUCT!
TIME AND AGAIN WE WERE TURNED AWAY BY THE HATED BEAR-FIGHTER!
BUT NO LONGER!
TODAY WE CELEBRATE ULTIMATE VICTORY!
HOOT! HOLLER!
BOOOOOO!
TODAY...AFTER THE LAST SECTION OF STANDING FOREST IS GROUND DOWN TO NOTHING...
...OUR TRUCKS WILL DELIVER FUZZY WIPES™ BRAND TOILET PAPER TO RETAIL STORES ACROSS THE COUNTRY.
AND FOR THE FIRST TIME WE WILL ALL WIPE OUR ASSES WITHOUT FEAR!
KNOWING THAT FUZZY WIPES™ STOCK WILL SOAR! AND THAT YOU MIGHT STILL HAVE JOBS BUT PROBABLY NOT!
YEAH!
WOO!
MOST IMPORTANTLY... AND WHAT WE MUST NEVER FORGET... IS THAT TODAY--
--I, JAXSON LOGGER... HAVE BEATEN SHIRTLESS BEAR-FIGHTER!
PART 4: TREES FALLING IN THE WOODS

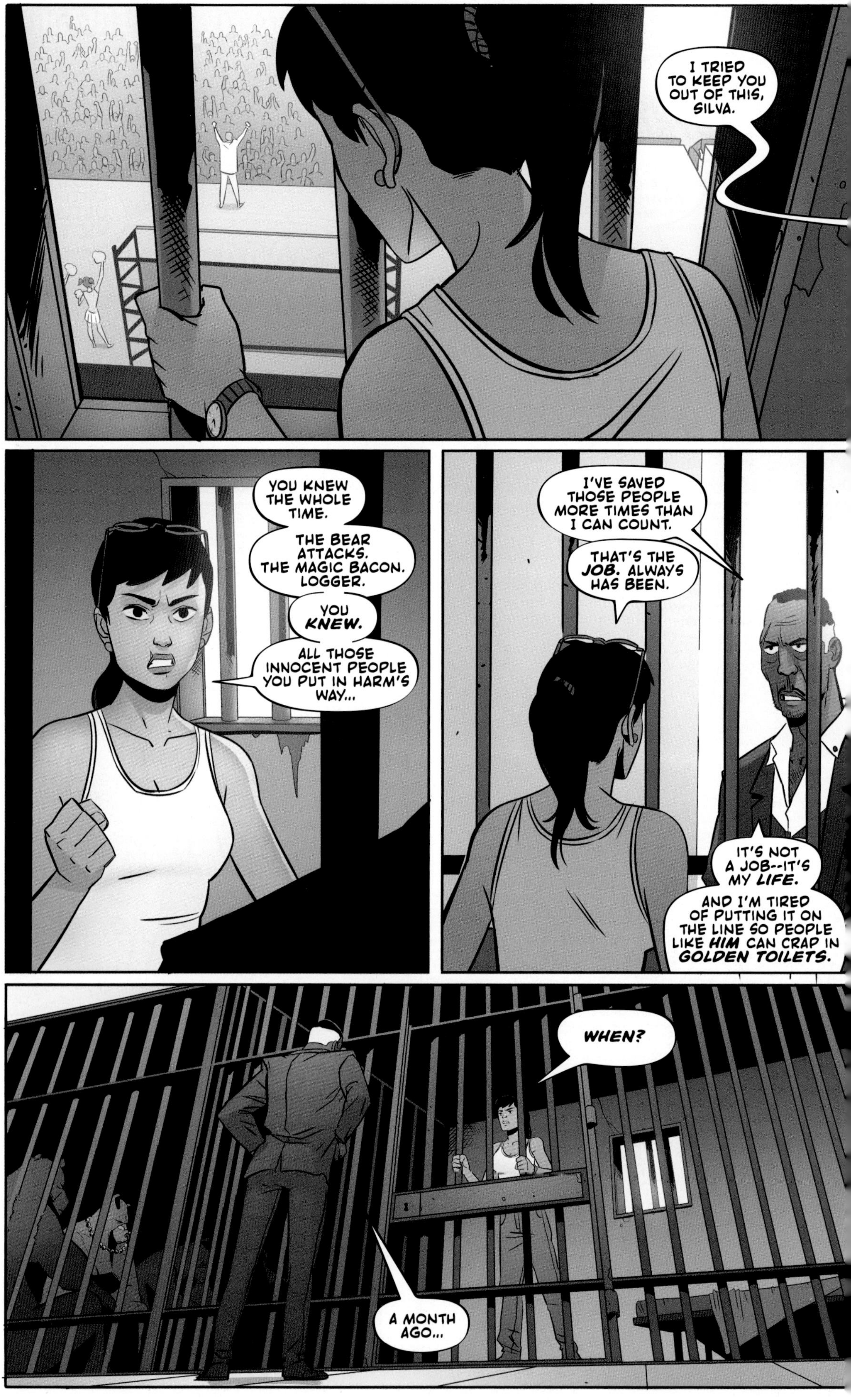
I TRIED TO KEEP YOU OUT OF THIS, SILVA.
YOU KNEW THE WHOLE TIME.
THE BEAR ATTACKS. THE MAGIC BACON. LOGGER.
YOU *KNEW.*
ALL THOSE INNOCENT PEOPLE YOU PUT IN HARM'S WAY...
I'VE SAVED THOSE PEOPLE MORE TIMES THAN I CAN COUNT.
THAT'S THE *JOB.* ALWAYS HAS BEEN.
IT'S NOT A JOB--IT'S MY *LIFE.*
AND I'M TIRED OF PUTTING IT ON THE LINE SO PEOPLE LIKE *HIM* CAN CRAP IN *GOLDEN TOILETS.*
WHEN?
A MONTH AGO...

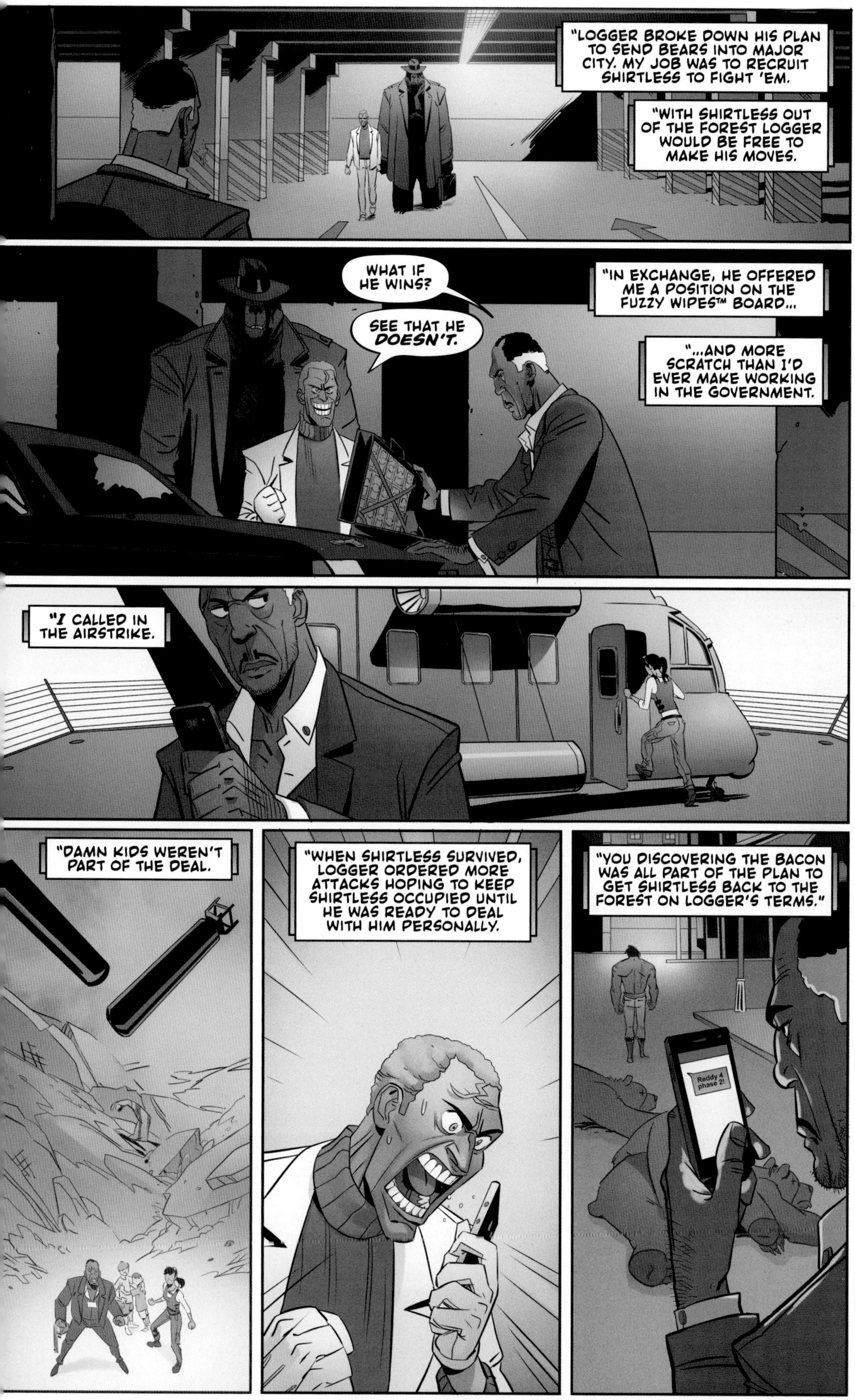
"LOGGER BROKE DOWN HIS PLAN TO SEND BEARS INTO MAJOR CITY. MY JOB WAS TO RECRUIT SHIRTLESS TO FIGHT 'EM.
"WITH SHIRTLESS OUT OF THE FOREST LOGGER WOULD BE FREE TO MAKE HIS MOVES.
WHAT IF HE WINS?
"IN EXCHANGE, HE OFFERED ME A POSITION ON THE FUZZY WIPES™ BOARD...
SEE THAT HE DOESN'T.
"...AND MORE SCRATCH THAN I'D EVER MAKE WORKING IN THE GOVERNMENT.
"I CALLED IN THE AIRSTRIKE.
"DAMN KIDS WEREN'T PART OF THE DEAL.
"WHEN SHIRTLESS SURVIVED, LOGGER ORDERED MORE ATTACKS HOPING TO KEEP SHIRTLESS OCCUPIED UNTIL HE WAS READY TO DEAL WITH HIM PERSONALLY.
"YOU DISCOVERING THE BACON WAS ALL PART OF THE PLAN TO GET SHIRTLESS BACK TO THE FOREST ON LOGGER'S TERMS."
Reddy 4 phase 2!

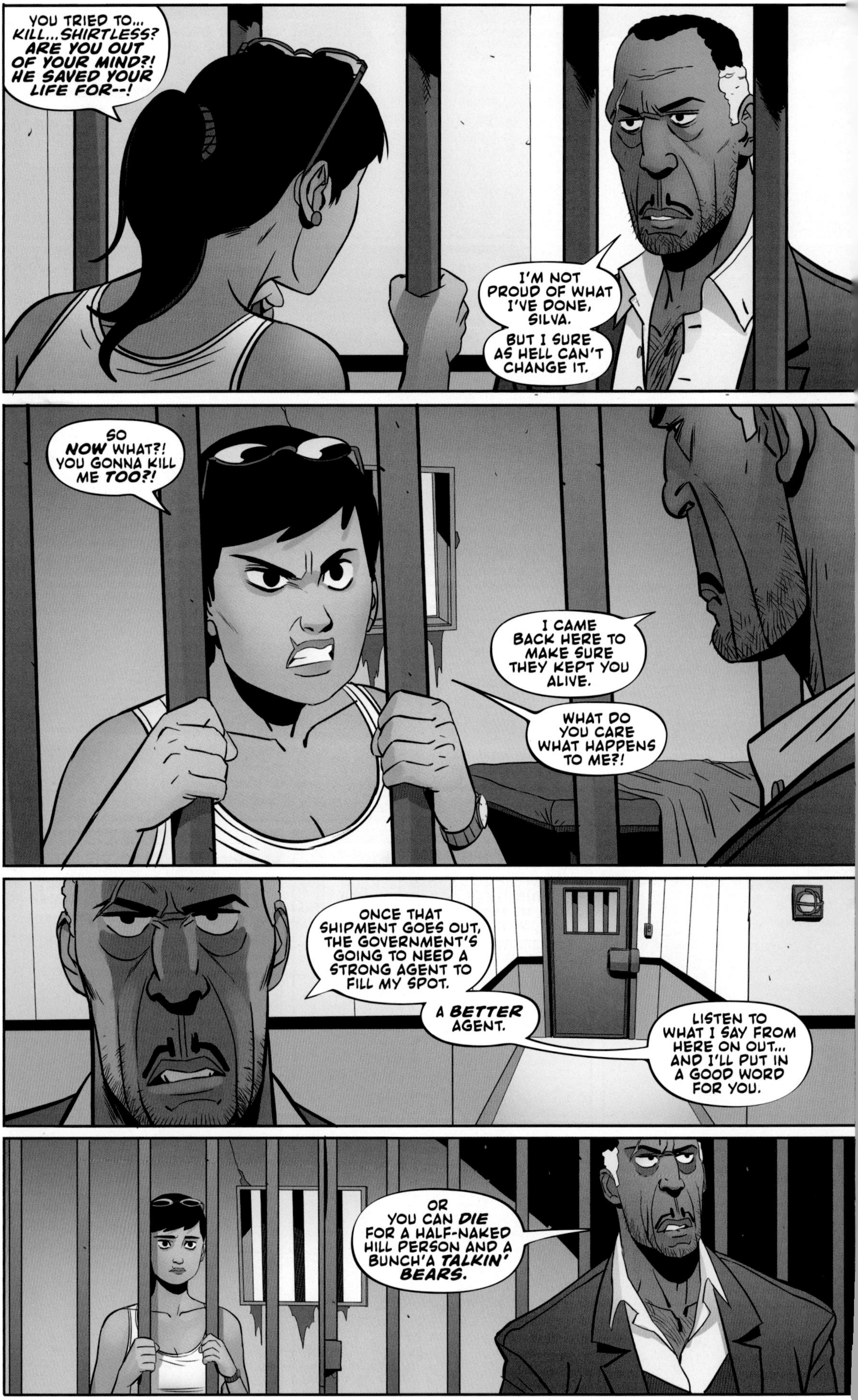
YOU TRIED TO... KILL...SHIRTLESS? ARE YOU OUT OF YOUR MIND?! HE SAVED YOUR LIFE FOR--!
I'M NOT PROUD OF WHAT I'VE DONE, SILVA.
BUT I SURE AS HELL CAN'T CHANGE IT.
SO NOW WHAT?! YOU GONNA KILL ME TOO?!
I CAME BACK HERE TO MAKE SURE THEY KEPT YOU ALIVE.
WHAT DO YOU CARE WHAT HAPPENS TO ME?!
ONCE THAT SHIPMENT GOES OUT, THE GOVERNMENT'S GOING TO NEED A STRONG AGENT TO FILL MY SPOT.
A BETTER AGENT.
LISTEN TO WHAT I SAY FROM HERE ON OUT... AND I'LL PUT IN A GOOD WORD FOR YOU.
OR YOU CAN DIE FOR A HALF-NAKED HILL PERSON AND A BUNCH'A TALKIN' BEARS.

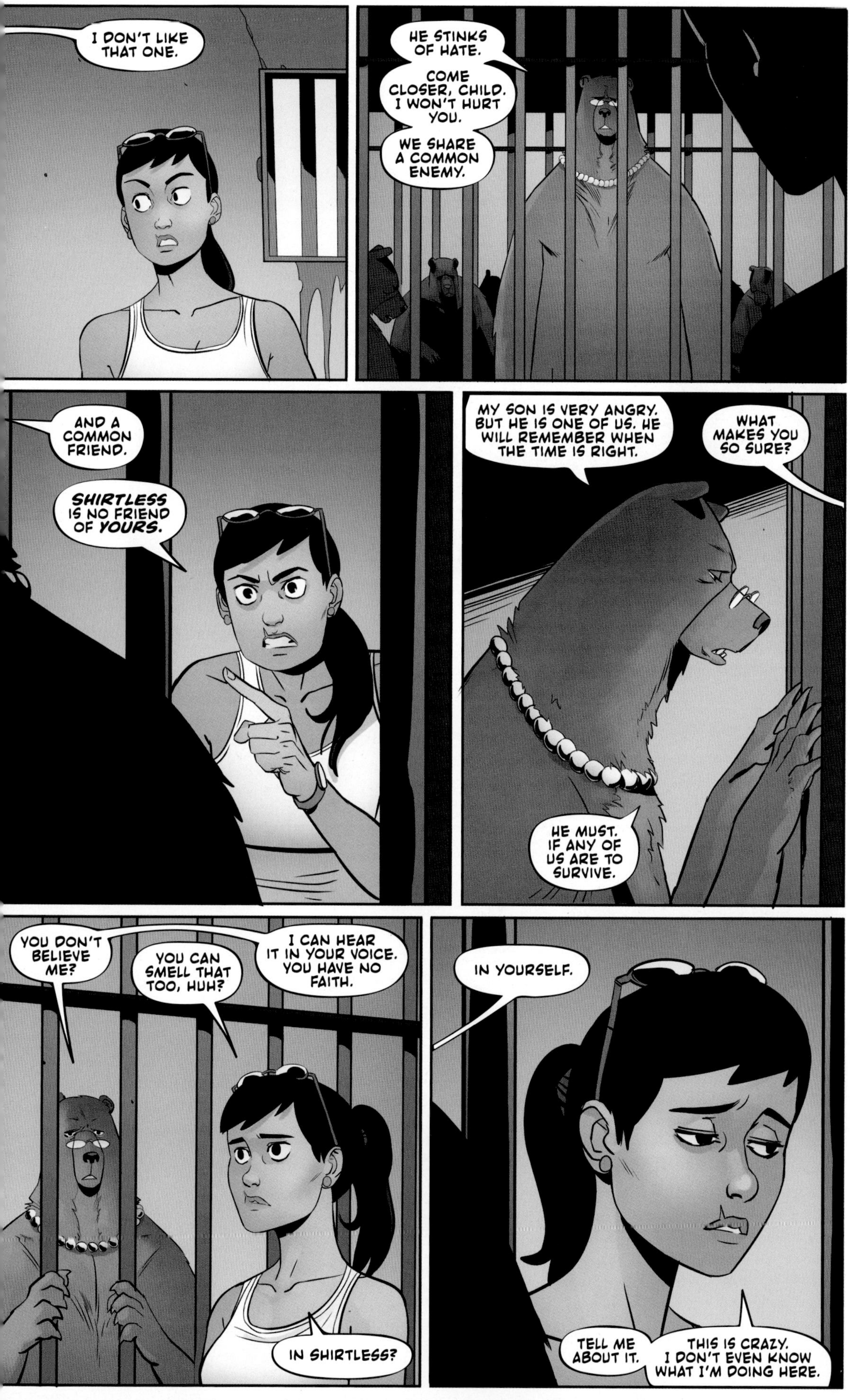
I DON'T LIKE THAT ONE.
HE STINKS OF HATE.
COME CLOSER, CHILD. I WON'T HURT YOU.
WE SHARE A COMMON ENEMY.
AND A COMMON FRIEND.
SHIRTLESS IS NO FRIEND OF YOURS.
MY SON IS VERY ANGRY. BUT HE IS ONE OF US. HE WILL REMEMBER WHEN THE TIME IS RIGHT.
WHAT MAKES YOU SO SURE?
HE MUST. IF ANY OF US ARE TO SURVIVE.
YOU DON'T BELIEVE ME?
YOU CAN SMELL THAT TOO, HUH?
I CAN HEAR IT IN YOUR VOICE. YOU HAVE NO FAITH.
IN SHIRTLESS?
IN YOURSELF.
TELL ME ABOUT IT.
THIS IS CRAZY. I DON'T EVEN KNOW WHAT I'M DOING HERE.

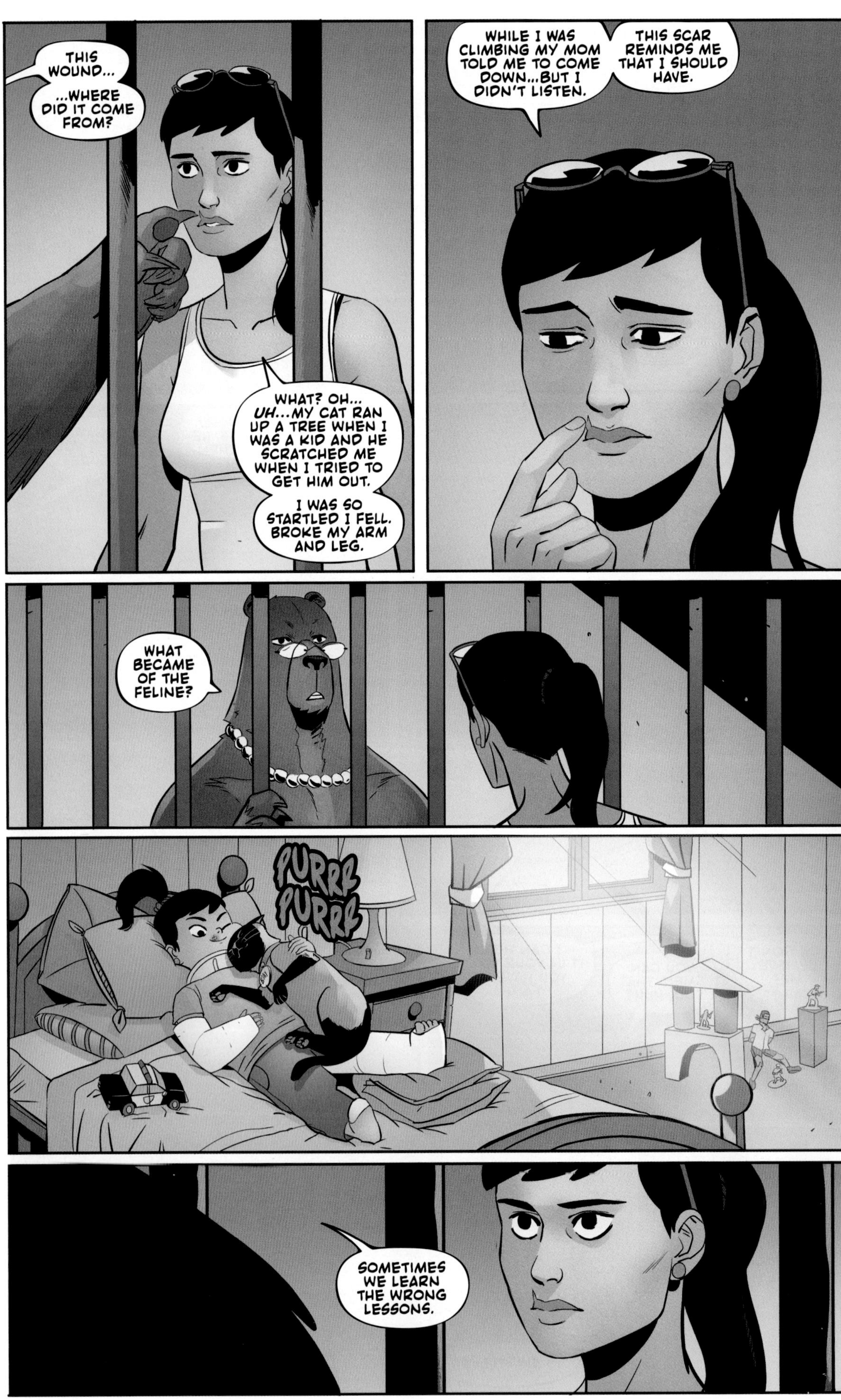
THIS WOUND...
...WHERE DID IT COME FROM?
WHAT? OH... UH...MY CAT RAN UP A TREE WHEN I WAS A KID AND HE SCRATCHED ME WHEN I TRIED TO GET HIM OUT.
I WAS SO STARTLED I FELL. BROKE MY ARM AND LEG.
WHILE I WAS CLIMBING MY MOM TOLD ME TO COME DOWN...BUT I DIDN'T LISTEN.
THIS SCAR REMINDS ME THAT I SHOULD HAVE.
WHAT BECAME OF THE FELINE?
PURRR PURRR
SOMETIMES WE LEARN THE WRONG LESSONS.

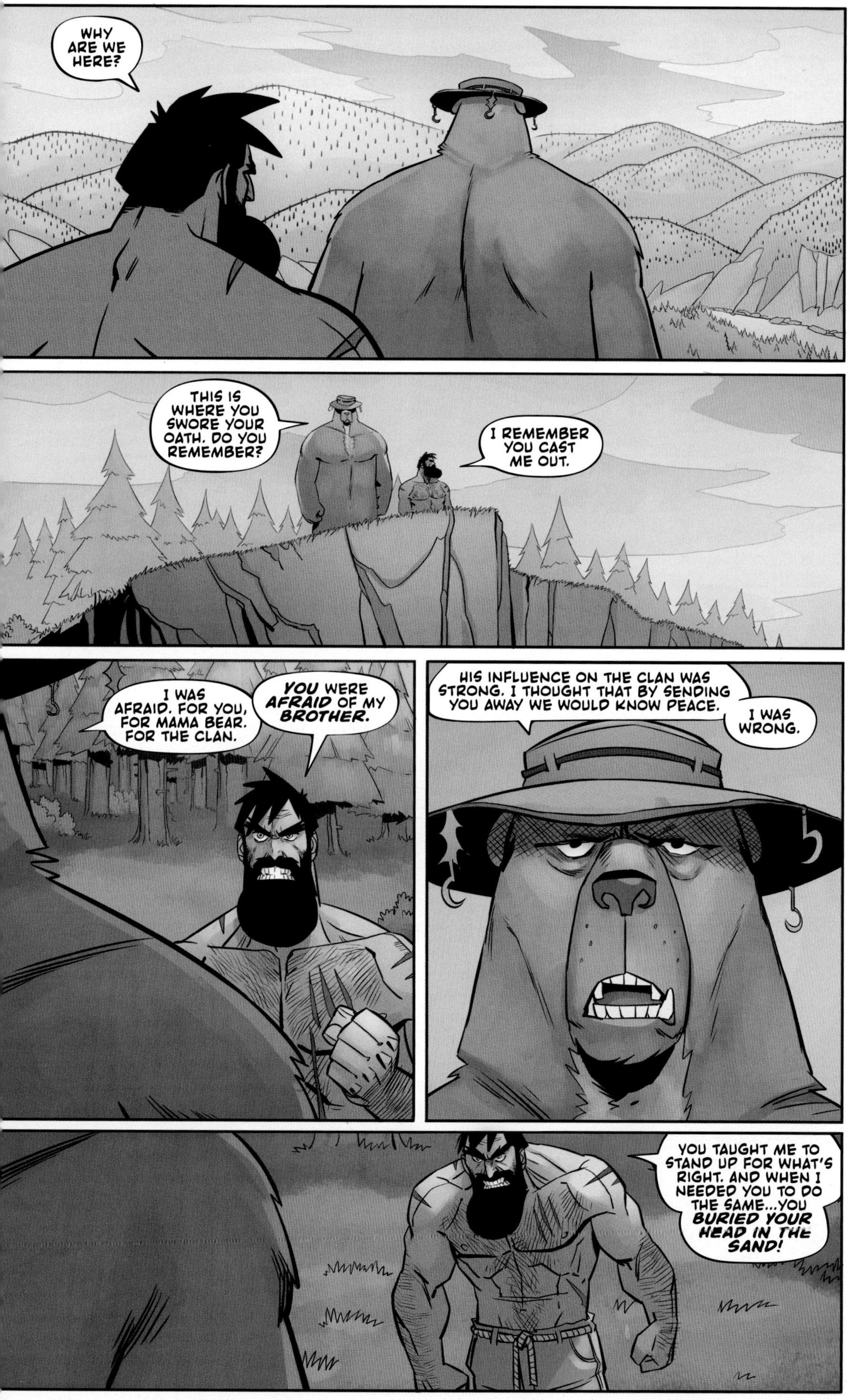
WHY ARE WE HERE?
THIS IS WHERE YOU SWORE YOUR OATH. DO YOU REMEMBER?
I REMEMBER YOU CAST ME OUT.
I WAS AFRAID. FOR YOU, FOR MAMA BEAR. FOR THE CLAN.
YOU WERE AFRAID OF MY BROTHER.
HIS INFLUENCE ON THE CLAN WAS STRONG. I THOUGHT THAT BY SENDING YOU AWAY WE WOULD KNOW PEACE.
I WAS WRONG.
YOU TAUGHT ME TO STAND UP FOR WHAT'S RIGHT. AND WHEN I NEEDED YOU TO DO THE SAME...YOU BURIED YOUR HEAD IN THE SAND!

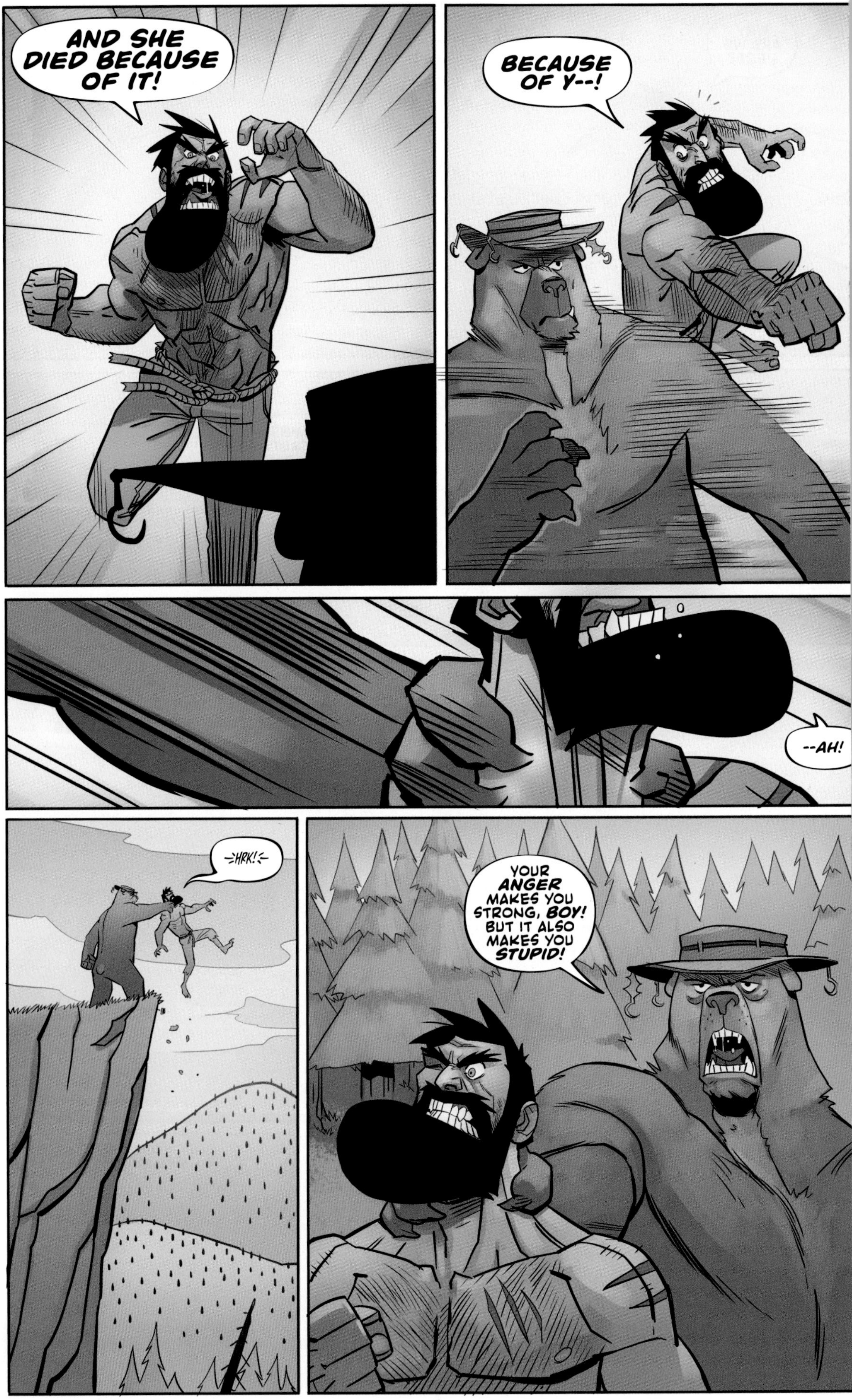
AND SHE DIED BECAUSE OF IT!
BECAUSE OF Y--!
--AH!
HRK!
YOUR ANGER MAKES YOU STRONG, BOY! BUT IT ALSO MAKES YOU STUPID!

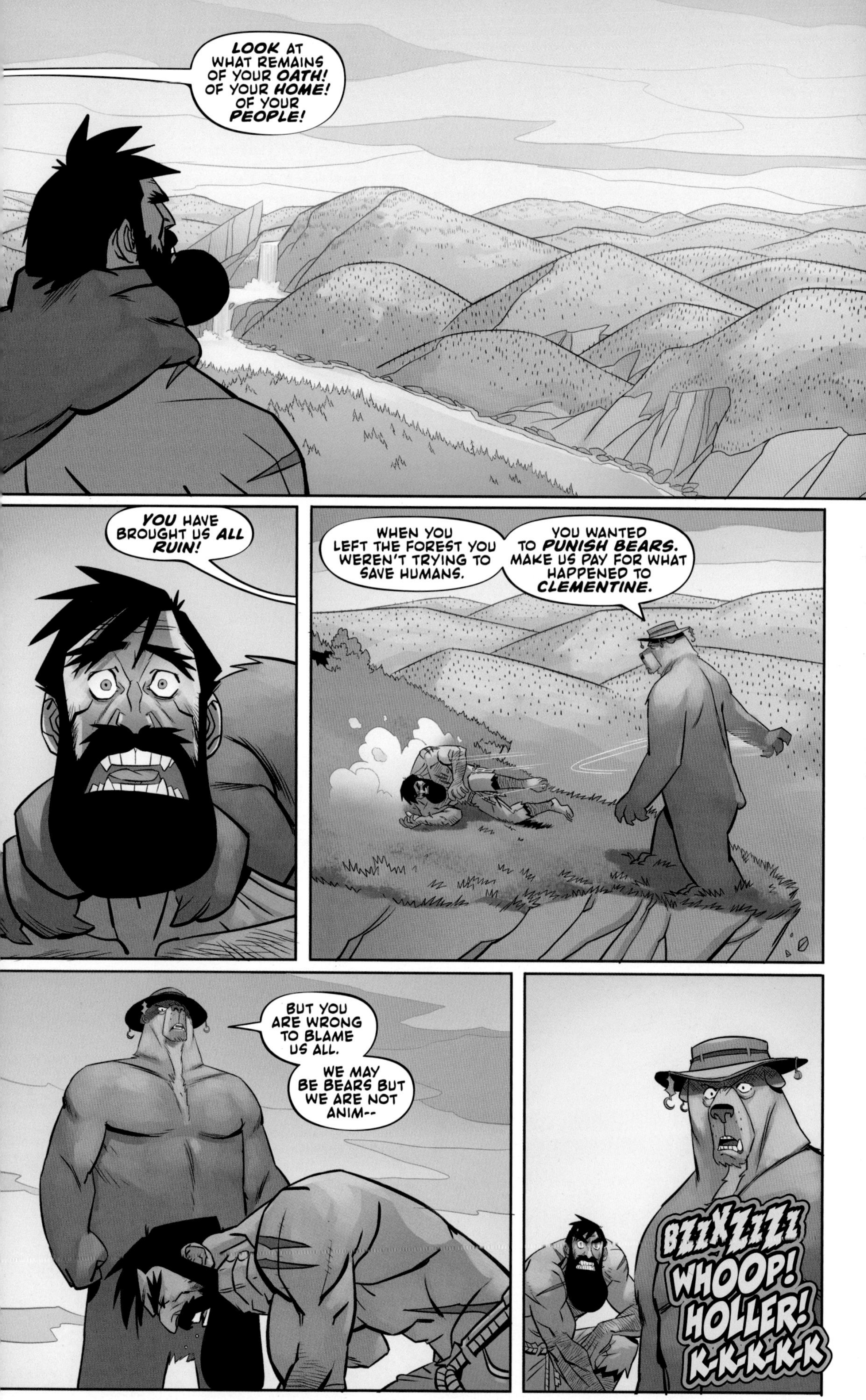
LOOK AT WHAT REMAINS OF YOUR OATH! OF YOUR HOME! OF YOUR PEOPLE!
YOU HAVE BROUGHT US ALL RUIN!
WHEN YOU LEFT THE FOREST YOU WEREN'T TRYING TO SAVE HUMANS.
YOU WANTED TO PUNISH BEARS. MAKE US PAY FOR WHAT HAPPENED TO CLEMENTINE.
BUT YOU ARE WRONG TO BLAME US ALL.
WE MAY BE BEARS BUT WE ARE NOT ANIM--
BZZZXZZZZ
WHOOP!
HOLLER!
K-K-K-K-K

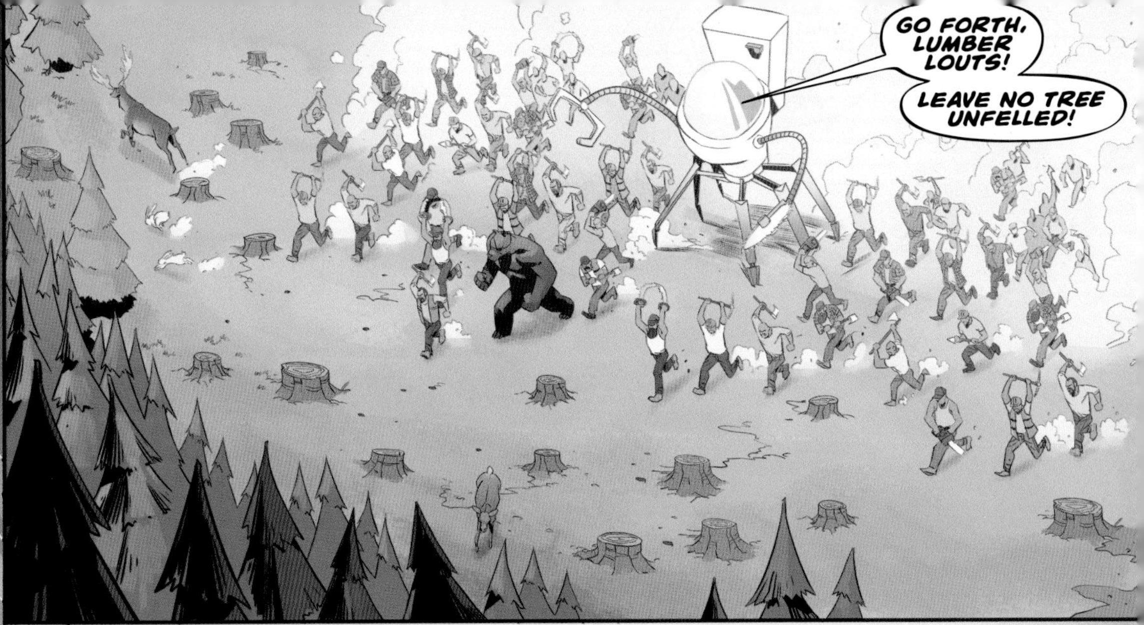
GO FORTH, LUMBER LOUTS!
LEAVE NO TREE UNFELLED!
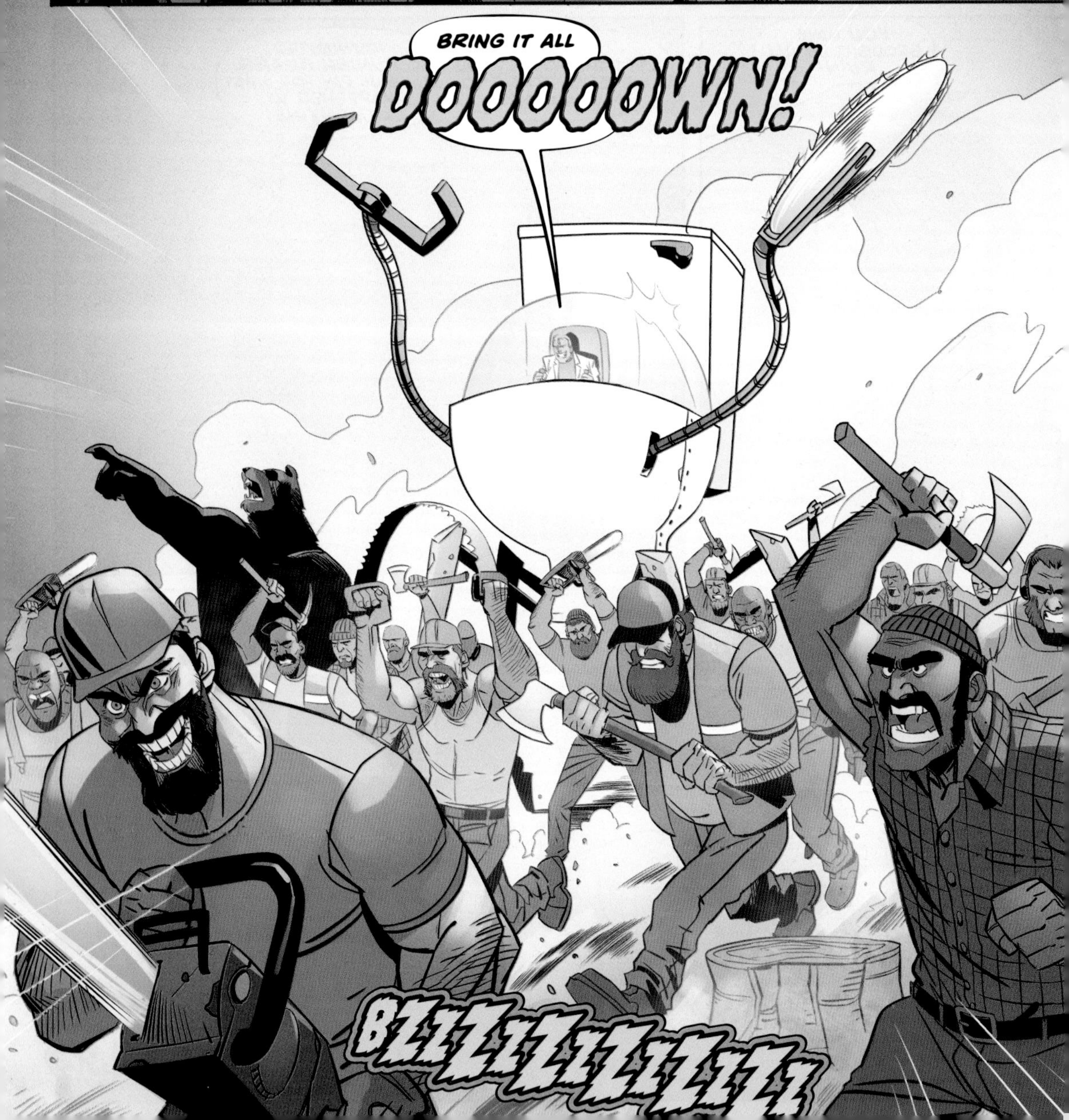
BRING IT ALL DOOOOOOWN!
BZZZZZZZZZZZZZZ

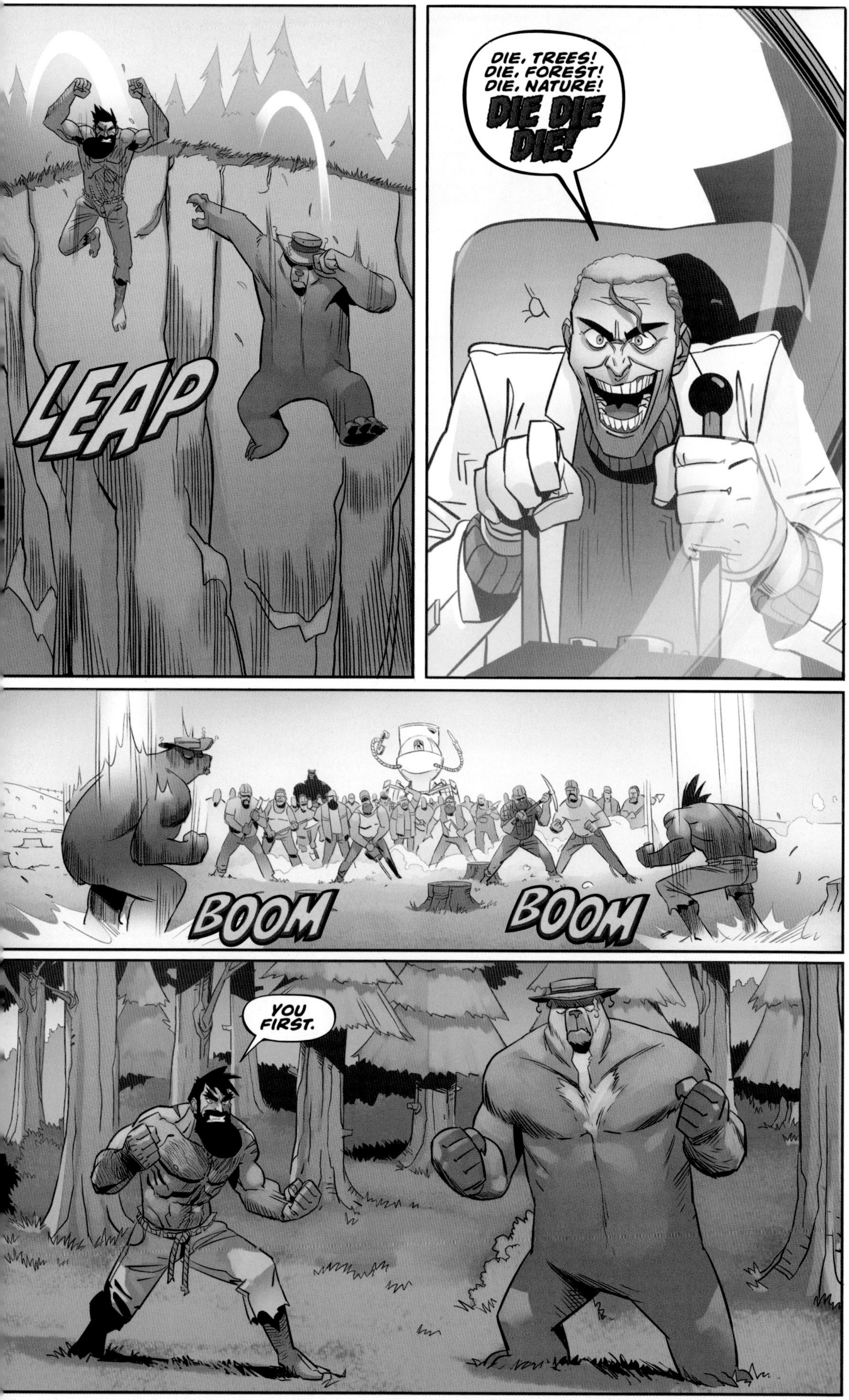
LEAP
DIE, TREES!
DIE, FOREST!
DIE, NATURE!
DIE DIE
DIE!
BOOM
BOOM
YOU
FIRST.

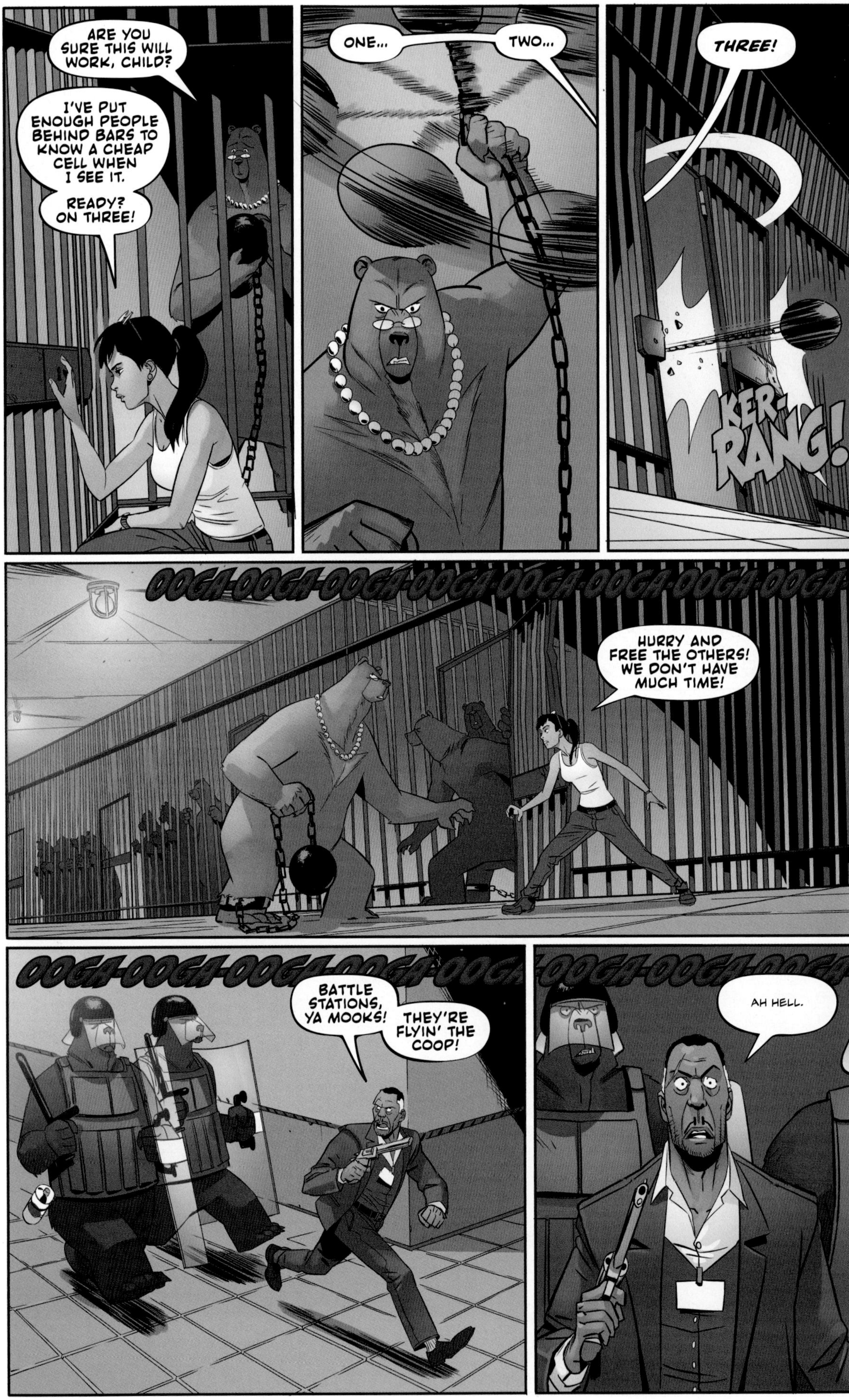
ARE YOU SURE THIS WILL WORK, CHILD?
I'VE PUT ENOUGH PEOPLE BEHIND BARS TO KNOW A CHEAP CELL WHEN I SEE IT.
READY? ON THREE!
ONE...
TWO...
THREE!
KER-RANG!
OOGA-OOGA-OOGA-OOGA-OOGA-OOGA-OOGA-OOGA
HURRY AND FREE THE OTHERS! WE DON'T HAVE MUCH TIME!
OOGA-OOGA-OOGA-OOGA
BATTLE STATIONS, YA MOOKS!
THEY'RE FLYIN' THE COOP!
OOGA-OOGA-OOGA
AH HELL.

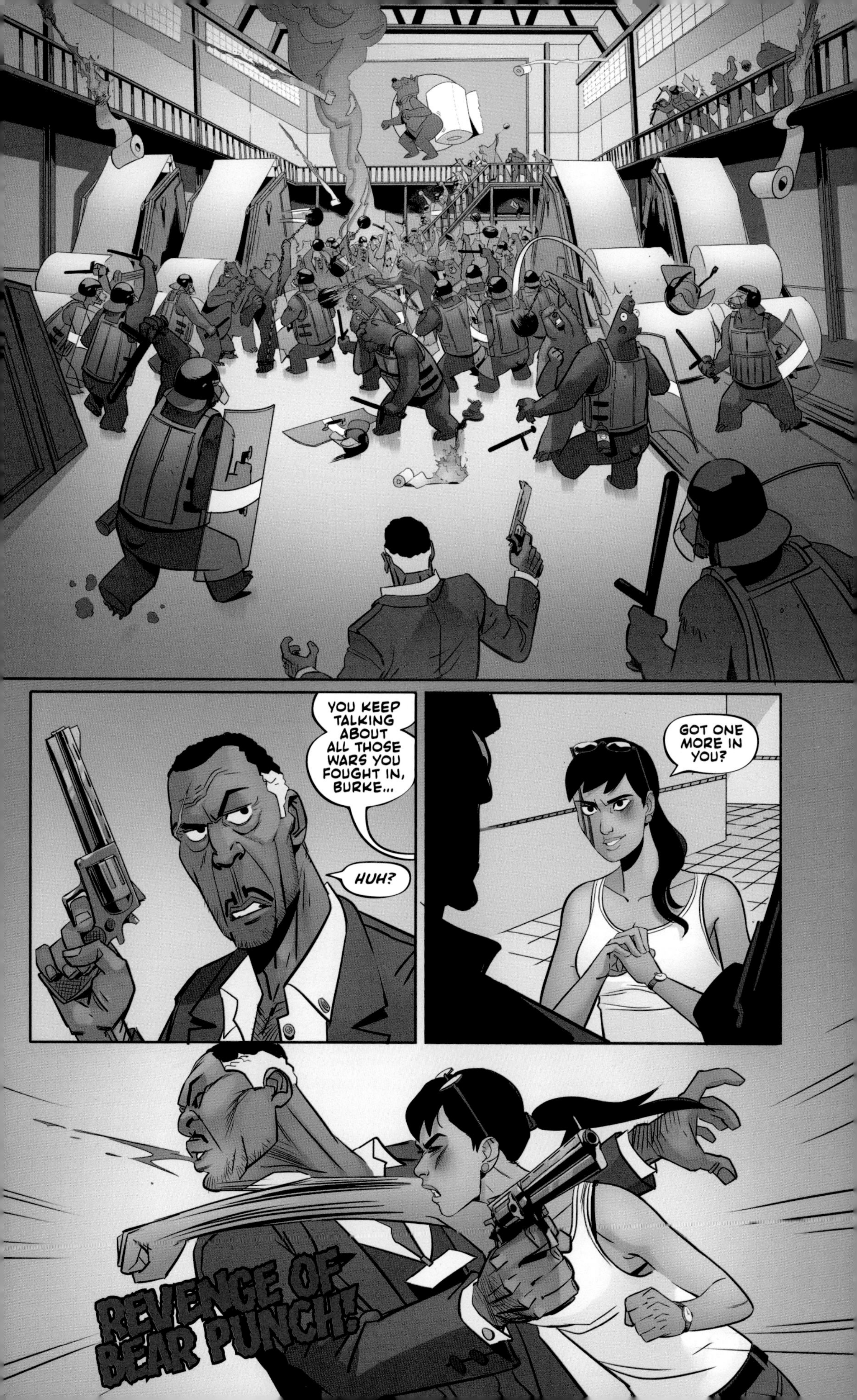

YOU KEEP TALKING ABOUT ALL THOSE WARS YOU FOUGHT IN, BURKE...
HUH?
GOT ONE MORE IN YOU?
REVENGE OF BEAR PUNCH!

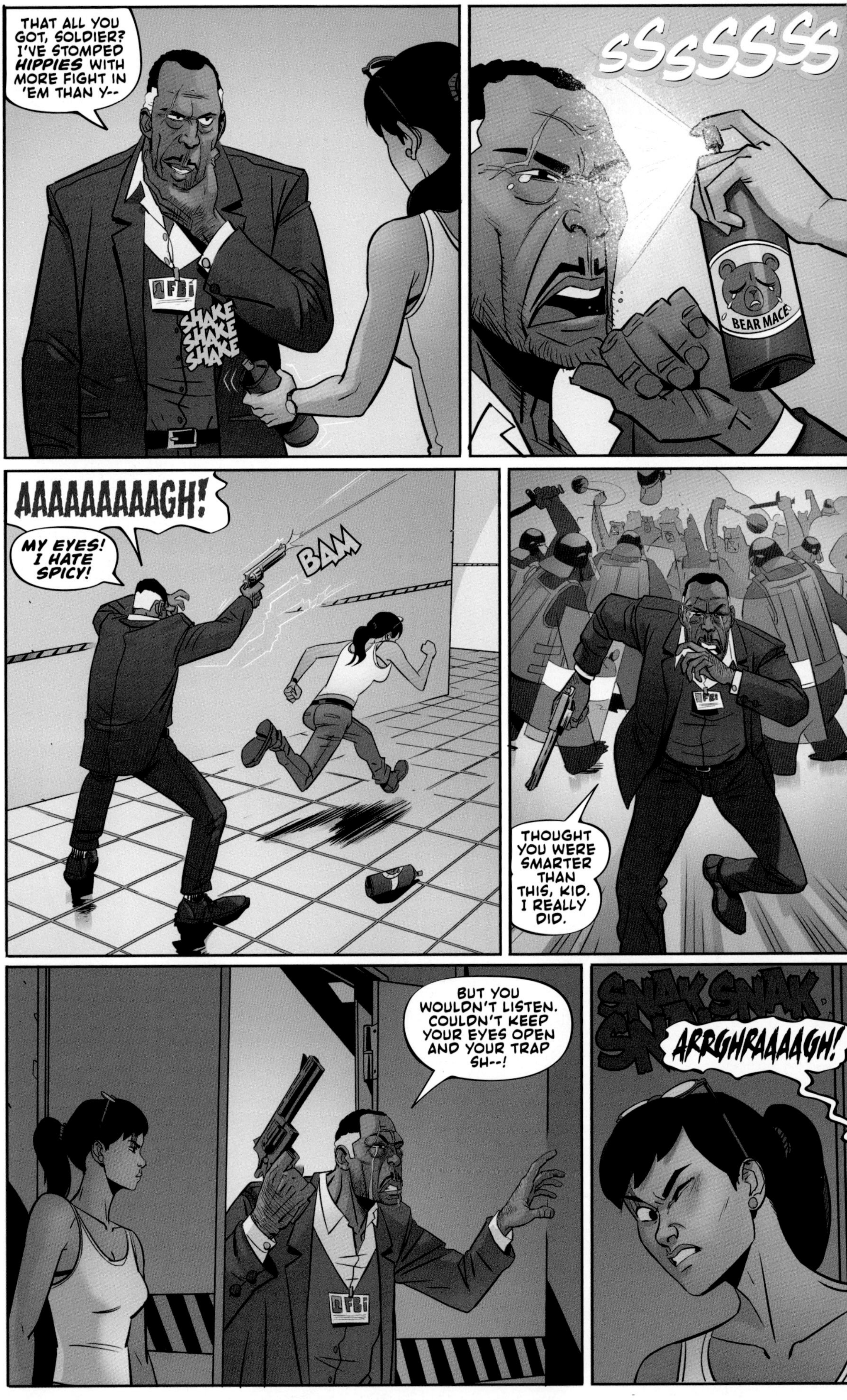
THAT ALL YOU GOT, SOLDIER? I'VE STOMPED HIPPIES WITH MORE FIGHT IN 'EM THAN Y--
SHAKE SHAKE SHAKE
FBI
SSSSSSS
BEAR MACE
AAAAAAAAAGH!
MY EYES! I HATE SPICY!
BAM
FBI
THOUGHT YOU WERE SMARTER THAN THIS, KID. I REALLY DID.
BUT YOU WOULDN'T LISTEN. COULDN'T KEEP YOUR EYES OPEN AND YOUR TRAP SH--!
FBI
SNAK SNAK
ARRGHRAAAAGH!

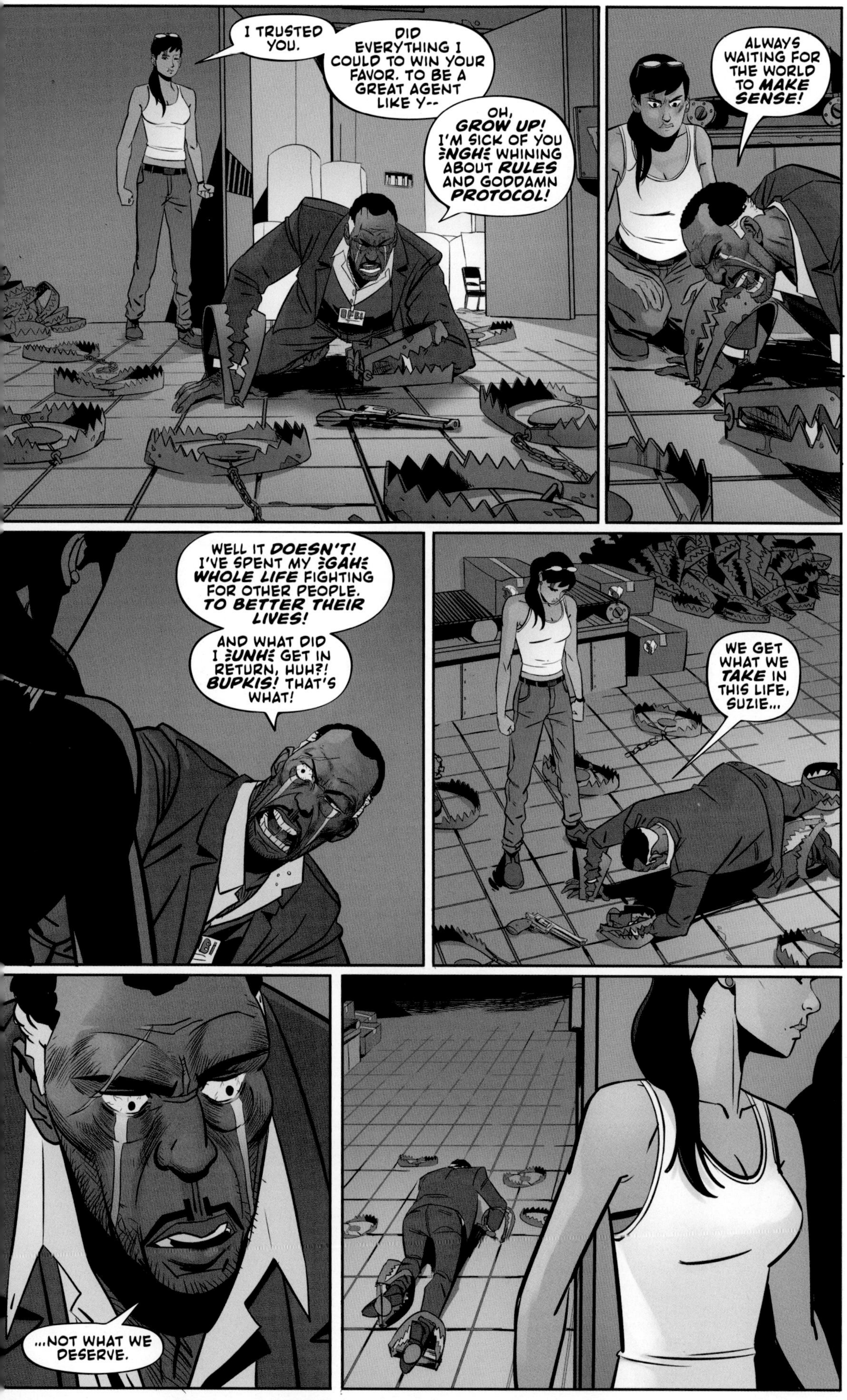
I TRUSTED YOU.
DID EVERYTHING I COULD TO WIN YOUR FAVOR. TO BE A GREAT AGENT LIKE Y--
OH, GROW UP! I'M SICK OF YOU NGH WHINING ABOUT RULES AND GODDAMN PROTOCOL!
ALWAYS WAITING FOR THE WORLD TO MAKE SENSE!
WELL IT DOESN'T! I'VE SPENT MY GAH WHOLE LIFE FIGHTING FOR OTHER PEOPLE. TO BETTER THEIR LIVES!
AND WHAT DID I UNH GET IN RETURN, HUH?! BUPKIS! THAT'S WHAT!
WE GET WHAT WE TAKE IN THIS LIFE, SUZIE...
...NOT WHAT WE DESERVE.

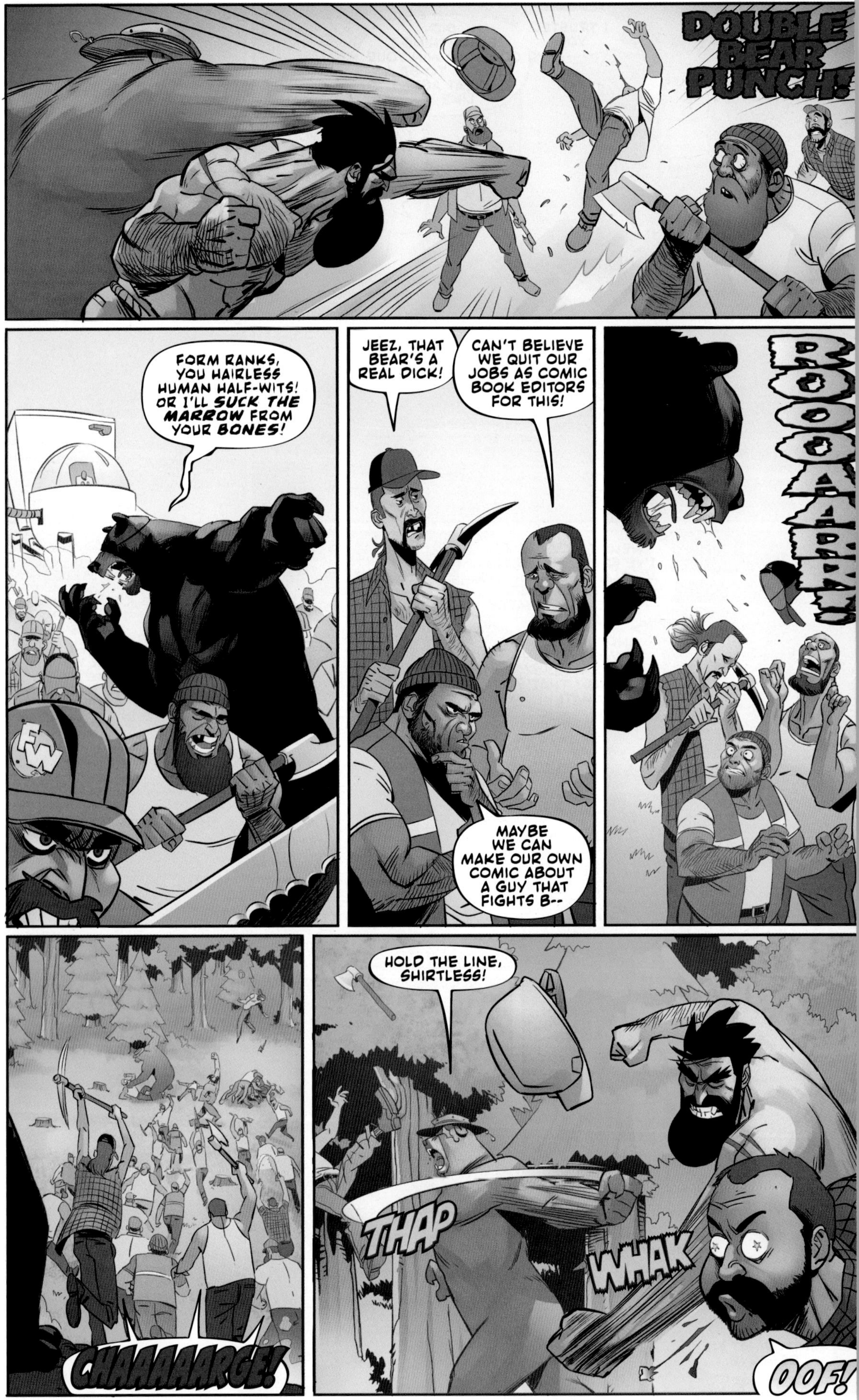
DOUBLE BEAR PUNCH!
FORM RANKS, YOU HAIRLESS HUMAN HALF-WITS! OR I'LL SUCK THE MARROW FROM YOUR BONES!
JEEZ, THAT BEAR'S A REAL DICK!
CAN'T BELIEVE WE QUIT OUR JOBS AS COMIC BOOK EDITORS FOR THIS!
MAYBE WE CAN MAKE OUR OWN COMIC ABOUT A GUY THAT FIGHTS B--
ROOOAARR!
CHAAAAARGE!
HOLD THE LINE, SHIRTLESS!
THAP
WHAK
OOF!

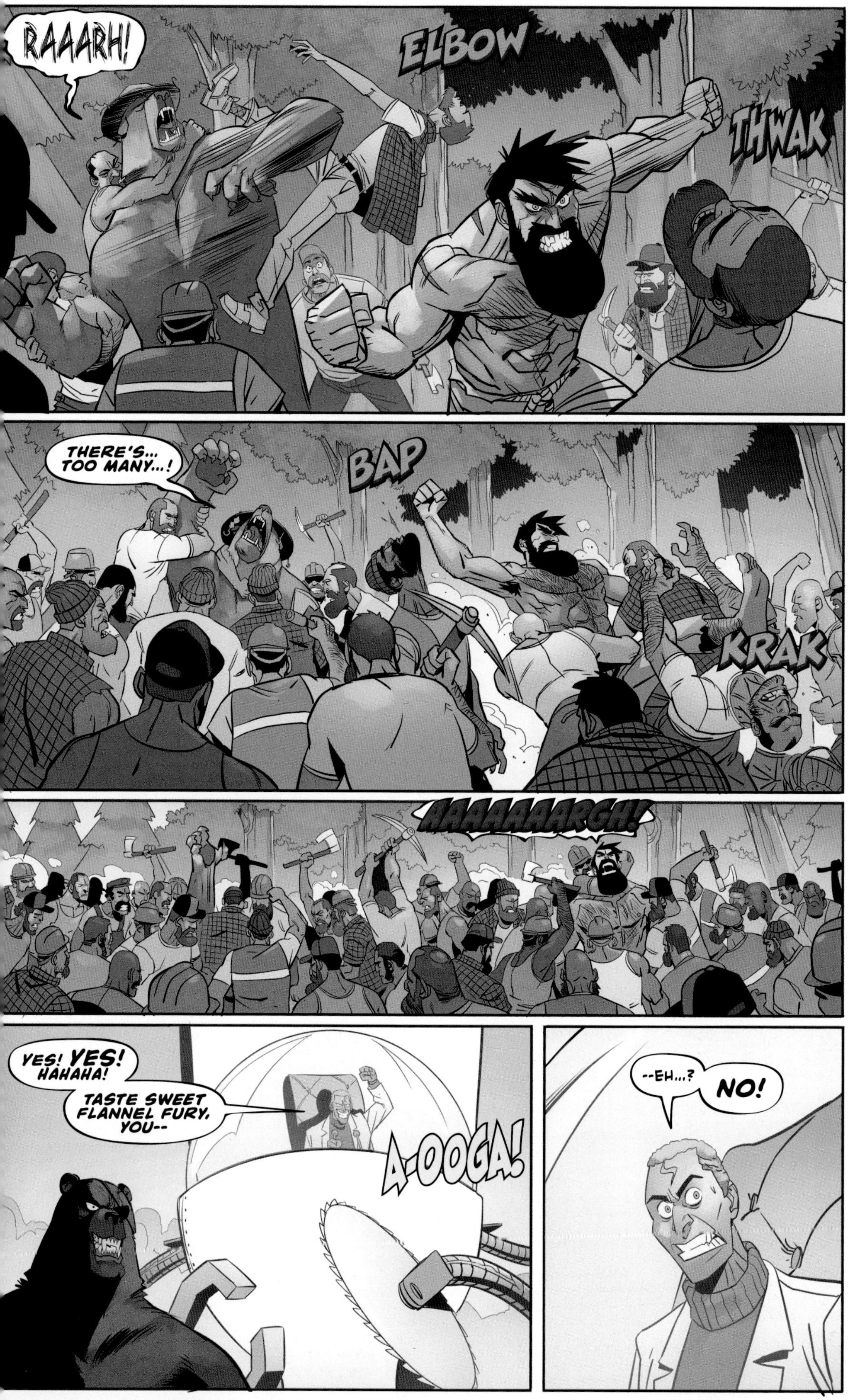
RAAARH!
ELBOW
THWAK
THERE'S... TOO MANY...!
BAP
KRAK
AAAAAAARGH!
YES! YES! HAHAHA!
TASTE SWEET FLANNEL FURY, YOU--
A-OOGA!
--EH...?
NO!

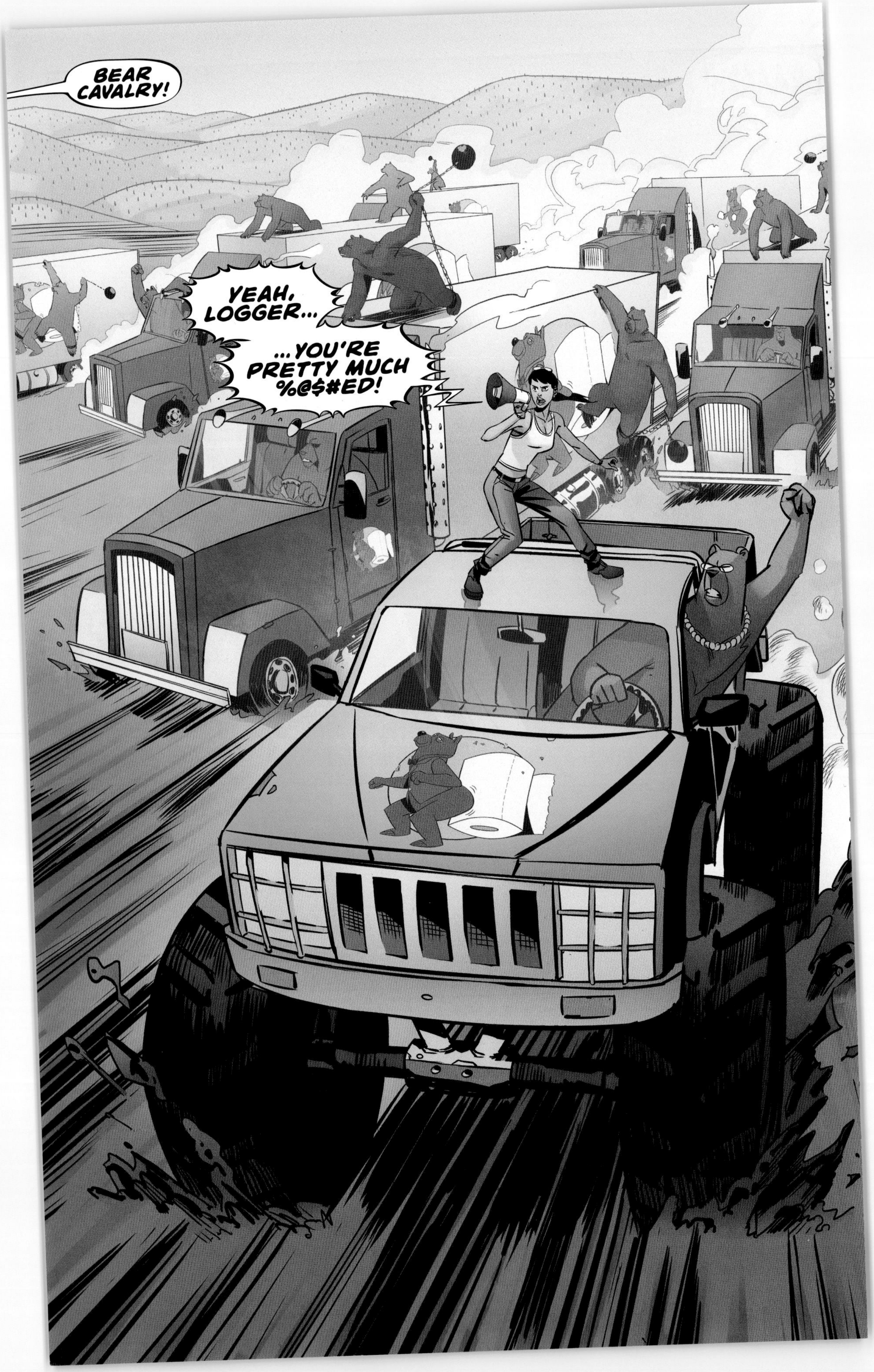
BEAR CAVALRY!
YEAH, LOGGER...
...YOU'RE PRETTY MUCH %@$#ED!

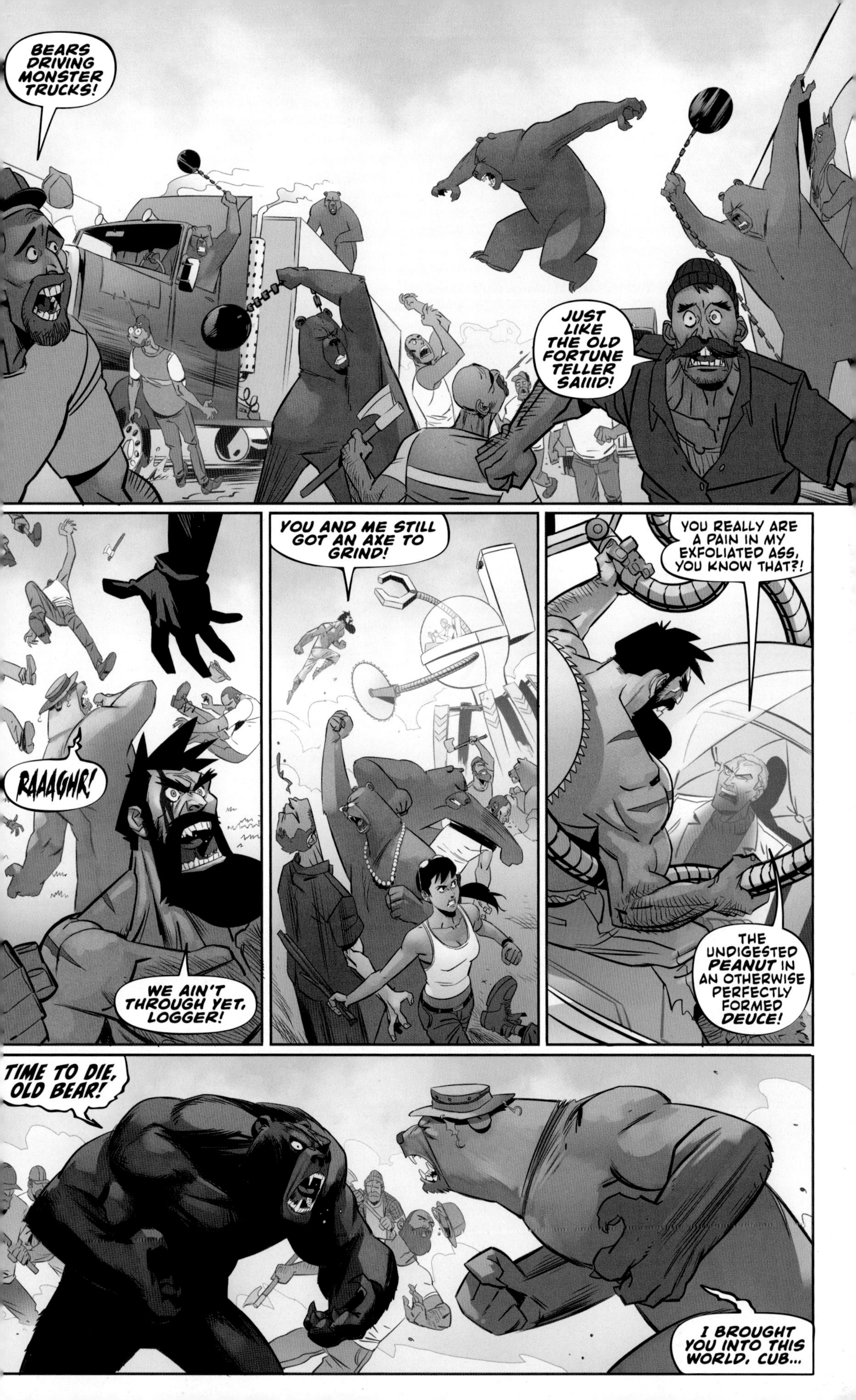
BEARS DRIVING MONSTER TRUCKS!
JUST LIKE THE OLD FORTUNE TELLER SAIIID!
RAAAGHR!
WE AIN'T THROUGH YET, LOGGER!
YOU AND ME STILL GOT AN AXE TO GRIND!
YOU REALLY ARE A PAIN IN MY EXFOLIATED ASS, YOU KNOW THAT?!
THE UNDIGESTED PEANUT IN AN OTHERWISE PERFECTLY FORMED DEUCE!
TIME TO DIE, OLD BEAR!
I BROUGHT YOU INTO THIS WORLD, CUB...

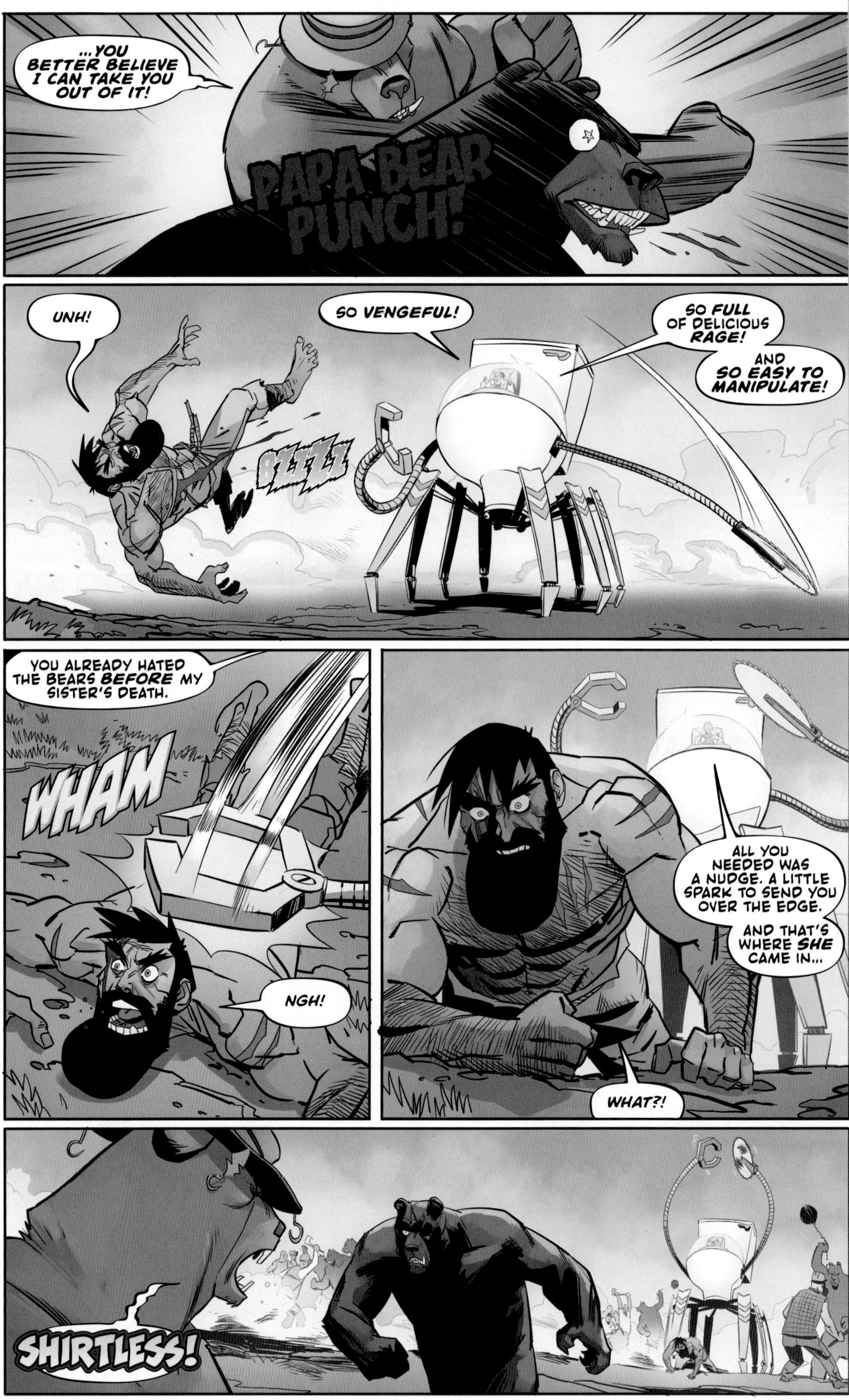
...YOU BETTER BELIEVE I CAN TAKE YOU OUT OF IT!
PAPA BEAR PUNCH!
UNH!
SO VENGEFUL!
SO FULL OF DELICIOUS RAGE!
AND SO EASY TO MANIPULATE!
BZZZZ
YOU ALREADY HATED THE BEARS BEFORE MY SISTER'S DEATH.
WHAM
NGH!
ALL YOU NEEDED WAS A NUDGE. A LITTLE SPARK TO SEND YOU OVER THE EDGE.
AND THAT'S WHERE SHE CAME IN...
WHAT?!
SHIRTLESS!

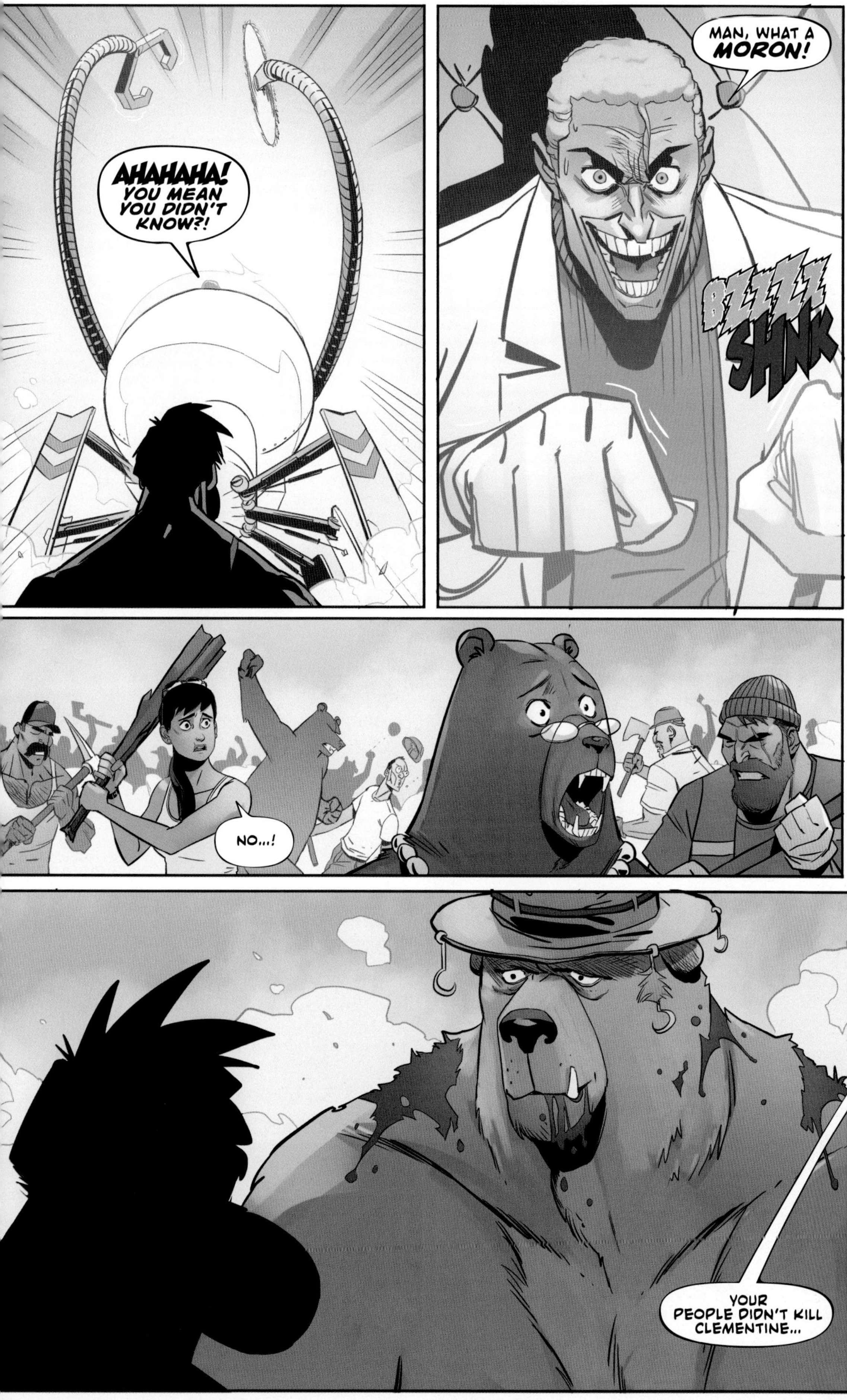
AHAHAHA! YOU MEAN YOU DIDN'T KNOW?!
MAN, WHAT A MORON!
BZZZZ
SHNK
NO...!
YOUR PEOPLE DIDN'T KILL CLEMENTINE...

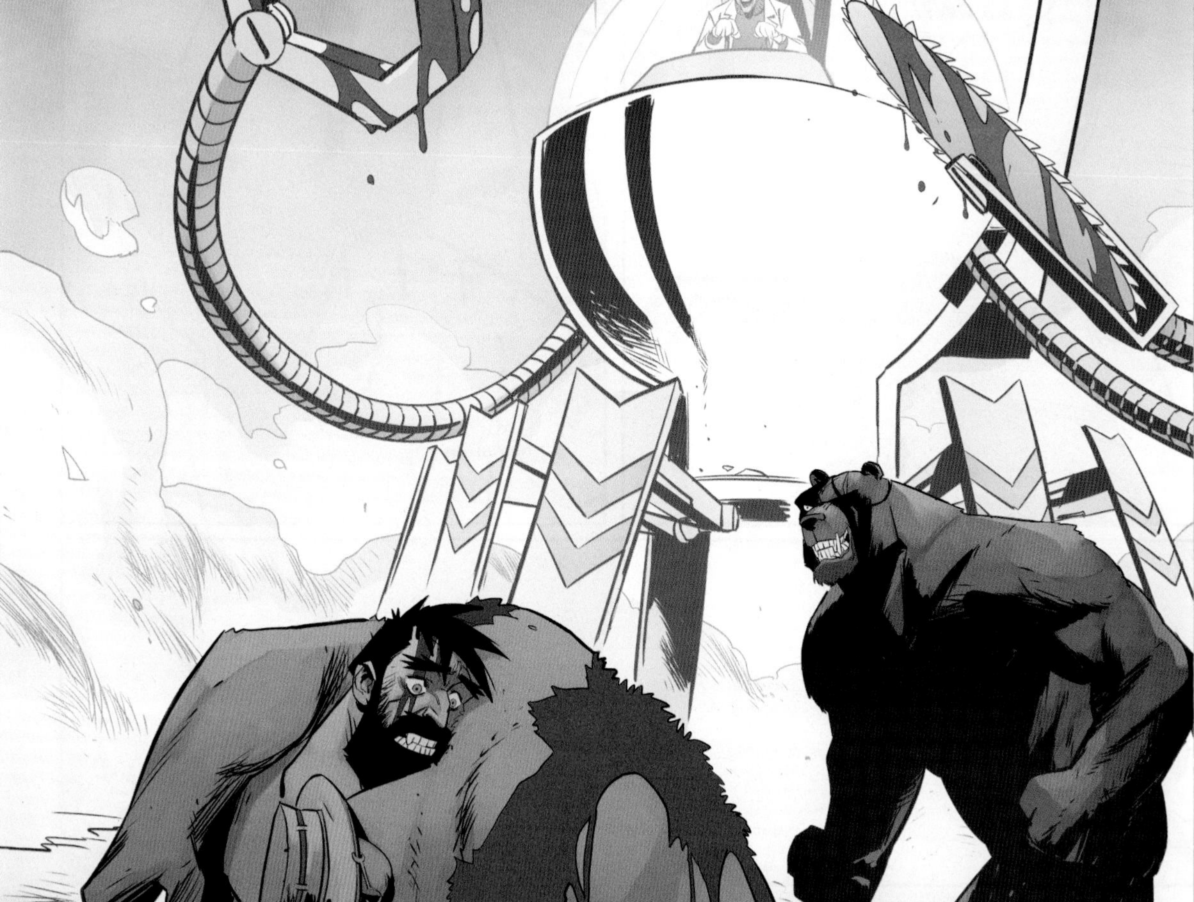

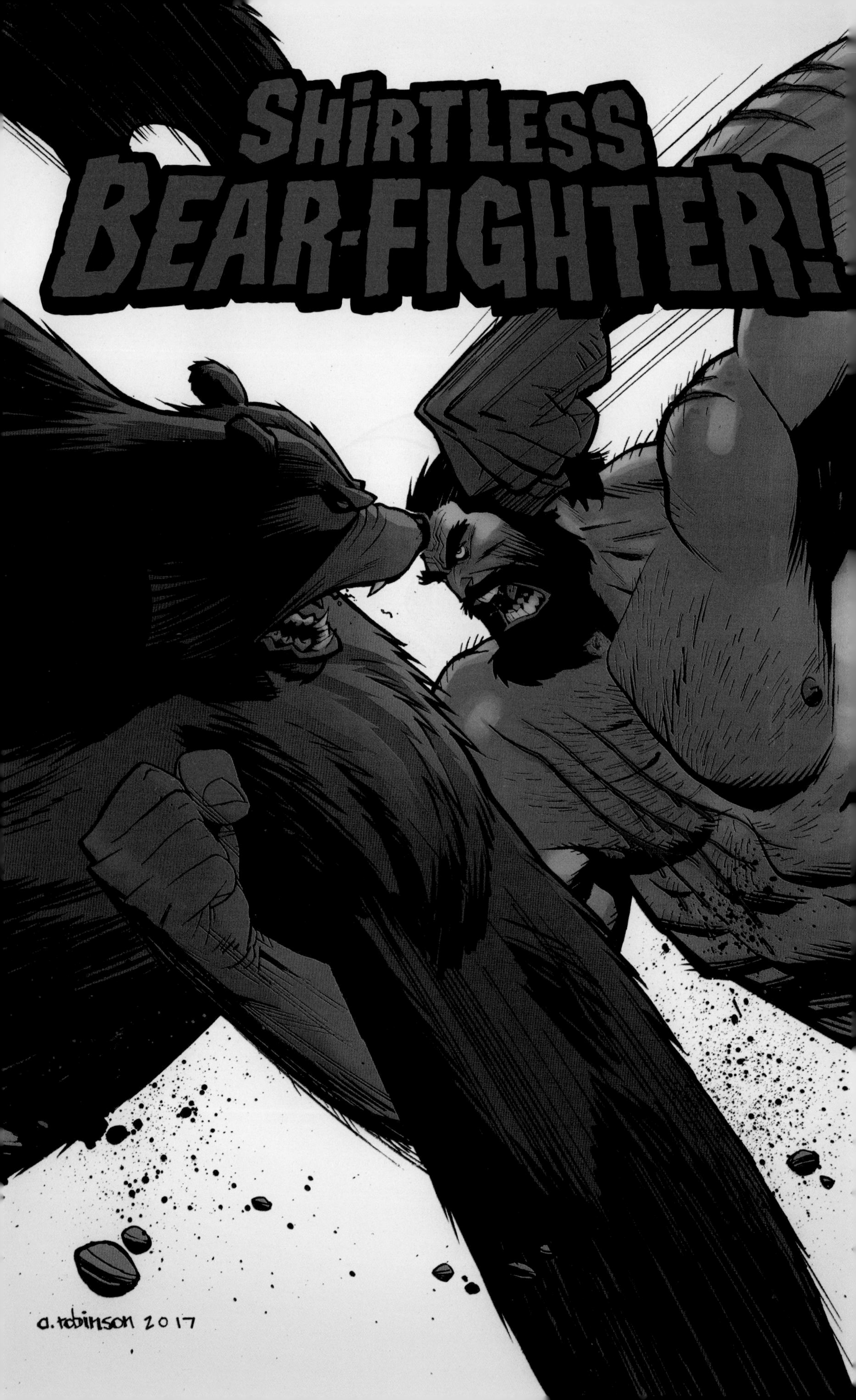
SHIRTLESS
BEAR-FIGHTER!
a. robinson 2017

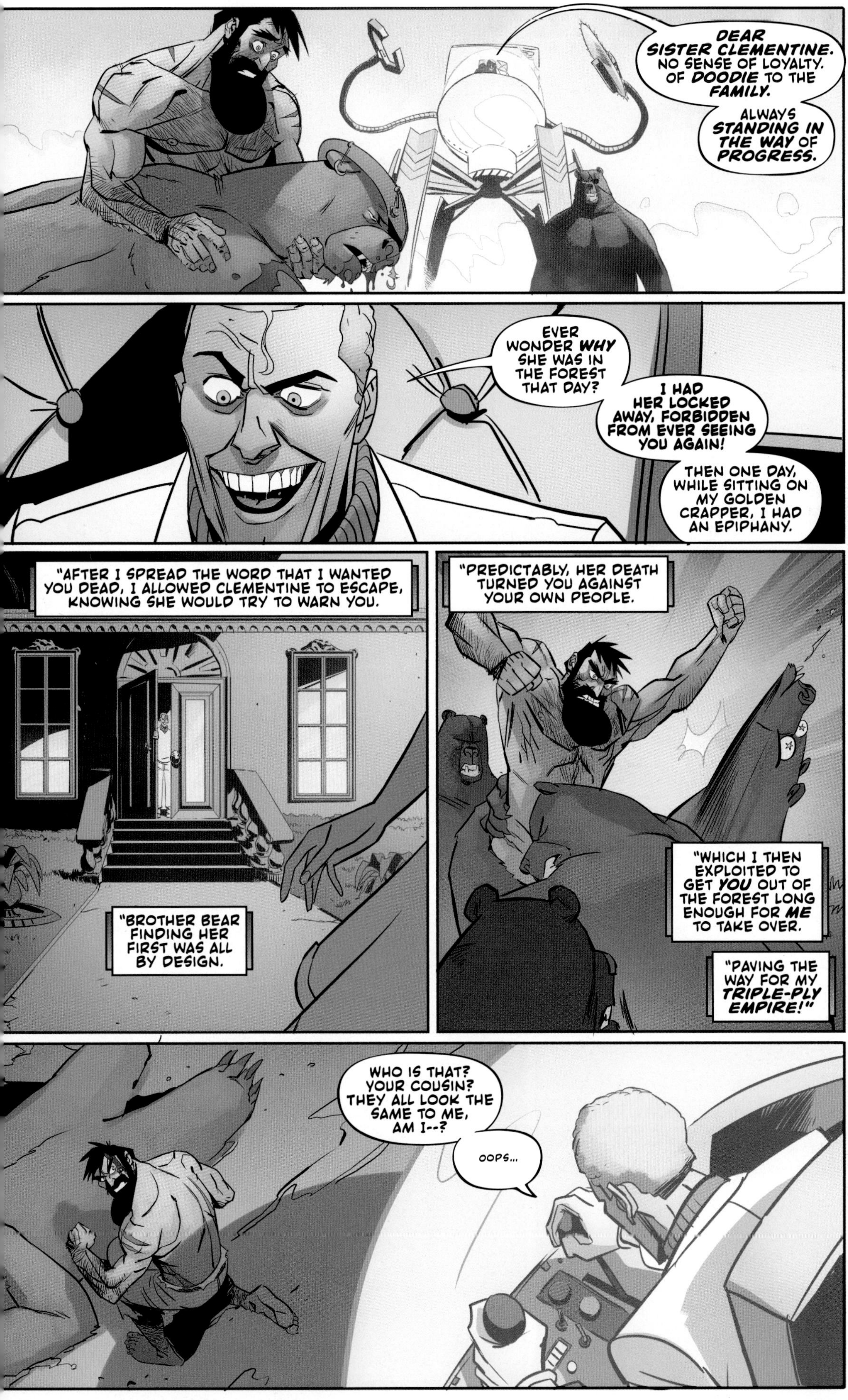
DEAR SISTER CLEMENTINE. NO SENSE OF LOYALTY. OF DOODIE TO THE FAMILY.
ALWAYS STANDING IN THE WAY OF PROGRESS.
EVER WONDER WHY SHE WAS IN THE FOREST THAT DAY?
I HAD HER LOCKED AWAY, FORBIDDEN FROM EVER SEEING YOU AGAIN!
THEN ONE DAY, WHILE SITTING ON MY GOLDEN CRAPPER, I HAD AN EPIPHANY.
"AFTER I SPREAD THE WORD THAT I WANTED YOU DEAD, I ALLOWED CLEMENTINE TO ESCAPE, KNOWING SHE WOULD TRY TO WARN YOU.
"BROTHER BEAR FINDING HER FIRST WAS ALL BY DESIGN.
"PREDICTABLY, HER DEATH TURNED YOU AGAINST YOUR OWN PEOPLE.
"WHICH I THEN EXPLOITED TO GET YOU OUT OF THE FOREST LONG ENOUGH FOR ME TO TAKE OVER.
"PAVING THE WAY FOR MY TRIPLE-PLY EMPIRE!"
WHO IS THAT? YOUR COUSIN? THEY ALL LOOK THE SAME TO ME, AM I--?
OOPS...

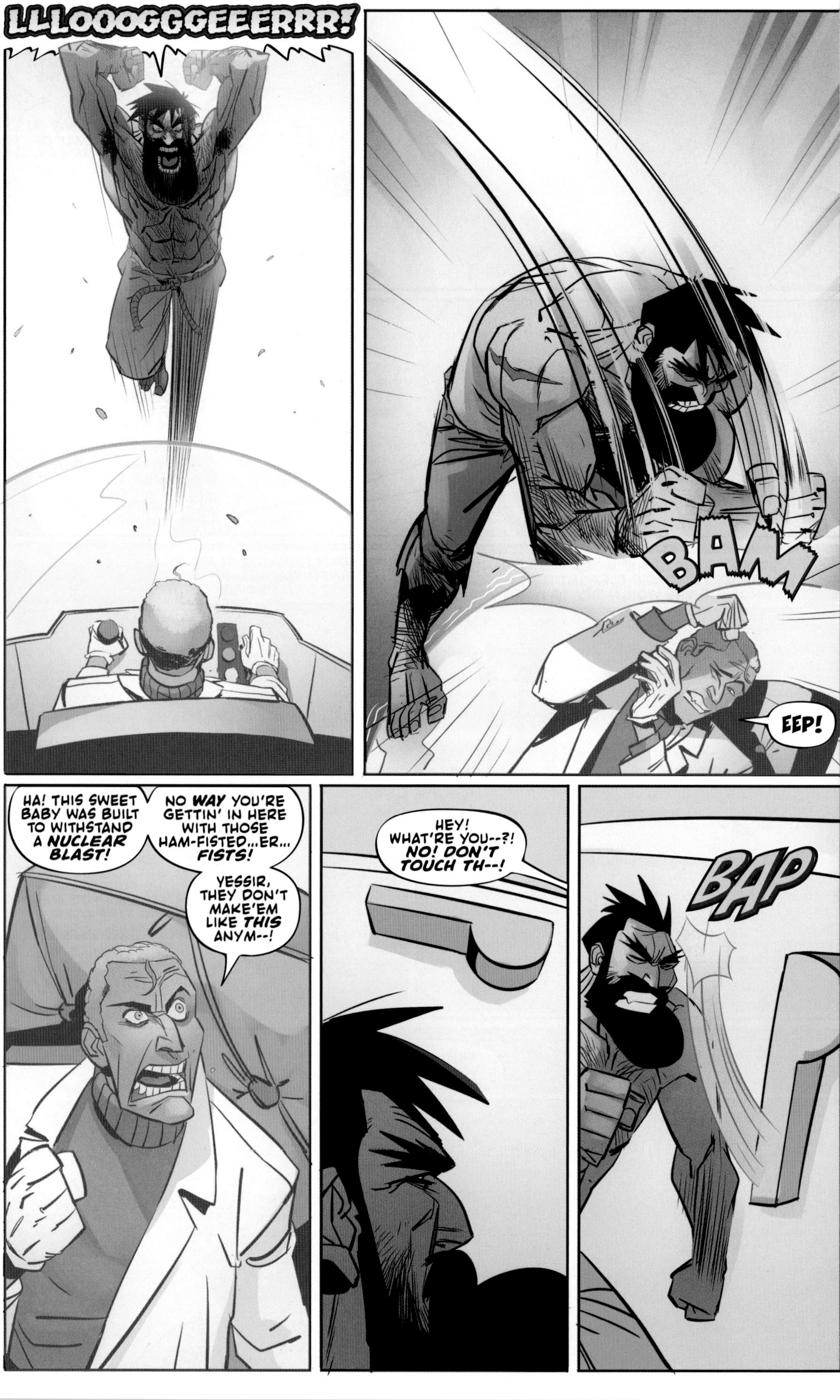
LLLOOOGGGEEERRR!
BAM
EEP!
HA! THIS SWEET BABY WAS BUILT TO WITHSTAND A NUCLEAR BLAST!
NO WAY YOU'RE GETTIN' IN HERE WITH THOSE HAM-FISTED...ER... FISTS!
YESSIR, THEY DON'T MAKE'EM LIKE THIS ANYM--!
HEY! WHAT'RE YOU--?! NO! DON'T TOUCH TH--!
BAP

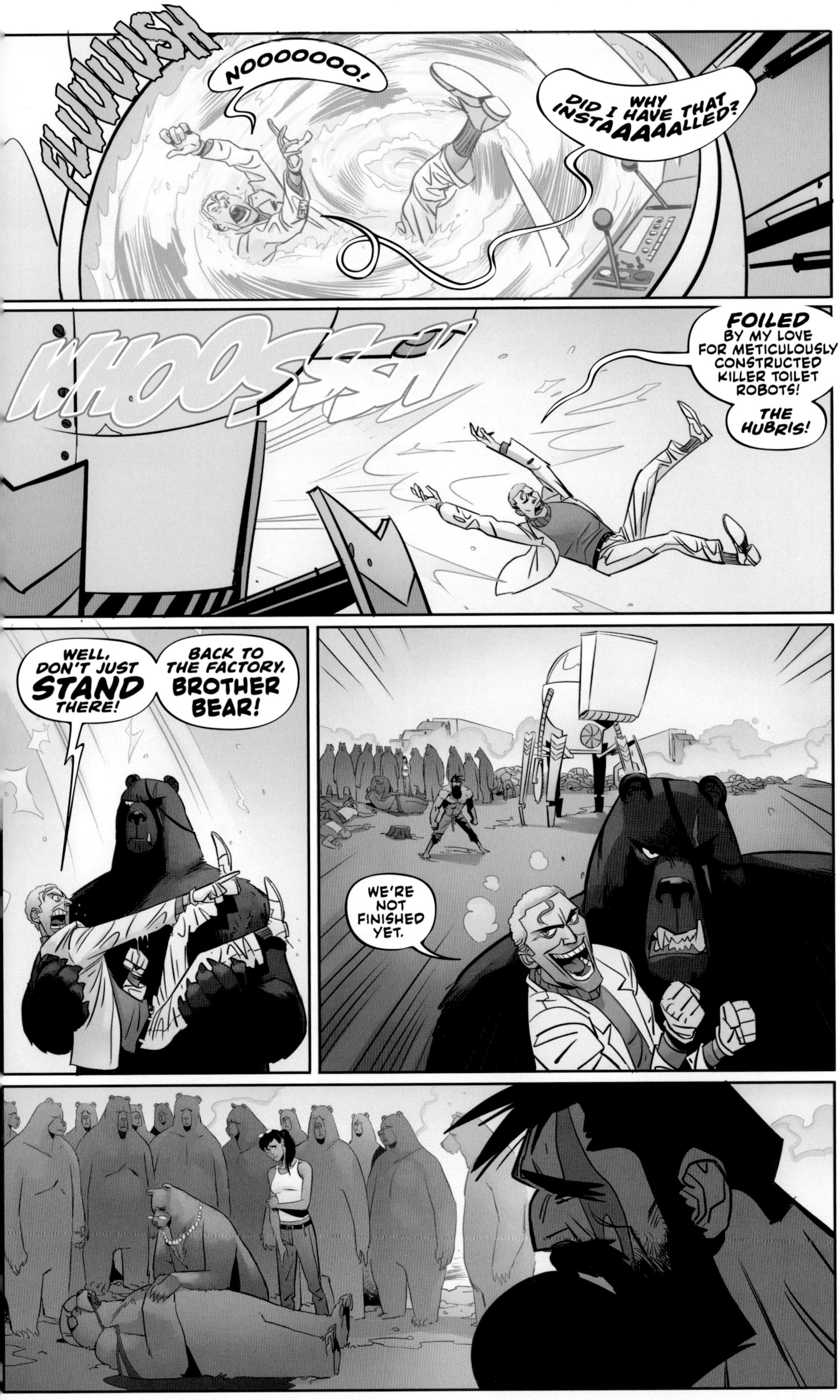
FLUUUSH
NOOOOOOO!
DID I WHY HAVE THAT INSTAAAAALLED?
WHOOSSH
FOILED BY MY LOVE FOR METICULOUSLY CONSTRUCTED KILLER TOILET ROBOTS!
THE HUBRIS!
WELL, DON'T JUST STAND THERE!
BACK TO THE FACTORY, BROTHER BEAR!
WE'RE NOT FINISHED YET.

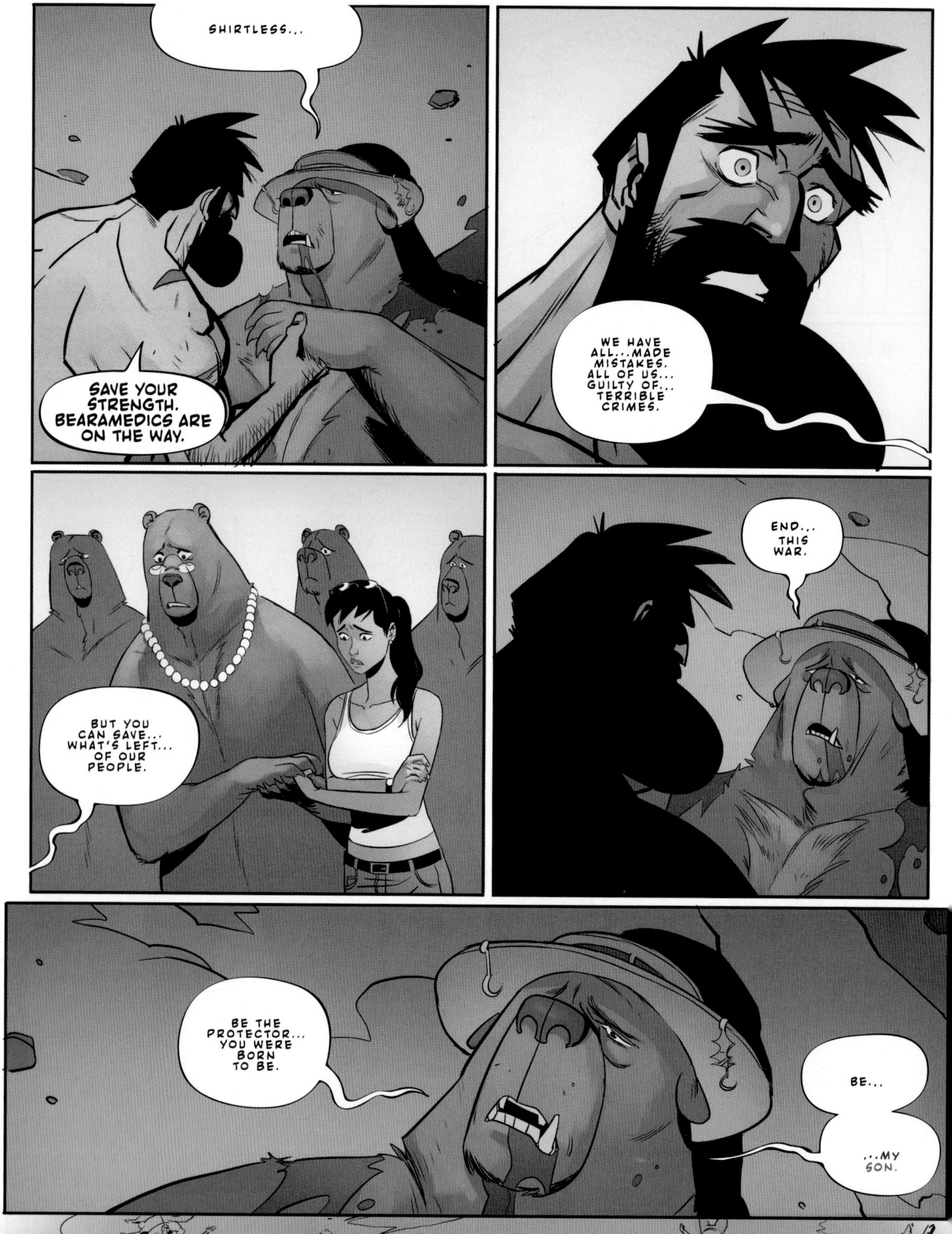

SHIRTLESS...
SAVE YOUR STRENGTH. BEARAMEDICS ARE ON THE WAY.
WE HAVE ALL...MADE MISTAKES. ALL OF US... GUILTY OF... TERRIBLE CRIMES.
BUT YOU CAN SAVE... WHAT'S LEFT... OF OUR PEOPLE.
END... THIS WAR.
BE THE PROTECTOR... YOU WERE BORN TO BE.
BE...
...MY SON.

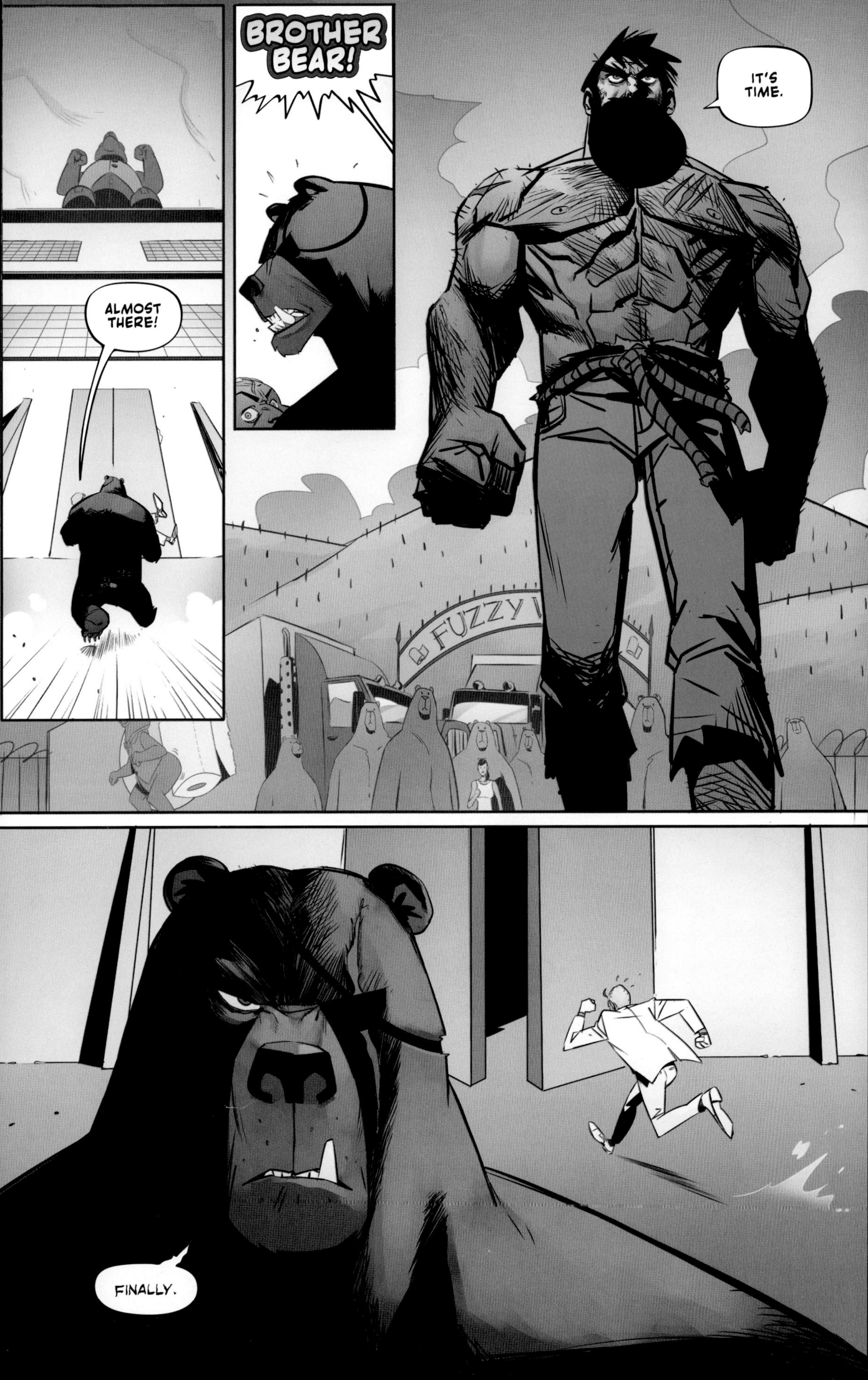
ALMOST THERE!
BROTHER BEAR!
IT'S TIME.
FUZZY
FINALLY.

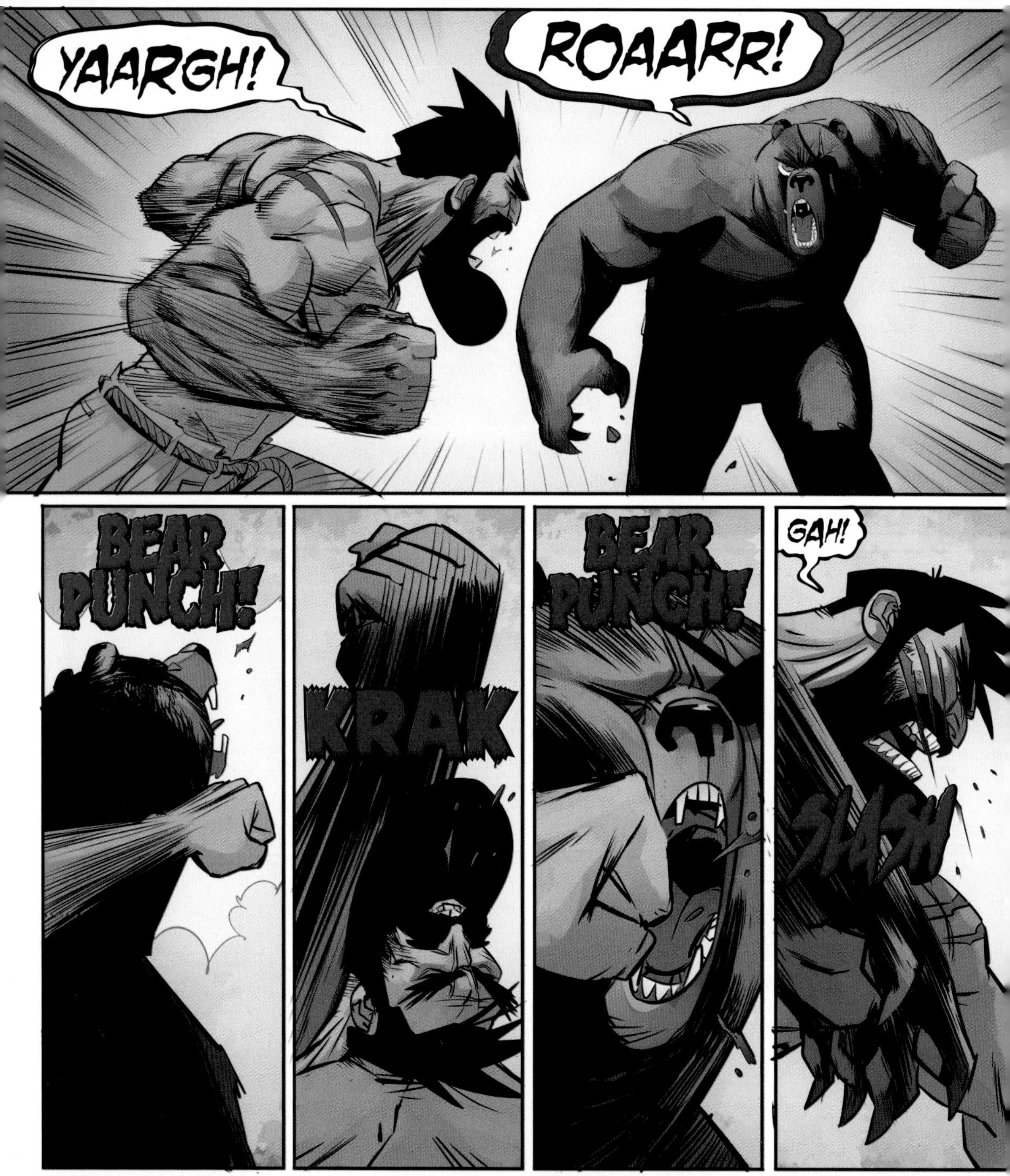
YAARGH!
ROAARR!
BEAR PUNCH!
KRAK
BEAR PUNCH!
GAH!
SLASH

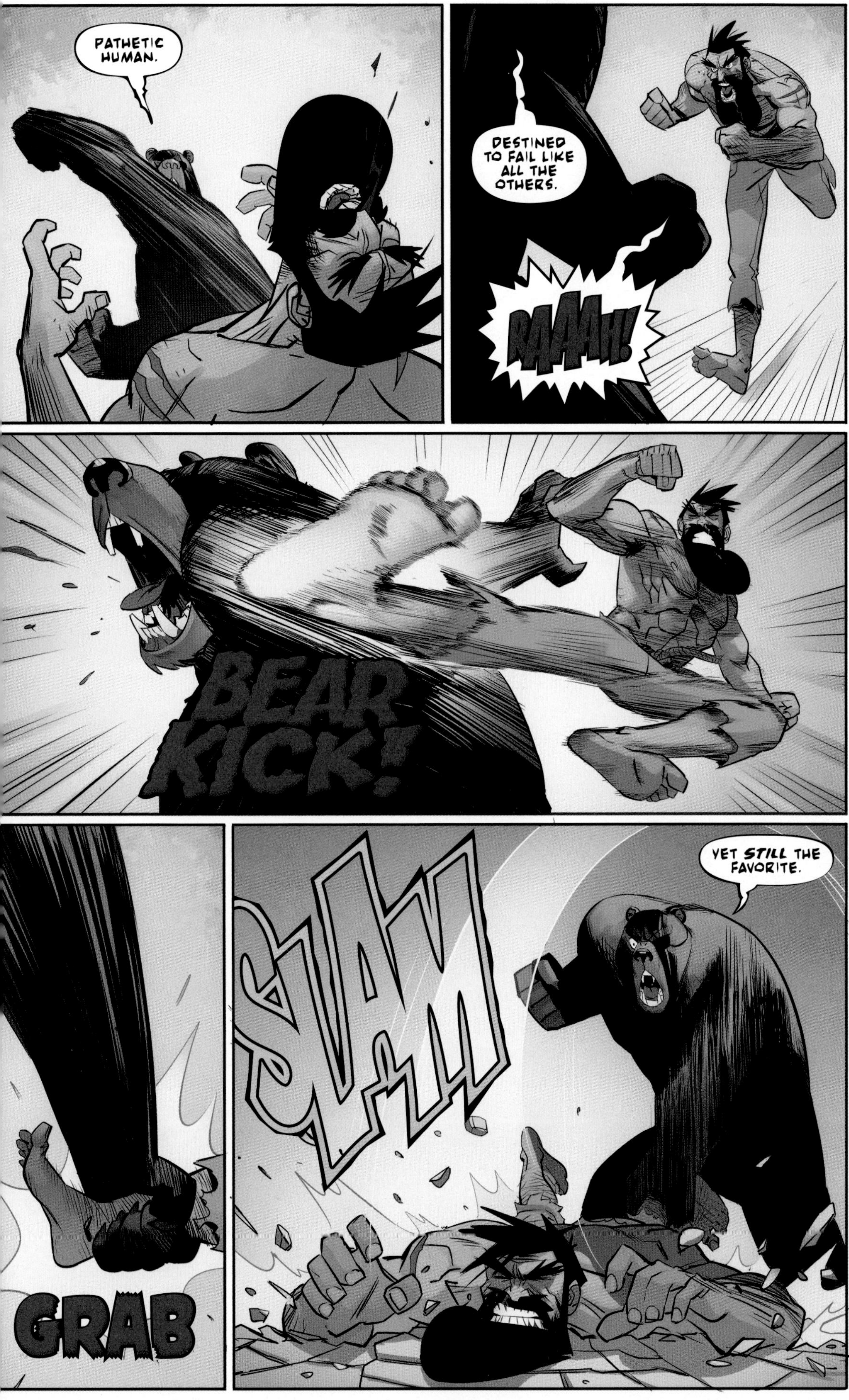
PATHETIC HUMAN.
DESTINED TO FAIL LIKE ALL THE OTHERS.
RAAAAH!
BEAR KICK!
GRAB
SLAM
YET STILL THE FAVORITE.

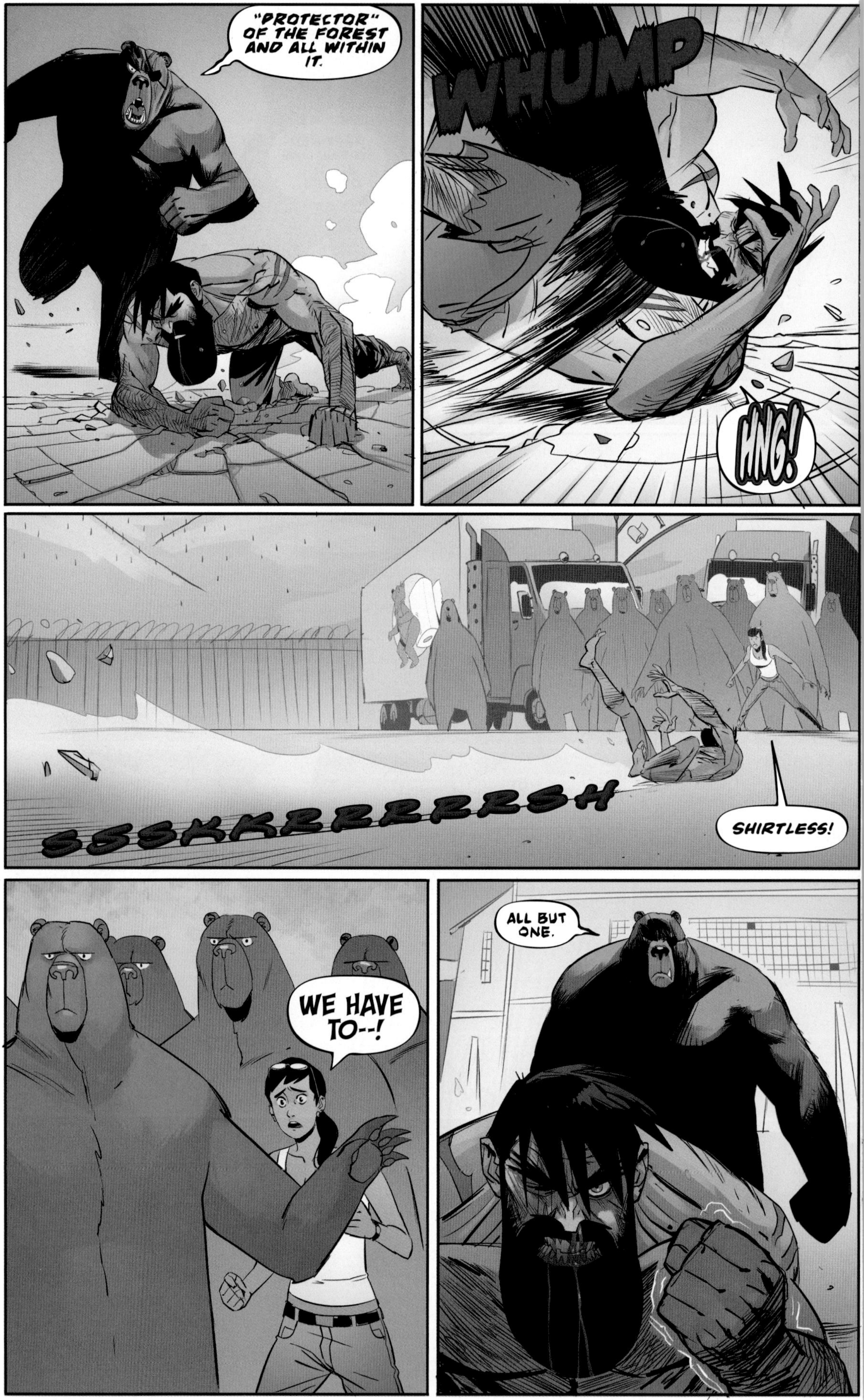
"PROTECTOR" OF THE FOREST AND ALL WITHIN IT.
WHUMP
HNG!
SSSKRRRRRRRSH
SHIRTLESS!
WE HAVE TO--!
ALL BUT ONE.

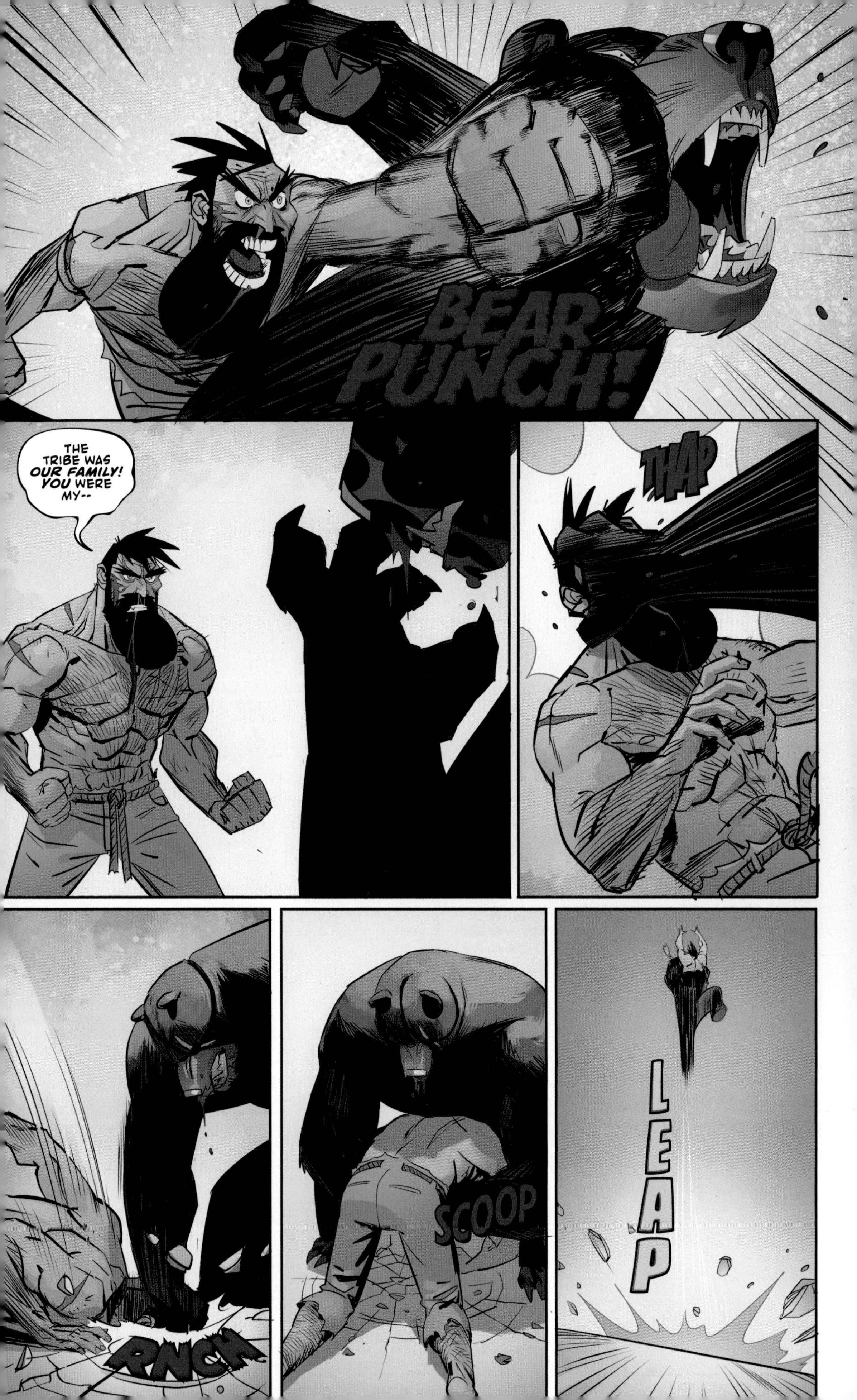

BEAR PUNCH!
THE TRIBE WAS OUR FAMILY! YOU WERE MY--
THAP
RNCH
SCOOP
LEAP

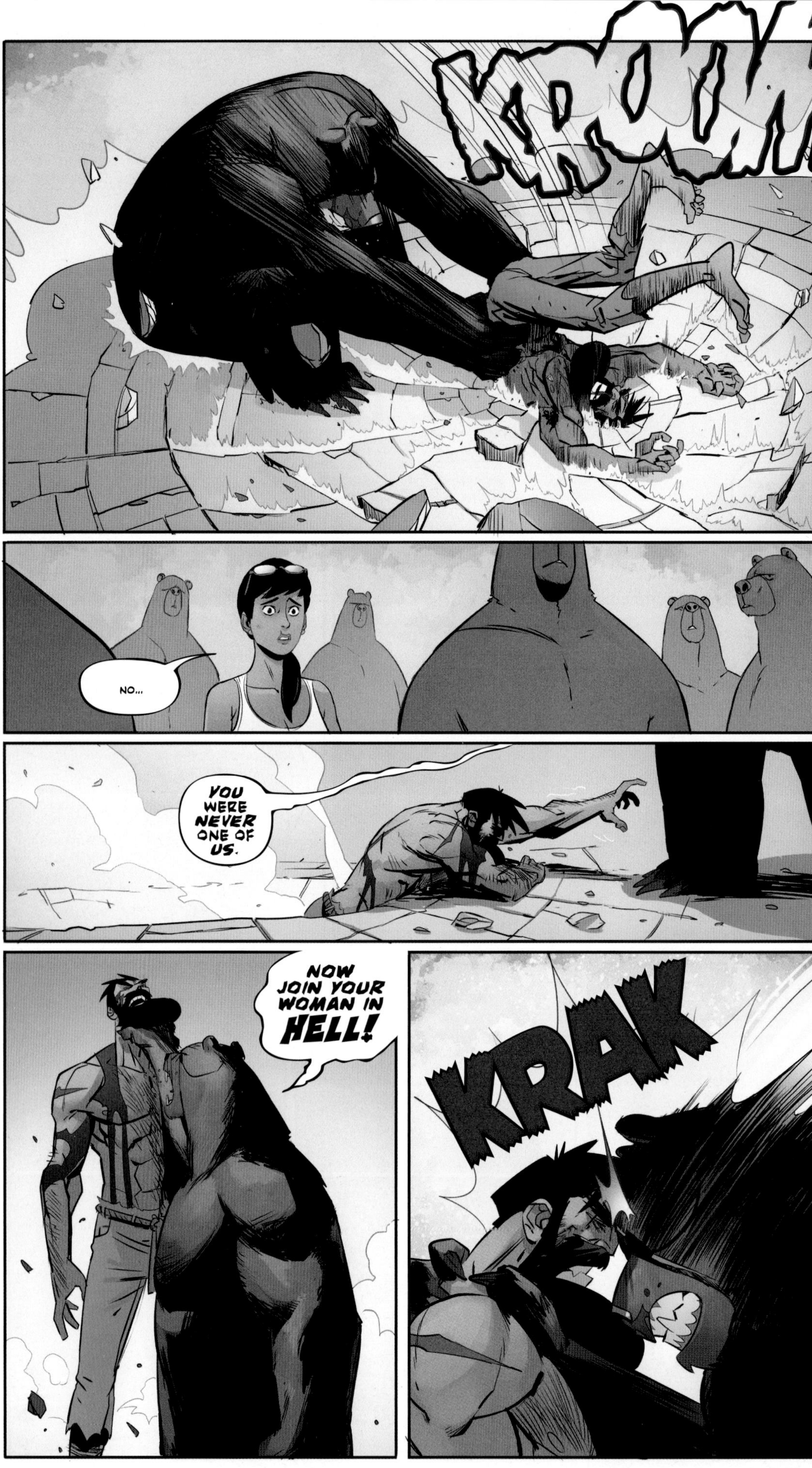
KROOM
NO...
YOU WERE NEVER ONE OF US.
NOW JOIN YOUR WOMAN IN HELL!
KRAK

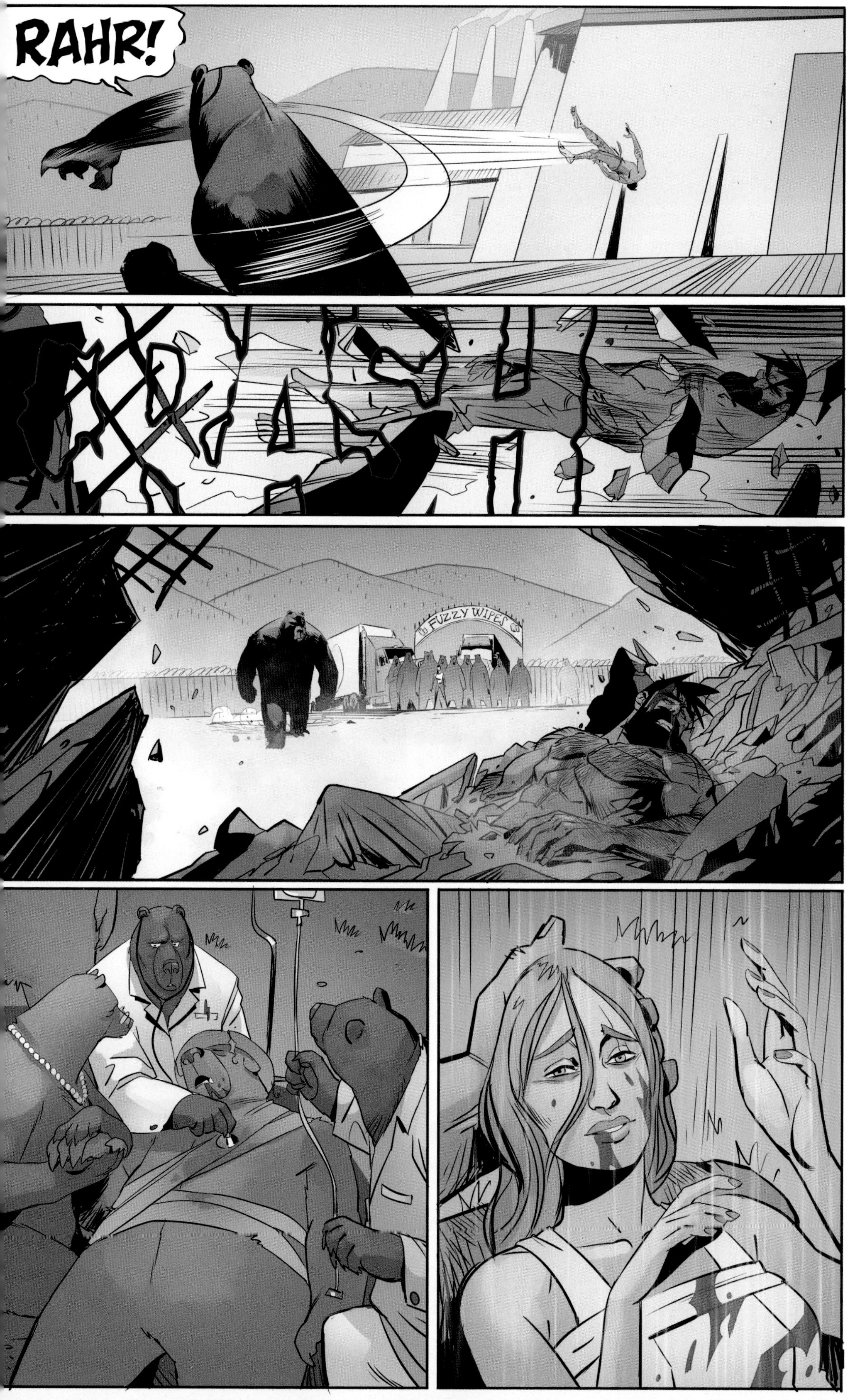
RAHR!
FUZZY WIPES

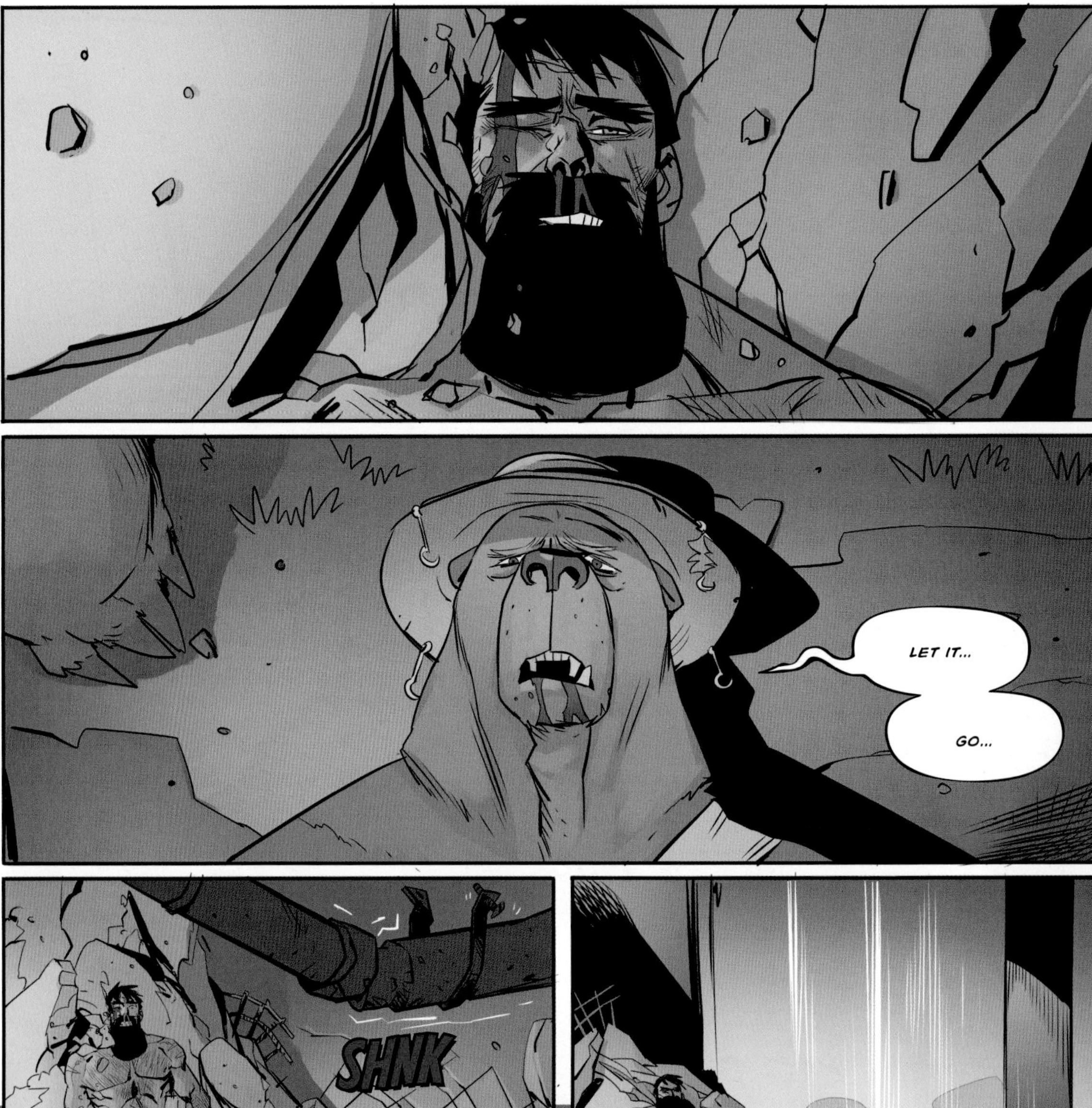
LET IT...
GO...
SHNK

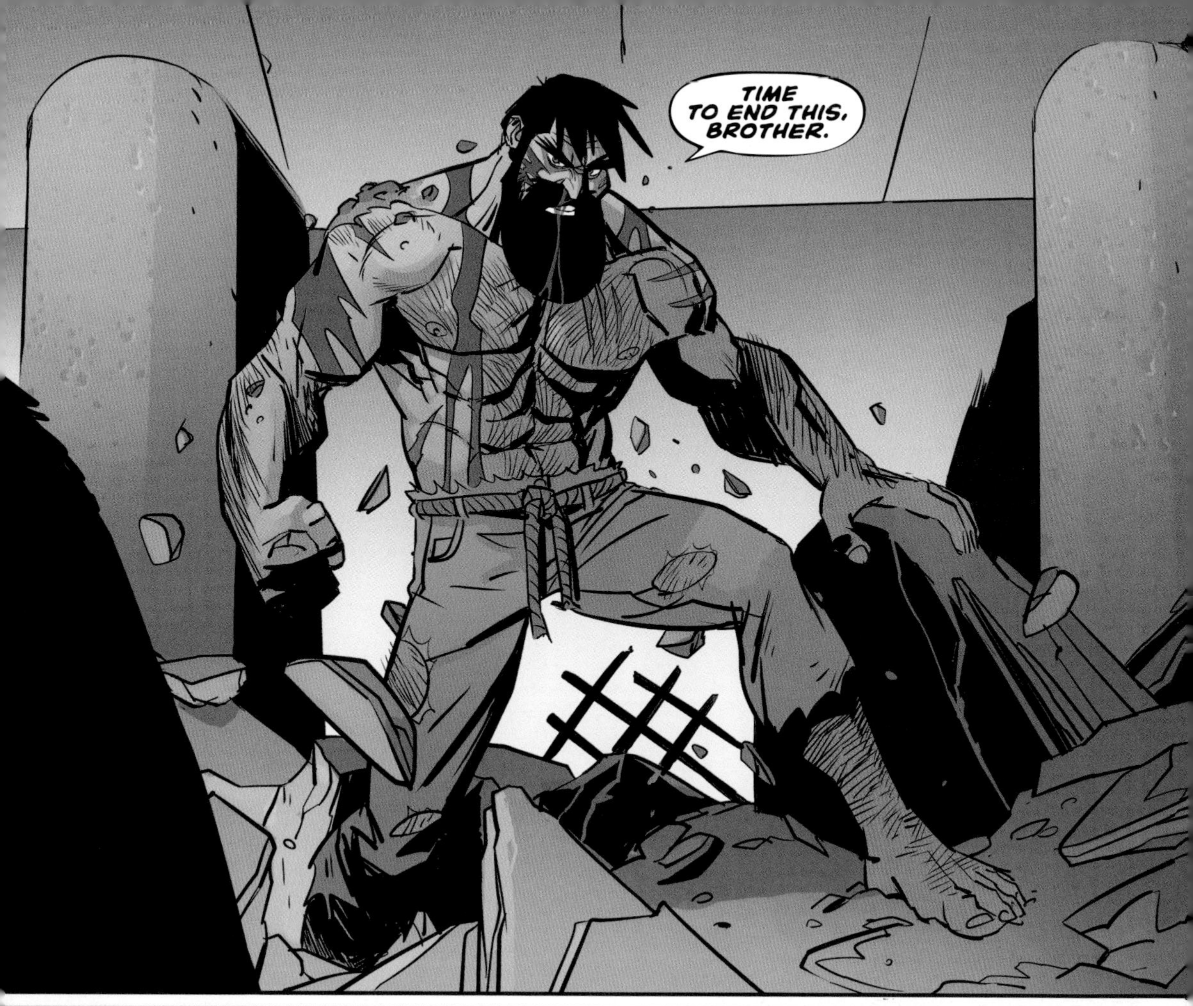
TIME TO END THIS, BROTHER.

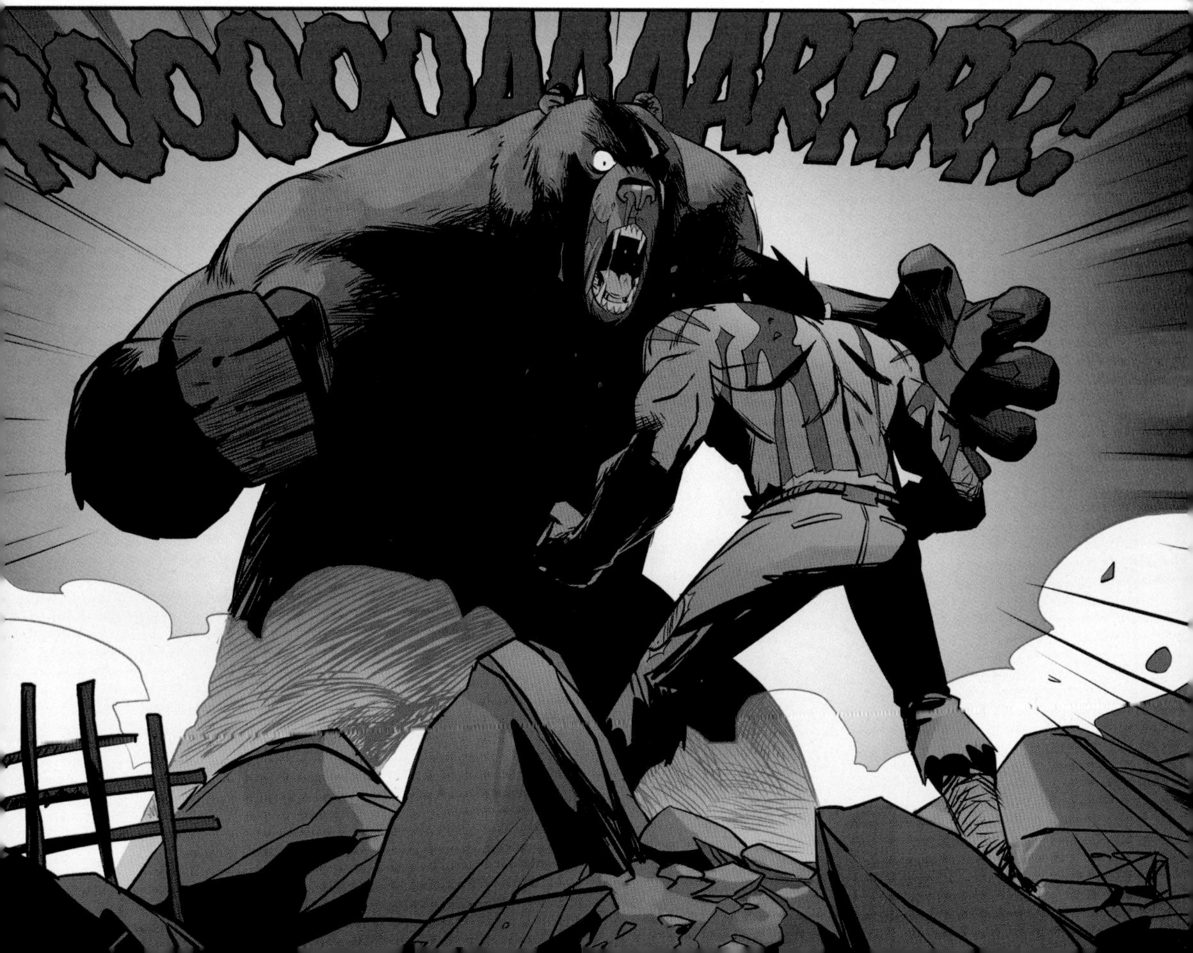
ROOOOOAAARRRRR!

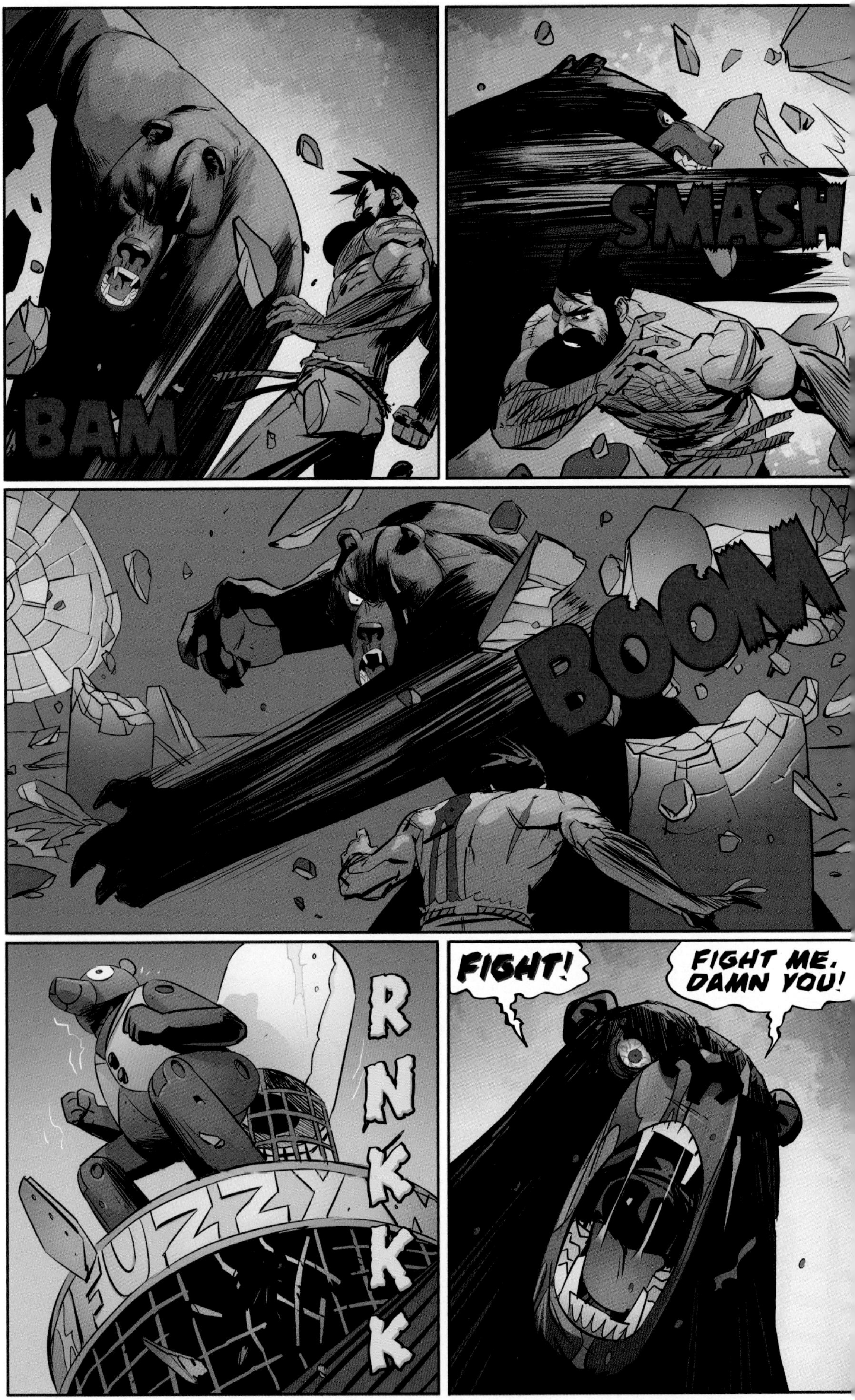
BAM
SMASH
BOOM
RNKKK
FUZZY
FIGHT!
FIGHT ME. DAMN YOU!

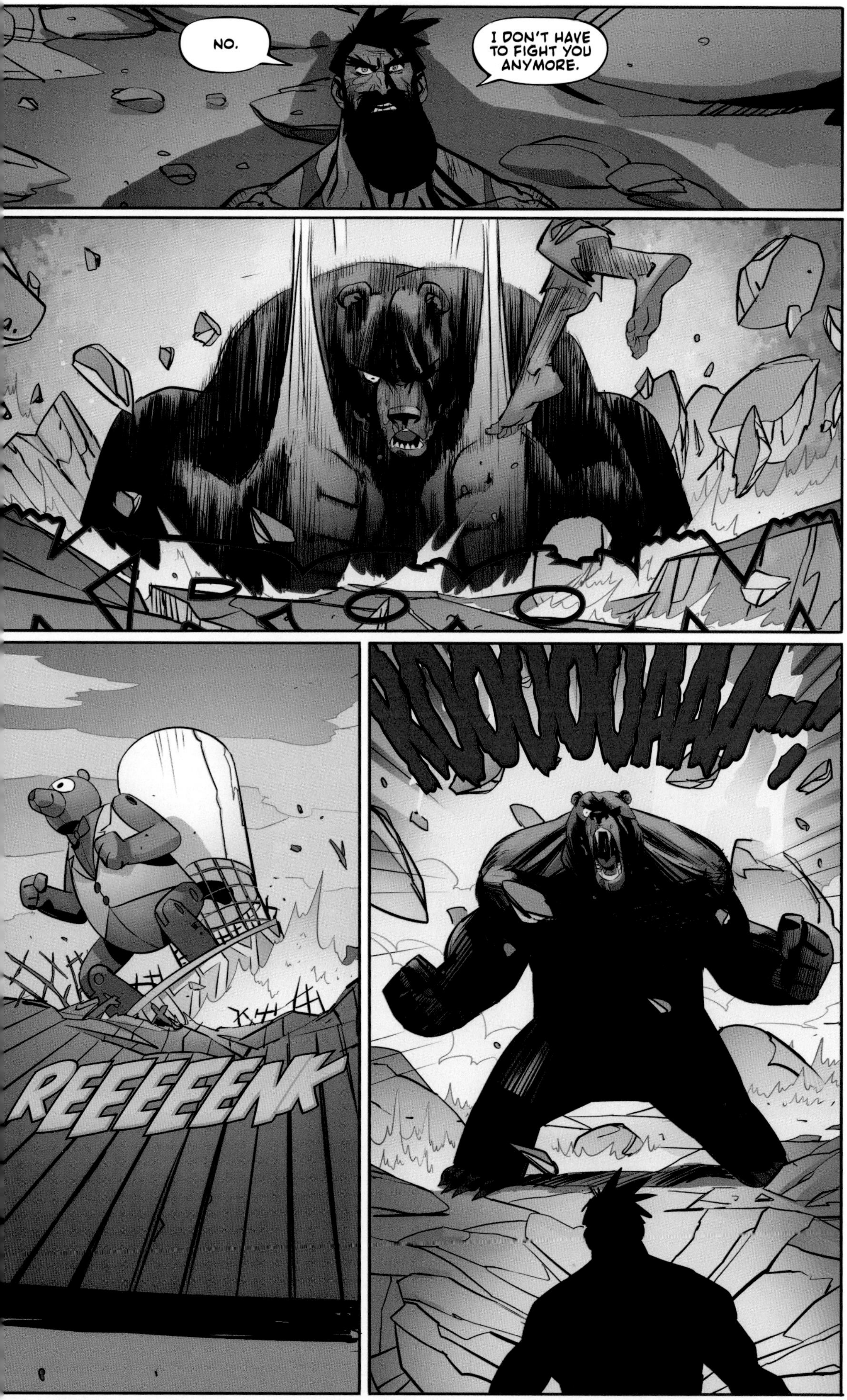
NO.
I DON'T HAVE TO FIGHT YOU ANYMORE.
REEEEEENK
ROOOOOAAAA...

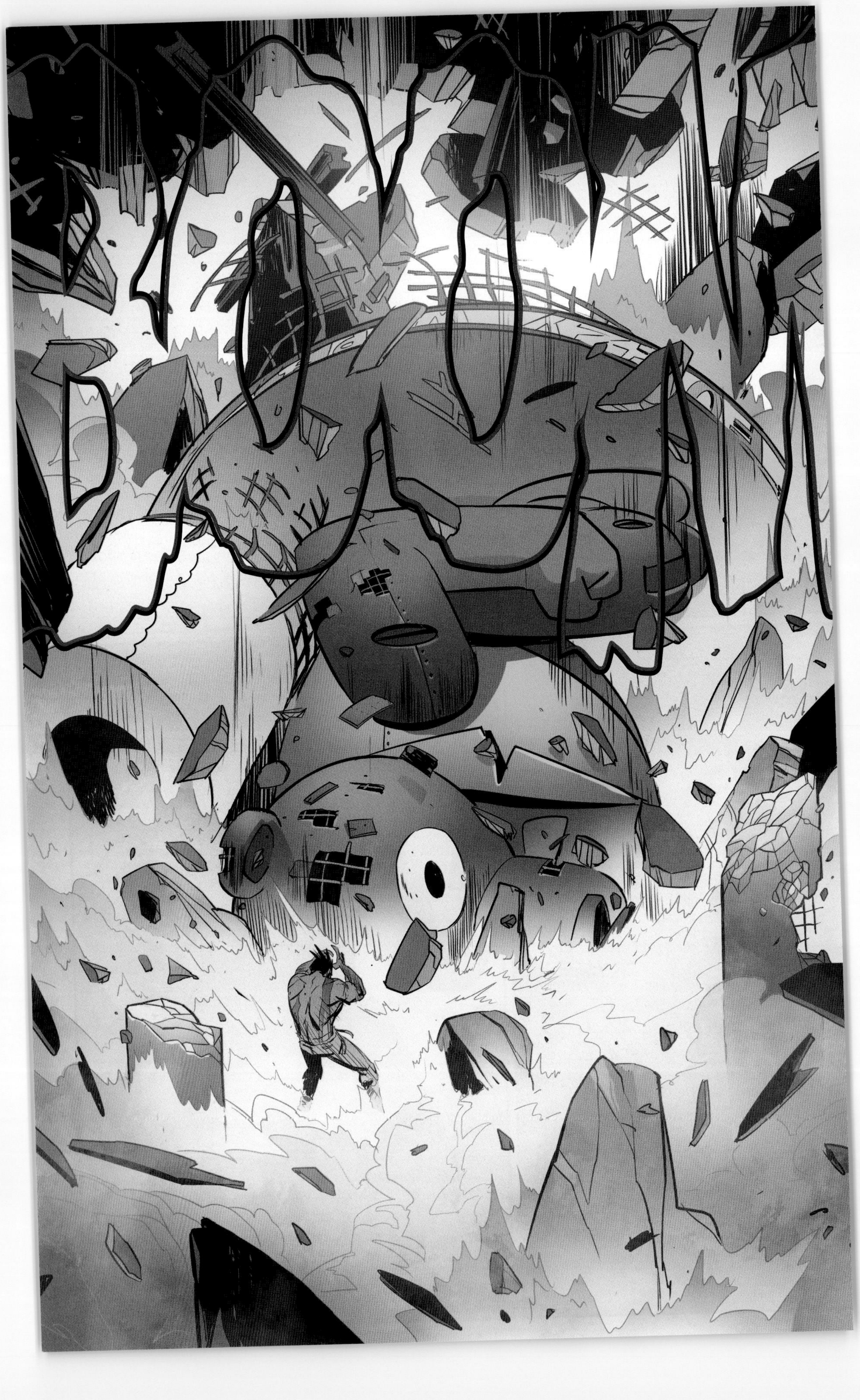

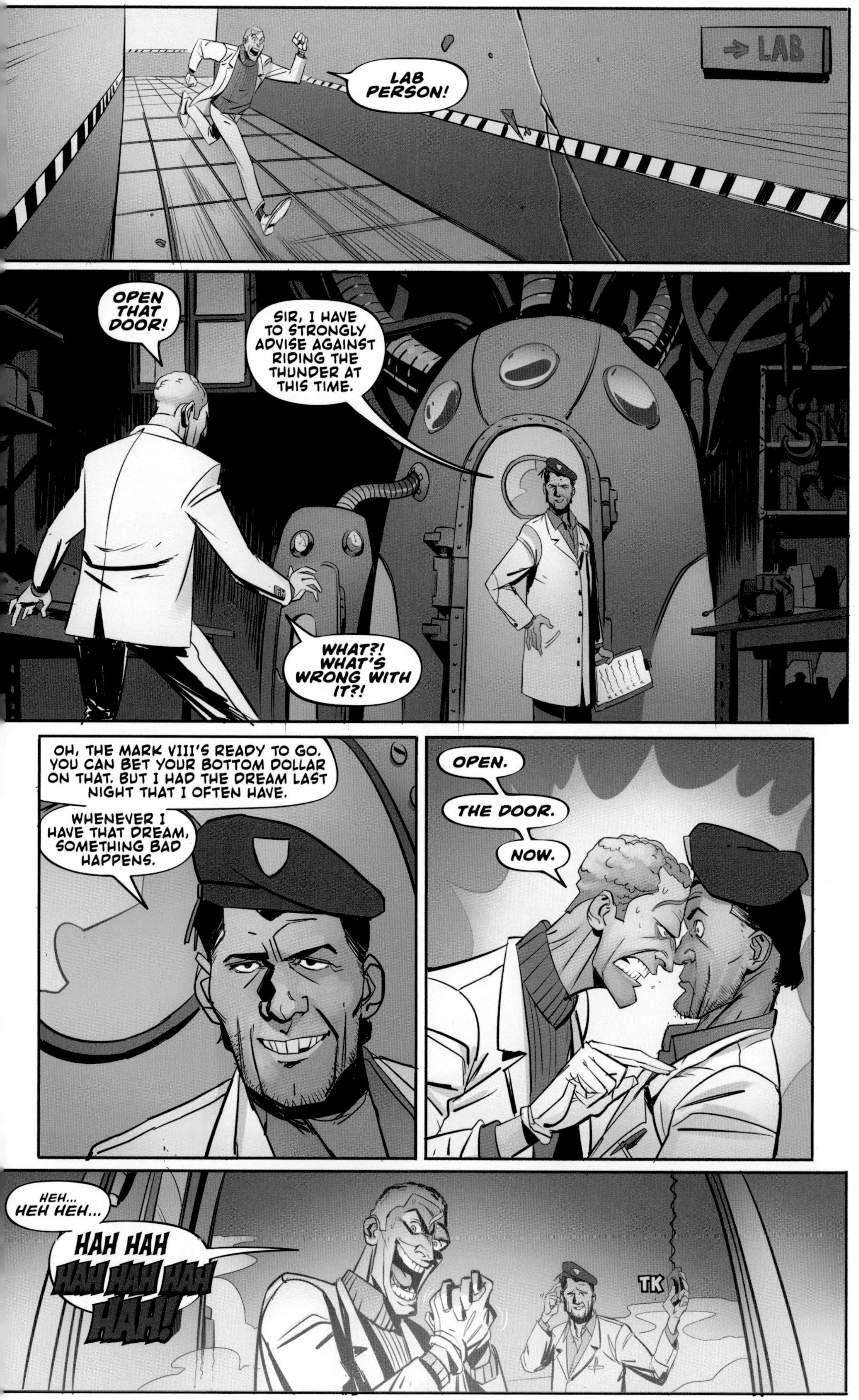
→ LAB
LAB PERSON!
OPEN THAT DOOR!
SIR, I HAVE TO STRONGLY ADVISE AGAINST RIDING THE THUNDER AT THIS TIME.
WHAT?! WHAT'S WRONG WITH IT?!
OH, THE MARK VIII'S READY TO GO. YOU CAN BET YOUR BOTTOM DOLLAR ON THAT. BUT I HAD THE DREAM LAST NIGHT THAT I OFTEN HAVE.
WHENEVER I HAVE THAT DREAM, SOMETHING BAD HAPPENS.
OPEN.
THE DOOR.
NOW.
HEH... HEH HEH...
HAH HAH HAH HAH HAH HAH!
TK

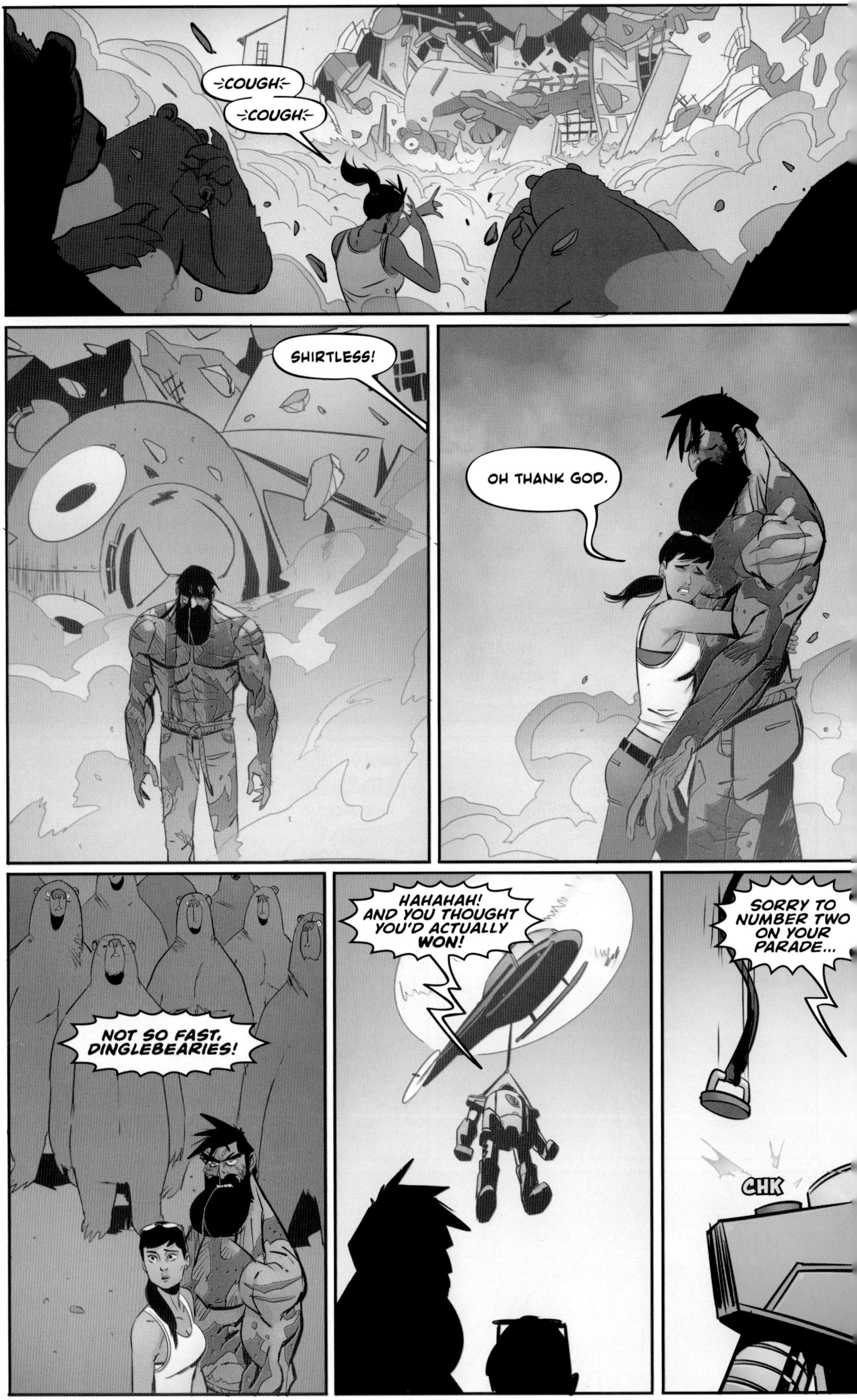
COUGH
COUGH
SHIRTLESS!
OH THANK GOD.
NOT SO FAST, DINGLEBEARIES!
HAHAHAH! AND YOU THOUGHT YOU'D ACTUALLY WON!
SORRY TO NUMBER TWO ON YOUR PARADE...
CHK

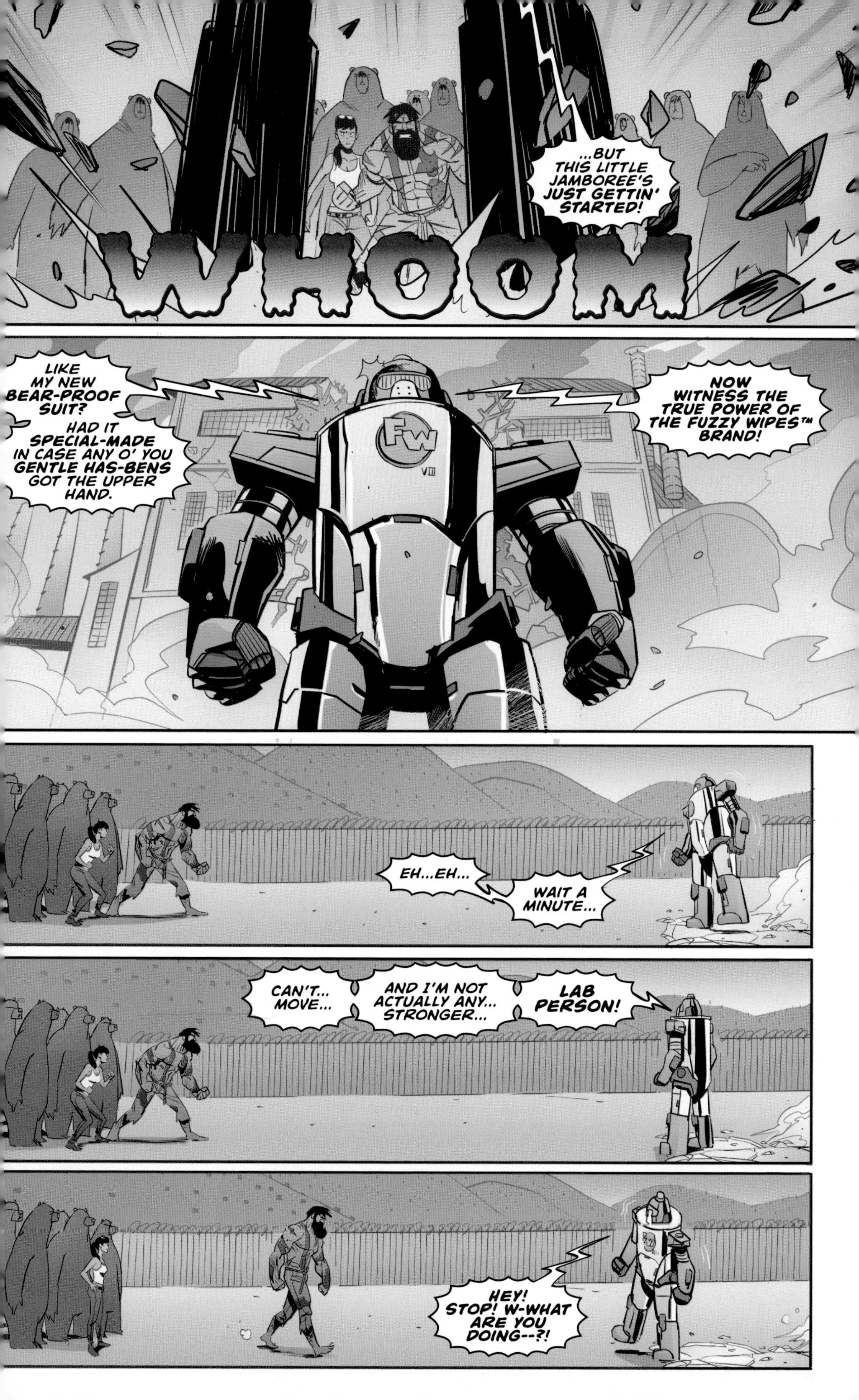
...BUT THIS LITTLE JAMBOREE'S JUST GETTIN' STARTED!
WHOOM
LIKE MY NEW BEAR-PROOF SUIT?
HAD IT SPECIAL-MADE IN CASE ANY O' YOU GENTLE HAS-BENS GOT THE UPPER HAND.
NOW WITNESS THE TRUE POWER OF THE FUZZY WIPES™ BRAND!
FW
EH...EH...
WAIT A MINUTE...
CAN'T... MOVE...
AND I'M NOT ACTUALLY ANY... STRONGER...
LAB PERSON!
HEY! STOP! W-WHAT ARE YOU DOING--?!

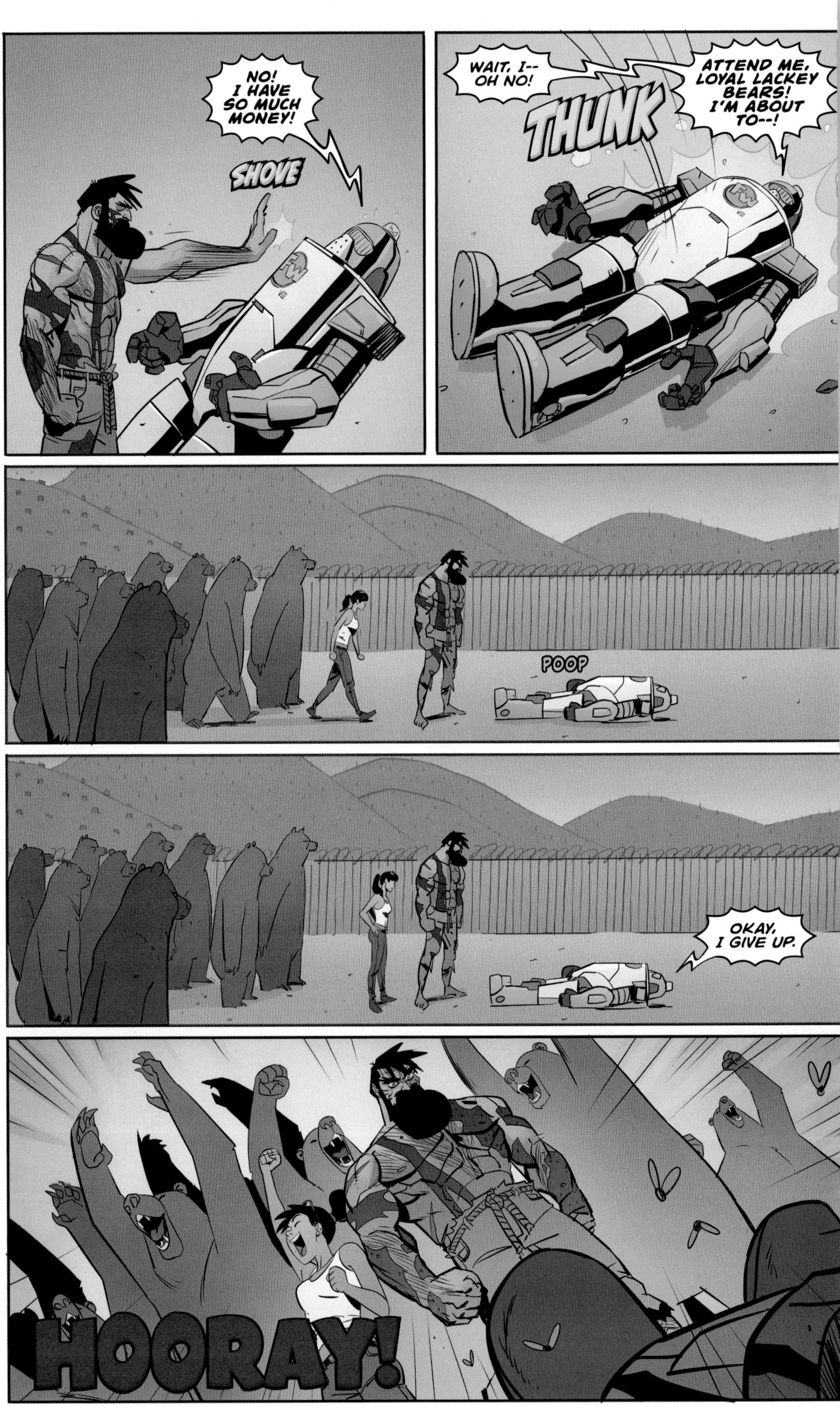
NO! I HAVE SO MUCH MONEY!
SHOVE
WAIT, I-- OH NO!
ATTEND ME, LOYAL LACKEY BEARS! I'M ABOUT TO--!
THUNK
POOP
OKAY, I GIVE UP.
HOORAY!

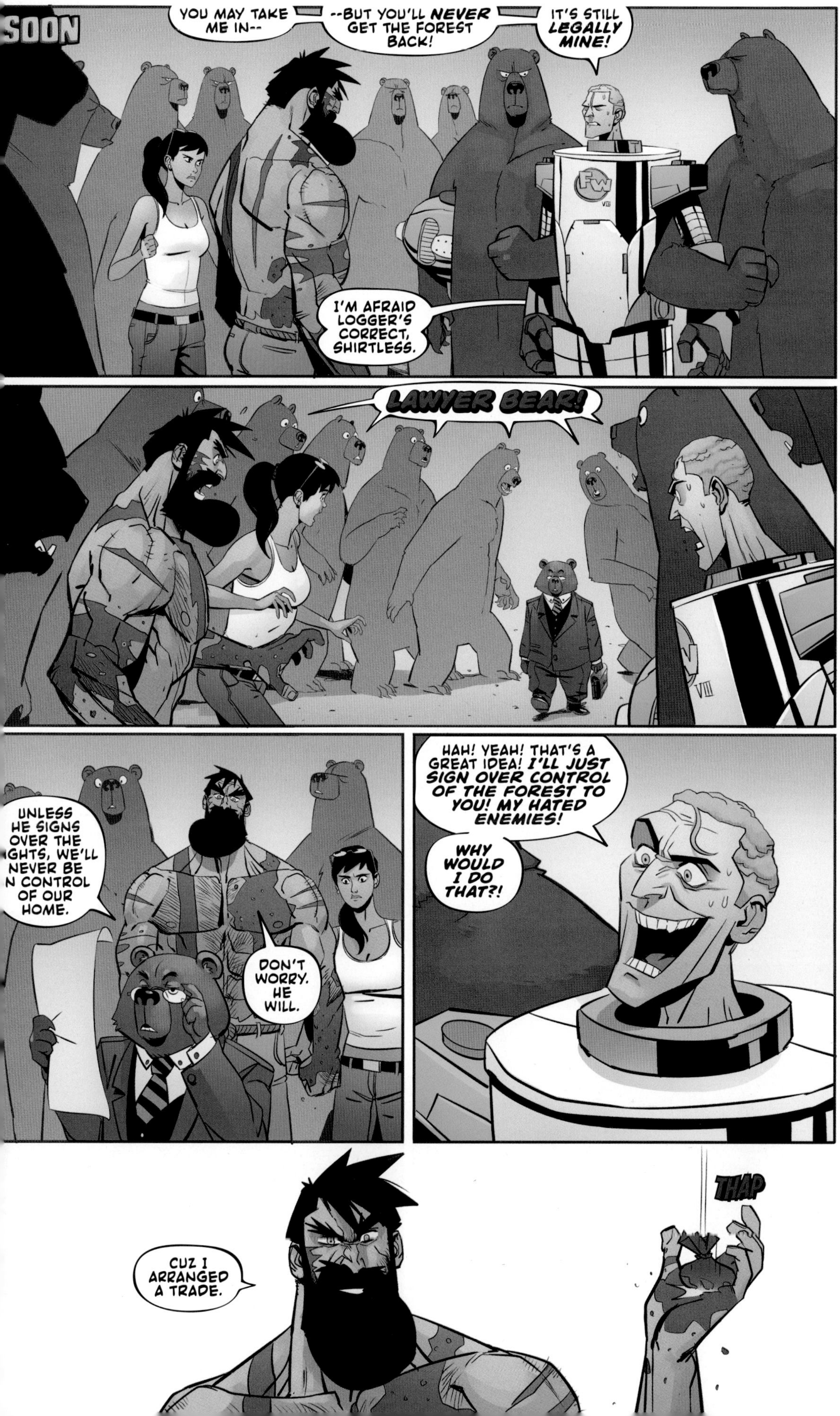
SOON
YOU MAY TAKE ME IN--
--BUT YOU'LL NEVER GET THE FOREST BACK!
IT'S STILL LEGALLY MINE!
I'M AFRAID LOGGER'S CORRECT, SHIRTLESS.
LAWYER BEAR!
UNLESS HE SIGNS OVER THE GHTS, WE'LL NEVER BE N CONTROL OF OUR HOME.
DON'T WORRY. HE WILL.
HAH! YEAH! THAT'S A GREAT IDEA! I'LL JUST SIGN OVER CONTROL OF THE FOREST TO YOU! MY HATED ENEMIES!
WHY WOULD I DO THAT?!
THAP
CUZ I ARRANGED A TRADE.

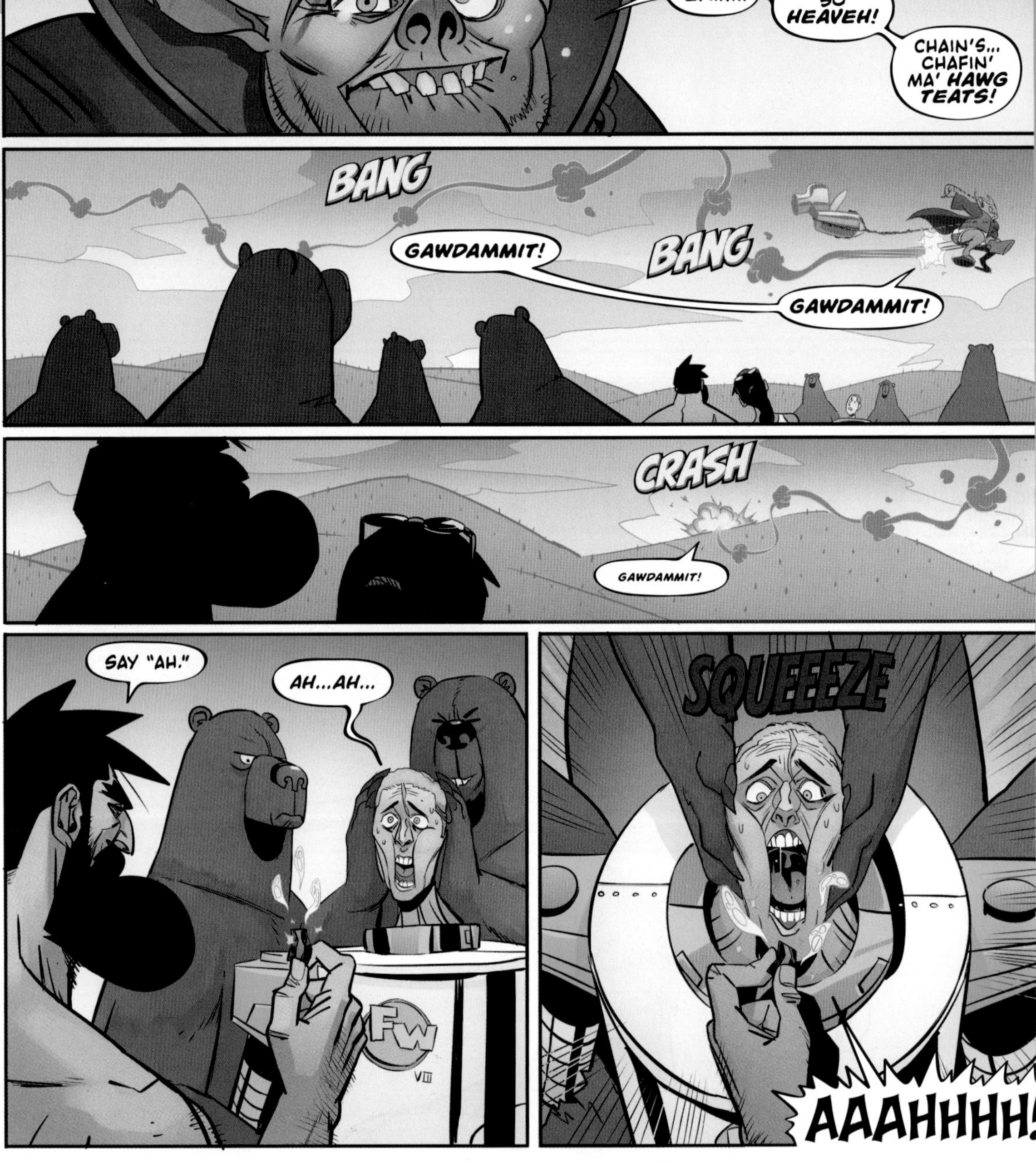
HEAVEH!
CHAIN'S... CHAFIN' MA' HAWG TEATS!
BANG
GAWDAMMIT!
BANG
GAWDAMMIT!
CRASH
GAWDAMMIT!
SAY "AH."
AH...AH...
FW
VIII
SQUEEEZE
AAAHHHH!

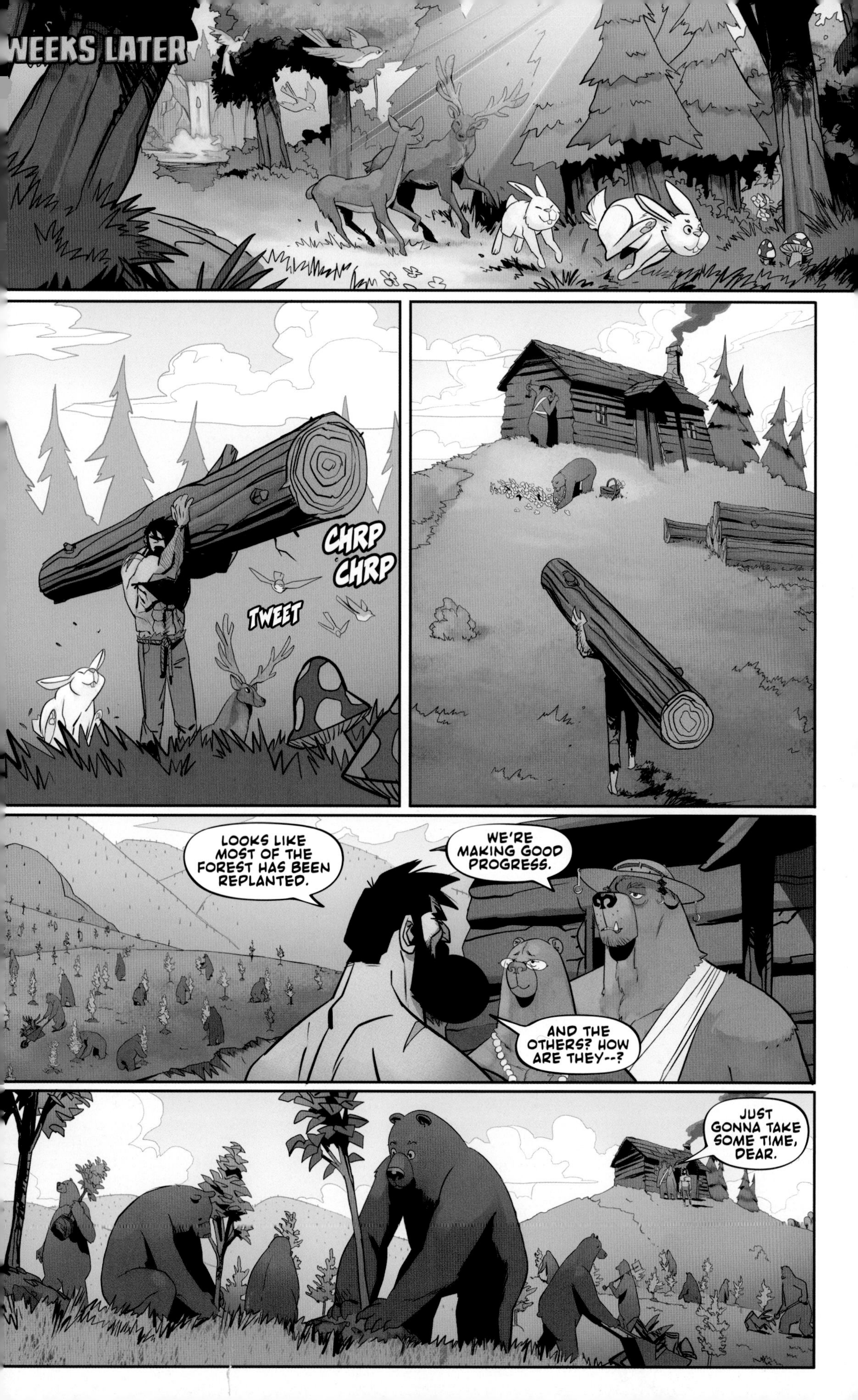
WEEKS LATER
CHRP CHRP
TWEET
LOOKS LIKE MOST OF THE FOREST HAS BEEN REPLANTED.
WE'RE MAKING GOOD PROGRESS.
AND THE OTHERS? HOW ARE THEY--?
JUST GONNA TAKE SOME TIME, DEAR.

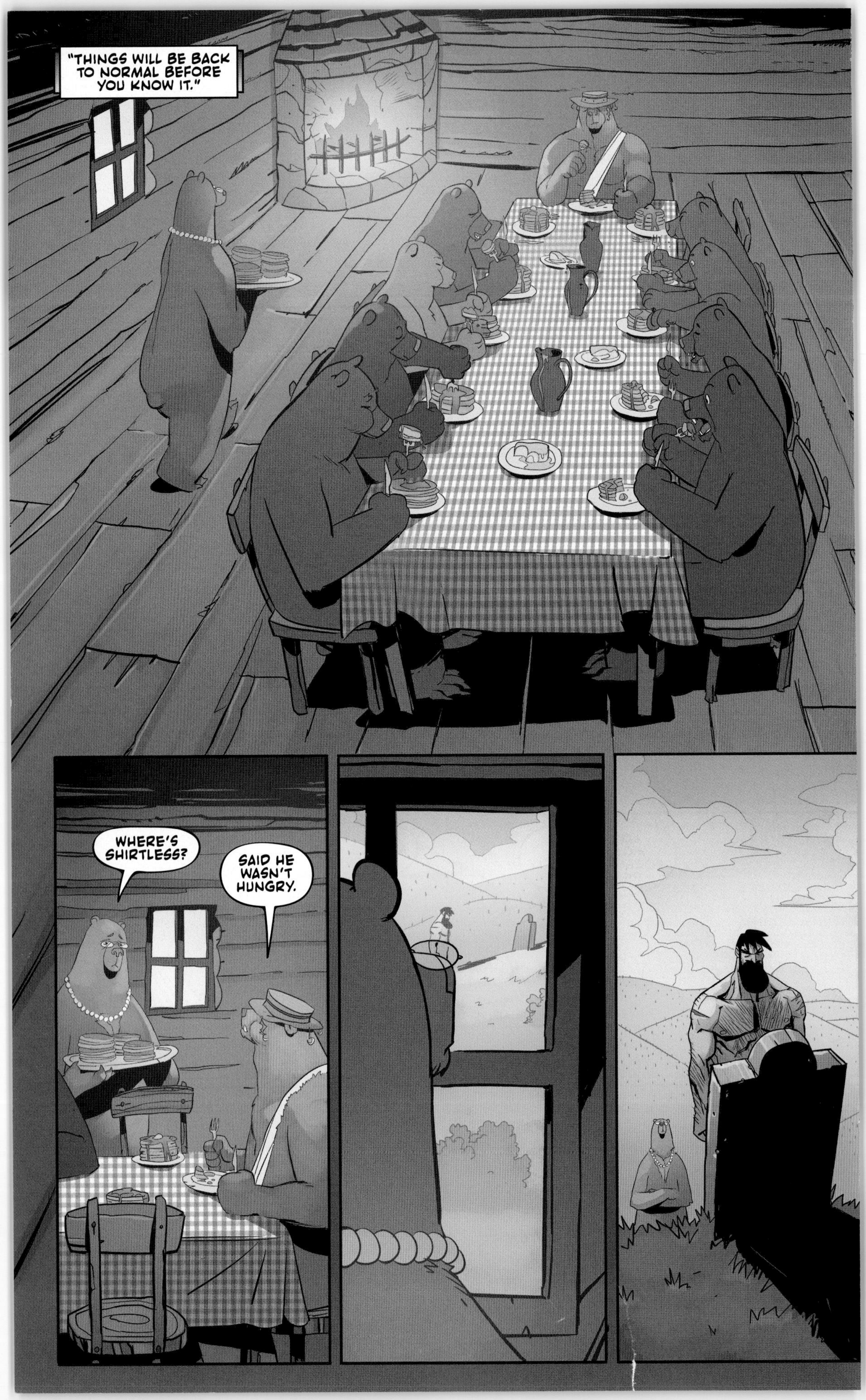
"THINGS WILL BE BACK TO NORMAL BEFORE YOU KNOW IT."
WHERE'S SHIRTLESS?
SAID HE WASN'T HUNGRY.

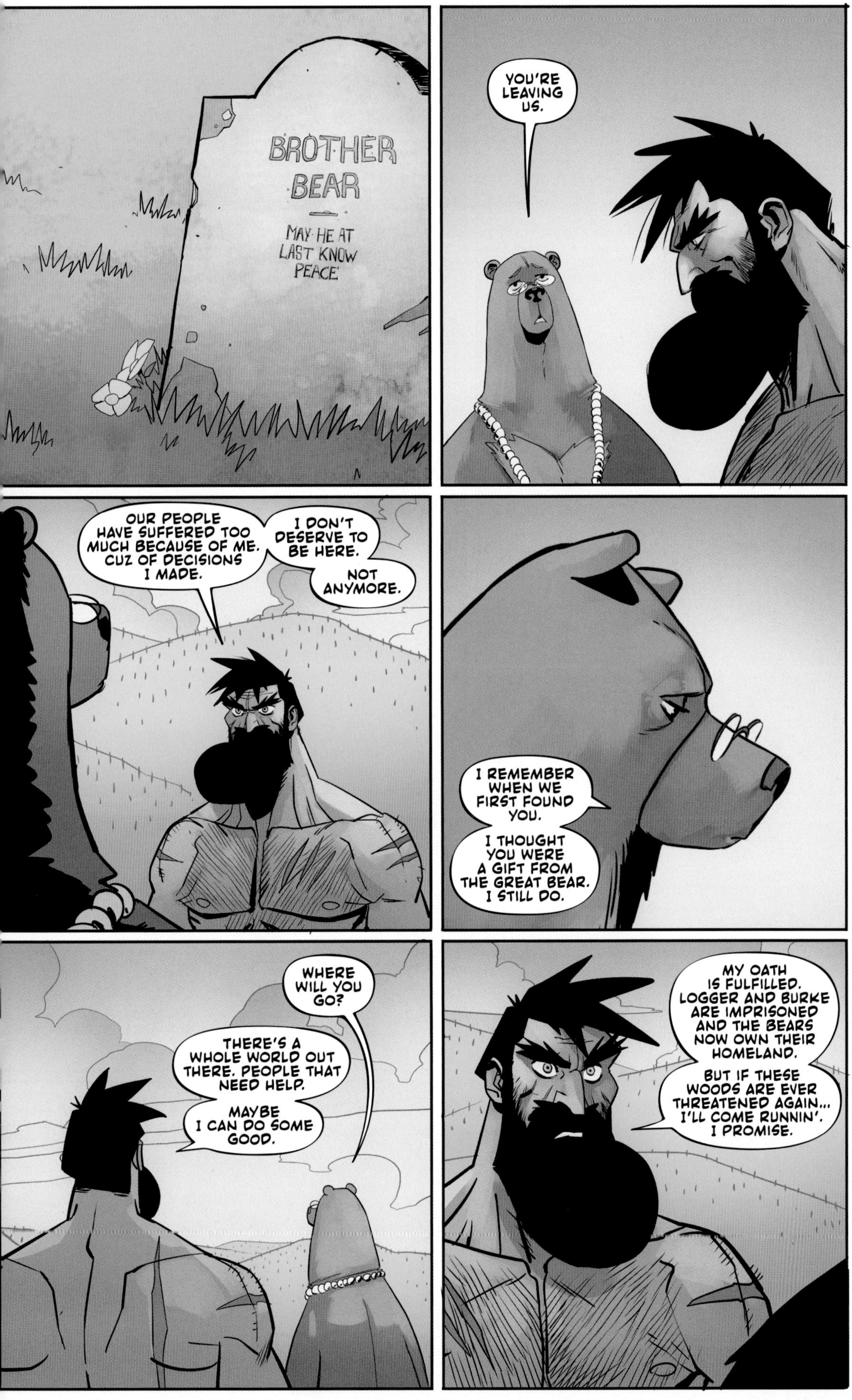
BROTHER BEAR
MAY HE AT LAST KNOW PEACE
YOU'RE LEAVING US.
OUR PEOPLE HAVE SUFFERED TOO MUCH BECAUSE OF ME. CUZ OF DECISIONS I MADE.
I DON'T DESERVE TO BE HERE.
NOT ANYMORE.
I REMEMBER WHEN WE FIRST FOUND YOU.
I THOUGHT YOU WERE A GIFT FROM THE GREAT BEAR. I STILL DO.
WHERE WILL YOU GO?
THERE'S A WHOLE WORLD OUT THERE. PEOPLE THAT NEED HELP.
MAYBE I CAN DO SOME GOOD.
MY OATH IS FULFILLED. LOGGER AND BURKE ARE IMPRISONED AND THE BEARS NOW OWN THEIR HOMELAND.
BUT IF THESE WOODS ARE EVER THREATENED AGAIN... I'LL COME RUNNIN'. I PROMISE.

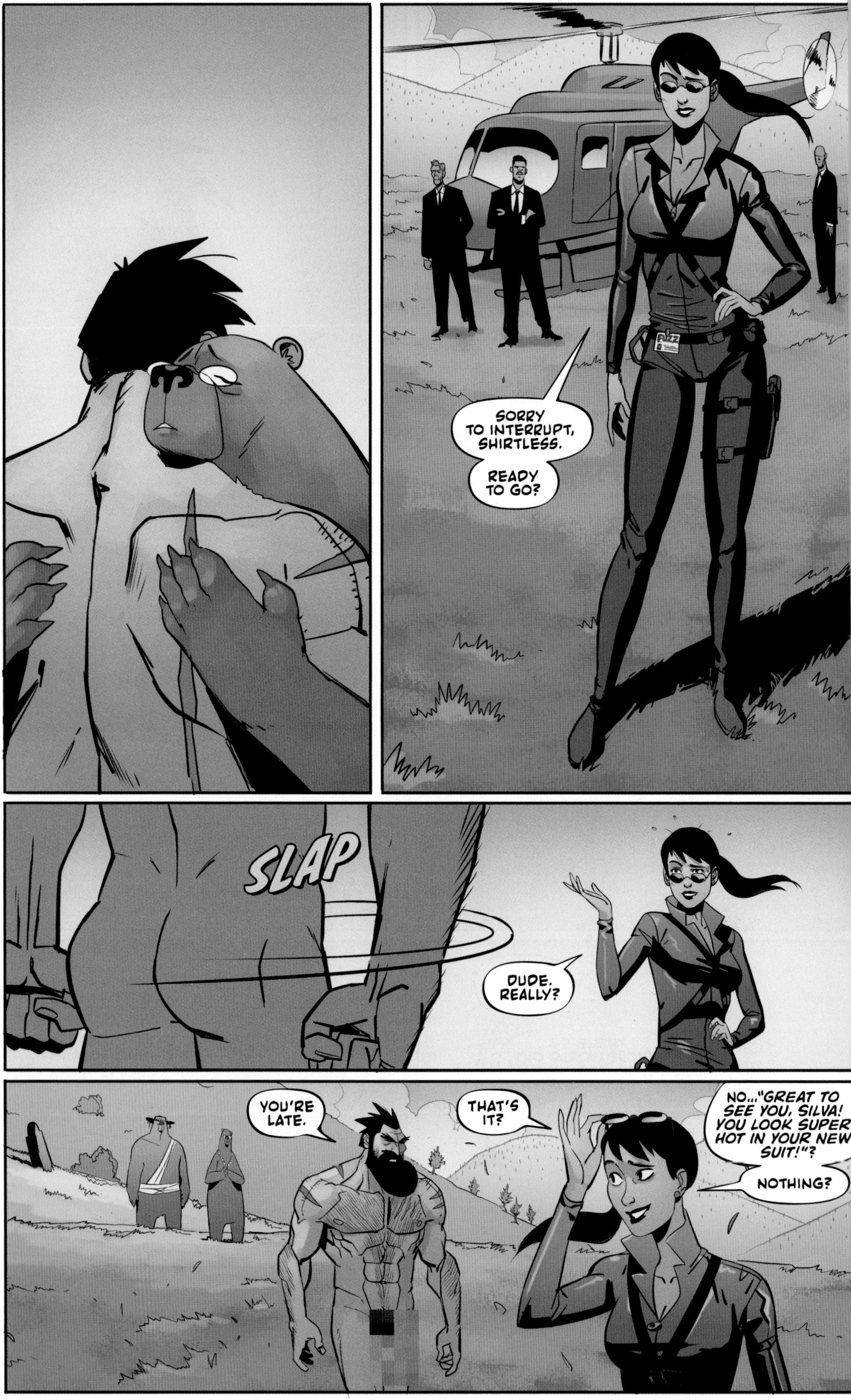
SORRY TO INTERRUPT, SHIRTLESS.
READY TO GO?
SLAP
DUDE. REALLY?
YOU'RE LATE.
THAT'S IT?
NO..."GREAT TO SEE YOU, SILVA! YOU LOOK SUPER HOT IN YOUR NEW SUIT!"?
NOTHING?

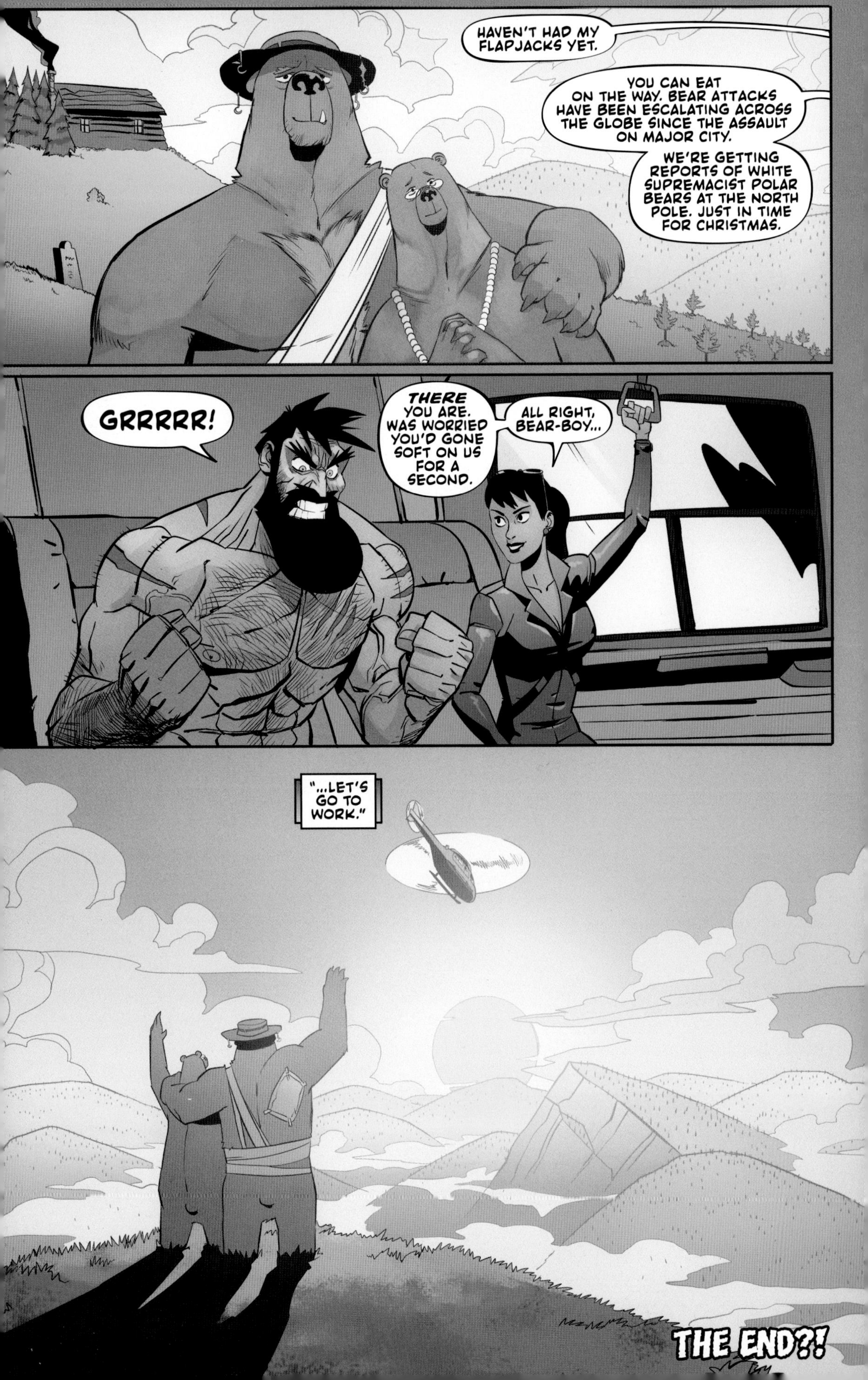
HAVEN'T HAD MY FLAPJACKS YET.
YOU CAN EAT ON THE WAY. BEAR ATTACKS HAVE BEEN ESCALATING ACROSS THE GLOBE SINCE THE ASSAULT ON MAJOR CITY.
WE'RE GETTING REPORTS OF WHITE SUPREMACIST POLAR BEARS AT THE NORTH POLE. JUST IN TIME FOR CHRISTMAS.
GRRRRR!
THERE YOU ARE. WAS WORRIED YOU'D GONE SOFT ON US FOR A SECOND.
ALL RIGHT, BEAR-BOY...
"...LET'S GO TO WORK."
THE END?!

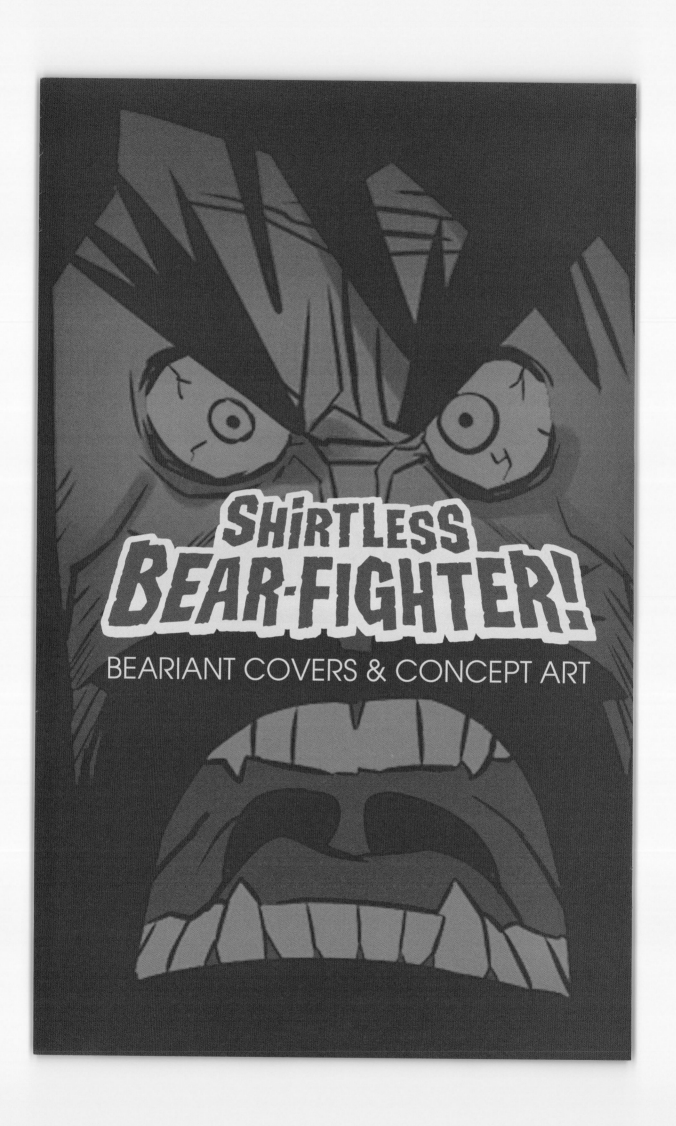

Shirtless BEAR-FIGHTER!

BEARIANT COVERS & CONCEPT ART

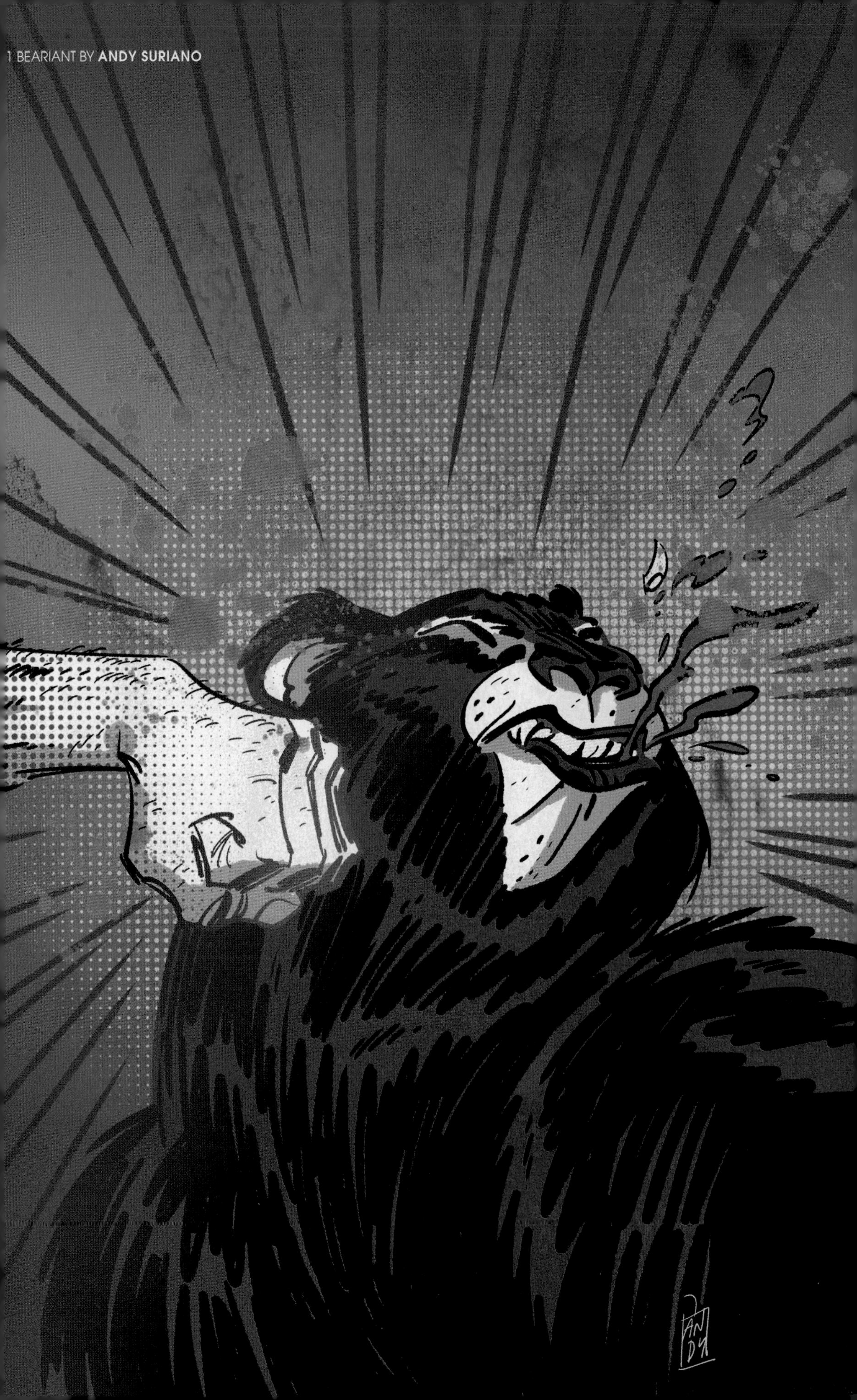
ANDY

1 BEARIANT BY **ANDY SURIANO**

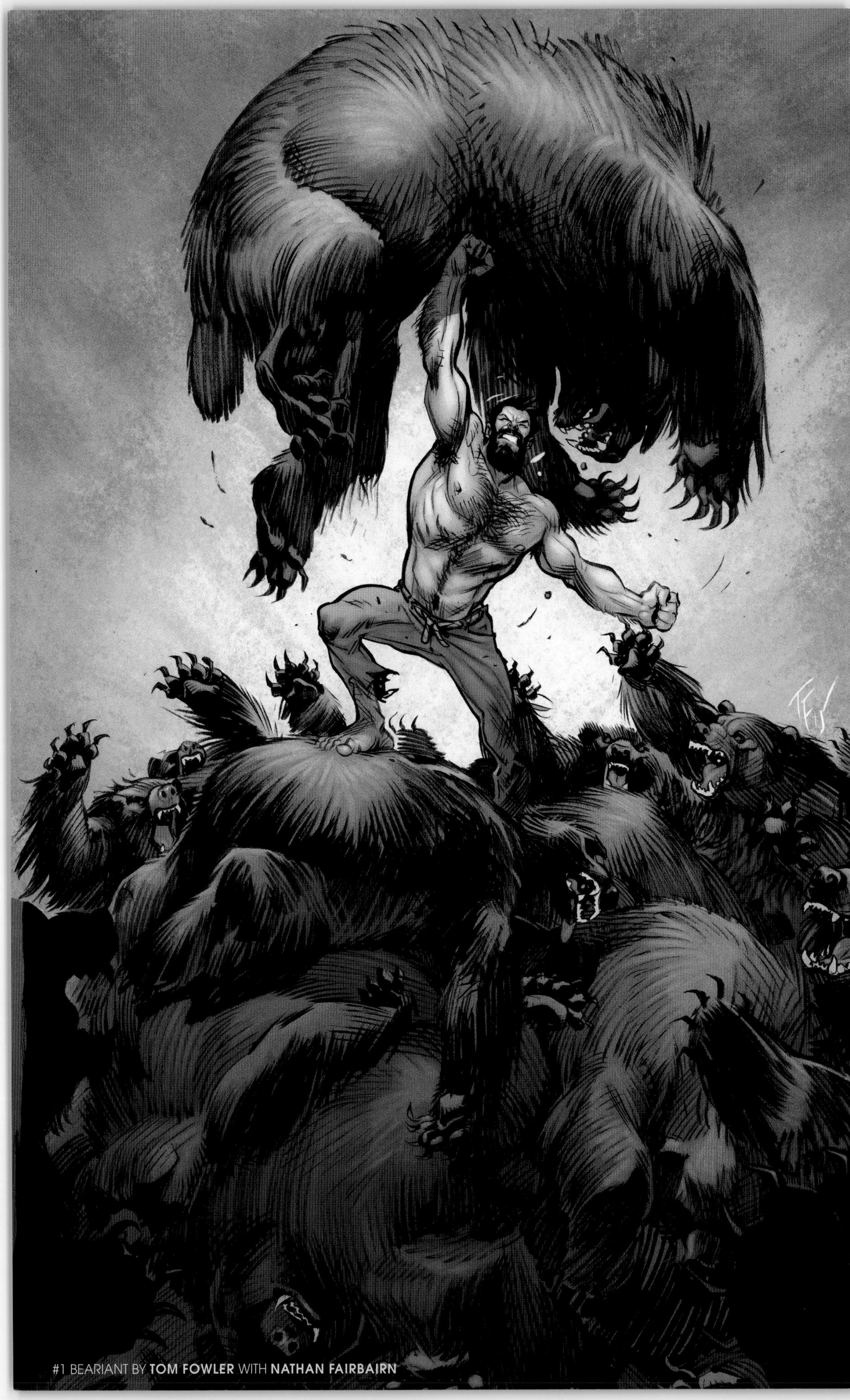

#1 BEARIANT BY **TOM FOWLER** WITH **NATHAN FAIRBAIRN**

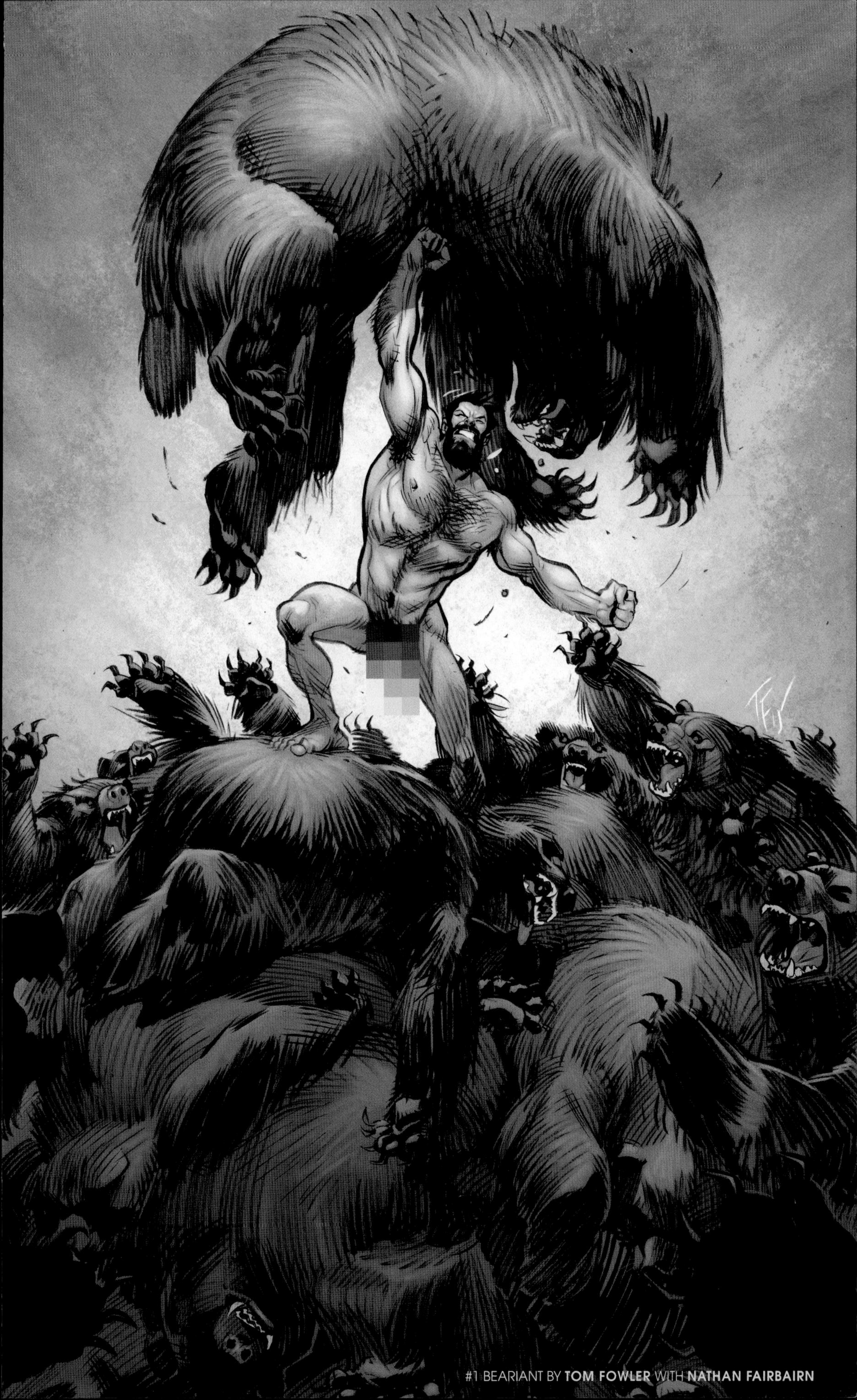

#1 BEARIANT BY **TOM FOWLER** WITH **NATHAN FAIRBAIRN**

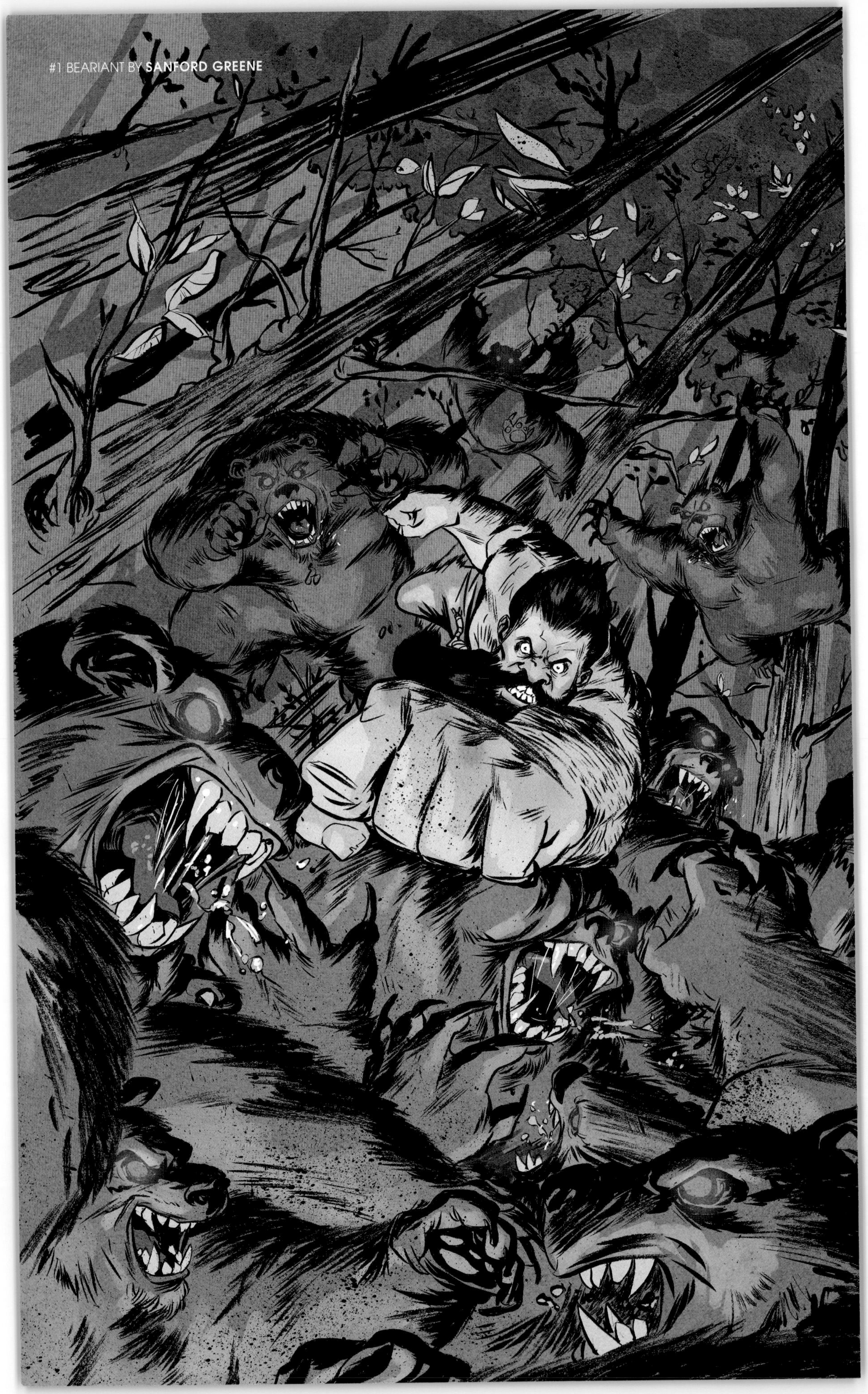

#1 BEARIANT BY **SANFORD GREENE**

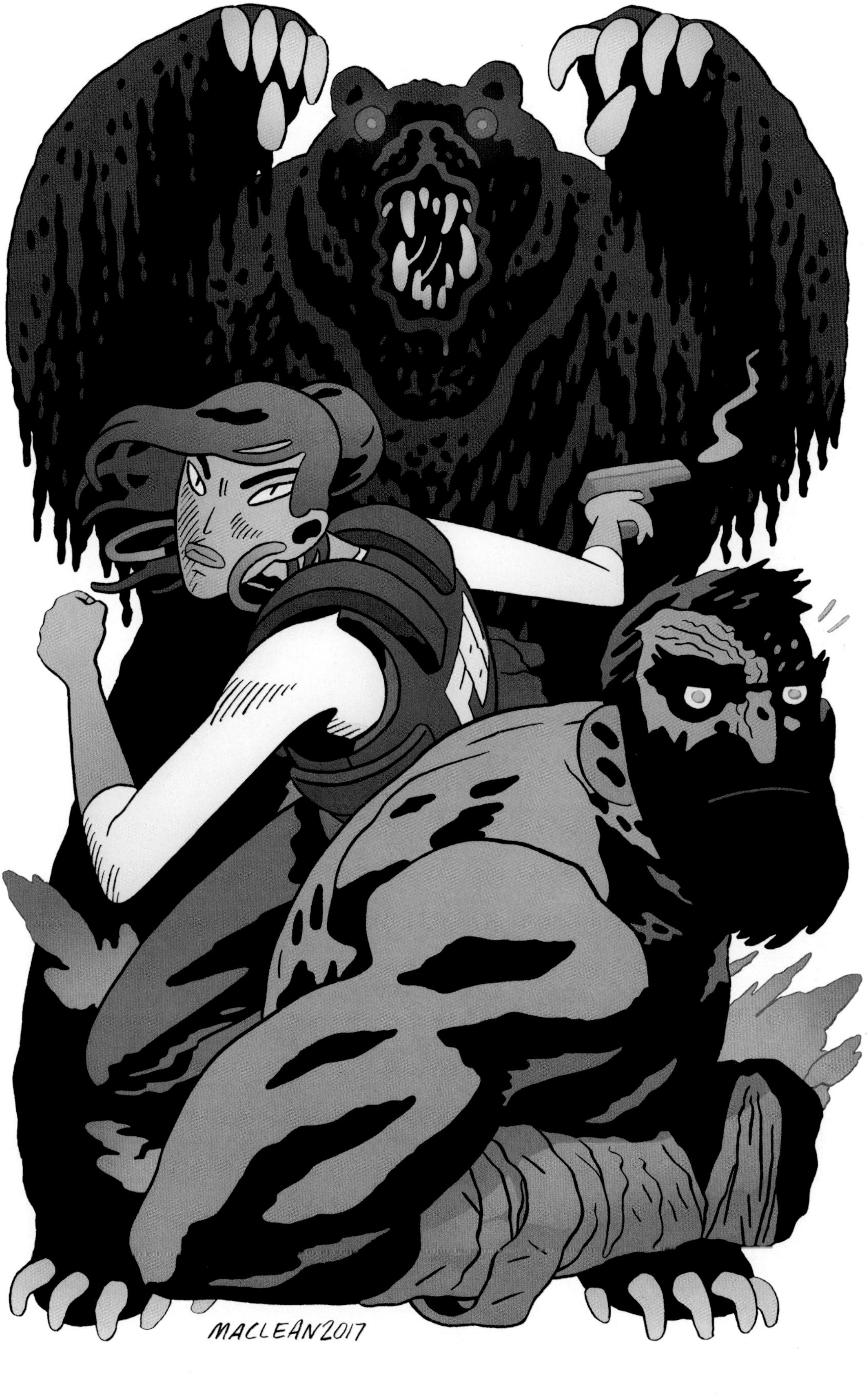
MACLEAN2017

#2 BEARIANT BY **ANDREW MACLEAN** WITH **MIKE SPICER**

#2 BEARIANT BY **NATHAN FOX**

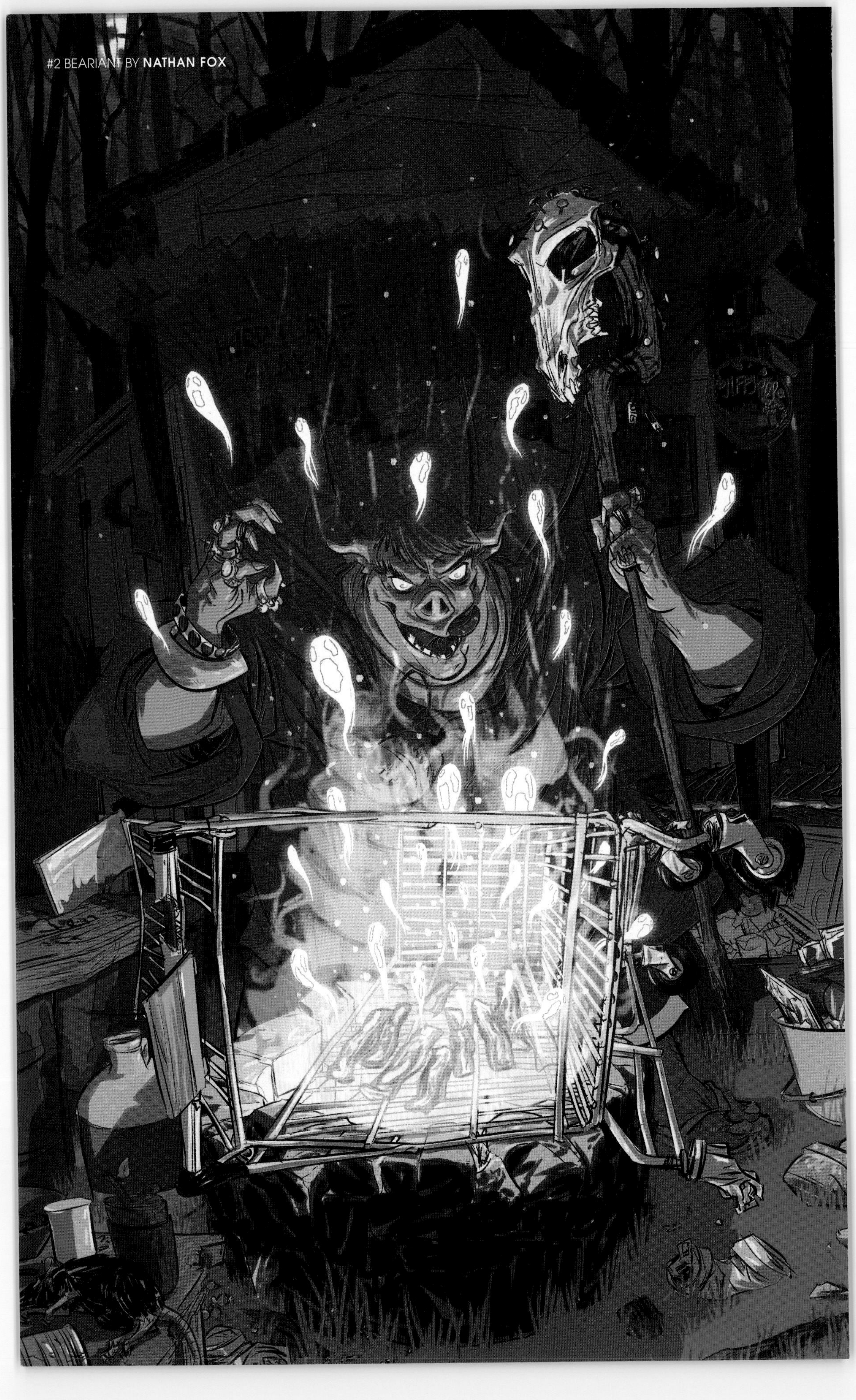

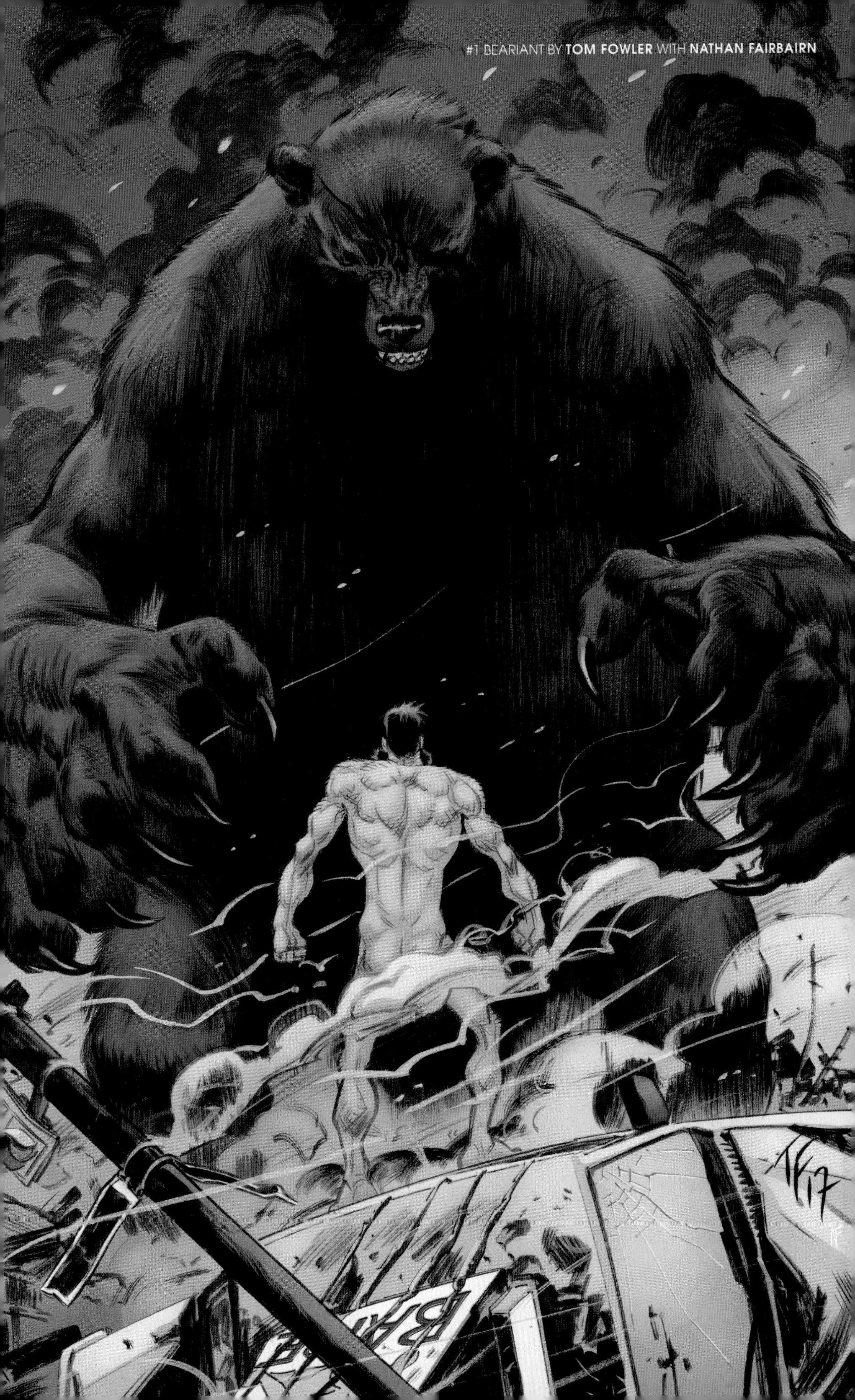

#1 BEARIANT BY **TOM FOWLER** WITH **NATHAN FAIRBAIRN**

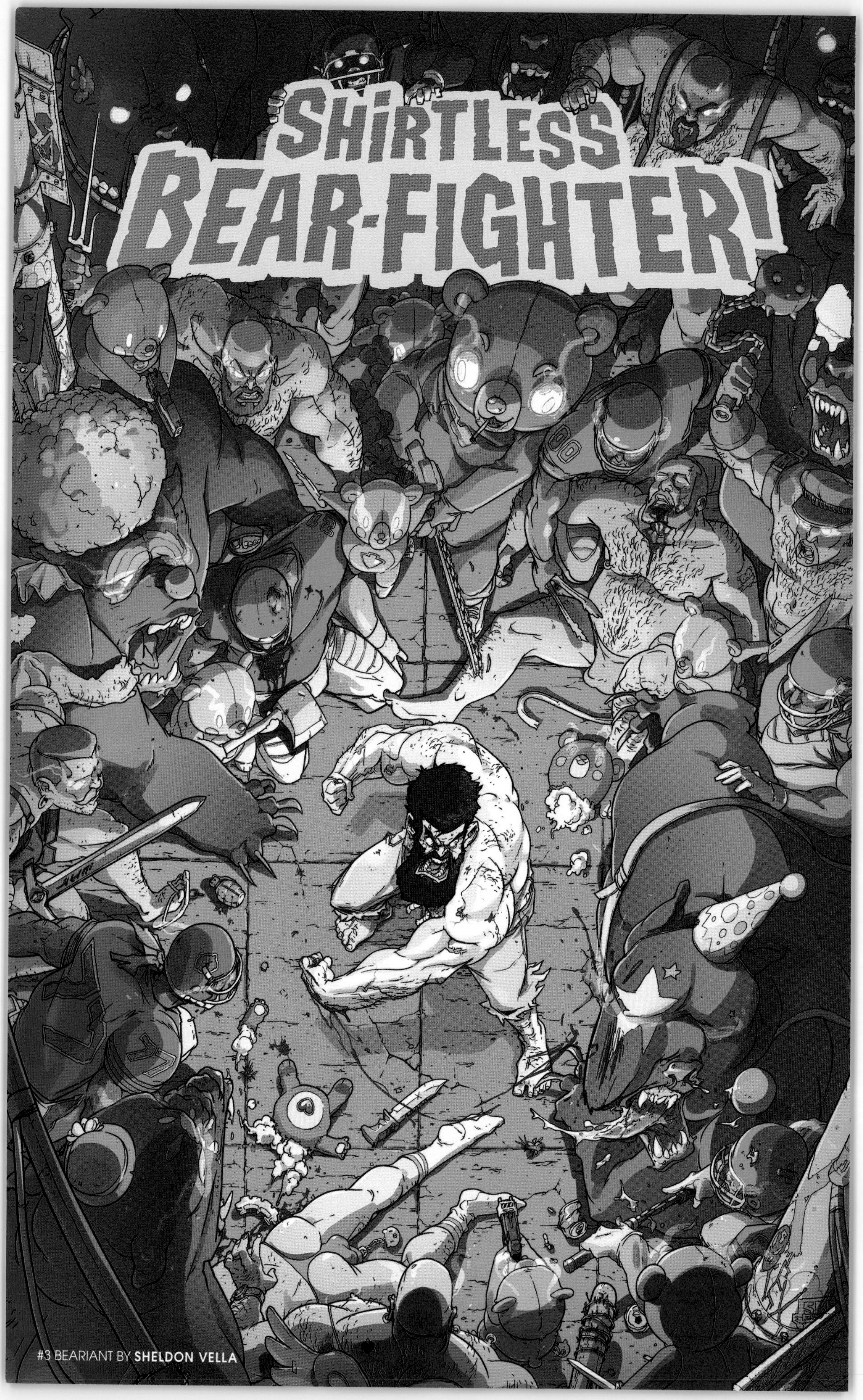
SHIRTLESS
BEAR-FIGHTER!

#3 BEARIANT BY **SHELDON VELLA**

#3 BEARIANT BY **JACOB CHABOT**

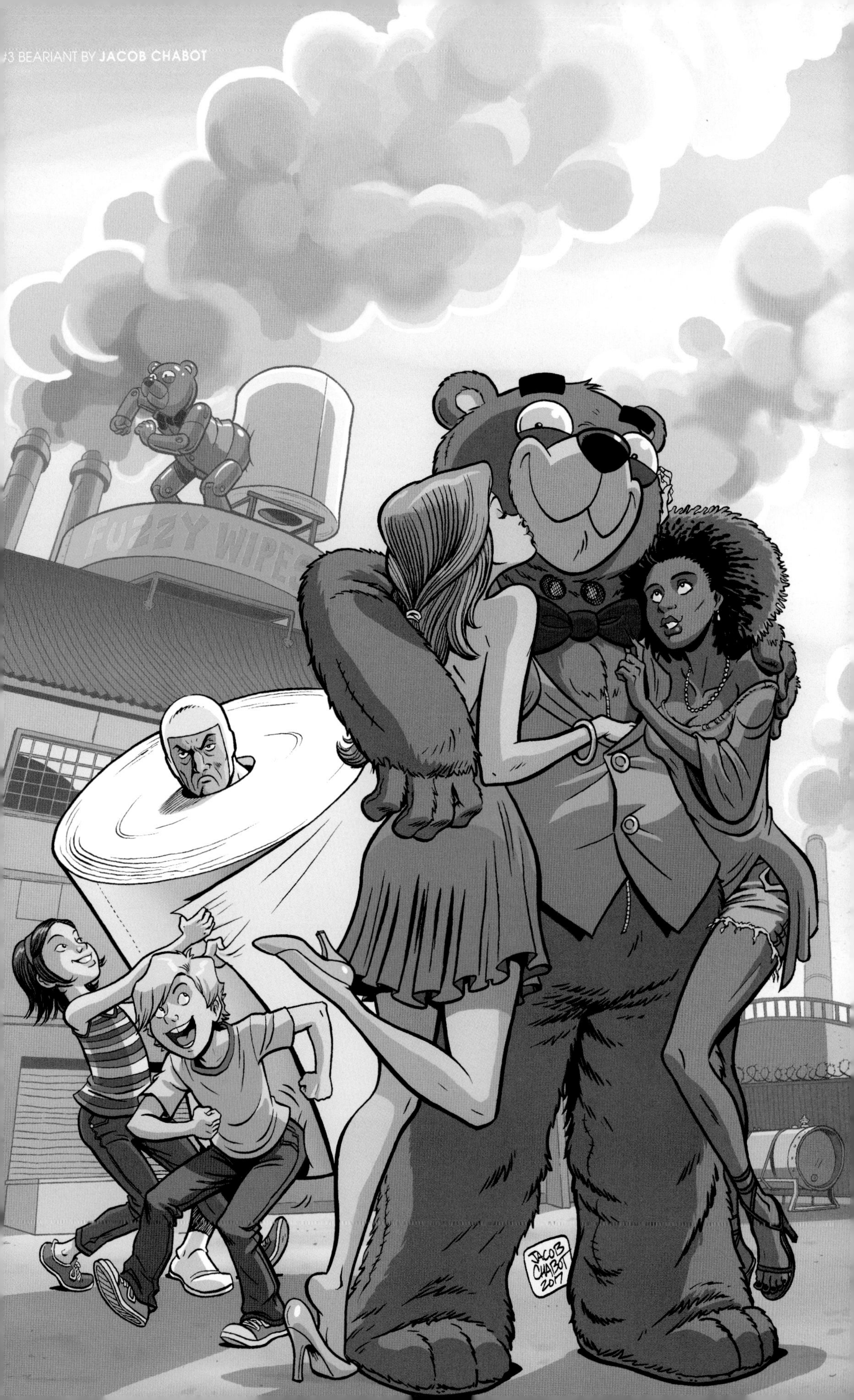
FUZZY WIPES
JACOB CHABOT 2017

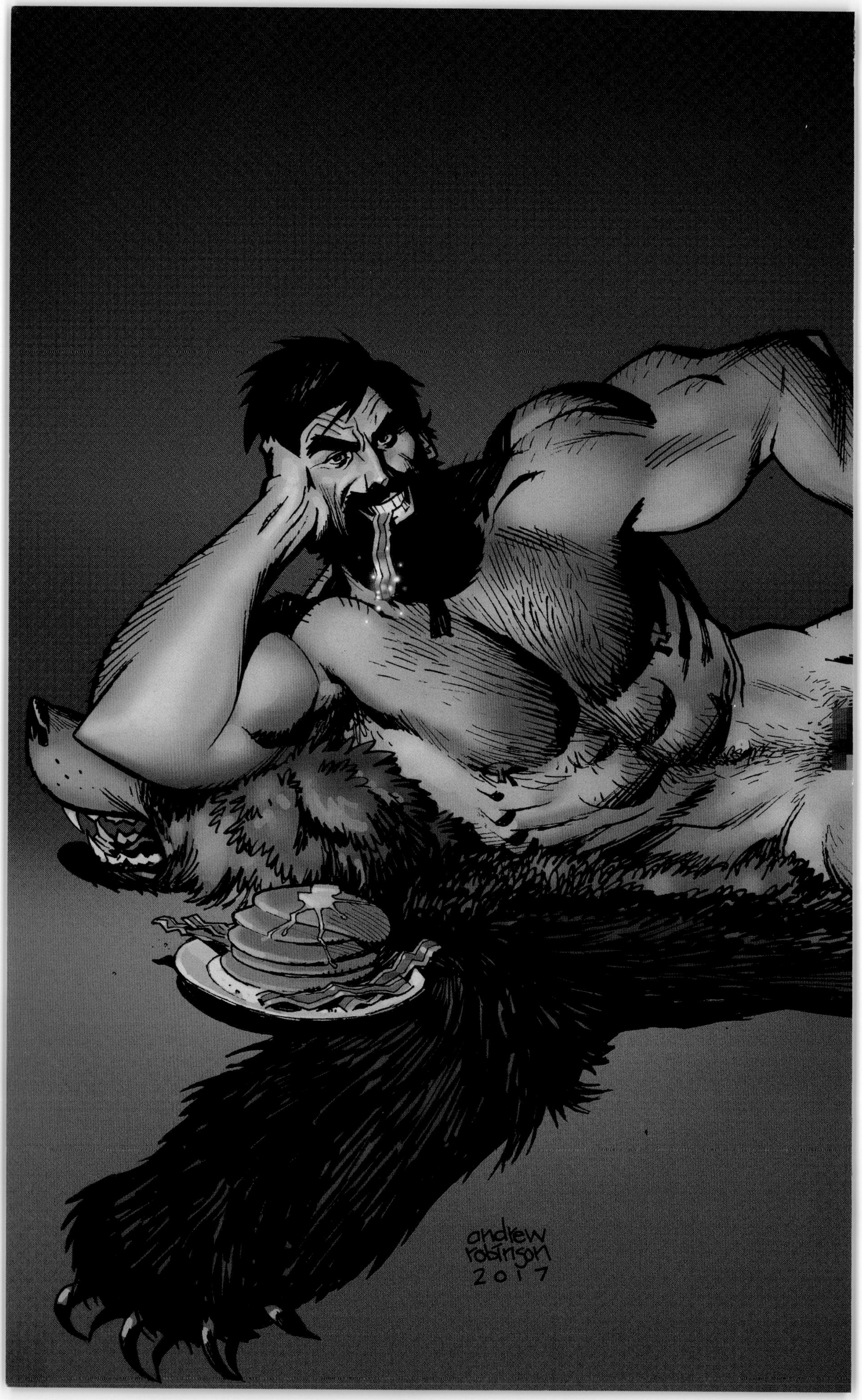
andrew
robinson
2017

#3 BEARIANT BY **ANDREW ROBINSON**

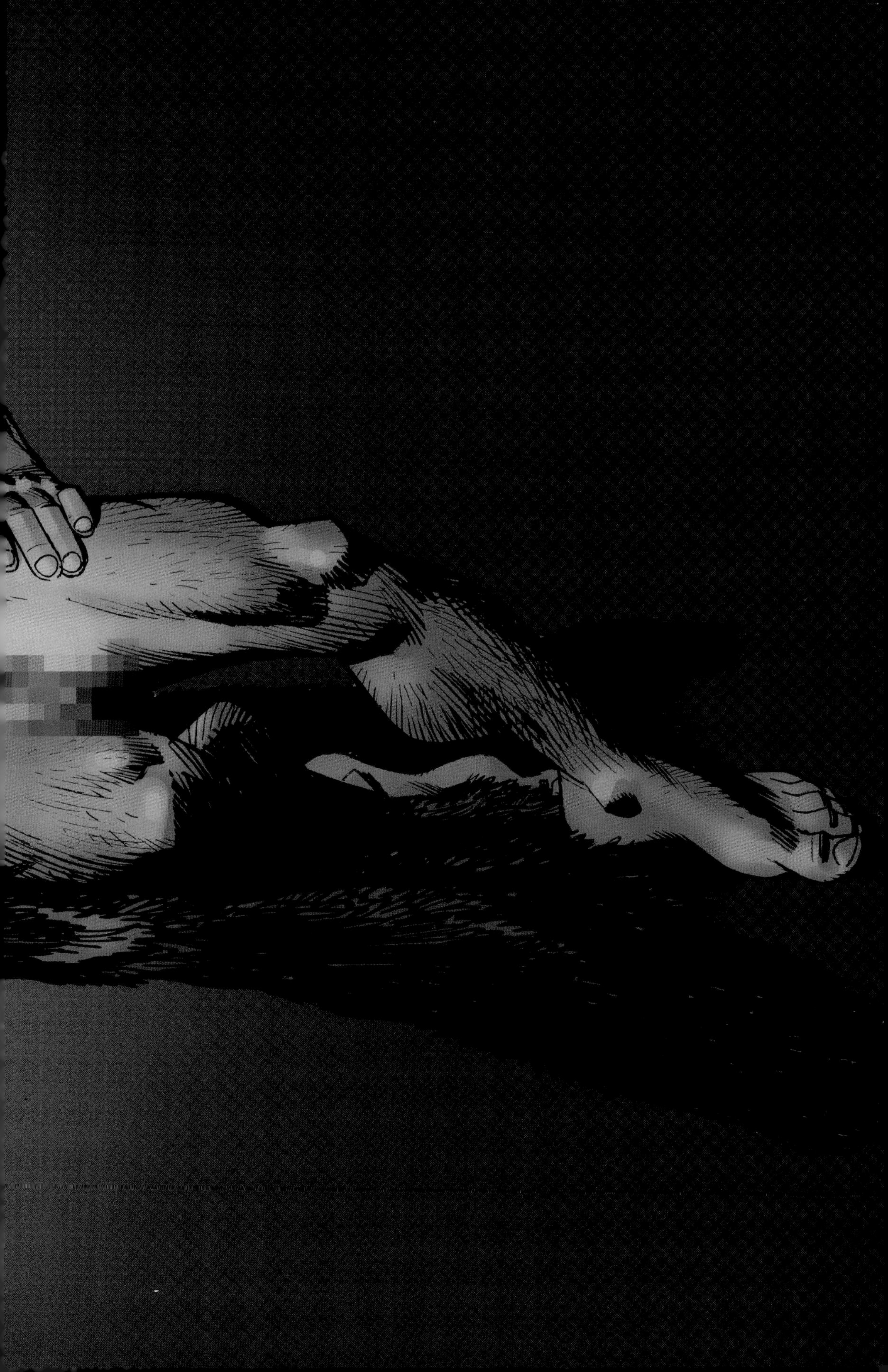

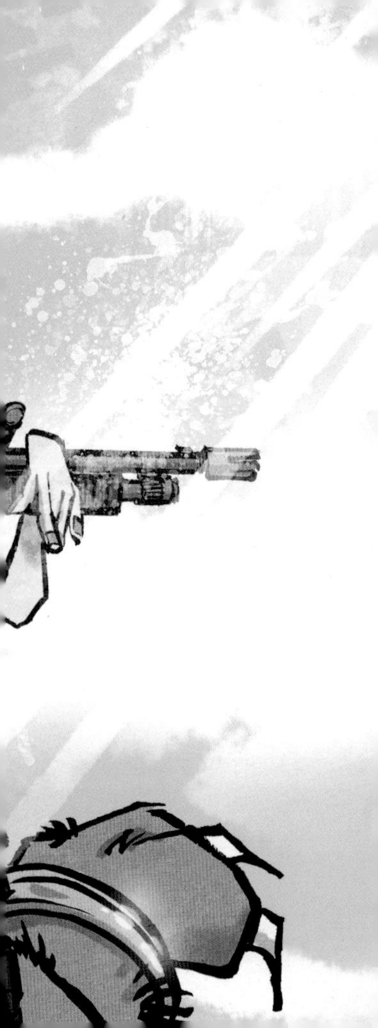

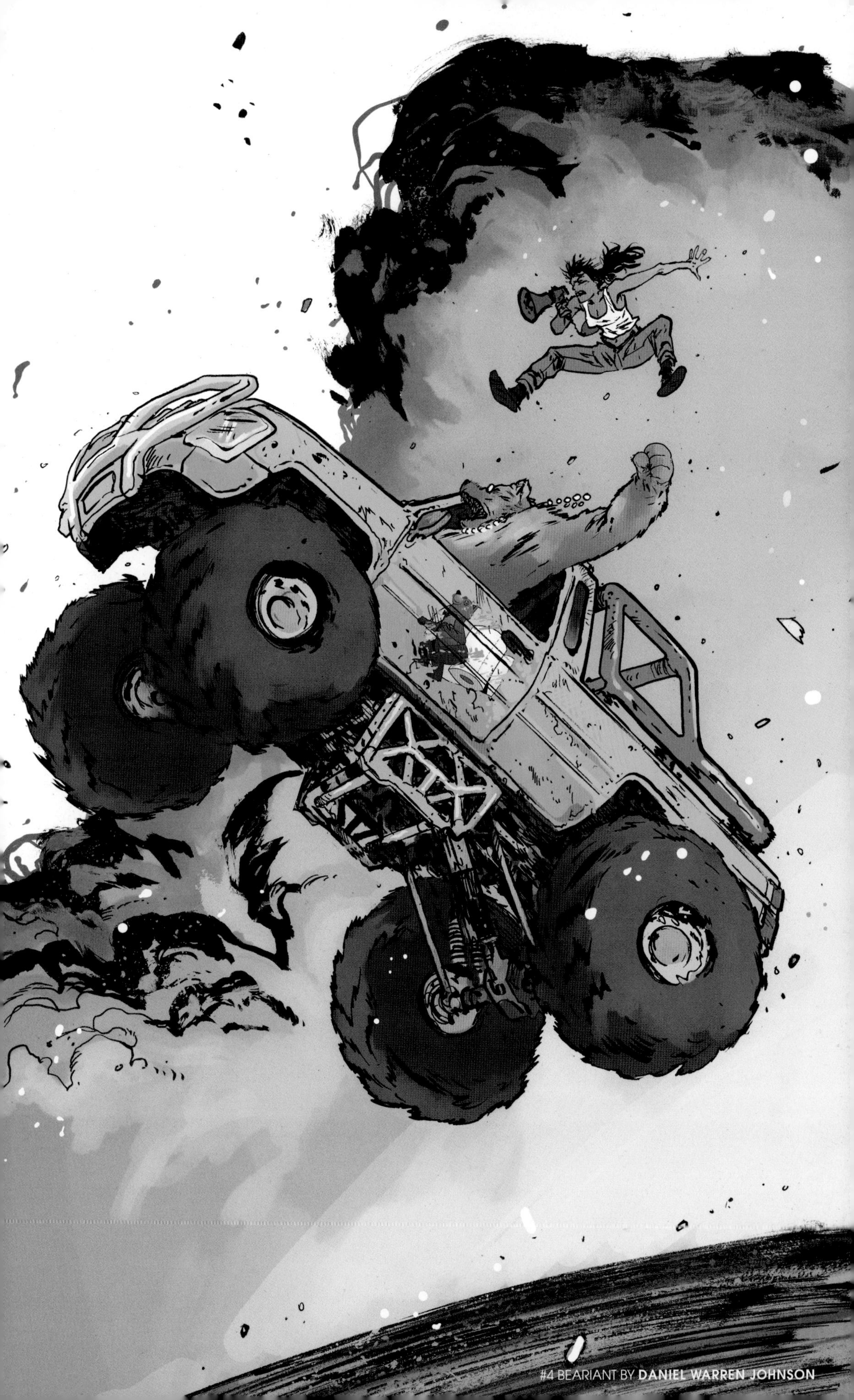

#4 BEARIANT BY **DANIEL WARREN JOHNSON**

PIN-UP BY **ROBB MOMMAERTS**

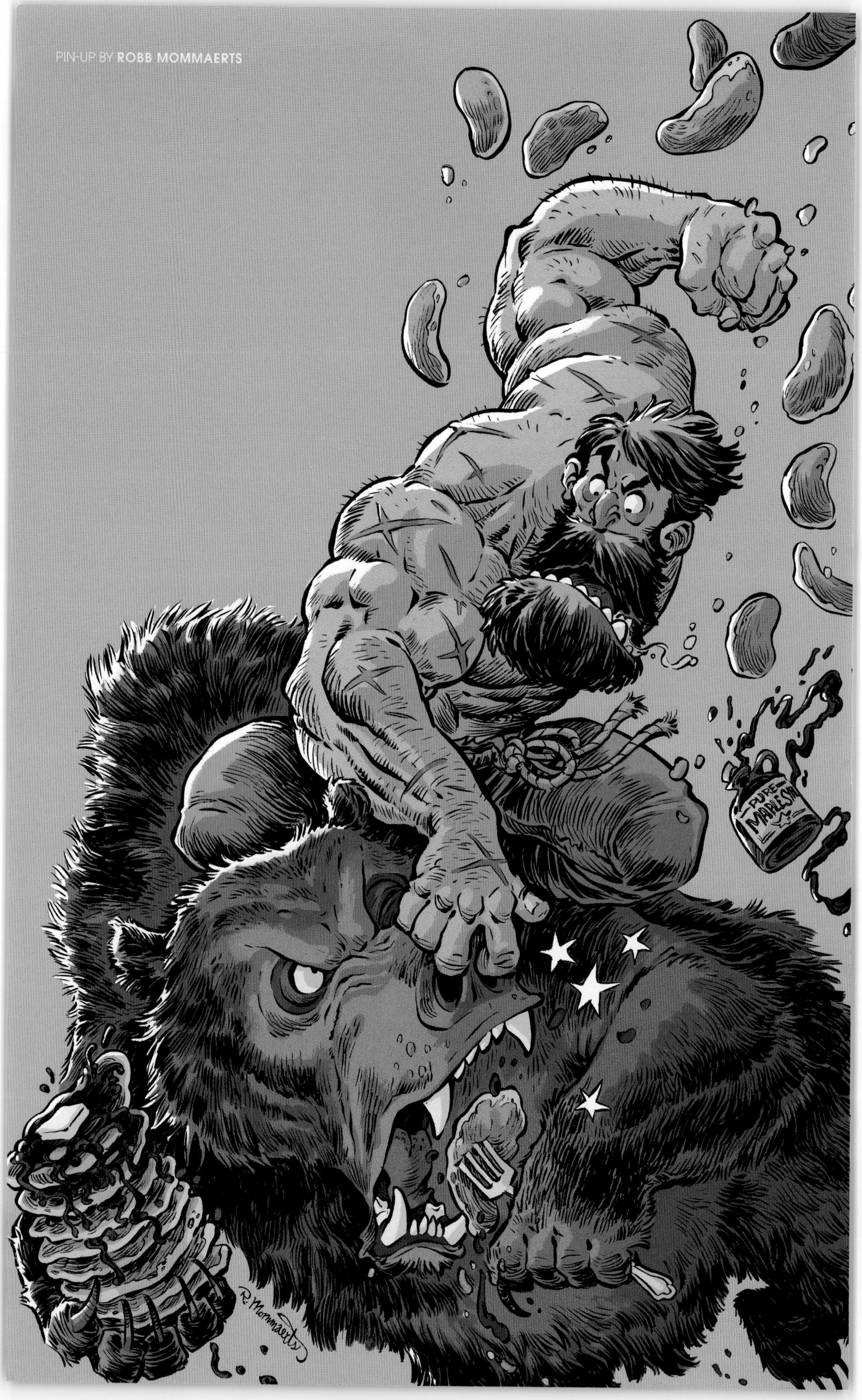
PURE
MAPLE
R. Mommaerts

#2 BEARIANT BY **SKOTTIE YOUNG**

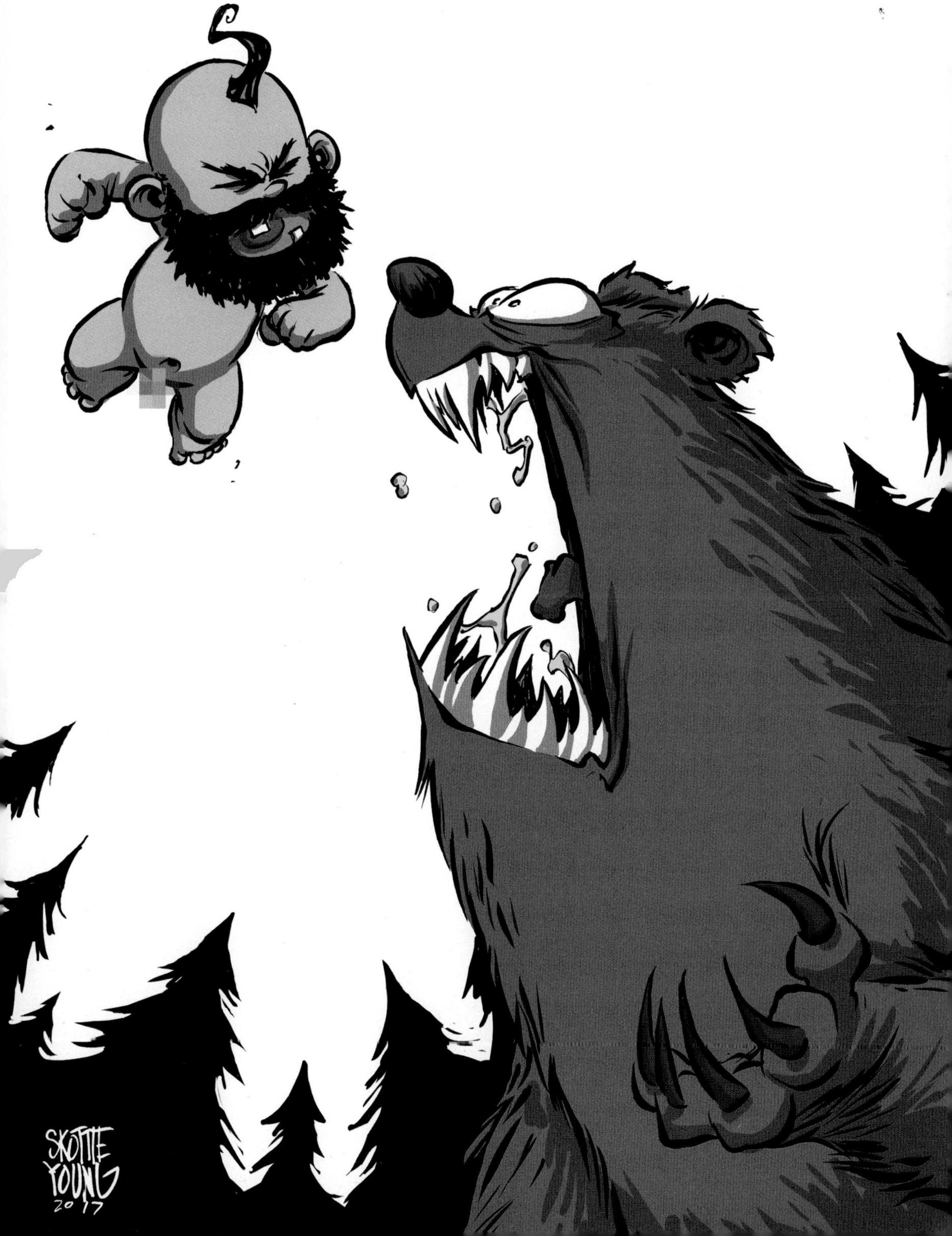
SKOTTIE
YOUNG
2017

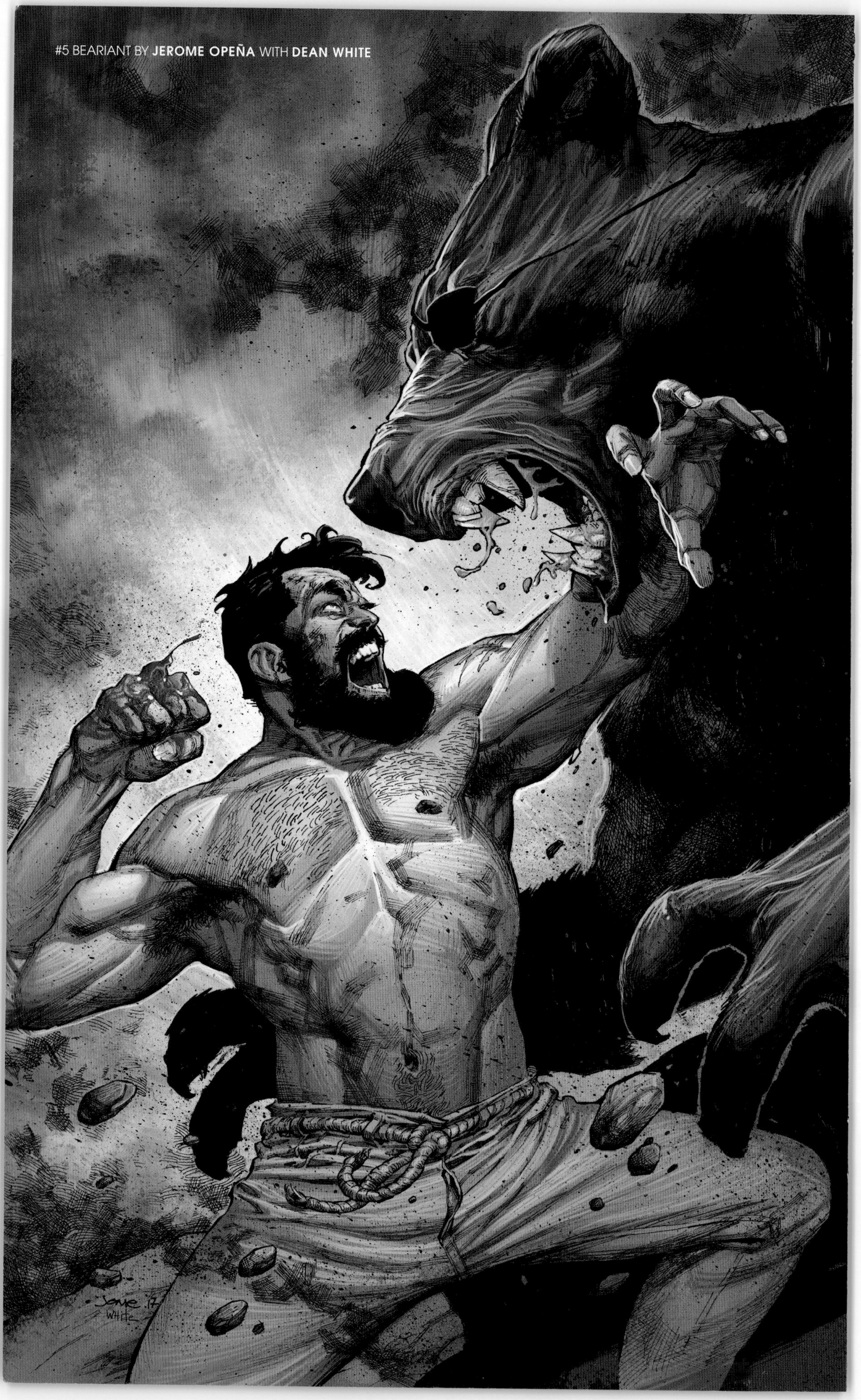

#5 BEARIANT BY **JEROME OPEÑA** WITH **DEAN WHITE**

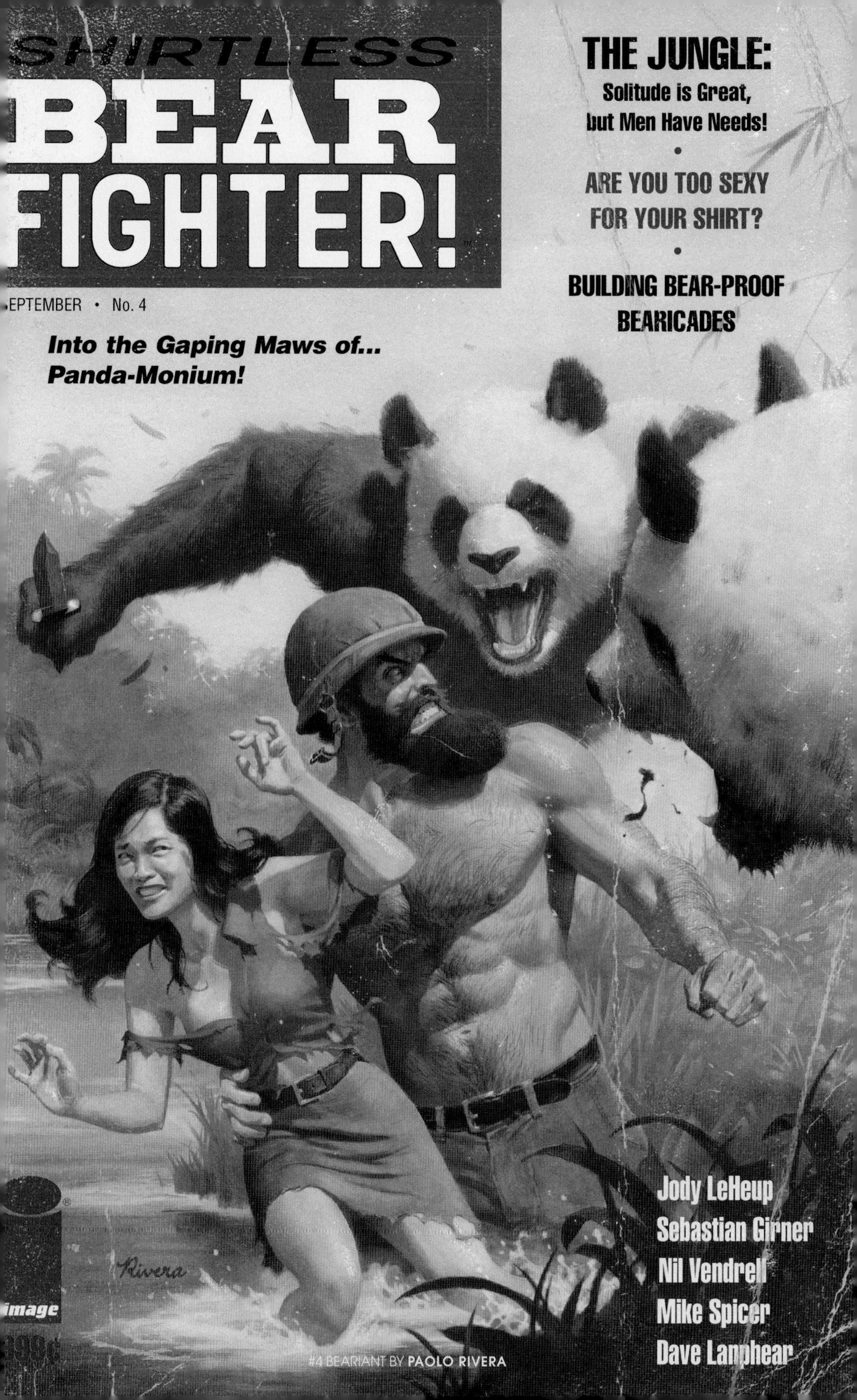
SHIRTLESS
BEAR FIGHTER!
SEPTEMBER • No. 4
THE JUNGLE:
Solitude is Great, but Men Have Needs!
ARE YOU TOO SEXY FOR YOUR SHIRT?
BUILDING BEAR-PROOF BEARICADES
Into the Gaping Maws of... Panda-Monium!
Rivera
image
Jody LeHeup
Sebastian Girner
Nil Vendrell
Mike Spicer
Dave Lanphear

#4 BEARIANT BY PAOLO RIVERA

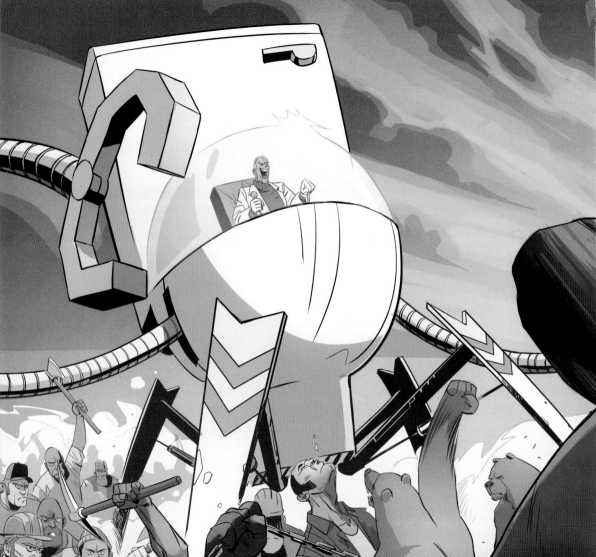

#5 BEARIANT BY **NIL VENDRELL** WITH **MIKE SPICER**

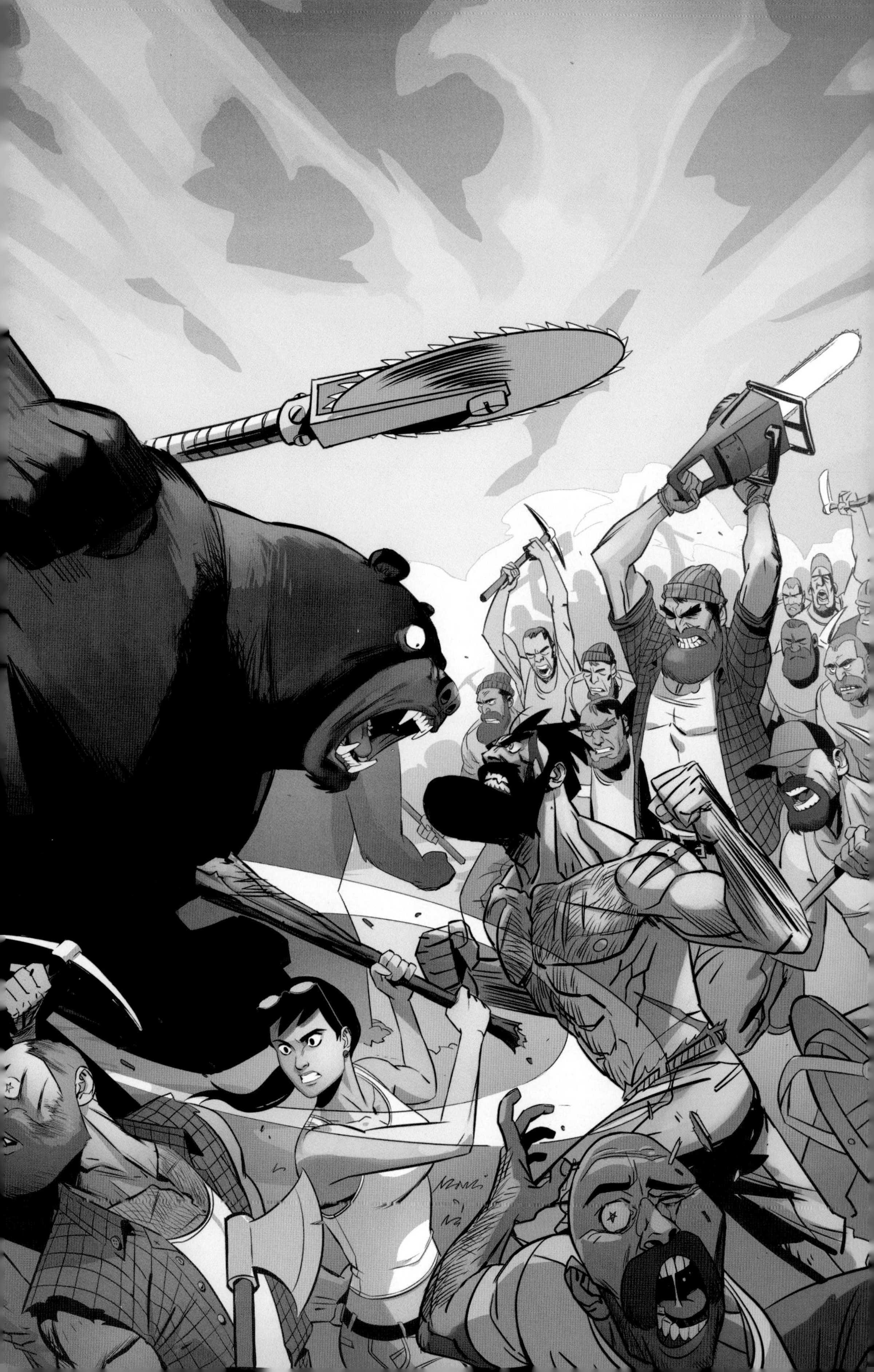

ART BY **NIL VENDRELL** AND **MIKE SPICER**

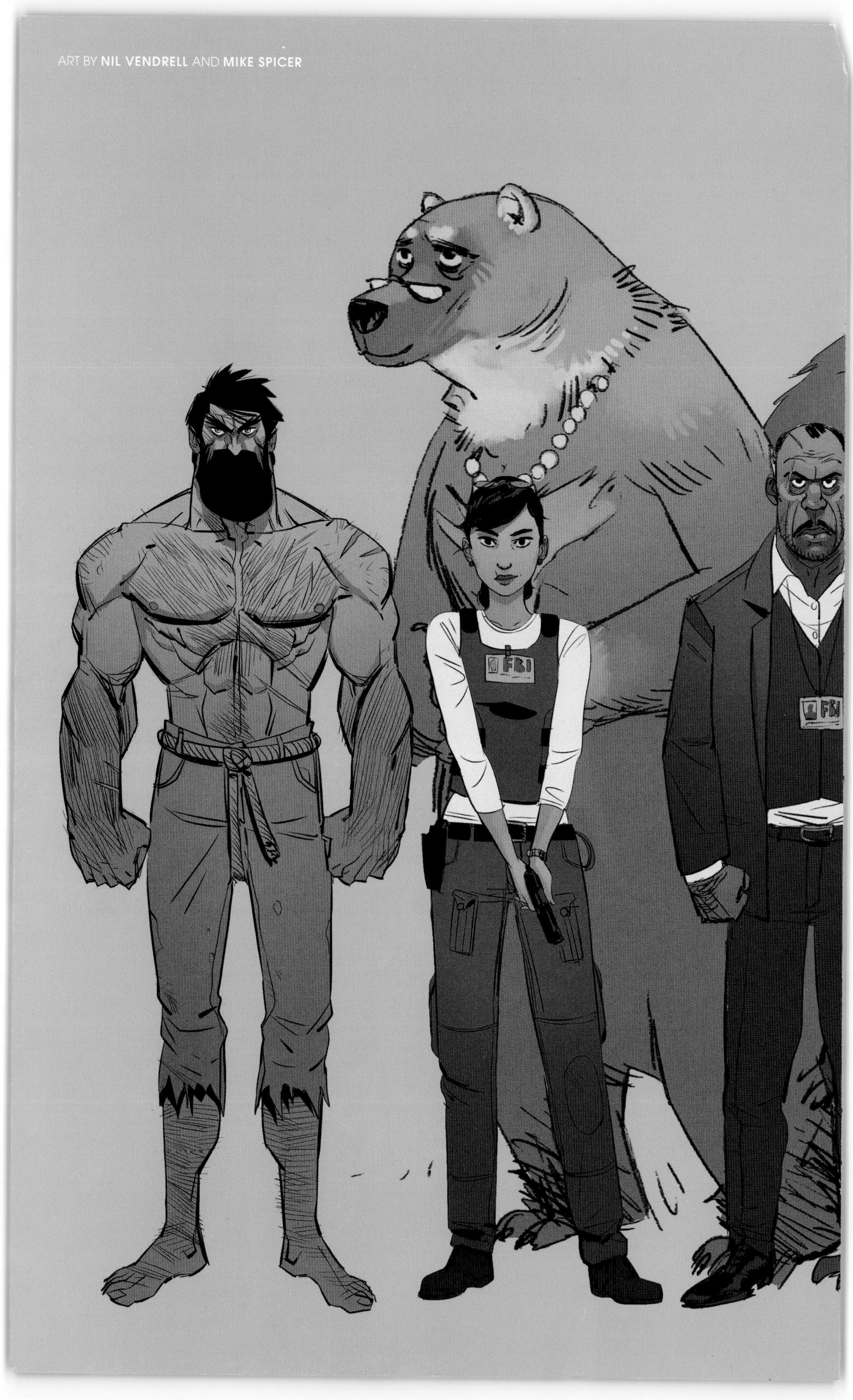
FBI
FBI

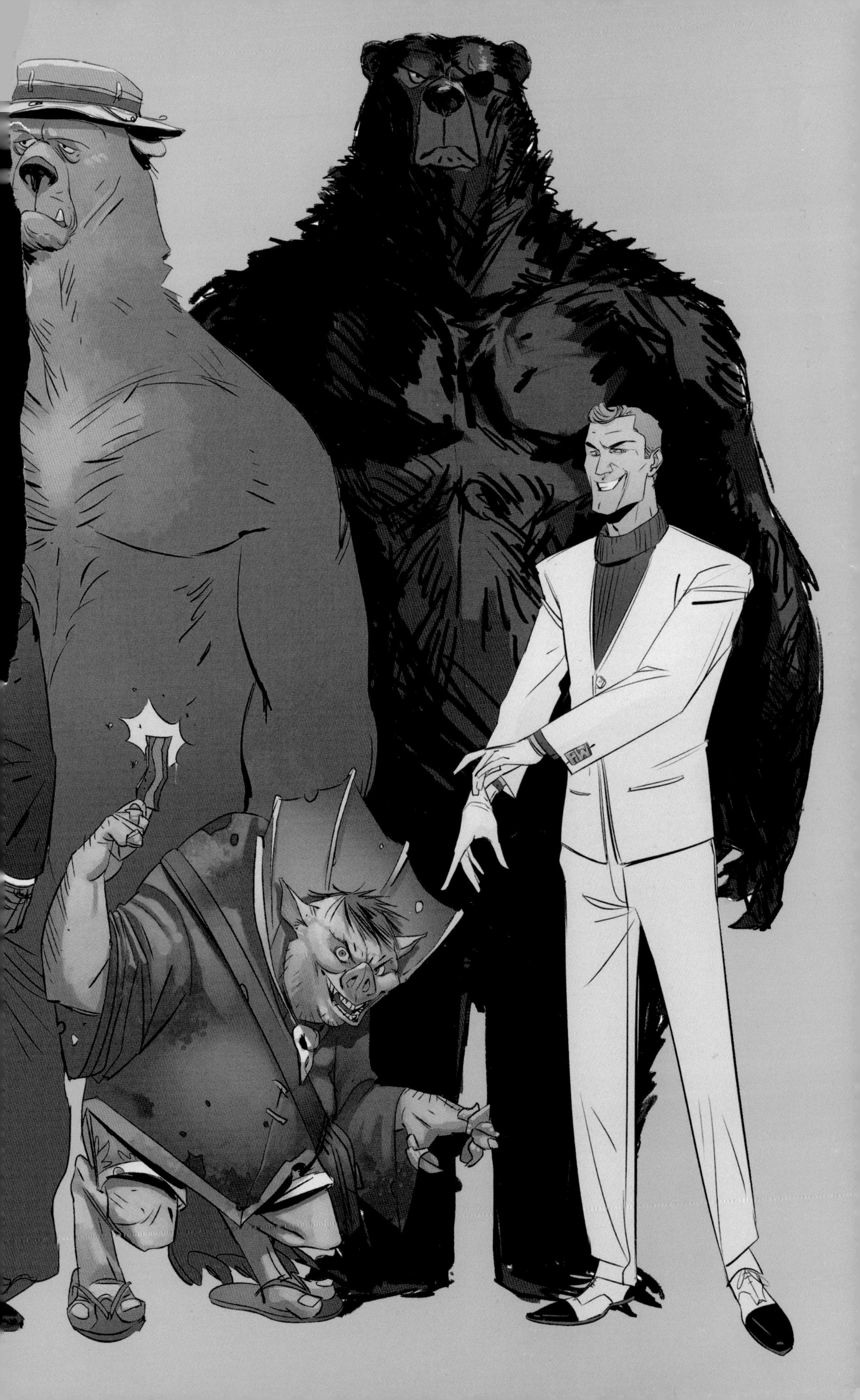

JODY LEHEUP

is the writer and co-creator of the IMAGE COMICS series *THE WEATHERMAN* with Nathan Fox and the co-writer and co-creator of *SHIRTLESS BEAR-FIGHTER!* with Sebastian Girner and Nil Vendrell Pallach. A Harvey Award nominated editor, Jody edited *UNCANNY X-FORCE, DEADPOOL* and *STRANGE TALES* for MARVEL and *QUANTUM AND WOODY* for VALIANT. He lives in Queens, New York.

SEBASTIAN GIRNER

is a freelance comic book writer and editor based in Brooklyn, NY. He is the editor of several creator-owned comic series published by IMAGE COMICS including *SOUTHERN BASTARDS, SEVEN TO ETERNITY, DEADLY CLASS, THE GODDAMNED,* and *DRIFTER.* Sebastian is the co-writer and co-creator of *SHIRTLESS BEAR-FIGHTER!* with Jody LeHeup and Nil Vendrell Pallach, and the writer and co-creator of *SCALES & SCOUNDRELS* with French artist Galaad.

NIL VENDRELL

is the artist and co-creator of *SHIRTLESS BEAR-FIGHTER!* with Jody LeHeup and Sebastian Girner. His illustrations have appeared in various webcomics and fanzines as well as the anthology *LAS VISIONES DEL FIN* published by *ALETA EDICIONES.* He lives in Barcelona, Spain.

🐦 @sbf_comic | 📷 sbf_comic | #WarOnBearror | fuzzywipes@gmail.com